WILDERNESS
REFORM

ALSO BY MATT QUERY AND HARRISON QUERY

Old Country

WILDERNESS REFORM

A NOVEL

MATT QUERY
AND HARRISON QUERY

EMILY BESTLER BOOKS

ATRIA

NEW YORK   LONDON   TORONTO   SYDNEY   NEW DELHI

EMILY
BESTLER
BOOKS

ATRIA

An Imprint of Simon & Schuster, LLC
1230 Avenue of the Americas
New York, NY 10020

First Emily Bestler Books/Atria Books hardcover edition July 2024

EMILY BESTLER BOOKS/ATRIA BOOKS and colophon are trademarks of Simon & Schuster, LLC

Simon & Schuster: Celebrating 100 Years of Publishing in 2024

For information about special discounts for bulk purchases, please contact Simon & Schuster Special Sales at 1-866-506-1949 or business@simonandschuster.com.

The Simon & Schuster Speakers Bureau can bring authors to your live event. For more information or to book an event, contact the Simon & Schuster Speakers Bureau at 1-866-248-3049 or visit our website at www.simonspeakers.com.

Interior design by Kyoko Watanabe

Manufactured in the United States of America

1   3   5   7   9   10   8   6   4   2

Library of Congress Control Number: 2024936004

ISBN 978-1-6680-2413-3
ISBN 978-1-6680-2415-7 (ebook)

This book is dedicated to every person's fight to keep a piece of their spirit wild and free.

"The child who is not embraced by the village will often burn it down to feel its warmth."

—*Unknown*

PROLOGUE

THERE'S A very particular kind of hot, coarse pain in the lungs that can only really be experienced after running from something that's trying to kill you.

The boy had never run that hard or that fast in his entire life. He'd also grown up at sea level. Even after spending several months in the Northern Rockies, a healthy thirteen-year-old flatlander will still get their ass kicked by extreme exertion at high altitude. But he ran as fast and as far as he could before his legs and mind gave out, when he collapsed onto all fours and crawled over to lean his back against a large, lichen-covered boulder.

He wasn't sure how long he'd been here. He could feel spit, snot, and tears pouring down his face.

He tried to look up the mountain to see if they were close, but his peripheral vision was just a shimmering blur. It was like looking through a paper towel roll. He couldn't see them coming, couldn't hear them, but even if he did, he did not know if he could keep going.

He noticed a sting in his hands and brought them up to his eyes, turning them over to examine them. Both were covered in blood, dirt, and the bone-white curls of freshly frayed palm skin. He looked down at a spot on his elbow that burned and found that most of the flesh between his elbow and wrist was just gone—replaced by blood caked in dirt and pine needles.

In that moment he remembered his younger brother getting a big scrape like that on his arm when he fell off his bike the summer before, and he remembered his elder brother calling it "road pizza."

Thinking of his brothers made him start to cry again in dry, wheezing sobs. He told himself he shouldn't cry right now, he didn't have time, and it wasn't going to help anything. In reality, he hadn't actually stopped crying much since he started running earlier that day.

He leaned his head back against the boulder and had to muster all the strength and discipline he had left to keep from screaming in frustration up into the dry, hot forest canopy.

He heard thunder in the distance—one of the brief afternoon lightning storms that thrashed against the granite mountains above tree line. He could picture the wrath in his mind. He'd seen and had actually been within quite a few of these high-country storms now. He'd grown used to so much over the last few months, so many things he'd never been exposed to until the morning he got torn away from his home and sent into these goddamned mountains.

After a long moment he pushed himself forward, wiped his face on his shoulder, and got a grip long enough to take stock of his surroundings.

He still had a long way to go down the mountain before he reached the stream, and then would have to follow the stream for another several miles. *When will this mountain end* had unintentionally become a mantra he asked himself again and again over the last hour. It was like some hellish treadmill covered in sharp-faced boulders, near-vertical walls of rock and scree, and house-sized snags of trees and deadfall. The boy had never known something so menacing and oppressive.

He wondered what the hell he was even going to do when he got back to camp. Would anyone believe him? *Did the other grown-ups know what the hell was actually going on up there?*

The dread of what was behind him shot a bolt of energy into his trunk and legs and the boy was up and moving down the mountain again. When he finally reached the stream that carved its way through the draw at the base of the valley, he collapsed into the fine gravel bed under the shallow, frigid water. He drank freely with his head almost entirely submerged. He was more exhausted than he'd ever been, but the water helped his body tap into a reserve of strength, and he kept going, splashing directly down the cold mountain stream in his frayed boots.

Eventually the streambed got too steep and rocky, so he had to go back up onto the boulder-strewn ridge a ways and maintain a parallel course with the creek.

The boy was lowering himself down a rock ledge when he heard a sound that shot a dump of adrenaline through his body with such force he instantly went numb, frozen in place.

It was the wailing.

It wasn't really a *wail*, as he understood the term before he got here, but there was no easy way to put it into words. It was a teakettle shriek, a pig being slaughtered, a piece of corrugated steel being tortured and bent by hurricane winds. Maybe it sounded different to everyone.

He dropped down to all fours and crawled under an overhanging shelf of rock, forcing himself up into the bit of cover it provided, willing himself to shrink as much as he could. He stared down at the creek and strained his ears to try to identify any approaching sounds over the babble and hum of the fast mountain water.

A blur caught his attention to his left. It was so startling it felt like his stomach lurched up into his throat, but he tried not to move more than his head, which he slowly turned.

He saw it then. A fox, a red fox had scrambled up into a small crag in the rocks, similar to the one he was taking refuge in himself. It wiggled and writhed its way into the hiding place, just the way he had. When it couldn't get any farther, the animal tried to go still, but the boy could see it was shaking as badly as he was.

The fox looked across the steep slope and locked eyes with the boy. They just sat there, the boy and the fox, eyes riveted on one another's, shaking in terror and dread. The boy knew they were hiding from the same thing.

After a long moment, the boy felt it.

The taste of cold steel filled his mouth; he could feel the zing of stomach acid boiling over his tongue and coating his teeth. Then the keening in his ears started, faint at first, but growing into a high-frequency shriek that throbbed behind his eyes. He felt the warmth before he realized his bladder had released.

He looked back to the fox and could see the small beast was wincing and flinching as well, making canine snuffing noises. The boy glared at the animal with fierce eyes, willing it to be silent.

More movement caught the boy's eye in the foreground along the slope between himself and the fox. He saw dozens of mice, voles, and small sage lizards running between the two outcroppings where they hid, down the incline toward the stream—away from them—jumping and skittering over the pine needles and rocks.

The boy felt something on his hands, and looked down to see that worms and centipedes were pouring out of the wet soil around him, writhing and gyrating once they reached the open air.

He looked over at the fox. It looked as though its senses were as besieged by the shrieking wail as his were—he saw in the fox's eyes that this was a misery that transcended species.

Right before the boy was about to pass out, the fox bolted from its hiding place. It exploded out into the open ground between them with incredible speed, bounding up the slope and between the trees so fast the boy could barely follow it with his eyes. The fox disappeared in a blur above the rock outcropping under which the boy was hiding.

The wailing stopped the moment the fox disappeared. The boy unclenched his jaw, shuddered, and almost began to cough as the shrieking and its paralytic effect washed out of him. But then he heard something else above him up the slope, near where the fox had disappeared.

It was an animal's frantic breathing and whining. The frenzied canine sounds grew in urgency until a deep, muffled crack punched across the forest, immediately ceasing the panicked noise—like a tree branch being broken underneath a blanket. He wanted to cover his ears, he wanted to wipe the tears from his eyes, but dared not move a muscle. Then he heard a wet rip and tear, and what sounded like a burlap bag of stones being tossed into the forest floor.

"Not the boy, just a fox."

Despite how different it had become, he knew the voice immediately. He knew who it belonged to. *What* it belonged to. Hearing the voice made him gag and dry-heave, which he tried to do as quietly as he could, clamping both bloody hands down over his mouth so hard he could feel his cracked fingernails cutting into his cheeks.

All he heard in response or acknowledgment to the voice was a guttural grunt from farther up the ridge. Immediately thereafter, he heard what sounded like a dozen hooves beating into the forest floor, then splashing and pounding as they charged their way down the stream, away from him, but in the direction he needed to go.

He didn't move until long after the echo of hooves traveled down the valley and disappeared entirely. He worked his way back down to the stream and felt the bite of cold as he plunged his torn, ragged boots into the water.

The boy saw a long, sharp piece of shale rock under the surface of the shallow creek, and picked it up. He gripped it tightly in his right hand, ignoring the burn of the splinters and fresh scabs in his palm cracking open.

In that moment he made a solemn promise to himself, one he would hold to until his last day if he survived this. It became his new silent mantra, repeating in his head over and over as he put one foot in front of the other, and kept moving.

If I actually manage to escape this place, I'll never set foot anywhere near the mountains again as long as I fucking live.

CHAPTER 1

SOUTHERN LOUISIANA

A RESTAURANT'S GREASE trap stinks in a way that's impossible to forget. The stench locks itself into a brain like initials carved into an old desk. Ben realized this in the days that followed his first close encounter with the vile waste.

He had found himself wedged into a small opening between a brick wall and a dripping, stinking grease trap behind a diner. He tried to stay as silent as he could as he watched the flashlight bob toward him down the weed-covered, trash-strewn alleyway.

He had not known it at the time, but the minute or so he spent in that hiding place would haunt Ben for a very, very long time. It was the first time in his life he'd been completely floored by dread. Paralyzed almost. He'd never felt anything like it before; he'd never felt his hands, joints, and mind completely seized up by shrieking, hysterical panic. It felt like black swamp mud filled his veins.

In the days that passed since that moment, he'd thought about it constantly. The grease trap's putrid citrus stench of rot, the inch-thick black grime on the bricks and cracked asphalt around the trap, the humidity in the air, the din and roar of his heartbeat in his ears, the shrieking cicadas, the cop slowly pacing down the alley toward him. He'd actually gagged on several occasions as he'd recall the sensation of the reeking burnt-orange grease running down the sides of his face, his neck, forming an adhesive slick between his shirt and shoulder blades.

To Ben, it felt like every excruciating detail of the moment was laser-burned into whatever part of the brain was right behind the eyes.

Ben had robbed a gas station a few blocks away from that diner and its disgusting grease trap. He'd only had an airsoft gun, the orange muzzle of which had been lazily Sharpied over in the dark on his walk toward the gas station. *Thing looks real enough*, he'd thought.

The lady at the counter certainly couldn't tell the difference. He grabbed about eighty dollars from the register and as many candy bars, jerky sticks, and packaged shitty pastries as he could carry. When he saw police lights start to pulse off the dirty windows of the abandoned old building across the street from the gas station, he bolted out the door. Ben ran as fast as he could until he saw the hiding place, and went for it.

He figured it was likely the cops had already seen him turn into the alley, but he dove behind the grease trap anyway. He thought about running once he'd wedged himself into the hiding spot, but he was shaking too badly. He was too exhausted, too dehydrated, too malnourished. His body knew it was already over. The grease and grime embraced him. Ben felt like he was stuck to a roach trap; those strips of adhesive brown tape the insects get trapped onto as they skitter across, then even more stuck as they kick and writhe until death takes them. Once the cop's flashlight got to within about thirty feet, all Ben can remember is that he started screaming.

He screamed that he didn't have a gun, he begged not to get shot, pleaded to be helped out from under the grease trap. He cried as he was put into the back of the cruiser. The next day, he cried more on the ride home from his arraignment in the back seat of Aunt Nicki's old Buick. Not once on the whole drive did she glance up at the rearview mirror to look back at him through the haze of cigarette smoke. Worse than the smoke was the razor-edged silence, the kind that was loaded with the assurance of beatings and pain.

Over the next week, Ben caught up with the buddies he'd grown up with in Lafitte, Louisiana. He regaled them with the tale of his days on the run. He told them about how he'd stolen his neighbor's johnboat and split off into the bayou, how he'd broken into private fishing camps where he drank good bourbon and robbed crab traps for his meals. He told them about how he'd finally run out of supplies and camps to raid, and about how he'd stashed his boat along a canal somewhere in

Plaquemines Parish, then hiked up Highway 23 in the dark with a plan to knock over the first gas station he came across, then finally about how that plan had gone pear-shaped and how he'd been caught by the constables.

He told them about how he'd kept his mouth shut throughout a blistering, night-long interrogation from multiple different detectives. He told them about the deals he'd been repeatedly offered, which he'd repeatedly refused. He said he'd told the detectives to go *fuck themselves*, that he'd *happily* do his time in Louisiana state's juvenile corrections, where he had plenty of friends he was excited to catch up with. Ben's buddies were proud of him. Their elder brothers were proud of him too. Part of Ben felt like a king, like he'd sunk a buzzer-beater three.

In reality, no detective interrogated Ben. No one offered him a deal. He hadn't been driven by some *outlaw spirit* as he'd stolen the boat, broken into the fishing camps, or knocked over the Chevron station. From start to finish, all he'd felt was fear and anxiety. He'd done it all to try to find somewhere safe to take his little brother, Wade, where their aunt couldn't find them—and he'd been scared shitless the entire time. He hadn't even considered how he'd sneak back to his hometown of Lafitte to get his little brother, let alone how he'd actually smuggle the small child away. The whole week was just a poorly planned cascade of fiascos, catalyzed by one moment of meteoric panic and rage. Panic for his little brother, and rage at being too small and not knowing how to protect him.

He hadn't even actually been brought to the Plaquemines Parish Sheriff's Office detention center in Davant, fabled among his friends, their elder brothers, uncles, fathers, and grandfathers. He spent his one night in "jail" locked in a sterile, fluorescent-lit room in the back of some double-wide that served as a district patrol office somewhere off state highway 23. He'd been relegated to this unique incarceration due to the late hour he'd been arrested and his only being thirteen years old. It felt worse to Ben somehow. It was insulting.

Ben spent several hours in that room disgusted by the stinking grease that still caked his upper body and head. He had been waiting for it to begin drying and crusting, hoping this would help abate its stench and allow it to be scratched away, but the nature of the wicked substance prevented that, so he tried to focus on how he was going to go about doing the one thing he'd always been good at: manipulating adults and talking his way out of shit.

He had read and thereby memorized the Bill of Rights and portions of several state statutes that he'd deemed potentially helpful based on their focus. He also had access to a collage of courtroom and interrogation scenes from television and movies he'd logged away over the years. However, over the last few hours Ben had started to see how truly useless that archive of surface-level information was. He'd sound like a damn fool just spouting off recitations of black-letter law without knowing when or how to use it. There was an operative nature to state law and constitutional rights; he knew they had to be employed in a particular sequence to specific facts. However, he didn't have any fluency in how to do that, and knew he'd sound like a dumbass to try. That aside, Ben did know that he was not required to talk to law enforcement without a lawyer present, especially as a minor, so he'd just have to rely on that as his mainstay for now.

Finally, the sound of slow, dragging feet in the hall outside preceded a massively obese corrections deputy who opened the door and trundled into the small space holding both a bottle of water and a bag of chips in one meaty, pink hand. Sweat glistened on his forehead and rendered swathes of his white uniform almost translucent under his arms.

Ben's panic had worn off at that point and had been replaced with exhausted irritation. He looked up at the deputy and spoke without solicitation for any such comment.

"I want a lawyer here if you fixin to question me."

The deputy just glanced at Ben with cold eyes as he set the water and chips on the collapsible camping table, the only thing in the room other than the flimsy, plastic deck chair Ben sat in. He spoke as he turned and headed back toward the door.

"Boy, you tink anyone here gives a fuck about anything yous gots to say?"

The officer talked with that raspy, Cajun twang that could make Ben's skin crawl. His mom, aunt, and all the men he'd been around as he learned the English language spoke with such a strong, French-peppered version of this accent that even most Louisianans struggled to understand them.

Ben wasn't sure why it grinded his gears so badly, hearing that insufferable parlance that afflicted so many of the white folk reared in the swamps south of I-10, like Ben himself. When Ben was tired or angry, he'd hear that same Acadian lilt flood into his own voice. It would come out from somewhere deep in his throat to sizzle into the skin of his words like a boiling acid, eating away vowels and rendering down consonants.

For the briefest of moments, Ben's subconscious urged him to withhold a witty response, but he had been alone for too long. Since he'd run away, he'd been deprived of any good opportunities to properly screw with a grown-up. He was as hungry for that opportunity as he was for the bag of chips in front of him. It's what he lived for. It was all he had.

Ben leaned back and rested an ankle on the opposite knee. He pushed back with his foot still on the ground, tilting the chair to lean back a bit onto only two of its flimsy legs.

"Maybe not your boss, but I spose I could say quite a few things that'd make *you* give a fuck, *Boudreaux.*"

The cop snorted through his nose, ceased his progress toward the door, and turned to face the boy. Ben knew it was very unlikely that this man's name was actually Boudreaux, but from the big man's accent alone, Ben knew—*that the cop knew*—that calling someone "Boudreaux" was a subtle way of calling someone a dumbass. This particular aspersion would only register as such to someone who grew up in Acadiana, someone who grew up in Cajun country.

The deputy narrowed his eyes and leaned his head toward Ben. Ben could see from subtle features on his face that the man's brain was attempting to gin up some response. He pointed at Ben as he replied.

"You still yappin, *couyon.* You said without no lawyah present you was gonna chut the fuck up, so how bouts you *chut the fuck up.*"

Ben made himself grin at the man before he responded—not a happy smile, but an amused smile. He couldn't put the differences between smiles or facial expressions into words, but he knew them all, had all their little nuances cataloged away, and he knew their different effects on grown-ups. He knew this difference between a happy smile and an amused smile was important right now.

"Well, *heavens to Betsy*, sir, I did not mean to hurt your feelings so badly. I think what's most important for us right now is for you to take in some *deep breaths* to try and *calm yourself down*, alright?"

The man clenched his fists and began to stride toward where the boy sat, as Ben knew he would.

At that same moment, Ben let the front legs of his chair fall and planted both feet on the ground. The noise and sudden movement made the deputy flinch. Ben stayed seated, leaned his upper body toward the man, pointed his face up to the right, and used his index finger to tap on his jawbone on the left side of his chin—making sure to maintain the same amused smile as he did so.

As Ben also suspected he would, the man checked his flustered surge toward the boy, looking confused and surprised as he came to a stop a few feet away. Ben kept tapping on his jawbone as he spoke.

"Land that hook right here, my man, right in the off switch. Come on, Boudreaux, *help reform me.*"

The man cocked his head to the side as lines around his eyes and forehead formed, slowly evicting the look of confusion and replacing it with a disgusted glower. He stared down at the boy and ran his hand up his neck to his chin, which he rubbed back and forth a few times.

The coarse rasp of the man's big palm against his two-day stubble sounded abnormally loud in the small room. Ben could almost *taste* his rage.

After a long moment, the deputy began slowly shaking his head as he backed away from the boy toward the door. He eventually forced an awkward smile as he reached back to open the door to leave, suggesting he'd found a few words. Ben already knew the gist of what was about to be said.

"*Whew*, boy, that lips gon' get you killed fore you turn eighteen, you know that, right?"

Ben leaned back again and began slapping a palm on his belly before the cop had even finished speaking, and shouted out his reply just before the door was slammed shut.

"Not before them clogged-up arteries get you, hoss!"

Ben's smile faded as he tried to will away the pressure building in his tear ducts. He felt his efforts fail as tears fell down his cheeks. He wiped them away aggressively with the sleeve of his shirt. He was wearing the same old T-shirt he'd had on for the last week; it had a cartoon version of the legendary lumberjack Paul Bunyan on it, grinning broadly as he held an axe over his shoulder in one hand and gave a thumbs-up with the other.

Ben was tough, he'd had to be, and was certainly no stranger to confrontation, but he was still just a boy being sworn at and threatened by a grown-up. A big fucking scary one, at that. He could talk shit and banter with anyone he'd ever met, *better* than anyone he'd ever met, but he could still be plagued by fear—the kind of red-hot fear that can only be felt by a kid.

Before the arraignment the next day, Ben learned that the prosecutor already had clear security camera footage of him pointing the fake gun at the terrified old woman behind the counter at the Chevron as he stuffed his pockets with cash and snacks.

Ben did not interrupt the flow of information the well-dressed lady appointed by the juvenile court to represent him decided to direct toward Ben's aunt Nicki. He knew he understood it far better than Aunt Nicki did, and had also gathered more than enough to grasp the fact that they had him red-handed, dead to rights. At one point the attorney asked Ben why he ran off and robbed a business. Ben didn't tell her about his plan to find somewhere safe for him and his little brother to live, somewhere quiet, somewhere without any adults, somewhere Aunt Nicki wouldn't find them.

He just shrugged and told her he didn't know.

CHAPTER 2

ONE MORNING, a couple of weeks after getting arrested, the strange voices coming from the living room were not actually what awoke Ben. The strange voices were how he would always remember being awoken, but he was really forced from sleep by the searing beam of light that shone into the bedroom he shared with his younger brother in his aunt Nicki's double-wide trailer.

That sunrise light was concentrated into a braid of fire by the dirt and mildew that caked the window on the eastern wall of the little room. It had often been the first thing to irritate Ben every day for the last five years. It was always the day's first bully and nuisance.

Ben rolled over, stretched his legs out, then pulled his knees toward his chest, hauling his tingling feet onto the bed from where they'd hung off the end of the mattress he'd outgrown years earlier.

Ben's little brother, Wade, was already awake, lying on his side on a filthy little mattress on the floor across the room, spooning a dirty, flaccid stuffed animal older than either boy. He was staring at Ben, waiting for him to wake up.

"Who that in the livin room with Aunt Nicki, *Pee-Pan?*"

Ben squeezed his eyes shut, responding in a half whisper.

"That ain't my damn name, Wade."

Ben felt bad as soon as his brother responded, hearing the embarrassment in the little boy's voice, but disregarded it as he tried to will himself back to sleep for a few more minutes.

"I mean *Ben*! Sorry, sorry, Ben."

The boys' mother had called Ben *Peter Pan*, a story she'd read to them before bedtime, even though she'd often pass out midsentence on the floor between their little beds long before the boys did. Wade never learned to pronounce the two words *Peter Pan* properly. *Pee-Pan* was as close as he could ever get. He was quite little when she died, and unlike Ben, he could not remember what she looked like, he could not remember her boyfriends or how angry she could get. One of the only things Wade remembered about his mother was her having called Ben that. Wade had told Ben once the year before, in the best way a small child was able to explain, that he could actually hear their mother's voice when he thought about the words *Peter Pan*—the sound having been stored away as some early trace code in his brain. So, in a way, Wade was lucky, as that magical name from that wonderful story was really the only thing she ever left behind for him.

Ben knew this; he knew what Wade meant by it. Ben knew his mother was not a saint, but he knew she used her hands and feet to hurt him far less frequently than Aunt Nicki did. And even when she did, he remembered how she would rock him afterward, crying and apologizing and saying sweet things. Ben knew that the nickname was the only special thing left in this world that was shared between him, his brother, and their momma. But it was still embarrassing to have his little brother calling him *Pee-Pan* in front of his friends—it being a nickname far more analogous to *piss bucket* than the fictional character's actual name. So, Ben had been trying to train it out of the small child.

Ben had stolen a nice copy of *Peter Pan* from the school library earlier that year. It was nicer than the one he remembered his mother reading them, better illustrations at least, and Ben would read it to Wade several nights a week until he could hear the little boy's breathing fall into the steady wheeze of sleep.

After Wade fell asleep, Ben would read through the 1984 copy of the ninth edition of *Webster's Collegiate Dictionary*, or one of the "new" tattered 2006 *Encyclopaedia Britannica* volumes the school library had gotten a month earlier. The collection was missing volumes 6, 17, and 29. This infuriated Ben, but he inhaled them nonetheless and cataloged their contents in his mind as though it were a chore.

The only books he derived real pleasure from reading were those about famous explorers and treasure hunters and the prizes they sought. Explorers like Cabeza de Vaca, Lewis and Clark, Frémont and Carson, John Wesley Powell, Shackleton, Cook, and the rest. On the treasure-hunting side, the Holy Grail, El Dorado, the Holy Lance, Quesada, Gaspar, Fawcett, Blackbeard, and of course his own hometown's namesake, Jean Lafitte.

Exploration and treasure-hunting was a comfort subject for Ben, and for some reason, it had been since before he could even read. His family never had the money for him to get into sports or hobbies, nor had any adult or peer in Ben's life ever taken the time to introduce him to those kind of things one does for recreation or enjoyment. As such, in Ben's thirteen years he'd not been introduced to the notion that it was a normal, human thing to seek out sources of personal, recreational pleasure. He did not have time or freedom for such a thing. Even so, for one reason or another, encountering any historic account of a person or group setting out into the wild to find something valuable or legendary had become one of his most profound sources of peace and private enjoyment. There wasn't a library or bookstore between Slidell and Lafayette that Ben hadn't spent hours in reading about these men and these things.

"They been talkin awhile now, B. Talkin *bout you.*"

Ben's eyes opened wide at Wade's words. He blinked through blurred vision and pushed himself up onto his elbows, shifting his position within the inveterate sunrise hell beam so that its mustard-yellow, dust-animated light seared into his chest and belly instead of his face. He began straining his ears to pick words out of the muffled conversation.

"What you mean *talkin bout me*? What're they sayin?"

Wade yawned as he shrugged.

"I dunno, somethin bout the trouble you're in, what to do about it."

Ben gestured for Wade to stay put, then slowly pulled the blanket off himself and crept to the bedroom door. He slowly turned the doorknob, then pushed the door open a few inches at the precise speed necessary to avoid a loud whine from the rusty hinges. *Not too fast, not too slow.* He'd done it many times.

The volume and clarity of the voices from the living room amplified immediately. Ben could hear his aunt Nicki and someone else. It was a man's voice, but he did not talk like a cop, or like anyone else who grew up in south Louisiana. More like a teacher, or a coach. Ben strained his ears and held his breath to hear what this strange man was saying.

"... *really one of, if not the best program in the country for boys like Ben. It's a type of program that falls under a category we'd call adventure-based therapy. Our model implements a wilderness expedition and survival approach for the purpose of therapeutic intervention, guiding at-risk youth, like Ben, and helping them develop the emotional toolbox to maintain a sustainable mindset of self-respect and self-reliance. And while I know you've already signed the guardian authorization, we have dozens of references who I would still encourage you to check in with—both parents of graduates and, of course, graduates themselves. Do you happen to know Frank Davis, who lives down the street and goes to school with your nephew?*"

Ben heard his aunt Nicki's reply come on the heels of a long, raspy wheeze, which he knew was her exhaling a thin band of Pall Mall cigarette smoke from the corner of her mouth.

"Yeah, I know Frank."

"*Well, Frank graduated from our program last year, as you might've known. We consider him to be quite a success story and a testament to the efficacy of our program. His maturity, discipline, work ethic, accountability, and dedication to school skyrocketed when he returned from Montana, and he's still doing quite well today.*"

Ben knew Frank. The kid had gotten sent off last summer to some weird juvie program out of state after he'd gotten busted stealing at the Dollar General. To Ben, Frank was a whole different dude when he got back. Stopped hanging out with his crew, got a weekend job, spent all his free time doing chores for his parents and studying, going to church. Ben just figured he'd gotten scared into a little Goody Two-shoes, right quick.

Ben heard his aunt's voice again.

"Yeah ... *I'll be damned.* He's a fine boy now, *night and day* compared to how he was before he got sent off. Only time I see him now he's doin chores for his momma or grandma or volunteerin down at the church. I didn't know he'd done this Montana thing, though. I thought he'd just gone to corrections, found Jesus o' some shit."

The strange voice responded.

"Yes, ma'am. Frank completed our program last August, and according to his parents, he's kept on the straight and narrow ever since. We're really proud of him. That's what we want for your nephew Ben. We don't want to see young men like Ben get sent to corrections. Your nephew's armed robbery charge is quite serious, even for such a young guy, so we'd like to avoid youth introduction to the justice system altogether. It has unpredictable outcomes, unlike our program. And as you know, we've already got the deferral authorization from the court, so Ben will have his charges dropped upon completion of our program."

Ben could hear his aunt take another long drag, and knew her words came through a cloud of smoke.

"Well, like I already said, he ain't gonna just up and go witch y'all. He ain't never left Louisiana. He ain't gonna like the sound a'this program, outside in mountains all day. Y'all best *mind that boy*, he's liable to run on ya, nasty little devil he is. He's got friends in juvenile corrections, probly over half his damn friends at this point. That's what he'll wanna do, and Lord knows I can't talk him into nothin no more."

"Well, Ms. Denton, Ben's thirteen. As his guardian you've made this decision. As I mentioned in our emails, we have highly reputable youth intervention transport specialists on staff who oversee the process of getting Ben from this house today all the way to our program headquarters outside White Haven, Montana. We'll get him there safe and sound, that's a guarantee. These folks specialize in working with youth who exhibit contentious and combative behavior, or unwillingness to voluntarily participate, and they're standing by outside."

Ben hadn't understood all of what the strange voice had said, but he understood enough, and his heart started pounding. Adrenaline crashed into his hands and face. He turned and leaned his back against the door, not caring about the noise it made as it slammed shut.

"Ben what's wrong, Ben you okay?"

Ben held his hand out toward his little brother and nodded.

"Yeah, Wade, just stay put. I'm fine. Just chill."

He could feel panic creeping into his mind. He felt like he was wedged into a small space between dirty bricks and a grease trap. He could smell the grease. He felt like he was eight years old again, getting dragged away from his mother's lifeless, pale body by his aunt Nicki.

"*Ben.*"

Wade's voice yanked Ben's attention back to the present.

"Ben, what's goin on out there?"

Ben got up quickly and moved toward his bed, when he heard his aunt's voice as she called for him. Ben was frozen. He was not sure what was going on out there, but he sure as hell didn't trust it. His aunt added a bit of snarl into her voice as she called for him again.

"*Ben, get out here now.*"

Ben looked over at Wade, who was sitting up in his bed now, eyes wide.

Ben saw his brother breathing fast, an easy thing to see in such a small, bony, malnutrition-stunted frame. He nodded at Wade as he spoke, only becoming more anxious as he heard the shake and fearful tenor in his own voice.

"It's all good, Wade, just stay in bed."

Ben's heart was pounding as he opened the bedroom door and slowly walked toward the living room. When he entered the smoky room, he found his aunt sitting on the couch, leaning over an information packet that was nestled among the empty beer cans and Styrofoam containers piled on the coffee table. Standing on the other side of the couch, facing Ben, was a man the boy had never seen.

He was tall. To Ben, he looked like some kind of fighter pilot or maybe a professional tennis player. He was probably in his early to midthirties, tan, with short, meticulously cared-for blond hair. He had a faded scar that traced the course of his jawbone on the back of his left cheek, closer to his ear than his nose. Same hair color he and Wade had. He was wearing Nike running shoes and a white polo tucked into khaki pants. The polo shirt had a logo emblazoned on the right breast, almost like a coat of arms. The man looked strong, chest and arm muscles well defined even through his loose-fitting shirt.

He smiled at Ben.

Ben did not know it at the time—*couldn't* have known it at the time—but every day for the rest of his life, without exception, Ben would be haunted by the first time that man smiled at him.

Time stopped. The smile sent a jolt of something strange into Ben's heart, like a well-measured mixture of calming trust and unbridled dread. His ears popped and then filled with a shrieking ring. He felt his bowels loosen and clenched his entire lower body to avoid shitting himself. Ben felt a dueling desire: he loved this man and he hated this man. In his mind, Ben could see himself burying his face into this strange man's chest and weeping with relief as he was enveloped, warmed, and protected by those strong, tanned arms. He could also see himself bolting out the front door, jumping off the porch, sprinting down the street, and leaping in front of a truck passing by on the state highway that bordered the trailer park.

He felt it all in the same moment. He felt the man caressing the back of his head as he embraced the boy and whispered calming things in his ear. He could feel his stomach in his throat and the impact of the grille and bumper of a semitruck, see his neighbors' faces as they winced and flinched away from his teenage body getting slammed, buckled, and shredded into the dirty pavement.

His jaw clenched down like a vise as he looked at that man's smile; he could feel his fingernails cutting into his palms. His joints were locked, his eyeballs were vibrating, he could almost *hear* the twisting, coiling tension in his muscles. His teeth felt like they were small, living things being tortured with electricity, little grubs frantically writhing to escape his gums. He felt like he was on the verge of laughing and weeping.

The second the man spoke—when the first audible syllable left his mouth—this cocktail of sensations flushed from Ben's head and out through his feet. It made him shudder and start to cough. He grabbed his chest, then looked back up at this guy, this beast. When Ben found his eyes, he looked almost sympathetic, as though he knew what his smile had just done to Ben, but that it was something that needed to happen.

"Hi, Ben, my name is Reid."

He extended his hand toward Ben as he took a few slow steps forward. Ben just stared up at him, awestruck, unable to process the physical and emotional experience he'd just lived through, he'd just *been trapped in*. Ben had heard of panic attacks before, but had never heard them described this way. Ben looked over toward his aunt with wide eyes.

"You just gon' stand there, hell's wrong with you? Sweet mother a'Christ, boy, *shake the man's hand*."

Ben looked back up at the tall man, and slowly took his hand in his own. It was like an oak branch coated in felt, like warm linen draped over steel. It felt electric, like it passed a current up Ben's arm.

Reid took a step away from Ben, leaned down and put his hands on his knees, then looked from Ben's aunt back to the boy.

"Ben, I'm the director of a wilderness reform school called Bear Springs Academy, based out of Montana. It's basically like a summer camp. Our program is for young men, like yourself, who've recently gotten into a bit of trouble. But it's not like jail or rehab. It's really more of an *adventure camp*. Hiking, camping, rock climbing, archery, white-water rafting, riding horses, fishing, trapping, cooking on open camp-fires, we spend all summer doing fun stuff like that. Does that sound like a cool way to spend a summer?"

Ben was speechless. He could barely hear through the yawn-rumble of panic in his ears. He looked back to his aunt as he struggled to mar-shal enough air into the top of his lungs to form words. Ben's aunt cut him off.

"Uh-uh, nah, *not dis time, boy*. You *goin* to this program. It's either this, or you go off to corrections up in Lafayette wit all dem otha fuck-ups. The court said we could defer da charge tru dis here program, an' dass *exactly what we gon' do*. Already signed the authorization."

She leaned back into her rancid couch, looking away and waving her hand dismissively as she finished her words. Tears started falling from Ben's eyes. He heard Wade's voice, could hear him shouting, then saw him in his periphery and looked over. Wade was crying, clutching the stuffed animal to his chest, demanding to know what was going on and where Ben was going.

Reid cast a sympathetic look toward Wade. It was so genuine it actu-ally cut through the malaise of Ben's panic, calming him for a moment. Reid looked back at Ben.

"I know this is a lot to take in right when you wake up, buddy, but there's really nothing to be frightened of. We're gonna go to the airport in New Orleans now, take a quick flight to Montana, and then you're going to meet the rest of the guys you'll be spending the summer and going on adventures with. These guys are your age and are from all over. These will be some of the best friendships you form throughout your entire life. This summer is going to be so fun it's going to *fly by*, trust me, and after a summer full of fun, learning, and adventures in the mountains, you'll be back just in time to start ninth grade."

Ben only heard every other word and processed even fewer. He'd begun slowly backing away from Reid, toward his little brother. He felt Wade's arms wrap around his abdomen, his little face pressing into the center of his back.

Reid stood back up to his full height, and a tight-lipped, empathetic smile spread across his face as he glanced from Ben to Aunt Nicki. He pulled an iPhone out of his pocket and put it to his ear, saying something into the receiver that Ben couldn't hear.

Ben realized he was shouting at his aunt. *Screaming* at her. He wasn't sure what he was saying, but she shook her head as she stared back at him with raised eyebrows. He'd never hated anything more than he hated his aunt in that moment. Wade was crying hard, his grip around Ben's trunk tightening with the heaving of his sobs. Ben was weeping now as well.

Suddenly the front door opened. Two more athletic-looking guys wearing the same white polo shirts as Reid walked into the living room, but these two were different.

They were older than Reid, by a decade or so. Something about them fascinated Ben for the briefest of moments. They shared some feature that was unique but unnamable. Something he'd never seen in the face of a man. They offered a curt nod toward Ben's aunt, then took positions on Reid's flanks with their hands behind their backs. Ben felt like throwing up.

Aunt Nicki stood abruptly and stormed toward the boys. She yanked Wade off Ben and carried him off toward her bedroom. Wade reached for Ben as he was carried away, the volume of his screams muffled abruptly when Ben's aunt slammed her bedroom door, leaving Ben alone in the living room with the three strange men. Ben had no idea how haunting that last glimpse of his terrified little brother would be over the weeks and months to come.

There was no way out. White light and darkness filled Ben's periphery at the same time. He couldn't breathe, he felt like the room was spinning. He stumbled toward the kitchen, unsure whether it was a desire for water or to throw up into the sink that was driving him.

Strong arms enveloped him before he broke the threshold into the kitchen. They were gentle, but firm, like they were carved out of wood. Ben began to thrash and scream. Everything Ben had ever bottled up and stored away came out of him in that moment. He kicked, punched, scratched, keened, and shrieked. He could hear one of the men repeatedly saying *you're okay, buddy, you're alright, we've got you, you're okay.*

The next hours were a complete blur. Ben remembered little other than hazy chapters, such as being in a Suburban with the air conditioner on too high, passing by black-water sloughs and refineries along the highway that pocked the southern Louisiana landscape. Then more enveloping arms, being at the airport, and then being on a plane. The men in the white polos were shadowing him wherever he went. They were repeatedly showing a clutch of papers to security officers and flight staff throughout the day of travel.

It was the first time Ben had ever been on a plane. He'd been looking forward to the experience for years, but by the time he was on this one, he was more exhausted than he'd ever been. The emotional overdose left him numb, feeling like he was watching himself from above. He slouched into the seat and fell asleep at some point as he was staring out the small window at big men in orange vests loading bags onto the plane.

CHAPTER 3

A LANCE OF pressure in Ben's eardrum woke him up. He squinted out the small window he'd been using as a headrest and saw an endless horizon of white and tan. He looked to his left to find Reid sitting in the aisle seat, holding a cup of water toward Ben. He gave Ben an apologetic smile.

"How you feelin, buddy? Here, you should drink some water."

Ben did. He could not remember ever having been so thirsty. He wiped his mouth, tossed the cup into the empty seat between himself and Reid, then looked out the window at a vast expanse of obnoxiously bright clouds.

"What do you like to do with your free time, Ben?"

Ben didn't respond. *Wouldn't* respond, if he could help it. He fixed his gaze on the clouds.

"Other than stealing boats and candy bars and breaking into people's cabins, what do you like to do for fun?"

Ben looked over at Reid, who was leaning on the armrest facing Ben with his whole body. He had a kind smile. It was the same as the first smile from earlier that morning, but not the same at all. Ben shivered and felt his eye twitch as he remembered how the man's smile had paralyzed him, how it had infected him earlier that morning. He issued the correction as he looked away, back out the window.

"Camps."

Reid cocked his head to the side a bit, either confused by the single word, or taken aback by the pure venom the boy had managed to lace into it. Reid began to speak, but Ben interrupted him again.

"We ain't got *cabins* in Louisiana, we got *camps*."

Reid smiled as he looked down at his hands, then back up at Ben.

"I was just messing with you, man. I'm never going to judge you. I got arrested for stealing when I was a kid, too, long time ago now. It happens, man, I understand."

Ben clenched his jaw. Reid took in a long breath through his nose before going on.

"Look, Ben, I know it was unpleasant, getting taken from home like that. I hate that part of this program, I really do. But if you'd have been given the choice, would you really have just come along with us?"

Ben used all his effort to fix his gaze at a random spot on a random cloud. Reid let out an audible sigh before speaking on.

"Before you know it, you'll be back with your little brother. His name's Wade, right? He seems like a sweet kid. Was he calling you *Pippin* or something? Is that like his nickname for y—"

"*Fuck you.*"

Ben had whipped around and leaned his whole upper body across the middle seat toward Reid. He'd snarled out those two words through clenched teeth before he even knew what he was doing. He was embarrassed by the quake he heard in his own voice.

Reid flinched his head and shoulders away from the boy with a flutter of blinks, appearing genuinely surprised and even a bit hurt or offended, rather than mad. It sent a subtle pulse of guilt into Ben, which faded quickly as Ben turned to look back out the window.

He felt tears come again. This time he was too resigned, too exhausted to resist them. He thought about his little brother, Wade. The tears were for him.

He thought about what Wade would do during those two-, three-, or five-day stints when their aunt Nicki would disappear—disappear without leaving pizza money, or any fucking notice. Ben had always been there for those unannounced periods of parental truancy. Wade had never done it alone.

Ben pictured Wade putting himself to bed on that decrepit mattress, waking up and looking through the double-wide trailer alone, flipping light switches, pouring himself water or just drinking out of the sink, climbing up on the counter to reach the microwave to make himself oatmeal, eating it alone with a dirty spoon.

Ben wondered specifically *where* in the trailer Wade would actually decide to go about the act of eating alone. Would he just sit on the floor? Would he sit on the couch?

Ben was not stressing over any precise concerns about how or whether Wade would survive or hurt himself. He figured he'd physically be alright, at least for the summer. Aunt Nicki's violence was likely to be stemmed a bit by her recent interaction with the authorities, as it often was for a few months after she was forced to interact with cops, lawyers, or child services staffers. The assistance she got from the state after agreeing to take in her sister's boys was her only income, and she almost just lost one of those cash cows. So she'd be wound up pretty tight about that close call, and would likely avoid doing anything to Wade that would leave a mark on his face or make him limp. She beat him less anyway, and never just for fun like she did Ben. So, the kid had *that* going for him, at least.

Rather, what plagued Ben's mind now was the mental image of his eight-year-old brother merely going about the mundane tasks of existence while scared and alone. This was enough to release a flood of grief and rage within Ben so strong he struggled to inhale. He pinched the bridge of his nose, leaned his head against the hot glass of the plane window, and wept in a way he had not wept in many years.

CHAPTER 4

BEN HAD spent the second half of the flight pretending to sleep as he prepared a monologue for Reid. This would be more of an *invective* or a *diatribe*, if Ben remembered the meaning of those words correctly. Something to truly blindside the man, something to establish the boundaries. He'd focused hard on choosing the characteristics he felt Reid would be most self-conscious about, then worked on appropriately balancing the subtle with the excessive within the attacks against each. Then he began arranging the most robust portion of his monologue, the onslaught against Reid's profession. He ran through the most appropriate language and facial expressions to accompany each phase, and cataloged several zinger counterpoints to correspond with the most likely comments Reid would try to splutter out along the way. Ben was trying to find a fitting place for the word *penchant* within a witty accusation of pedophilia he'd been cobbling together when he realized something and stopped himself.

He cast a quick, one-eyed glance toward Reid from his fake-sleeping position and halted all resistance against the disappointing conclusion he'd just reached. He let the conclusion wash over him and had to stop himself from sighing audibly as he did so.

He couldn't show his cards now. He needed to embody the deviant urchin, embrace the role of the juvenile delinquent. Ben had been so shaken at their first meeting—so emotional and on such poor footing— he felt the opportunity to shock and to frighten this man had been taken from him. He felt he was *owed* that chance, like it was something he was entitled to. Ben also felt, however, that he needed to fight that craving, resist the urge to brandish his best weapon. He didn't know exactly why, but he felt deeply that it was in his best interest to simply be the troubled, ignorant shithead this man thought he was.

Once they'd arrived at the airport, Ben, Reid, and the two elder henchmen who made up Ben's escort detail left the plane, and Ben found the warm smile of the stewardess incredibly difficult to understand, let alone return.

As they made their way toward passenger pickup, Ben side-eyed the two other men, who, he had somehow gathered during the sordid morass of the day, were named Javier and Gordon. What he saw in them was something intimidating, and rare. Javier sported a large mustache and goatee, while Gordon went clean-shaven. From their eyes and the ways they carried themselves, Ben got the feeling that when things got sporty and violent, for these two, everything else in the world went into slow motion, except for them. For some reason, the notion of *violence* came to his mind from their relaxed hands, their eyes, their shoulders, the way they walked through the crowds. It was something he had never seen, he had no baseline for it, nothing to compare it to. There was no anger though, no rage, which, to Ben, had always been a prerequisite for violence. It was just violence, all on its own, humming calmly throughout their features.

Ben watched other travelers engaged in what appeared, to them, to be the familiar routine of picking up their baggage. It overwhelmed the boy, which quickly turned into annoyance.

"I ain't got no other clothes."

Ben was almost surprised he'd spoken the words himself. They came out of nowhere.

It seemed to surprise Reid as well, who stopped walking and looked down at Ben with a comforting, almost relieved smile. He put a strong, warm hand on Ben's shoulder.

"Don't worry about that at all. We've got clothes, shoes, boots, hats, packs, and everything you'll need all summer long, buddy. You'll even get to take it all home with you after you graduate in August."

Ben slowly recoiled from Reid's contact, leaning his upper body away from the man.

"Who's payin for all that, all this shit, this program or whatever? Aunt Nicki ain't payin, not a chance in hell a'that."

Reid nodded once before responding.

"Your tuition at Bear Springs and all other expenses are covered by our scholarship program. Very generous people from all over the world donate to our program so we can help all kinds of young guys, from all kinds of backgrounds. Because of the scholarship donations, we can help more kids than just those few whose parents can afford a program like this. They make it so we get to try and help any kids who need help the most."

Ben looked away from Reid.

"I don't need none a'y'all's help."

Reid slowly walked around where Ben stood so he could face the boy.

"Well, Ben, judges back in Jefferson Parish *and* Plaquemines Parish think you do, and judges get to make calls like that in the world we live in. So, at least for now, can you just give it a try? I promise you, buddy, you're *going to have a good time.*"

Ben glanced up at Reid, then back into the throngs and clusters of travelers again.

"Ain't like I gotta choice."

Reid squinted his eyes over a tight-lipped expression, then gestured with his head toward the doors that led outside.

"Come on, let's go meet Jimmy, Daniel, and Nicholas. They're outside at passenger pickup with the camp van we'll be taking from here to Bear Springs."

It was warm and bright outside. They made their way toward a white Sprinter parked along a curb that had a Bear Springs emblem on the side matching those on the shirts of the counselors. Outside the van were three more large, tanned men sporting the same polo shirt Reid was wearing. One of them had a ponytail and a toothy smile that annoyed Ben immediately. The other two reminded Ben of Javier and Gordon; older, stoic, and dangerous. There was also another kid with them.

This other kid sat on the concrete, arms wrapped around his shins, pulling his knees into his chest. He stared blankly into the sliding door of the large white van. He had black, disheveled hair. He looked kind of like an El Salvadorian kid who was a class ahead of Ben at his middle school.

Ben watched Reid exchange pleasantries and an excruciatingly awkward fist bump with the ponytailed asshole, before taking a knee in front of the kid sitting on the ground. He held out his hand to introduce himself. The kid looked up at Reid but did not extend his own hand.

Javier and Gordon did not say anything to the other counselors as Javier got behind the wheel of the van and Gordon got into the front passenger seat. At the same moment, the other, elder pair of men moved ahead to a new-looking white Toyota Tacoma parked in front of the van with the same Bear Springs emblem on the front passenger door and climbed in.

Ben made a note of that as the last counselor approached him, the smiley bastard with the ponytail. His voice was even more obnoxious than his appearance, *talking like a surfer would in some damn Nickelodeon cartoon,* Ben thought. He bobbed up and down on the balls of his feet as he spoke.

"Hey there, Ben, I'm Jimmy. I'll be one of your counselors this summer. I'm really stoked to get up to Bear Springs. I think you're going to love it, man. We're gonna have some *really* great times."

Ben looked at the van, pointing to it as he spoke without looking back at Jimmy.

"This our ride?"

The forced enthusiasm which Jimmy spoke with made Ben cringe inside—it made him want to kick Jimmy in the nuts or stomp on his knuckles.

"*Yahhh, man,* this is our Sprinter, pretty friggin sweet, right?"

Ben yanked back on the handle of the sliding door before Jimmy had finished his sentence, feeling the air-conditioning on his face as he worked his way to the farthest-back bench.

Reid called after Ben.

"Hey, Ben, buddy, I want you to meet Rodrigo. He's one of your fellow campers. Y'all are gonna be good friends by the end of this summer."

Ben looked and saw Rodrigo standing now, staring into the interior of the van. Other than looking deeply exhausted, he displayed no discernible emotion whatsoever. The boys locked eyes and acknowledged one another by quickly cocking their heads back, almost in unison. Ben looked away out the window as Rodrigo sat on the other end of the back bench from him and did the same out his window.

CHAPTER 5

THE DRIVE from the airport in Bozeman to Bear Springs Academy was long. Longest drive Ben had ever taken, so far as he knew, but it was not unenjoyable. He had never seen mountains before, let alone western Montana's shockingly large, horizon-sprawling vistas of granite spires and crags that drove into the sky above aprons of pine and aspen forests, and the rolling seas of sage and cheatgrass that flooded away from the topography. Nor had Ben ever seen houses of the kind they passed on the outskirts of Bozeman and thereafter along their drive.

To Ben's eyes, these were massive, gaudy fortresses made up of giant stones and logs. Goddamn *castles* nestled amid bronze statues of elk and trout, flamboyant gates and archways where long driveways snaked away into the large properties, flanked by fountains and water features. Some of these mansions had what must've been *miles* of copper gutters—Ben saw more copper on *one goddamned garage* than he and his friends would've been able to strip from *hundreds* of the abandoned commercial properties that littered the southern Louisiana landscape.

Ben was completely foreign to and awestruck by all these trappings of the Patagonia-clad gentry of the modern West. So much so that he'd almost forgotten the horrible circumstances of how his day had begun. Ben glanced over at Rodrigo, wondering if he was equally smitten by the scenery, or equally shaken by how his day had started.

He found the boy had not moved an inch—hunched into the window of the van as though he were willing himself to shrink away and fuse into the bench of the vehicle itself—staring out at some point in the immense landscape, but staring out at nothing at all.

Neither of them spoke a word the entire drive. Reid and Jimmy sat on the bench behind Javier and Gordon and would excitedly point out elk, pronghorn, or deer they'd spotted in the meadows or valleys along the road. None of these sightings earned a response, despite how fascinated Ben truly was to see these animals. He'd force himself not to move his head to follow the big mammals as they'd pass by, force himself to avoid betraying any physical indication of interest in anything these two louts had to say.

Javier and Gordon were almost as silent as the boys. Although at one point, Reid asked both of the men up front something Ben could not hear, but he did hear Javier respond in his raspy voice as he said *wouldn't bet a busted trace-chain on it.* Shortly thereafter, Reid asked the pair another question Ben could not hear, but he did hear Gordon respond with *of that, I am certain as all fuck.*

Though Ben was still, as always, he was paying very close attention to everything. They'd spent about three hours driving along the Clark Fork River on Interstate 90 since leaving Bozeman, heading mostly northwest going what Ben had to guess was just under the 80 mph speed limit, clipping along at a trucker's pace. He reckoned that was somewhere near the two-hundred-mile mark when they left I-90. From there he noted being on Highway 93, then Highway 200 along the Flathead River, then Highway 56 passing Bull Lake, then Highway 2, which took them on their first east then southern tacks, and then finally a long, winding county road Ben did not catch the number of.

Eventually they turned into and drove under one of the large, gaudy ranch archways that Ben had grown accustomed to over the past seven hours, and Reid announced their arrival at camp. Ben checked back over the four-hundred-ish-mile map he'd completed in his head, then stowed it all away in his mind as he vaguely pondered why these lazy goddamned Montanans hadn't bothered cutting a road between Highway 200 and Highway 2.

Ben would soon answer that question for himself as he became more familiar with the infallible, dispassionate nature of this wild high country. But as he arrived at Bear Springs Academy, he did not yet grasp the

Rocky Mountains' resolute disregard for the comfort and convenience of man.

The long driveway they took now was lined with tall poplar trees and snaked its way toward yet another imposing mountainscape, visible but with flat detail due to the fading evening light. The van stopped in front of a massive log-and-stone building Reid told them was called "The Lodge," as he opened his door and hopped out of the van.

Ben stared out through the van's window, overwhelmed by the beauty of what he was looking at. The castle of a building had interior lighting that made it look warm and inviting in the twilight. Ben could see a number of other barns and cabins behind this lodge; smaller but equally lavish and cared for. All of them were sturdy-looking structures built with large timbers and barn wood, with tall veneers made of tire-sized stones. Every building Ben could see was surrounded by its own manicured garden filled with flowers, shrubs, and shocks of wild grasses. Behemoth pine trees stood individually or in small clusters throughout the sprawling, landscaped grounds and lantern-lit pathways that weaved between the buildings.

Ben and Rodrigo pulled themselves out of the Sprinter van and stood there looking at the grounds in silence. To Ben, it all kind of looked like a mountain-cowboy version of Hogwarts.

Ben had seen several of the Harry Potter movies at a friend's house a few years earlier. He had never derived enjoyment through fantasizing, or by *pretending* as a young boy. He could never take himself into another world with Legos or fake swords. However, for months after seeing those movies, Ben lay in bed at night frustrated by the story of that fictional British kid getting swept away by magical, kind wizards to live in a castle. *Why bother even trying to construct some sympathetic narrative if you're just gonna go and give the magical little bastard a clean house, his own little bedroom, and three square meals?* Ben had wondered. Why not *build* the sympathy by giving the main character clusters of infected burns after being used as an ashtray, or a few mornings of being woken up by kicks and stomps from his aunt's naked, laughing boyfriend? Why not have the main character getting swept away from an aunt's fists and smoke, or the oppressively hot bayou country, or the perpetual, maddening screech of cicadas, or the acidic musk of pulp mills and oil refineries braided into the humidity you breathe?

As Ben looked up at this grand lodge, he felt a strange pang of nostalgia for those nights spent thinking about that lucky asshole Harry Potter. It wasn't the old frustration with the unreasonableness of the exposition though; it was a jolt of excitement and relief. It was a jolt of *vindication*. Ben—the one who *actually deserved* sympathy and rescue—had been swept away and sent to a castle after all. He felt shame at this emotion, and forced it from his mind easily by thinking back on the goons tearing him from his brother as they both shrieked and wept.

He took in a deep breath and begrudgingly noted the relief and dopamine release that accompanied the crisp, clean, cool air filling his lungs.

The boys were led by the endlessly enthusiastic counselors into the lodge. The fancy décor and size of everything in the entryway was a sensory overload for both Ben and Rodrigo. The massive double doors of the lodge opened into a cathedral of a room where a monstrous staircase led up like a causeway to a landing the size of Aunt Nikki's living room, then again to the second floor. Ben noted the four elder men—Javier, Gordon, Nicholas, and Daniel—peel away from the group toward the staircase, where each took an old, worn cowboy hat from a polished-bronze tree that seemed specifically designed to cradle them. The tender yet intentional way the men put their hats on suggested they'd been longing to do so, ever since whenever it was they'd set out from this place on their deviant-roundup operation.

Reid and Jimmy led the boys down a long hallway lined with photographs, new and old, of smiling groups of teenagers in rafts or on top of mountains. These photos hung under a dozen moose, elk, and deer trophies, their antlers seeming to reach across the hallway toward one another to form a canopy of bone overhead. The sounds of excited voices up ahead drew both boys' attention down from the photos and large, decapitated beasts.

They were ushered into a large room lined with bookshelves, big and small oil paintings in ornate frames, lamps, and huge windows.

Several rows of large leather couches and chairs formed a horseshoe around an open area at the foot of a massive stone fireplace where a crackling fire leapt and flared. There were about a dozen other polo-clad counselors—all fit, tanned, athletic-looking men who appeared to be in their midtwenties to midthirties—buzzing around the room with smiles and irksome positivity.

Ben counted twenty-six other teenage boys already in the room, sitting or milling around among the awkwardly invigorated adults. Ben began sizing up those of them within view and found most of them were staring around the room doing the same. They were Black, Hispanic, other white kids, and even one kid who, to Ben, looked Hawaiian or something. The only similarity between this group of boys was their collective glower.

They were all from vastly different cultures, families, and cities throughout the United States, but in that moment—milling around in what they would learn to call the "Great Hall" within the lodge—they were all connected by one harmonious current; they all shared a sense of discomfort at this ostentatious setting, and some type of rage toward the traumatic circumstances that had forced them from their homes and into this room.

A chipper, skinny blond guy virtually skipped over to Ben and Rodrigo carrying a large stainless-steel tray filled with foil-wrapped lumps. His smile was warm and friendly but *intense*. Every word he spoke sounded as though it were about to be followed by a fit of giggling.

"Hey, guys! I'm Riley, one of the counselors here at Bear Springs. You guys look *hungry*. Grab a burrito—we've got chicken, steak, or veggie."

Rodrigo grabbed one without reading the label or looking at the man's face, then stalked over to one of the leather chairs near the fire, where he promptly began devouring the meal.

Ben watched him go, then looked back at Riley. He held the young man's gaze as he used both hands to grab four of the burritos. He watched the counselor flick his eyes down at the serving tray and saw his smile falter briefly as he did this. Ben spoke as Riley stared down at his large helping.

"*Good lookin out*, Riley."

Ben barked out the words, intentionally abrupt and sharp, much louder than was necessary.

Ben felt satisfaction when he saw the young man's flinch and flurry of blinks, obviously startled at the timing and volume of his words. Ben turned on his heel, strode away, and listened eagerly for words of reproach as he did so—some kind of admonition for his tone or attitude offered from Riley or another counselor.

Ben really hoped it would come. He really hoped he'd have an early opportunity to feel these counselors out through confrontation while he was on good ground.

Ben stuffed three of the burritos into the pocket of his hoodie as he made his way toward the farthest vacant seat from the fireplace, where he sat and began inhaling the fourth. He could sense the gazes from several of the other boys on him as he began to eat and could guarantee the gaze of all the adults.

When he finished the burrito, he looked around the room for a trash can. He saw one across the room next to two of the cheery counselors. They were both overusing hand gestures as they engaged in animated conversation about something that Ben just knew down to his bones would be unbearably fucking ridiculous. He stood and strode toward them. He walked calmly but with confidence, focusing on crinkling the foil that had wrapped his burrito into a little ball as he approached them.

When he was a few paces away from the trash can, he looked up and found both of the counselors looking at him, smiling and shifting their posture as though to welcome him into their conversation as a friend. Ben offered the closer one a slow nod and a warm smile, a smile he made sure reached his eyes.

The man was a shorter, muscular, and rather hairy guy. Looked like a wrestler. Ben could see the guy become disarmed by his smile, see the subtle flush of tension leave his shoulders, see kindness and what was almost excitement mix together in his expression. The man took a small step toward Ben and extended a hand. Ben held his gaze, and before he even finished speaking the words *Hi there, my name is*—Ben dropped the foil in the trash can, spun abruptly on his heel, and walked back toward the chair he'd occupied a few seconds earlier.

He could hear the surprise in the man's voice as his introduction was cut short and his sentence sputtered out into a mumble. He could almost *feel* the look of embarrassment or indignation he assumed, *hoped* the man was exchanging with the other counselor. Again, Ben waited for words of admonishment or reproach, waited for some kind of scolding for his rudeness to punch out across the large room. Again, he really hoped those words would come; he hoped for the opportunity to make these adults look petty, stupid, and overly sensitive.

None came by the time Ben sat, intentionally slowly, back into the same chair. He was disappointed, but he accepted the lack of confrontation. To Ben, it either meant that these adults were weak, or they were even more patient than he'd given them credit for.

If it was indeed the latter, that meant this would be an enjoyable challenge. He'd have a chance to employ some of the more advanced strategies he'd rarely bothered using on the short-tempered, idiotic teachers and adults he was used to. He looked around the large room and across the faces of the boys and counselors alike and, at least for a brief moment, felt that this summer might not actually be such a nightmare after all.

CHAPTER 6

WHILE IT was something entirely foreign and new to all the anxious boys brooding around the Great Hall that evening, Bear Springs Academy had actually opened its doors way back in the summer of 1892, the same year the Great Northern Railway finally blasted and carved its course through the unforgiving landscape of northwestern Montana.

In the 131 or so years since that first summer, young men from all fifty U.S. states—as well as the territories of Utah, Oklahoma, New Mexico, Arizona, and Alaska, prior to their statehood—had graduated from the program. Its doors opened to boys from all around the continental United States, and it was far ahead of its time in accepting anyone of any color or background, be they Black, white, brown, Native, Christian, Jewish, rich, poor, or otherwise. Given this progressive policy for the times, those families with either the money or a segregationist inclination, or both, as was often the case, would not have considered sending their boys to spend a summer at a place like Bear Springs Academy. Thus, out of necessity, for the first decades following its inception this institution operated more like a seasonal boarding home for troubled youth and orphans, as opposed to the status it presently enjoyed as a therapy-forward rehabilitation program—this being a model and reputation it began developing around the midtwentieth century.

Through the latter half of that century, national segregationist proclivities began to wane, while at the same time general public interest in as well as the demonstrable efficacy of behavioral programs increased.

As support for inclusivity and for cognitive behavioral therapy rose, established institutions such as Bear Springs Academy were well situated to accommodate deferrals from state criminal courts interested in alternatives to traditional juvenile corrections programs. In the early 1980s, with a secure stream of funding from grants and private sources, as well as an increased availability and dependability of recreational outdoor winter gear, Bear Springs started running a spring class in addition to its traditional summer program. Since its first summer, 4,612 young men representing virtually every cultural and ethnic diaspora that has existed in the United States since the late sixteenth century—as well as dozens of different Native tribes who were here long before then—had graduated from Bear Springs Academy.

Unbeknownst to any one of those thousands of young men, any current or former members of the Bear Springs staff, and even to the boy with the watchful eyes sitting in that Great Hall himself, Benjamin Thibodaux was *profoundly* different from anyone else who'd ever been through this program before.

Indeed, Ben was profoundly different from almost every living person in the world. The entire global demographic of people with whom Ben could reasonably be described as bearing any real, meaningful similarity to likely only numbered in the mere hundreds.

Every individual person has unique qualities. *The same snowflake has never fallen twice,* as it's said. Fingerprints, retina patterns, disabilities, moles, sexual kinks, aspirations, all the products of one's nature and one's nurture—every individual is a salad of experiences and qualities that make them unique, to be sure. But there are some who truly are set apart from the rest. There are some born with something nameless and exquisite, something impossible to predict, duplicate, or really even explain. There are those rare few born with minds so exceptionally wired that they simply eclipse the observable mean that exists throughout the rest of the entire species. Those born with minds that have a resting power so extraordinary it can seem unnatural.

There are several reasonable ways people would have aptly, albeit simply, described *Ben's thing.* Some would have referred to it as a master-level aptitude for human interaction, others perhaps as simply an extraordinary social intelligence. However, no one had ever bothered to try. It was just *Ben's thing*.

It was just something about him, something that manifested in a way that was unsettling, often even shocking, to most of the adults the boy had ever communicated with. To most adults who interacted with Ben, it felt like you were meeting the only other person in the world who was also fluent in that secret, fucked-up language you use when you're talking to yourself.

If Ben had grown up with decent role models, teachers, or schools—or even just in semiregular contact with any adult who bothered affording him some base level of sincere attention—he likely would have started being referred to as *uniquely intelligent* by the age of two. By the age of five, adults would have begun regularly employing terms like *child prodigy* or *savant* to describe him. By the age of eight or nine, he'd have likely found himself playing Franz Liszt on the piano in crowded amphitheaters, or perhaps doing simultaneous chess exhibitions against a dozen adults, or maybe on some university conference circuit amusing academics with complex proofs or working memory challenges.

Even if none of those things came to pass, even if Ben had just grown up under the wing of someone only mildly interested in fostering his abilities, the ambient backdrop to all his childhood memories would've been an awareness that adults were impressed by him, in a *good* way, and that he was special, in a *good* way.

Ben, however, did not grow up under any of those conditions, nor did he enjoy any sincere or even base level of attention from any adult in his life. Apart from a few caring moments from his mother before she died, he never experienced what genuine interest, nurturing, or encouragement from any elder person felt like.

Ben's cognitive abilities were never guided, honed, encouraged, or tested. He had never taken dives into challenging curriculum or been introduced to stimulating subject matter. Indeed, Ben had spent a tragically significant portion of his thirteen years and several months thus far simply being ignored as he went about his days in states of fear, anger, and immense stress and anxiety that he had no idea were abnormal. There was no exposure to *eventualities* or *opportunities* associated with his intelligence; those were not even workable concepts in his mind, just more English words with definitions he had memorized. Those things that stimulated his uniquely powerful mind were most often just associated with mere survival.

Ben's mind, therefore, had thus far not been *refined* in the sense that there was any level of volitional sculpting. It was something feral, something that simply *was*, as opposed to something truly operative. Like the fists on a large athletic man, or the teeth on a bobcat. This brain, its bottomless archive, and its propensity for lightning-fast calculation and recall had just been pulsing along in a level of stagnation, thrashing against the inside of this skinny, angry, terrified boy's skull.

Thus, it is a farcical thing to compare the person Ben was as he sat in the garish Great Hall that evening to some hypothetical child prodigy being courted by Ivy League universities at the age of ten. The dramatic *contrast* was actually what was most notable. Like that which exists between the nameless mutt living off garbage and roadkill in the industrial outskirts of some town in central New Mexico, and the upland hunting dog from a prestigious bloodline living off venison and probiotic dog food while sleeping on a Tempur-Pedic bed with its name monogrammed into it. The differences are immeasurable, and the extent of their similarities is mostly just a matter of physiology.

But Ben did know he was different, or at least that he *had* something others did not have. He certainly never considered himself a savant or prodigy in the traditional sense, and he saw the countless similarities between himself and other guys his age he grew up with. Ben knew that, at the end of the day, he was still a boy who could be deeply frightened, and overwhelmed, and often driven by emotional impulse or recklessness.

He also had not developed any kind of maturity that would allow him to fully take advantage of his unique mind—which Ben's seventh-grade guidance counselor referred to as "a blessing from God *and* the devil." As such, Ben usually employed his cognitive power to simply press people's buttons, manipulate, push boundaries, and challenge what he had decided was very likely the worst and most dangerous part of this world—a feigned poise present in virtually every adult he'd ever met.

Ben scored only slightly above average in writing, mathematics, and social studies. He could read something once and be able to recite it verbatim forever, but he had not figured out how to really employ that to his academic benefit. Perhaps more accurately, he had just never seen why that was even something worth doing.

Be all that as it may, there was something Ben would, and often did, use his mind to do. Something Ben felt it was virtually guaranteed that others his age *could not* do. Ben was able to subconsciously log away the ways adults spoke and communicated, their words and phrases, and the body language and facial expressions that accompanied different moods or subject matter. Whether it was something he saw on TV or in real life, an actor in a movie scene, a politician on the news, a lawyer in court, a teller at the bank, or a teacher at his school, Ben could store it away—the gestures, the language, the timing of the delivery—just like it was someone's name. He didn't even know what some of the words or phrases he had stored away in his mind really meant, he wouldn't bother recalling them to use while writing a paper for school, but he knew how to use them in conversation.

Perfectly.

As a result, when Ben wanted to, he could communicate in a way and with a composure, maturity, delivery, and grasp of language that were often jarring to adults. In some cases, even terrifying. He had the ability to embody an entirely new person and engage in a level of mature conversation that would absolutely floor most adults who thought, up until that moment, that they had just been engaging some normal teenage boy in thoughtless conversation.

There is a group of several dozen people in this world—completely unaware of one another or their own membership in this group—who regularly reflect back on their interactions with this boy named Ben, years after they happened, with goose bumps on their skin. As soon as that haunting conversation had ended, however, Ben had not thought about any one of those people ever again.

Ben figured that most human beings, upon reaching the age of twenty or perhaps twenty-five, simply became manipulative and full of shit. He saw it as something similar to getting taller, hair graying, simply a biological progression. To Ben, all adults wore a facade, and as soon as he met or even stood near an adult, he'd immediately begin his testing, prodding, and reflex checks.

Ben derived a profound satisfaction from these quiet investigations. Likewise, he felt real fascination and even true joy at seeing the disbelief, shock, and sometimes even fear he could force into an adult's face when he'd morph into someone intellectually superior and with more social grace and intelligence than they had. He probably enjoyed it more than anything else in life. He could also protect himself by being that way, and he could protect Wade.

He'd never met anyone like Reid, though. Ben had met good and bad men—murderers, rapists, thieves, dealers, coaches, athletes, preachers, teachers, junkies of all stripes—and had most of them figured within a minute of hearing them talk.

Not Reid. Ben sat in that leather chair staring up at the fireplace and could almost feel Reid's gaze on him, like it was a unique radio frequency. He could almost taste it and was mostly successful as he tried to suppress a shudder at the memory of the paralyzing effect of Reid's smile in his aunt's trailer.

Ben did not believe in God, magic, or an afterlife. Likewise, he did not exactly put much stock into science, rationalism, or the Socratic method. He did not have particular grievances or disbelief in those constructs either; he just hadn't been exposed to them on any level that went deeper than their definition; he hadn't been equipped with the knowledge or mental tools to give any of those lofty concepts much consideration.

Ben just usually knew when something was cool or when something was screwed up, and he usually knew which long before the people around him did.

He felt there was something unnatural and predatory about Reid. Ben was not sure why or how, but he got the impression that Reid casually, yet consistently and with deep focus, worked to hide whatever that unnatural, predatory quality was.

The fact that Reid was able to paralyze or hypnotize Ben with a single smile was not the only reason Ben felt that way about him either, even though he'd sure as shit never experienced anything like that before.

Something else radiated off Reid. It was like a humid stench, or static electricity just above the surface of a fleece blanket. A vibe, as Rodrigo would later describe it—a *super sketch-ass fuckin vibe*.

He glanced over at Reid, saw him wiping his hands and stepping away from the other counselors to survey the room. He watched him take in a deep breath and prepare to speak.

Ben clenched his jaw in anticipation several seconds before Reid's strong, calming, confident voice punched across the room. Preparing himself to hear Reid's voice shot a strange feeling into Ben's gut and the back of his neck, like the one you get as you watch the tip of a needle before a nurse sticks it into your arm.

"Alright, guys, gather round, gather round, let's get these seats up in front filled up."

The exhausted, edgy boys slowly congregated closer to the open floor before the fireplace where Reid now stood, flanked by the smiling Bear Springs staff in a formation that would satisfy a naval officer.

"Alright, fellas, as most of you know, my name's Reid, I'm the camp director here, and on behalf of myself and the rest of this amazing team, I'd like to welcome you all as the 2023 summer class of the one, *the only*, Bear Springs Academy!"

The counselors all erupted into raucous cheering—clapping, whistling, laughing, jumping up and down. One of the insufferable motherfuckers was actually *fist pumping*. They were in their own world up there. They'd all gone totally febrile. It was excruciating to watch.

The contrast between the group of counselors standing before the hearth and the group of boys staring back at them was so stark and profound it was like they were on different planets. The boys did not make a sound. Some shifted uncomfortably or slouched, but most remained motionless. All of them watched the fevered joviality of the adults with a mixture of exhausted resignation, confusion, and disbelief.

Except for Ben.

Ben was watching the other boys. He was taking *their* measure. These ridiculous theatrics created a wonderful opportunity to do so. Ben watched one of the Black kids up toward the front—who he'd learn later was named Trent—drop his face into his hands and start rubbing his temples. He watched Rodrigo slowly shaking his head, staring at the counselors through squinted eyes.

Reid fell into a well-rehearsed, prosaic spiel about the therapeutic objective of wilderness therapy and reform, which flowed seamlessly into an overview of their calendar over the next twelve weeks. He went over the rules of the place, the activities schedule, bear safety, meal times, the one-on-one therapy requirements, their strict rule against cell phones and internet access while here, and so forth. It would seem, however, that at least half of their time this summer would actually be spent on backpacking or rafting expeditions in the national forests or national parks around northern Montana.

Reid also told them about the current spring class of Bear Springs Academy—the group of guys who had been here since March and were slated to go home soon. They were all in the mountains with a few other counselors completing their last *solo nights*, which, Reid began to explain, represented the final step in their program.

Reid's voice dropped an octave as he began discussing this topic of the *solo night*. His didactic, high school coach vibe quickly fell away, replaced by a pensive, almost religious ardor. A thick air of reverence fell over all the assembled counselors. One man held his hand over his heart, closed his eyes, and stared up at the ceiling as he nodded slowly. A few locked their fingers in front of them and hung their heads as though in prayer. Several pairs put their arms around one another's shoulders and nodded slowly at Reid with deep credulity in their eyes.

The man explained how each boy would be chosen to go on their *solo night* toward the end of the summer once the staff determined that their minds, bodies, and spirits were ready. The boy would be given his camping gear and guided to an area in the wild where he would be left alone to make a fire, cook his dinner, then spend the night under the stars, without a tent, in silent reflection. The next morning, the counselors would go to retrieve him, and he would leave behind his old self, and come back as a different man. Ben listened as Reid—with great solemnity and painfully drawn-out and unnecessary detail—described the final threshold each boy had to cross on his journey toward self-mastery, discipline, temperance, and *becoming a man.*

The topic finally, mercifully changed as Reid brought up the spring class again, the group of guys currently in the mountains, who they'd all get an opportunity to meet in a few days when they came back down to catch their rides to the airport. Their rides to freedom. Ben looked forward to that, getting the measure of those who'd already been here for several months. Ben wondered if they'd all be like Frank from back home, and wondered if *he* would end up like Frank. Ben had an intense aversion to that thought, but a simultaneous curiosity about it as well. Kind, helpful people who followed rules certainly seemed to have an easier time in life, after all.

The twenty-eight boys were eventually broken up into seven *fire circles*, delineated by color, for the purposes of lodging while at what the counselors called "Bear Springs Basecamp." Each fire circle had its own cabin, shared between four boys and a counselor. They were then ushered out of the Great Hall and out into the night, where they followed the lantern-lit walkways to their cabins.

The boys were all speechless when they entered the cabin. Ornate, large rugs lay over the dark, well-oiled wood floors. Large paintings of alpine valleys, trout, mountain men, and wagon trains passing through flowering prairies hung in lavish frames, illuminated in soft yellow light cast from small, angled lamps mounted above each frame. The embossed baseboards and trim around the windows and doorways looked hand-carved. The boys each had their own bed and dresser, all spaced apart nicely, two against each wall. Their dressers were full of socks, underwear, pants, shirts, sweaters, hats, and shoes—all the right size. There was a large bathroom in each cabin with two toilet stalls and four shower stalls. The beds were already chosen for the boys, likely to avoid conflict, Ben assumed, and there was a separate large bedroom at the back of the cabin where the counselor slept.

They were nice digs. Undeniably so. Nicer bedrooms than any of the boys had back home, nicer than most had ever even seen in real life. It was so surreal that it only amplified their delirious exhaustion.

Ben was in the *green fire circle*, along with Rodrigo, whom he'd already met, the Black kid named Trent Williams, and another white kid, tall and lean, named Billy Axelson.

Ben had noticed Billy as soon as he'd arrived in the Great Hall several hours earlier—he wasn't just the most dangerous-looking kid in that room, he was the most dangerous-looking *person* in that room, adults included. Ben, Rodrigo, and Trent were thirteen, Billy was fourteen. Jimmy, the obnoxious dickhead with the ponytail Ben had met at the airport, was their cabin counselor. Jimmy insisted that the boys engage in a "what's your name, where ya from" kind of introductory session before being allowed to go to bed.

Turns out Rodrigo was from Albuquerque, and had gotten arrested for breaking into a used car dealership one night and firebombing the office with Molotov cocktails. Said they'd ripped his dad off. He was the middle child of five, all of whom still lived with both their parents, who only spoke Spanish. Trent was from Lansing, Michigan. He lived with his dad, who worked for the post office, and had an elder brother who'd moved into his own place a few years earlier. Trent had been arrested in a car he'd stolen with a bunch of copper he and some buddies had stripped from abandoned buildings on the outskirts of Lansing.

Ben nodded approvingly at the end of Trent's introduction.

"My buddies and me strip copper, too, lots of it sitting around in old places no one uses anymore. It's good money, no one's using it, so why not, right?"

Trent grinned and nodded back at Ben.

"For real. It's just sitting there, ain't harming anyone by taking it and selling it. What's the big deal?"

Jimmy interjected and cut off Ben and Trent's exchange with some empty comment about trespassing and private property. Ben and Trent looked back at one another as Jimmy spoke, grinned, and shook their heads, but stayed quiet.

Billy only spoke a few words that first night. Jimmy prodded the large boy to tell the others what it was like growing up in Texas. Billy did not do so, but he did offer up a two-word correction in response, before falling back into his impenetrable silence.

"*West* Texas."

The other boys regarded Billy warily, almost as though he had some kind of contagious affliction. He was a lot taller and more muscular than most fourteen-year-old dudes Ben, Rodrigo, or Trent had ever met. Billy also spoke with this sharp cut at the end of his words, those very few he spoke, that was something just a step down the scale from a snarl. He also had a flat gaze that was menacing yet vaguely unfocused at the same time. To Ben, the boy's eyes were those of the unfortunately unsurprised, the reluctantly initiated.

The three boys would not have all described the feeling in the same way, but they all got pretty much the same impression of Billy that first night. Those repulsive, heinous things you have read or *heard about* people doing but have *never actually seen* someone do in real life—for Billy, that was a much shorter list than it was for most people.

The boys all went through the process of changing out of the clothes they'd arrived in and into their new pajamas, which would've been much more awkward if they weren't all so exhausted. Jimmy then had to coax and usher them into the bathroom to have them brush their teeth, which Jimmy somehow did make awkward despite their exhaustion. Ben, Rodrigo, and Trent all gave Billy a wide berth as they moved around the cabin that first night, quietly bonding through the anxious glances they all periodically cast in his direction, or the exasperated looks the three boys would exchange in response to most things Jimmy said.

Billy was snoring loudly within thirty seconds of Jimmy turning off the light and shutting his bedroom door.

The quiet camaraderie Ben, Rodrigo, and Trent had developed in those first hours together faded as quickly as the light. In those first few moments of darkness, all three were again just young guys, in a strange place, uncertain about the experience to come, and very, very far from home.

Rodrigo stared at the ceiling for a while with an arm under his head. It was all so wildly unfamiliar. The smell of the pillow, wind in trees that sounded far away, the hum of the electric floor heaters. He glanced over toward Jimmy's room to confirm that the door was shut, then sat up and leaned toward Ben's and Trent's beds against the other wall.

He whispered as loudly as he could, "Yo, you guys awake?"

Trent sat all the way up in his bed, while Ben propped himself up on his elbows.

Rodrigo glanced toward Jimmy's door again as he spoke in another loud whisper.

"These counselors are weird, man, right? Do they seem normal to you?"

Trent looked toward Jimmy's door, then at Ben, then back at Rodrigo, and slowly shook his head from side to side.

Ben looked at Trent, then at Rodrigo. He did not bother whispering. "Nah, *they sure don't.*"

CHAPTER 7

B EN *THIGH . . . bo . . . docks . . .* Thibodaux? That's a pretty weird last name, B."

Hearing someone call him "B" made Ben think of his little brother, Wade. It made him think of the startled shame in the little boy's face as Ben would scold him for calling him *Pee-Pan* in front of other people, the repentance in the little boy's voice as he'd whisper *sorry, B.* Wade really had tried hard to make the change, as hard as a little boy could, at least. He forced the guilty recollections out of his mind.

Ben finished tying his boots—thinking of how he had to tie Wade's dirty little shoes every morning, knowing his aunt would not be doing that this morning, or the next—then looked up at Trent. The taller boy was inspecting the name placard that had been placed on the bed assigned to Ben the night they'd arrived in their cabin for the first time, several days earlier. He could see Trent's mouth silently sounding out Ben's last name.

"It's pronounced *Tib-a-doe.* It's an Acadian name. Cajun, you know? It's French, I guess. Town in Louisiana named Thibodaux too. Mom used to tell us the town was named after our great-great-great-granddaddy or somethin."

Trent and Rodrigo, who was sitting on his bed, both tried the name out loud a few times as pronounced by Ben, speaking over one another but getting it mostly correct.

Rodrigo shrugged.

"Frenchies got some weird names, bro."

Ben smiled at Rodrigo as he stood and stretched out his arms.

"Does that mean *Gut-tear-ezzie* is a French name too?"

Trent laughed. Rodrigo grinned and rolled his eyes.

"It's pronounced *Gu-tier-rez,* you alligator-riding fuck."

All the boys chuckled together. Trent picked up Billy's placard, holding it so all three could read his full name. Ben read it out loud, but very quietly, despite having all watched him leave the cabin a few minutes earlier.

"Billy Axelson . . . ol' Axe, eh?"

Trent tossed the placard back onto Billy's bed, then looked up at the clock on the wall.

"Shit, we gotta scoot, gotta muster at the Lodge Pole in five minutes. Time for some more *bull*shit log-carrying or somethin."

The boys groaned and shuffled out of the cabin and down the steps from the little porch. It was a short walk to the Lodge Pole from their cabin. Ben looked up at the mountains looming above Bear Springs as they walked. In a few days, the boys would be going on their first overnight expedition into the mountains. Ben would not betray this reality, but he was genuinely excited about it. He'd already grown a bit bored with the Bear Springs routine, as he had logged most of its patterns and had opened mental files on each of the counselors and all his classmates. He would need to eventually get his hands on one of the handheld radios the counselors used to communicate, but that was a dull heist to look forward to.

Over the past several days since they'd all arrived at Bear Springs, Ben, Trent, and Rodrigo fell in fast together. It could've been the collective stress at the experience plus sharing a cabin, or the fact that they all truly enjoyed one another's company. They were already starting to communicate silently like brothers or childhood friends. Particularly Trent and Rodrigo. Those two had fallen into an almost sibling-tier friendship that seemed to exceed any bond existing between any boys in the program.

Billy, on the other hand, had maintained the same stern reticence as he had the first night. Likewise, the boys maintained the practice of giving Billy a wide physical and conversational berth whenever they were around him. Billy only ever spoke when he was asked something directly. The boys could tell Billy intimidated the guys from the other cabins, as well. Even the counselors. It wasn't just his massive, calloused, scarred hands; he also just had the air of a grown man, or at least someone much older than the rest of the boys at the camp.

While the strangeness of the environment around them and the nuance of the "Bear Springs Basecamp" program had not yet abated, Ben, Trent, and Rodrigo had certainly begun to jibe with the routine.

Breakfast was in the mess hall of the lodge at 7:30 sharp every morning, then the boys did some kind of activity as a full class until lunch, often referred to as the *lesson* of the day. The first day they'd done archery, a task at which no boy appeared particularly adept, with the exception of a kid named Hector who said he used to bow hunt with his dad, and Trent. Within twenty minutes, Trent was shooting more bull's-eyes than not at fifteen yards with a heavy recurve bow. The second day they'd broken into small pairs for a shelter-building in the forest above basecamp, using sticks, rocks, and tarps. This activity, likewise, seemed very natural to Trent, his shelter ending up considerably stronger, larger, and sturdier than any of the rest. On the third day, they'd each been given large, expensive-looking backpacks and gone over how to pack the necessary gear for their upcoming "expeditions," two of which would be five days long, and were shown how to adjust all the straps so the packs would fit comfortably once heavily loaded.

After lunch the boys all had a couple of hours of "downtime" when they had to stay around basecamp, and during which time they cycled through their individual therapy sessions. The boys each had to do one of these therapy sessions every other day. There were four therapists on staff, and none of the boys in any one cabin saw the same one, seemingly by some design, Ben considered. He saw a therapist named Jessie, who looked much like all the rest.

During Ben's first therapy session with Jessie, the man spent most of their first hour asking questions he found to be quite shallow and predictable.

However, Ben engaged in this process with the best feigned sincerity and interest he could muster. He took careful note of the painfully obvious sense of relief and pleasant surprise Jessie betrayed as their first session went on, which suggested to Ben that this man had been warned—presumably by Reid—that Ben was a bit "challenging." Ben intended to continue these therapy sessions with doctored sincerity and enthusiasm, at least until necessity arose to adjust the strategy. Ben wished he could be a fly on the wall to observe Reid's reaction as Jessie told him how productive the therapy sessions were going, and how pleasant, honest, and open Ben had been.

After the downtime and therapy session block that took place after lunch, upon the tolling of a large and very loud bell, all the boys mustered under what was called the Lodge Pole in the center of the compound to engage in some other full-class group activity until dinner. This Lodge Pole was basically just a big wooden post in the ground surrounded by benches, with predictable, shallow slogans carved into it. Reid had introduced the Lodge Pole to them as some kind of totem or symbol of their collective strength and resolve. The boys hadn't quite figured out what this block of time was meant for yet, but it seemed as though the activities during this time could be just about anything.

The first day was a stupid team-building exercise where they all introduced themselves, basically a larger version of what they did in their cabins the first night. The second day they were broken into new groups, each tasked with collectively carrying a "team pole" on their shoulders up a trail as the counselors got them to sing goofy chants about determination and perseverance and other kitschy bullshit. That was exhausting, and Ben could sense the rising irritation and ire of the group toward the end of the exercise. After dinner, the boys broke into their *fire circle* cabin groups and engaged in more activities with their individual cabin counselor, as well as additional counselors who'd occasionally join in for this portion.

To Ben, this postdinner, pre-bedtime evening block seemed like some kind of group therapy effort, wherein the counselors would get the boys to share experiences and discuss broad concepts together. Stale bullshit like "right and wrong" or "honesty."

Ben had determined that the handful of counselors who did not preside over their own little *fire circle* cabin, in addition to the program's therapists, all shared a large bunkhouse within the grounds that looked like a beefier version of all the others. He had not precisely pinned down the location where Reid and his four elder henchmen slept. There were no other outbuildings that seemed plausible for lodging, so he was very confident they had quarters somewhere in the lodge, as there was a considerable second-story wing of the sprawling building that was strictly off-limits to the boys. On his second day there, Ben had tested the doors at the top of the large staircase and found them locked tight.

He ran through the pattern and routine of the place as he walked with the other three boys from their cabin to the Lodge Pole and was not surprised to find that he was already fairly bored by it. At the same time, he was fairly bored with his life at home as well, so he looked down at his feet, and followed along the path quietly.

CHAPTER 8

B RING IT in, guys. Bring it in."
Reid stood under the Lodge Pole, using his arms to usher the throngs of boys dragging their feet into the area. He was a bit too far away to be certain, but Ben felt like Reid was staring directly at him.

The boys sat on the benches in silence and, as they knew would happen, Reid went about explaining the stodgy lesson and message embodied by today's bizarre activity that would fill the time between now and dinner, without actually mentioning what the activity would be. The boys were then led down a trail into the forest about a quarter mile to an area none of them had been before. At the end of the trail, they found a series of large stone benches surrounding a very large firepit, marked by the charcoal remains of bonfires past.

Rodrigo nudged Ben with his elbow, then gestured with his head toward a rack where a dozen large, doublehanded saws were resting, and beyond where a number of large tree-trunk-sized logs were laid out. Rodrigo rolled his eyes, held up two fingers, made a sawing motion with the same hand, then pointed to the firepit. Ben took in a deep breath through his nose and shook his head slowly in recognition of Rodrigo's meaning. Ben was impressed, as he hadn't actually caught this one yet himself.

Even though he'd only known the lanky boy for around a week, Ben had grown to recognize Rodrigo as one of the most perceptive people he'd ever met. Rodrigo could walk into a room, an outdoor area, or a group of people and know what was going on faster than everyone else—everyone else except for Ben, most of the time.

Within seconds of walking into the clearing, Rodrigo surmised that they'd be broken into pairs to use the doublehanded saws to cut the logs into firewood-sized pieces and then burn them in a bonfire. He was also able to communicate this forecast to Ben in just as brief a time without speaking.

And Rodrigo was exactly right.

Ben was paired up with a gangly kid named Marcus who he'd learned a few days earlier was from somewhere in California. He had been arrested after stealing one of his middle school teacher's cars, then crashing it through a neighbor's fence and wrapping it around a tree in their backyard before running from the police for two miles. Finally they caught up to him and hit him with a Taser.

They spent the next three hours working in the dry heat of the Montana summer—sawing the tree-sized logs into two-foot rounds, stacking those smaller logs neatly near the firepit, and then repeating the process. Reid and the other counselors walked among the boys as they worked, offering trite words of encouragement and brief lectures on the importance of teamwork, foresight, planning in life, and "preparation for uncertain times ahead." Obnoxious and uninvited shit like that.

After the last logs were stacked, they all marched back to the mess hall, where the boys quietly but aggressively ate their dinner of pasta and salad. After dinner, Reid announced that they'd all be going out together for a bit, instead of breaking up into their smaller *fire circle* groups like normal. The boys watched as the other counselors hefted large bags with marshmallows, graham crackers, and chocolate and led them down the trail toward the firepit. There was more buzz in the air on this walk than Ben had seen within the group thus far, some of the boys talking excitedly, laughing openly, declaring their affection for s'mores and campfires.

When they arrived, Reid gave some prepared speech about the importance of working together with others to prepare for times ahead, working with others to achieve a mutual goal, and the benefits of community efforts. Then several of the counselors made a flamboyant show of lighting the large bonfire, passed out metal stakes, and the boys and counselors mingled as they all went about the process of making and devouring s'mores.

It was the happiest Ben had seen the group since arriving. Even he couldn't help but enjoy the atmosphere and, especially, the treat. After all, Ben had never eaten a s'more before, without speaking, and with far less discernible emotion than the others.

Ben was standing alone, a few yards from the closest person and the large fire, when he heard the footsteps approaching behind him. He recognized the footfalls and the length of the stride, and he had been hoping for a moment like this to present itself. He didn't take his eyes away from the fire as he turned his head slightly so as to speak over his shoulder.

"*Reid*, you finna sneak up on me?"

Ben heard the abrupt change in the man's pace—the uncertainty betrayed by the slowness in his next step. He knew there was a chance it wasn't Reid, and if it wasn't, he'd be comfortable explaining his comment away. But he knew it was Reid now. It felt nice being right and successfully giving the strange man a little start, *very* nice, and Ben grinned into the fire. He glanced up at Reid when he'd finally walked up to stand next to him.

Reid stared back at Ben with a narrow-eyed look of curiosity.

"How'd you know it was me? Do I have a distinct smell or something?"

Ben looked back into the fire, shrugging slightly and cocking his head to the side.

"*Somethin.*"

Ben could hear Reid offer a snort of amusement, and then felt suddenly scared. He was scared because he remembered the way that he'd felt paralyzed by Reid's smile when he'd first met him in his aunt's living room. He remembered wanting to run into Reid's embrace and run into oncoming traffic at the same time—simultaneously seeing himself weep in Reid's arms as Reid comforted him, while also seeing himself ripped apart by the bumper of a truck on the tar-stinking highway outside his aunt's trailer park. He remembered that this was a bad man and tensed his shoulders and lower back in order to suppress a shudder as he continued to stare into the flames.

"Jessie said you guys have had a couple very productive therapy sessions so far."

Ben glanced up at Reid, shrugging as he responded.

"I guess. He seems nice."

Reid nodded and was quiet for a long moment before responding, seeming to use the silence as though it were its own full sentence.

"You wouldn't be intentionally insincere in therapy sessions with Jessie, right? You wouldn't just be saying things you think a therapist wants to hear, would you? That just doesn't seem like the kind of guy you are. Am I right about that?"

Ben felt a bolt of panic course through him but forced it away quickly. This fuck didn't have proof of that, he *couldn't* know that, *and even if he did, so what?* Ben steeled himself, assured by having outwitted older, scarier adults than this preppy frat-lord of a camp counselor. He could mess with any adult's head, and he'd been craving the chance to dunk on this asshole Reid since the minute he'd met him—since the minute his screaming little brother had been torn away from him and he'd then been torn from his home.

Ben finally heaved his shoulders up and held them there for a moment, then let out a long exhale as he looked back up at Reid.

"Ohhh come now, *cher*, thass beaucoup crazy. You'd think a fancy therapist with a fancy degree at a *fancy place like this* woulda seent right through that kinda shit awful quick, would they not?"

Reid squinted at Ben. Ben could see, as he'd seen so many times before, the surprise in this adult's face at his response, and the accompanying struggle to think of their own. It was all about footing, and Ben enjoyed the small, rare pleasure of conversing with someone *not from* southern Louisiana. Adding just a dash of Cajun slang into a clever, smart-assed comment always left them off-balance.

Ben held Reid's gaze as long as he could, then looked back toward the fire and focused all his attention on Reid's breathing, trying to discern the abrupt inhalation that would suggest Reid was about to speak. When he heard it, he waited a fraction of a second, timing his next comment to perfectly cut Reid off, just as Reid sucked in the necessary air to form his first word.

"Besides . . ." Ben spoke the word sharply, held his hands out to his sides briefly in a gesture of contrition, then clasped them in front of himself as he turned his body toward Reid and looked up into his eyes, relishing the familiar surprise on the man's face. As he spoke, Ben adopted a contemplative pose and cocked his head in a way he'd seen adults do in movies when they were thinking hard about something.

"Not sure I could even tell ya what *insincere* means, Reid."

The smile was gone from Reid's face now. Ben forced himself to hold the man's gaze, even though he felt scared, felt like he was playing with fire. He knew this man was bad, he just didn't know why.

Reid finally looked away from Ben toward the fire with an awkward grin. Ben had that facial expression stored away in his mind, as well. Ben knew it meant an adult was somewhere in the spectrum between embarrassed and angry. Then his face changed, and Reid eventually looked over toward Ben with his friendly, confident smile.

"The rest of the guys are lucky to have you here with them. We're all lucky to have you here. You're a good kid, Ben."

Ben was surprised by the warmth in Reid's response. He was annoyed by it as well. *This fuck face was gonna to be tough to crack*, he thought. Ben realized his facial expression was betraying his emotions when he saw Reid's smile grow a bit wider, reaching his eyes.

Ben looked down at a round stone embedded in the hard-packed dirt between his feet, feeling Reid's eyes on him. Ben kicked at the stone lightly, then looked up at Reid.

"Reckon I wouldn't be here if that were the case."

Something like pity crossed into Reid's expression. He shook his head as he spoke.

"Your character doesn't have to be defined by a few silly mistakes, Ben. When you meet the spring class tomorrow, you'll see, those are different guys than who they were when they got here. They came here boys, and they're leaving as men."

Ben had forgotten about that—about the other class of Bear Springs prisoners who were up in the mountains. He felt a bolt of excitement remembering that he'd get a chance to meet them. Assess them.

Reid had just started into another sentence when excited voices pulled their attention toward the trail that led back down to the lodge, where a gaggle of other counselors and a therapist Ben recognized were making their way toward Reid. A few of the counselors were on radios, while two jogged up to Reid and told him something that appeared urgent.

To Ben, they looked scared as they spoke. Reid's expression morphed into one of iron focus. Without saying another word to Ben, Reid yelled for a few of the other counselors who'd brought them up to the bonfire, and barked out some orders to them while he joined the other Bear Springs staffers as they all ran back down the trail.

Ben saw a few of the other boys watch the scene with worry on their faces, though some watched with what appeared to be amusement. He saw Billy sitting alone on one of the stone benches across the fire. Billy paid no attention to the commotion and remained fixated on the flames. He looked more youthful in that moment than Ben had ever seen him. He looked like he was an actual fourteen-year-old, instead of a hard, street-reared man that he could come across as.

Ben skewered a marshmallow, grabbed some chocolate and graham crackers, and walked around the fire toward the bench where Billy sat. When he was only a few paces away, Ben watched Billy's shoulders slowly tense and his hands ball into fists inside the front pocket of his hoodie. Ben slowed his pace. Billy did not look away from the fire.

"Sup, Billy."

Billy turned his head slightly, glancing over toward where Ben had stopped, squinting his outside eye as he did it. He held Ben's gaze for a moment, then looked back into the fire, only speaking the single word once he'd fallen back into his original posture.

"*Yah.*"

Ben heard the slight inflection of inquiry Billy put onto the end of the word, and Ben knew the single word translated to: *What do you want?* Ben took another step toward Billy and held the food items toward the bench.

"Got some s'more fixins, want one? They're pretty damn good. Never had one till tonight."

Ben could see Billy take in a slow, deep breath, but just barely. He responded without moving his gaze.

"Nah."

Ben nodded and just watched the quiet boy. He looked very far away in his mind. He looked dangerous.

In that moment, Billy reminded Ben of his aunt's neighbor's big mutt that spent every day chained to the old, dying cypress tree behind their trailer. Ben had spent many hours watching that mean dog, the way it would pull its ears back and put its tail down when another neighborhood dog would trot up to say hello, the way it would side-eye the uninvited dog visitor before snapping its jaws into its face.

Ben figured he'd try one more time to connect.

"Your buddies back home ever call you Axe?"

Billy looked up at him then. Ben recoiled inwardly and concentrated on not letting his body acquiesce to his brain's warning as he felt the urge to take a step backward when Billy's cold, gray eyes met his.

"No one calls me that. *No one.*"

Ben just nodded in response, allowing himself to finally move away from the large boy, trying to maintain some composure and mumbling something about *catchin ya later* as he did.

All the other boys were buzzing around the fire, proposing ridiculous theories as to what had the counselors all worked up. Bear, wolves, mountain lion, Bigfoot, and other potential sightings near camp had been offered.

A moment later Jimmy stood on one of the benches and shouted over the fire as the remaining counselors began corralling the group of boys.

"Alright, fellas, that's a wrap for tonight. Let's start heading back toward the cabins, time to call it a night! Let's get into formation!"

Jimmy started shouting out colors, delineating where everyone was supposed to go. When all the boys were going somewhere together within the general boundaries of Bear Springs, the counselors made the group walk "in formation." Basically, it was just all twenty-eight of them walking in a two-row column, sixteen guys on each side, with four of the fire circles on one side, four more on the other. The counselors shouted out colors and sides so that everyone always ended up walking next to someone new. A *bonding strategy*, Ben figured. One of the boys at the front of the formation had to carry the Bear Springs summer class flag, and the other had to carry the base where it was mounted. The counselors had the boys bring the flag everywhere they went as a group within the camp, then plant it at the base of the Lodge Pole before dinner every night.

Ben felt tired as the group worked its way back down the trail from the fire. The sugar high had the boys buzzing, and loud jokes and good-humored shit-talking echoed and strafed through the dark woods like the headlamps and flashlights carried by the counselors. Ben walked quietly and watched the light of the large bonfire behind them dance on the dark trunks of the ponderosa and spruce trees, wondering what his little brother was doing and what he'd eaten that night. Then, he wondered where Reid had run off to.

CHAPTER 9

THE WALK back to their cabin was only about fifteen minutes long, but it seemed sufficient for the slap-happiness of the bonfire to wear off. By the time they had made it back into the warm lantern glow of the basecamp grounds, Ben, Trent, and Rodrigo had grown as quiet as Billy.

Javier—one of the elder counselors, or *youth intervention transport specialists*, as Reid had branded him and Gordon back in Aunt Nikki's trailer—stood sentinel at a junction in the flagstone pathways that veined throughout basecamp, where the class began splitting and breaking into their respective cabin groups. Since arriving here, Ben had not seen any of the four intervention specialists wearing the matching garb they'd had on when Ben was taken from his home, which the other staff, and Reid, all still wore daily. Javier had a chambray shirt tucked into slim, dark jeans, both deeply worn, and roper boots that looked older than the man himself. Ben's jaw tensed whenever he was around Javier or the three other older counselors due to what he saw as potentially explosive force and tension coiled into their shoulders. The strange man stared up into the dark mountains with razor focus that only broke as Ben walked by and they gazed at one another. Javier's dark eyes glinted under the brim of his gambler-style cowboy hat, which dipped forward as the man nodded at Ben. Unsure exactly why, he felt the gesture came from a place of respect, so he returned the nod.

Jimmy waved the boys into the cabin and stayed by the door as they all filed in, then addressed the room in his obnoxious lilt that Trent had started calling the *Jimmy bro-bro voice*.

"Alright, fellas, I've gotta go help the other counselors with something really quick, alright? No leaving the cabin unless there's a real-deal emergency. Some of the other staff are hanging out outside in the common area for a while so they'll know if you try to pull a fast one on me, got it, bros?"

Ben hated the way Jimmy never stopped smiling as he spoke. It was fake. Forced. An anxious smile.

Billy, Rodrigo, and Ben responded by silently continuing to take their boots and dirty outdoor clothes off and getting into their pajamas.

Trent threw his boots toward the foot of his bed and cocked his chin toward Jimmy.

"What's goin on, Jimmy? Why'd Reid and the other counselors dip like that? Bear snatch up one of the counselors or somethin?"

Jimmy pumped his palms toward Trent in a calming motion, which came across as incredibly awkward and unwarranted given the lack of any real interest in Trent's voice.

"Ahhh, nothin to worry about, bros, we'll fill you in tomorrow, but just keep it cool for a half hour, alright? I'll be right back. Get ready for bed because when I'm back it's lights-out, bros!"

None of the boys responded with anything more than an eye roll.

A minute or so after Jimmy had left, Ben noticed Rodrigo in his periphery slowly get up from where he was sitting on the foot of his bed.

Ben looked over to see what he was doing, and saw Rodrigo carefully scanning the far side of the room with squinted eyes, taking slow steps forward as he did it, seeming fixated on the floor, the dressers, the closet door, the walls.

Trent looked at Ben, then followed his eyes toward Rodrigo, and barked a question toward Rodrigo's back.

"*Fuck you doin*, Rod?"

Ben noticed that Billy, likewise, had also started watching Rodrigo and following his gaze across the far side of the cabin. Billy slowly stood, then fell in with Rodrigo on his flank. Usually the second the group got back to the cabin, Billy either went straight to the bathroom or immediately to bed, and never paid any attention to what the other boys were doing or discussing. This was very much out of the ordinary—enough so for Ben to drop the hoodie he was trying to put on and stare at Rodrigo's and Billy's backs.

Trent reiterated his previous question.

"Yo, what the hell are you two lookin at?"

Billy didn't move anything but his eyes, switching his gaze between Rodrigo's face and the areas where Rodrigo was looking.

Rodrigo responded in an almost urgent whisper over his shoulder.

"Somethin ain't right in here, man. This ain't the way we left the cabin. I don't know what, but somethin's different. Somethin's wrong."

Trent looked at Ben with a mixture of confusion and concern, then back at Rodrigo, who had begun focusing on the large armoire on the far side of the cabin where all four boys kept their backpacks and camping gear.

Ben did not see what Rodrigo saw, but he trusted Rodrigo's instincts, even after spending only a few days with him. He reminded Ben of a hunting dog in that moment—frozen in point, muscles revving in the red, about to tear into a covey of quail hiding in a patch of willows. Without thinking, Ben began to move to Rodrigo's side.

Within a few seconds, Ben, Trent, and Billy all flanked Rodrigo as he slowly approached the large piece of furniture. Rodrigo looked back at the other three boys with wide eyes as he extended a shaky finger toward the armoire.

"Somethin's in there, bro. I ain't playin. *Somethin's fuckin in there.*"

Before the last syllable had even left Rodrigo's mouth, Billy was moving across the room. He moved so fast it made the other three flinch. They took a full step back as Billy ripped the doors of the armoire open so hard that one tore completely off the hinges and clattered onto the wooden floor.

Ben heard the distinct utterance of the word *shit* from an unfamiliar voice as Billy reached past the coats and packs on hangers, into the back of the armoire. Billy heaved his body backward and the head, then torso of a shocked-looking boy came tearing out of the armoire. Billy had full-handed grips of the kid's collar, and held him entirely aloft in the air as he spun around, then slammed him hard into the ground, pinning him in place. The kid hit the ground with such force

Ben could hear the wind blasted from his lungs before he started coughing.

Trent and Rodrigo dropped down to their knees on Billy's flanks, each putting hands on the intruder's shoulders and upper arms, as though Billy needed their help to keep the terrified kid pinned to the ground. Trent and Rodrigo then both started rapid-fire lines of inquiry, demanding to know who the kid was, and what the hell he was doing in their cabin. Billy remained silent, pinning the kid to the floor with his large, man-sized hands smashed into this new kid's collarbones.

The kid looked between the three others with feral, terrified eyes, but he didn't try to fight them. He looked about their same age. He had dirt on his face and dried blood near his scalp and below his right ear. His hands and forearms were covered in scrapes, blood, and dirt. His clothes were filthy as well, spackled in mud and burrs. He looked like he'd just pulled himself from the depths of a landslide.

Ben watched the kid catch his breath enough to begin trying to speak, adding a third voice into the pastiche of Trent and Rodrigo's frantic interrogation. Ben approached and stood over all the boys, speaking with a sharp volume and tone he rarely used around people his age, and hadn't yet around this particular group.

"*Hush now, fellas, that's enough.*"

Rodrigo, Trent, and the new kid all shut up immediately, looking up at Ben with a mix of surprise and apprehension—as they would a schoolteacher or coach who was scolding them. Billy just loosened his grip on the kid's collar a bit, but did not look away from the kid he was pinning beneath him.

Ben pointed down at their prisoner before asking his first question.

"You happen to be a member of the *spring* class?"

Trent and Rodrigo looked up at Ben briefly with wide-eyed shock on their faces, then back down at the kid on their cabin's floor, unconsciously loosening their grips on his sweatshirt. Billy even glanced toward Ben, then back at the newcomer with his head cocked to the side a bit. The kid took a few breaths and began to nod as he stared up at Ben.

"Y . . . Yeah, I am."

Ben nodded, then responded with a bit of warmth and understanding in his tone.

"*Alright.* So, you come in here fixin to steal our shit? This some kinda graduation prank, loot the new guys' fresh gear or somethin?"

The kid looked even more confused now. Billy's grip on the kid's collar tightened again, which appeared to expedite his response.

"Nah, nah, man, this is *my fuckin cabin,* or at least it was until a week ago when we went up on the last expedition. That was my bed right there, I swear to God, bro. I didn't even know there was a new group of dudes at basecamp."

Trent and Rodrigo looked up at Ben, appearing almost eager to hear his response. Ben squinted down at the kid, and everything clicked in his head. Ben responded just as the kid was starting to speak again, adding some edge to his tone he knew would make the kid shut up.

"So you cut and run? That why you're creepin round like this? That why the counselors are all hot and bothered tonight, they out lookin for you?"

The kid used silence to respond in the affirmative, switching his gaze frantically between Ben and the three boys pinning him to the ground. He licked his lips and a new kind of desperation came into his eyes, as well as new tears.

"You can't turn me in, please, man, *please,* you gotta let me go. Come on, just let me up and I'll dip out right now and you'll never see me again. I just came back here cause I needed some new boots and pants, I swear. You can't let them find me, man. *Please,* just let me go and I'll leave."

Trent released his grip, stood up, then put his hand on Rodrigo's shoulder for a moment, prompting him to do the same.

Trent responded to the kid but was looking at Billy while he did it.

"We ain't gonna snitch, you're free to go."

Everyone's attention went to Billy in that moment, as though they all just remembered there was an unpredictable bear in the room with them. To all four other boys' relief, Billy just unclenched his white-knuckled grip on the collars of the kid's pullover sweater and stood up slowly. The room was so silent, the popping in Billy's knees as he stood seemed loud to the other four boys.

Billy towered over the boy still lying on the floor of the cabin, whose palms remained out before him in full surrender. Billy just stared down at the kid, and for the first time since the other three boys had met him, he spoke without being asked a question first.

"Why'd you split?"

Even the newcomer seemed startled at hearing the large boy's voice, but eventually he started shaking his head from side to side as he responded.

"Dude . . . you don't get it, this place, this place ain't . . . them counselors, man, they're straight-up evil, this place is fucked, it ain't right."

The kid was crying now, and his hands started shaking like twigs in the wind. Tears were streaming down his cheeks, and heavy sobs were starting to shake his chest.

They all stared down at the crying boy. His fear, his apparent dread, was infectious. Ben felt tendrils of panic lick his mind, and could feel Trent and Rodrigo looking at him, probing him for a reaction.

All four boys' attention went to Billy when he took a step back from where he stood towering over the prone, crying boy. He then looked down at the kid's feet with an appraiser's focus. His feet were barely contained in soaking-wet, frayed boots, the sole of the left one almost completely torn away, holding on by just a strand of cracked rubber.

They all watched Billy as he stepped over the kid, walked over to the armoire where the kid had been hiding, and grabbed Rodrigo's brand-new pair of hiking boots with one hand.

He half turned back to the boy, but stopped to face Rodrigo and held his gaze with an expressionless mask. Ben and Trent looked at Rodrigo just in time to see him nod once at Billy. Billy then strode back toward the scene of the interrogation, dropped the pair of boots between the kid's legs, looked the kid in the eye, then walked slowly into the bathroom. The boys all stared after him in silence until they heard the shower turn on.

Rodrigo took a step toward the kid, who flinched and covered his face as Rodrigo extended his open hand toward him. When the kid gathered Rodrigo's intent, he warily took his hand and let himself be hauled to his feet.

He stood there, looking between Ben, Trent, and Rodrigo with a defeated, apologetic glower that made Ben feel embarrassed. The kid wiped his eyes on his filthy sleeves, then picked up the boots and looked toward the door.

Trent gestured toward the wall on the other side of the cabin with his head.

"You should boogie, Jimmy'll be back soon, but you should use them back windows. Counselors patrolling tonight. Might see you if you use the door."

The kid looked at all three boys warily, then nodded slowly as he began backing away from them and moving toward the windows on the other side of the cabin, speaking as he moved.

"Yeah, word, good lookin out."

The kid tucked the boots under one arm and reached for the window with his other hand, but froze when Ben spoke, and looked back at them.

"What did you mean, *they're evil* and *this place ain't right*? These counselors kiddie diddlers or somethin? This whole clown show actually some kinda sex-traffickin operation? You gotta give us somethin more to work with here."

The kid clenched his jaw as he appeared to consider what to say. He didn't look at Ben, he looked past him, and when he spoke, his voice shook.

"*Nah*, ain't like *that*, but you gotta just trust me, as soon as you get the chance, you fuckin split, alright? You fuckin run, and you don't stop runnin."

The three boys stood in silence as they watched this newcomer haul open the window, climb through, then drop down out of sight. Ben strode across the room and shut the window, then Trent and Rodrigo joined him to stare out into the darkness.

They could see their new acquaintance creeping through just outside an arc of light being cast off by one of the lanterns that lined the pathways between the cabins and the lodge.

The shouting that came from the other side of the cabin was faint, but it still startled all three boys enough to make them jump. It was muffled shouting from outside, an adult's voice. They couldn't hear what exact words were being spoken, but as soon as they heard them, the kid must have as well, because he exploded into a sprint.

The three boys all ran to the other side of the cabin to use a different window to follow the running kid's path. They heard more shouting now, from other adults, and could see a half dozen counselors running through the darkness after the fleeing kid. They were so much faster than him. When one counselor got close, they watched as the kid threw Rodrigo's boots at him, one of which connected squarely with his forehead. But it didn't matter, the counselors were on the kid from every angle like a pack of wolves chasing down a bleeding, exhausted moose. The boys could hear the kid screaming now. They couldn't pick out anything coherent from the screaming, other than the tone of it: pure terror.

One of the counselors tackled him around the waist, and within seconds there were four or five others on him, each with a limb, helping carry the writhing, shrieking kid toward the lodge. There were other counselors flanking the scene now—a mass of white-polo-clad staff, Jimmy and others Ben recognized among them—buzzing around the terrified, weeping, thrashing kid as he was dragged toward the lodge. The frantic procession disappeared from view, but boys could hear the kid's dreadful noises echo out across the grounds of the camp and into the dark forest beyond.

The sound of the kid's screaming was abruptly cut when he was dragged into the lodge—replaced by the eerie quiet of the big valley. The immediacy of the audible change was actually startling to Ben. It was like the mountains themselves threw a wet, lead blanket over the chaos, dousing it, replacing it with the inveterate cadence of crickets and wind on distant ridgelines.

The boys stood in silence for several long moments after hearing the echo of the kid's last, shrill wail die out in the foothills beyond the camp. All three then erupted into chatter—it wasn't actual discussion, it was just how young men sometimes communicate when they witness something crazy—a stream of profanities and declarations of disbelief, spoken over one another.

They had barely noticed Billy come out of the shower, stroll across the room, and look out one of the windows. They did, however, notice when Billy spoke. It was only one word, but was more than enough to shut them all up.

"*Listen.*"

They all stared at Billy. He was looking out the window into the darkness. He only wore a towel around his waist. Ben noticed, for the first time, what he knew right away to be cigarette burns pocked across both of Billy's large shoulder blades. Ben had some cigarette burns of his own.

Then they heard it. None of the four boys had ever heard that noise in real life, but they all immediately knew what it was. The sound itself, and the emotional response that accompanied, was programmed into their bones.

Somewhere on one of the dark ridgelines that crept out like fingers from the trunks of the large mountains looming above Bear Springs Academy, wolves had begun to howl.

CHAPTER 10

W E CALL it the *solo excursion*. You've heard us talk about it before. It represents the final chapter in a young man's journey here at Bear Springs—the final step in developing a level of self-respect, self-awareness, and self-reliance that you'll carry with you for the rest of your lives. The instructors here decide when each of you is ready for your solo excursion. It's when you take everything that you've learned in this program and set off to spend a few days alone in the wilderness. We make sure you're entirely safe throughout the process, but even so, for most of our graduates it is still a very emotional, very profound ordeal. And that's a good thing, it should be."

Reid moved from where he'd been speaking and strode under the Lodge Pole, across the row of benches where all the boys were assembled. He pinched his chin between his thumb and index finger, as though he was deep in contemplation on what he'd just said, and what to say next.

He stopped, spun on his heel to face the group, and looked up with an expression of amused acknowledgment, almost an embarrassed smile.

"Last night, I assume you all heard a good deal of commotion in the dark outside the cabins. It was pretty hard to miss!"

The counselors—some sitting among the boys, most standing in clusters behind Reid—all broke into smiles and warm laughter, some shaking their heads as they chuckled to themselves.

"All that commotion, gentlemen, was the sound of a young man's emotions as he approached that final great feat—the sound of a young man, just like you, facing that last hurdle of this program. Sometimes, the profound nature of the *solo excursion* can be very, very overwhelming . . ."

Reid and the rest of the counselors donned solemn expressions, all appearing to nod in acknowledgment as though they'd gone through it themselves.

"One of our spring class graduates, Michael, became a bit overcome during his solo excursion. He lost himself in the experience somewhat and ended up wandering back down here to camp. It was fairly *dramatic* when we found him, but once we all got together in the lodge, he quickly calmed down, centered himself, apologized, and found the strength in himself to go back up there and finish that last, important step in our program. We're so proud of Michael—his strength, his decision to go back up there, to get back up on that horse, is what this program is all about. He faced adversity, he struggled with it, and he prevailed."

All the camp staff started clapping in response to that, some offering cheers and whistles. Reid patted at the air to calm them, and went on, speaking louder and with more gusto.

"And it gives me great, *great* pleasure to introduce to you guys, not only Michael himself, but the entire spring class of Bear Springs Academy, all of whom just arrived back at basecamp this morning!"

The camp staff erupted into raucous cheering and applause now, and the boys watched as a column of guys their age came jogging down the path toward the Lodge Pole, as though they'd been waiting behind one of the barns for their cue.

They were all wearing white polos with the Bear Springs Academy emblem on the right breast, tucked into khaki pants. They all had their large backpacks on as well. One of the boys at the very front—Michael, whom Ben recognized immediately—carried the large flag with the Bear Springs blazonry fluttering out over the heads of the other boys trotting along behind him.

Even more shocking to Ben was the demeanor of this group of boys. They all had huge smiles plastered on their faces. As they came into the area around the Lodge Pole, Ben watched as they began cheering, fist pumping, and clapping. When they reached the Lodge Pole itself and the staff members surrounding Reid, they broke out of their formation and all began embracing the staff members with hugs, two-handed handshakes, and high fives. More than half of these new guys had tears rolling down their faces, while all of them exuded a stirring and almost debauched elation as they smiled and worked their way through the cluster of staff members. They all exchanged hugs of a duration and intensity that, to Ben, were unreasonably passionate for any two guys to exchange—with the exception perhaps of a son and father or pair of brothers who'd been searching for one another since they'd gotten separated years earlier in the flames and chaos of a siege.

Ben watched Michael set the flag down into the mounting post at the base of the Lodge Pole and walk toward Reid with open arms. He was smiling, tears were pouring from his eyes. He looked as though he were embracing his own father when they connected. He buried his face into Reid's chest, wrapped his arms around him, and they held one another like family members in a hug as they spun around in a full circle, clapping each other on the back.

Ben was stunned. He couldn't imagine himself, or anyone else in his summer class, feeling any kind of positive emotion like this toward the staff. It was also just embarrassing as hell. Even if they did end up having a positive experience, when leaving a place like this—a carceral program they were physically forced to attend—*for the love of God just shake the man's fucking hand and leave*, Ben thought. *No experience at a place like this could warrant such unbridled foolishness and affection.*

Ben looked around at his cabinmates and the other guys in his class. He found they were almost all sporting looks that betrayed internal cringe as they took in what was to them such an excruciatingly awkward scene. Some were looking at each other in disbelief. Ben saw Billy glance off to the side—away from the loud, platonic spectacle of excitement—then slowly shake his head a few times as he stared up at the mountains.

The guys from the spring class and the Bear Springs staff eventually quieted down, and they all turned to face the watchful, confused group of new guys of the summer class.

The one they called Michael—the kid who was weeping and pleading with Ben and the other guys in his cabin hours earlier as he desperately tried to escape this place—stepped toward the group. He faced the summer class with a smile that was jarringly warm and friendly, at least for those few who'd stood witness to his wild, animalistic efforts to flee just the night before.

"Well, guys, I really want to apologize about the scene I made last night. I got overwhelmed by this experience, and, well, believe it or not . . . I was up there, enjoying my solo excursion, and was just so stressed by the prospect of leaving this place to go home. I'm just going to miss it so much, the staff, my buddies, deep down . . . *I just didn't want to leave.* Thankfully, Reid and the others were able to calm me down, and get me back up on that horse to finish the last mile of this amazing race! I know it might seem hard now, but by the end of the summer, you guys are going to be best friends, and more importantly, you are going to be champions of your own destiny!"

Michael threw his fist into the air, and all the spring class guys and staffers erupted yet again into energetic cheering and celebration. Ben stared at him in slack-jawed awe, leaning forward over his crossed arms to scour every detail of his face and body language for a sign, any indication that this was some kind of front or facade.

There was nothing. Everything about the kid suggested he was content, excited, and genuinely happy. Ben looked over toward Trent to find he was already looking back at him with wide eyes. He had shock in his face, and a bit of fear as well.

Ben didn't hear much of what Reid and a few of the other counselors said after that. He just watched in a state of bewilderment as the spring class guys nodded along, slapped each other on the backs, and applauded everything that was said. Eventually, Reid bellowed something along the lines of *get in here, guys,* and all the staffers and polo-clad boys smashed themselves into a large huddle. Ben heard a deep voice yell a count of three from within, then everyone screamed, "Bear Springs forever!" in unison.

It was so loud it seemed to echo out across the valley with carried sound for a full ten seconds.

Ben remained in a daze as he watched several of the counselors break away from the group and lead the procession of ecstatic boys in their matching uniforms toward the row of Sprinter vans behind the lodge, then watched as they loaded their bags into the vans, then themselves, and drove a full circle around the Lodge Pole, all the boys cheering and waving from the windows as they went, shouting words of encouragement to the remaining boys and praise toward the staff, before accelerating down the drive.

Eventually, after Reid droned on about harnessing their enthusiasm and diving headfirst into the benefits of this program, Ben gathered that their afternoon activity fell into some kind of "survival skills" category. The boys were led into the woods until they reached a large clearing with a broad, flat area at the center covered in sand. In the sandy clearing, a group of counselors had set up bow drills, strings, cords, and what appeared to be an assortment of other twigs and sticks.

The boys were all silent as a large, muscular counselor named Freddie lectured them about how to make a fire with sticks and how to rig a few different kinds of snares and traps for small game. He used the items as he explained the methods, being unnecessarily operatic with his hands, gestures, and voice as he did so. Ben wondered if the other boys were as shocked by the previous encounter with the spring class as he was. He wondered how any of them could possibly be listening to a word this big, man-bun-rocking fuck had to say.

Ben found himself in a small group with two other young guys named Hector and Sam, whom he'd only met in passing. He was almost relieved to find that they were as disinterested and seemed as mentally distant as he did. The counselors went from group to group, reiterating the process of making a fire and setting up the traps as the boys stared at them blankly, and were then beckoned into giving it a try for themselves.

The cooler air of morning was being burned away by the dry, dusty heat of midday. This, in conjunction with the counselors' petulant earnestness, made Ben feel violent.

He eventually found, though, that the mundane physical tasks were a nice reprieve from thinking about the bizarre spectacle he'd just beheld, the fear at seeing that kid—Michael—in a state that he could only describe as either the greatest bit of acting he'd ever seen, or absolutely fucking brainwashed. Ben struggled with the bow-drill fire starter but found the technique behind snares and traps straightforward enough.

The smell of smoke hit Ben's nose, and he looked over to see Trent hunched over a small but crackling fire, a clutch of counselors around him issuing congratulations on his "stellar bush craft." Trent looked unamused, and caught Ben's gaze. Trent widened his eyes a bit, slowly shook his head, and mouthed the words *what tha fuck was that.* Ben could only shake his head in return, then went back to fiddling with the cords and sticks necessary to construct what Freddie had called a "Graves motion snare."

The rest of the afternoon, and dinner, were a blur for Ben. Only once they'd gotten back to the cabin and engaged in some *cabin time* with Jimmy, the high king of dipshits, did Ben notice some clarity coming back into his mind. Jimmy had them all individually slog through an explanation of what they thought the word *perseverance* meant. Billy, as usual, refused to offer more than four or five words, despite Jimmy's prodding, and they were soon, to Ben's great relief, getting ready for bed.

Moments after Jimmy shut the lights off, told them good night, and closed his door, Rodrigo and Trent were propped up on their elbows, hissing urgent whispers across the room, most of which were some variation of *what in the fuck was that shit, bro.*

Trent looked over at Ben, gesturing at him with his head.

"Seriously, B, what the hell do you make of that shit, you saw that motherfucker Michael last night, he wasn't *sad to leave* or whatever bullshit Reid tried to spit about him, that dude was tryin to get *the fuck* out of here, that dude was *shook.* What the fuck happened to him? What the fuck did those assholes do to that dude in the lodge last night after they caught him?"

Ben just shook his head, staring into the darkness of the far wall.

"I dunno, man, honestly . . . I ain't gotta damn clue."

All Billy did was lift his arms up to put his hands behind his head, but it was enough to grab the other three's attention. He'd never done anything but snore through Ben's, Rodrigo's, and Trent's deliberations after lights-out. They all shut up and stared at him.

After a few long moments, Ben pressed.

"What do you make a'that wacky shit, Billy?"

Billy inhaled slowly through his nose, then exhaled for what felt like a full minute before responding.

"Kid got broke."

The other boys looked to one another in the dark for further understanding, then eventually all back at Billy. Ben pressed him for more.

"Whatchu mean, *got broke*? Like they beat him into submission last night?"

Billy shrugged from his prone position, almost indiscernibly, then spoke more than he had since they'd all met.

"Don't always gotta beat someone to break em. The right words can do it. Coulda been fists, coulda been words, both, whatever it was, *they broke that kid lass night*. It was easier for the rest of em. Broke em over the last few months. Whoever ol' Mikey was, he held out till last night, but he gone now. They gon' try to do it to the rest of us, too, that's how places like this work. Bust ya down till your last fuse pops, last bitta you's *gone*."

The boys sat, shocked, both by the length of Billy's contribution to their conversation, and at the meaning in what he'd said. To their surprise, Billy went on.

"The wolves could hear it, though. They heard im wailin, they heard somethin wild, like them, they tried to tell him to hold out. Wasn't enough though . . . I ain't never seen it go down that fast, ain't never seen someone broke that quick. Like a switch got flipped. Whatever went on in the lodge last night, well . . . had to've been some wicked shit."

Ben felt real fear now. He couldn't have put it into words, but he *felt* what Billy was saying. He figured some kind of abuse was the only way to rip the fight out of a kid like that, but to change him into the cheerful Boy Scout he saw today, that was another thing entirely. Ben's mind couldn't grasp what it would take to do something like that, but he figured it wasn't anything good. He figured it had something to do with Reid.

Rodrigo snorted, grabbing Ben's and Trent's attention. They watched as he stared down at the comforter of his bed and ran a hand over it slowly. He put his hands behind his head as he lay back down, then spoke, and what he said was haunting to Ben.

"They're gonna have to fuckin kill me, bro. *Straight up.*"

Trent and Ben just stared at Rodrigo, frightened by where his mind led theirs.

Billy was the one to finally respond, doing so without moving at all, speaking up at the ceiling.

"Straight up."

CHAPTER 11

JESSIE LEANED back in his chair and rested his chin on his palm, strumming his fingers on his lips. The fingers partially obscured the composed, genial smile Jessie wore as he listened to Ben's answers to his shallow questions.

That calm smile was a good thing to see, Ben thought. As were the occasional nods and follow-up questions. To Ben, these were tells. Jessie felt Ben was being sincere. Jessie, no doubt, felt like he was *really getting somewhere* with Ben, and that is exactly what Ben wanted.

About a week had passed since the night of the bonfire and the furor that followed the boys finding the terrified kid hiding in their cabin. About a week since Reid had confronted Ben about the sincerity or honesty of Ben's engagement with his therapist Jessie. Ben had no idea how Reid could have picked up on such a thing, but it made him nervous. It also made him focus on really selling the level of engaged buy-in he wanted Jessie to see in him.

Because Jessie was an important piece of the puzzle, Ben had decided. He needed this therapist asshole wrapped around his finger, and the effort was going well.

"Well, Ben, are you excited for the next few days?"

Ben knew he was referring to the upcoming backpacking trip, the group's first expedition away from basecamp. Ben actually *was* excited, to an extent. He saw it as a good opportunity to learn more about the counselors, more about what was actually going on here. At the same time, he found himself staring up at the big mountains above basecamp quite often, and genuinely looked forward to exploring them. Coming from bayou country in south Louisiana, such wild alpine country was as foreign to him as Mars, or the bottom of the ocean.

Ben looked down to a knot of wood on the leg of Jessie's chair, putting his hands together between his knees as he did so, and shrugged as he responded.

"I dunno, I guess so."

Jessie leaned forward a bit as he responded, "It's beautiful up there, Ben. These expeditions are a great way to bond with the other guys, get to know the counselors better, and get to know *yourself* better."

Ben almost shook his head and cringed at the cheeseball cliché, but forced himself to glance up at Jessie and offer his best version of a nervous, reluctant smile.

"Yah, I guess it will be pretty cool."

Jessie smiled and nodded in response.

"It *will be* pretty cool, Ben. I promise you'll have a great time."

Ben saw this as a good opening for a probe.

"Did you ever go up into those mountains as a kid, Jessie?"

As he stared at Jessie's face, Ben saw something the moment he finished his question. For just *half* a second, like a switch had been flipped, all emotion drained away from Jessie's face—his lips slackened as all the skin on his face relaxed; his eyes left Ben's and focused vaguely on some spot near Ben's scalp. He looked a million miles away. He looked like Rodrigo had on the seven-hour drive from the airport in Bozeman to Bear Springs.

Then, just as quickly, the color, life, and kindness flooded back into Jessie's face. He focused again on Ben's eyes, smiled, and nodded.

"I sure have, they're beautiful. No place like it anywhere in the world. You're gonna love it up there."

Ben donned a nervous smile before pushing a bit further.

"Are Javier or Gordon or any of those other guys going to come with us on expeditions, or are they not really *normal* counselors?"

Jessie put his elbows on his chair's armrests and steepled his fingers, looking amused.

"They're just counselors as well, Ben, as *normal* as all the rest. A bit older, perhaps, but just as normal."

Ben looked confused.

"Then why don't they dress the same, or do daily lessons with us, go on hikes or outings, eat with us, or live in the cabins like all the other counselors? Why do those guys get to live in the lodge with Reid?"

Jessie's eyes narrowed almost imperceptibly, but the expression did not evolve into anything beyond mild surprise.

"Well, Ben, we have different jobs and responsibilities. The four of us trained therapists see to the one-on-one time with you guys. Those four are professional interventionists and have been here quite a bit longer than any of us cabin counselors and therapists and, as you may have noticed, are not as spry *as us young bucks*! Although I assure you, at the end of the day we're all just normal Bear Springs counselors. Those four just keep an eye on things around here until your return."

Ben nodded. He wasn't entirely sure why he'd thought to ask Jessie that line of questions, but it felt like the right time, and it sure felt like the right *way* to explore the hierarchy of the place a bit, and that had certainly paid off.

Jessie spoke as he stood.

"Well, Ben, I feel like we've been making some *really good* progress over this last week. These sessions have been *just great*."

Ben looked up at the man with another nervous smile, trying to appear as though he were a bit bashful, and shrugged. Jessie gestured toward the door of his office with his head.

"Alright, bud, as discussed at breakfast, you've all gotta be back at your cabins by one o'clock sharp to finish packing before you all set off this afternoon."

Ben grabbed his book and left through the outside entrance to Jessie's office on the ground floor of the lodge, and with a half hour to spare before one o'clock, he would head to the library to return his book and check out another. He worked his way around the large building along the vibrant, bee-filled flower gardens that lined the walk toward the front doors that led toward the Great Hall, and the library therein. The library was Ben's favorite part of this place. The boys could borrow any book they liked from the massive shelves, so long as they signed it in and out, and Ben had spent most of his free time since getting to Bear

Springs poring over them. Few Bear Springs *students* did this, it seemed, based on the plume of dust that accompanied almost every book Ben had removed from the shelves.

Their loss, Ben thought. There was a shocking number of very rare books in here, which, besides the dust, were all in wonderful condition. Ben had already found, and read, first-edition *first printings* of Stephen Crane's 1895 *The Red Badge of Courage*, Upton Sinclair's 1906 *The Jungle*, and Lew Wallace's 1880 *Ben-Hur*, as well as a half dozen first-edition *later* printings of famous titles that might be even more rare and cherished, one of which was Mark Twain's 1884 *Adventures of Huckleberry Finn*. It was magical. Ben had no idea of the present values of these books. He was not a rare book appraiser, rare book merchant, or rare book collector.

Ben was, however, something of a rare book *thief*.

He'd made some good cash pilfering abandoned old houses and camps throughout the bayou country near home, including one long abandoned and decrepit plantation house where he found a first edition of Louisa May Alcott's 1868 *Little Women*, which he'd sold to a fancy little man at a fancy little shop up in New Orleans for *$200*. That was the most money Ben had ever made in his life for anything. He didn't even care that he'd gotten his eyes ripped out on the deal, which he assumed he had. That book dealer told Ben to come back to him with *any* first-edition books he "came across in the future," and that he'd pay good money for them.

Ben intended to make it through this summer and head home with a *fine haul* of first-edition books to take right into that book dealer's shop. He'd already smuggled nine out of the library to hide in his dresser at the cabin.

He nodded at one of the other Bear Springs "intervention specialists," Nicholas, when he entered, who returned the greeting with a warm smile and a nod of his own. The older man was sitting at one of the large oak tables in the center of the room with a notepad and a stack of large, old books with leather bindings that Ben knew did *not* come from any of these shelves he had access to. He made a quick mental note of that as he signed his name and the date on a ledger on the wall, making sure as he did to catch the eye of Nicholas, who smiled and nodded once more. Nicholas was often in the Great Hall during the day and had already grown used to Ben's fondness for the books that lined the walls. He had readily accepted Ben's offer to return his book to its correct location on day one, and was thus very used to the routine now, as was Ben.

Ben made his way toward the spot in the shelves where he'd left off the day before.

He ran his finger across the spines of all twenty-six volumes of *Time* magazine's 1973 *The Old West* series, then the fourteen volumes of Shelby Foote's *Civil War* history, then slid the book he was holding back into its place within the series. Ben had been *really* looking forward to getting his hands and eyes on the next books down the line. One of these was a legit 1858 first edition of DeWitt C. Peters's *The Life and Adventures of Kit Carson, the Nestor of the Rocky Mountains.* Ben had been a fan of Kit Carson and his many celebrated adventures since he'd first heard of the man when he was about Wade's age, so he might even keep this one for himself. Ben used both hands to carefully remove the old book from the shelf, while also grabbing the one next to it that had a similar size; the *decoy book*, which appeared to be some catastrophically dull screed on old mining technology.

Ben was deftly snugging the first edition into a comfortable position behind his belt when he heard something small fall over and make a *clunk* in the dark, vacant space where the books had been.

He set the decoy book down next to a lamp on one of the reading tables nearby, then reached into the dark slot, feeling blindly until his fingers landed on a small, thin piece of wood, just a bit larger than a playing card. He pulled it out and confirmed that's what it was. He turned it over in his hand and saw some faded writing on the other side in what appeared to be pencil lead. He leaned down into the glow of the lamp and held it closer to his eyes, where the faint, flowery cursive writing came into focus a bit more.

It's all so S. E. B. can keep the lantern lit
    Silas left a bit upstairs for the rustlers to keep them sane and tend
to the flame

Nothing left for them other men, they age, they're just S. E. B.'s
working stock
   Hightail west, find Buckle Creek a few drainages over
   Follow it up to Buckle Glacier, then up over Caravan Pass
   That don't work, try any other damn way
   That don't work, kill yourself & make your case at St. Peter's gate
   Lord knows, it's a strong case

—H.R., 1917

He put the little piece of wood in his pocket and snatched up the old book just as Nicholas glanced up at him. Ben smiled at the man as he began thumbing through pages of the book one at a time, as though trying to find a place he'd left off. As soon as Nicholas went back to his own reading and note taking, Ben got a desperate urge to sneak the wooden note card out of his pocket and read it again, but an equally dire internal warning *not to*. He ran his fingers along the outside of his pocket, tracing its shape.

He glanced up at the bookshelf where he'd found it; all American history, biographies, journals, and nonfiction. He decided the most likely explanation of its existence was that it had been used as a bookmark by some previous owner of one of these old books, and then it had fallen out into the shelf. It was a perfect size and thickness for such a purpose. He scanned the titles along the spines, pairing each with the publication and edition date he'd already unintentionally memorized. Almost half the books in the shelves were from before 1917, which did not help narrow things down much.

A soft *chime* came from the large grandfather clock across the room. Ben knew well this meant it was either fifteen or forty-five minutes past the hour, but looked at his watch anyway to see that it was, indeed, 12:45 p.m. He scooped up the decoy book and tucked it under his arm.

Nicholas's shock of gray, curly hair bounced a bit as he looked up at Ben over his tortoiseshell reading glasses.

"Another book today, Mr. Thibodaux?"

Nicholas was the only adult at Bear Springs Ben had heard pro-

nounce his last name correctly. It unnerved him—made him wonder if
all four of the elder interventionists and Reid sat around sharing details
about all the boys with one another. He also spoke with what Ben assumed was the accent of a well-educated academic from New England,
and always wore a starched white shirt under a waxed barn jacket to
round out the rugged intellectual aesthetic. At the same time, there was
something happening at the edges of his eyes and in the way he moved
his hands that suggested this man could move very, *very* fast if he wanted
to. Ben answered him as he began filling out the library ledger.

"*Yeah*, gonna see what all these gold miners were gettin themselves
into round these parts back in the day."

Ben froze when Nicholas spoke.

"Benjamin . . ."

Ben turned, eyebrows inquisitively raised, putting great care into not
letting the rare book in his pants create a profile through his shirt.

"Have you really read *nine* books in the last *nine* days?"

Ben was getting called out but played his part well by trying to hide
an embarrassed grin.

"Ten actually, sir. I'm a skimmer, you know, don't get through every
single word, but readin's always been m' favorite thing to do. Others,
they tease me for it, so I try to do my readin on my own downtime, it's
just something I enjoy."

The air of suspicion left Nicholas's face and was replaced with something Ben felt landed somewhere between amusement and pretention.

"*Well then*, what're your thoughts about the book you read yesterday,
about General Sherman, what would you have to say about his legacy,
his military doctrine?"

Is this weasel really fixin to test me, Ben wondered. But looking into
Nicholas's face, Ben realized that was not what he was doing. This man
had the essence of a coiled snake, but he had *no idea* Ben was stealing
books, Ben could see that, he could read that reality off every part of this
man's body. *He's not trying to test you*, Ben concluded. *This son of a bitch
is trying to embarrass you.*

Ben suppressed an amused grin and kept his face expressionless.

"Well, that depends, sir . . ."

Nicholas let out a contemptuous snort of air.

"Oh, *does it now*, Benjamin. Upon what, might I inquire, does that *depend on?*"

Ben did not shroud his accent.

"Pends on who's askin."

Ben waited for that *lovely* moment when an interjection was just a *little too* early to be deemed an actual interruption, but *just late* enough to sting someone. Nicholas's lips began to form the first word and Ben spoke, staring into the space between them.

"If a *southern* contemporary of Sherman's were asked that, I would expect animosity, if not outright anger toward the scorched-earth tactics employed by Sherman as he campaigned through Georgia and into the Carolinas, given how novel and, thus, how *jarring* those tactics would've been for people of the time to behold. If a *northern* contemporary were asked, they'd likely argue that such tactics were called for given the dire need to end the Civil War, and the institution of slavery, both of which had already lasted far longer and brought about more death and suffering than anyone, anywhere at the time, could have imagined possible. I see some merit in both assessments but tend to side with General Sherman on the matter. At the end of the day, unfortunately, when a dog is wild, angry, and hungry enough, and you've tried everything else but its jaws are still clamped down like a vise . . ."

Ben looked up into Nicholas's eyes.

"Sometimes, the only thing you can do is just *beat it to death.*"

Ben would've bet good pocket money his answer would astonish this guy, but he did not appear shaken at all. Nicholas's eyes narrowed a bit, and if there were anything less put into it, his subtle grin would've been completely imperceptible, even to Ben's keen eye. Several awkward moments passed until Ben felt he needed to say something.

"I've gotta jet, sir. Gotta go get packed for camping. I'll stop by to swap books out when we're back day after tomorrow."

Nicholas did not speak. He just nodded slowly as he pointed a single finger at the door.

Ben wandered out through the lodge, then into the bright sun as he made his way toward his cabin, watching the other boys and staff strolling around about in pairs or small groups. *These interventionist dudes are something else*, Ben thought. He hadn't even been here for two weeks yet, but as he looked around and worked back toward his cabin, he realized he was starting to get a hang of the routine of this place. It made him feel an unpleasant, fuzzy mixture of comfort and foreboding.

When Ben caught sight of his cabin, he saw Jimmy leaning on one of the live-edge pillars supporting the front porch, gazing up toward the mountains with that idiotic smile, rocking his ridiculous, big eighties-style mirror shades. He looked over and saw Ben approaching, smile widening as he did.

Over the last week, Ben had decided Jimmy was a genuine, organic moron. He didn't attempt to shroud any of his personality or intelligence from this fucking nitwit, as he did with Jessie, Reid, the guys in his class, and the other staff members, with the new exception of that pretentious, albeit intimidating bookworm, Nicholas. Jimmy had the emotional intelligence of a child, and Ben saw no reason to avoid treating him as such, at least when it was just the two of them communicating.

Ben shook his head and stared down at his feet. The moment Jimmy's larynx activated and he began to shout what Ben was confident would be some vibrant salutation, Ben shouted back at Jimmy, loudly, cutting him off.

"*YES*, James . . ."

Ben let a moment of silence hang in the air as he looked up at Jimmy. Ben was not surprised to find the fluttered blinks and the blank, dumb look that fell upon Jimmy's face whenever Ben cut him off like that. Trent and Rodrigo had even started to notice it.

"We leave this afternoon for the camping expedition. I'll be sure to follow the packing list you put on the whiteboard, *down to the item*. Please, James, would you get the door for me?"

Ben gestured toward the door to their cabin as he took the steps up to the porch. Jimmy reached for the screen door and held it open as he muttered his response.

"Y . . . yeah, man."

Ben found Rodrigo, Trent, and Billy in the cabin. Each had an array of clothes, outerwear, cooking utensils, and other assorted camping gear a comfortable position with these new, massive bags on their backs, Ben remembered the piece of wood from the library with the message on it that he'd put in his back pocket. He pulled it out, angled it to catch the sun, and read it slowly due to the unfamiliar, formal cursive handwriting.

Ben couldn't make sense of it, and tucked the piece of wood back into his pocket as he vaguely heard conclusory notes in Reid's voice. He stared up at the mountains they were heading into, musing over the message. His breath caught in his throat when he realized he was staring west.

Hightail west, find Buckle Creek a few drainages over . . .

Could the author of this note have been a student *here*, writing a warning about *this place*? *No way*, Ben thought. It was just an old bookmark, with a message from over a hundred years ago, if that date was even to be believed. He ran his finger along the outline of the piece of wood as he ran through the message again and again in his mind, finding no hard links to Bear Springs, or even Montana. *Buckle Creek, Buckle Glacier*, and *Caravan Pass*. He'd scour the maps on the walls of the lodge when they got back, and if any one of those unique geographical names were to the west of camp, then it would indeed be something more than an old message scribbled on a bookmark. Ben looked over at the lodge, wanting badly to go review the maps immediately, but he pushed the matter from his mind.

Before long, the group set off in the single-file line formation they took when on trails, counselors interspersed between the boys cracking stupid jokes, encouraging participation in sing-alongs, and making idle chatter about the ecosystem and landscape. The group had gone on quite a few shorter day hikes over the past week to get a feel for their backs, but had not yet hiked with them fully loaded, so more exasperated groans and grunts hovered over this particular line formation than usual.

It only took an hour or so for the group to reach a point in the long, sloping pine forest above basecamp that marked the farthest they'd yet traveled from "home" on previous outings. Rodrigo, Trent, and Ben all exchanged a variety of anxious grins and shrugs.

spread out on their bed, all lazily stuffing it piece by piece into the large backpacks they were provided for these multiday outings.

Rodrigo grinned and cocked his head toward the door as Ben passed by him.

"You've got that fucker pretty well trained, eh? Getting the door for you and shit—what else can you get him to do?"

Ben chuckled in response but said nothing as he fell in among the others and began packing the final items into his large pack. They wer setting off, Ben thought, feeling a bit of excitement.

They were setting off on an adventure.

Trent cinched down some straps on the top of his pack, lifted it and hoisted it onto his back. He let out a long whistle before speak

"This thing is heavy as hell, and we're supposed to cart them all way up those damn mountains?"

When Ben and Rodrigo finished stuffing everything from the list into their own packs, they also groaned at the weight. Billy his pack onto his back with ease, buckled the lumbar support arou waist, and silently strolled out of the cabin—making it appear as it weighed no more than a shirt.

Since the night after they'd found the elder boy trying to Billy hadn't spoken more than a word or two at a time, and or it was absolutely necessary. Ben, Trent, and Rodrigo had of about how awkward his one-on-one counseling sessions must therapist.

Jimmy led the four boys toward the Lodge Pole, wher counselors were mustering their respective four-dude squ their large packs. Reid was there with some of the other sta all clad in hiking boots and what appeared to the boys to of expensive nylon outdoor clothing.

When everyone had gathered, Reid gave the group a what was to come, reiterating the "expedition plan" that cussed at length at dinner over the past several days. Th five-mile hike from basecamp up to some alpine lake wh camp and spend two nights, and head back home day

As the boys shifted their weight from foot to fo

As tough as these three boys were—as much rebellious bravado and disinterest as they went about their days here trying to maintain for one another—they all felt real excitement. None of them had ever been on a backpacking trip, let alone in the remote Montana wilderness. All the pictures of the alpine landscape they'd seen around camp, all the discussion about protocols to follow if various predators or moose were encountered, all the survival lessons, it all left them equal parts anxious and excited for their first real overnight trip.

The ridgeline got steeper over the next hour, eventually turning into long switchbacks. It didn't take long for all the boys in the group to fall into a silent ruck, eyes glued to the forest floor and trail before them as they navigated the roots and rocks jutting from the trail. Eventually, without much warning, the group crested the large mountain ridge and turned to follow its spine farther upward into the mountain. The incline was more gradual, and the boys could afford to look around themselves a bit more, and the landscape was much less monotonous.

The other side of the ridge was not like the one they'd trudged up all afternoon—it was far more open, pocked with clusters of aspens, streams, and rock outcroppings, and dropped a long way down into the next valley. The view, however, was what made every single one of the boys stop in their tracks from time to time. It was breathtaking, even to the grumpiest cynics among them. Ben felt like he could see for a hundred miles across the vista of granite peaks and deep river valleys among a sea of endless mountains.

After a while hiking up the ridge, the group reached a merciful downhill aspect, where the ridgeline opened into a large bowl of meadows and wildflowers. The morale of the group notably lifted as they reached the small but noisy stream that spilled from the lake they'd be camping on.

As they rounded a large rock outcropping, the lake came into clear view. It was as lovely to Ben as the first view. Maybe the most beautiful thing he'd ever seen. The evening light made it look red and gold, and the surface was glimmering with ripples and rings as trout feasted on the clouds of small gnats and bugs that rose in swirling columns above the water.

Reid and several other counselors walked out ahead of the group, gesturing toward an area near the shore where a large, blackened stone firepit sat surrounded by long benches made from logs and stacked flagstone. They shouted instructions as to where the boys should go about setting up tents. Ben, Trent, and Rodrigo paid them no mind, transfixed by the scenery.

After a long moment Trent turned to face the other two boys, catching their attention. He gestured over his shoulder toward the lake with his thumb.

"Aight, well . . . this is actually pretty fuckin cool, right?"

Ben and Rodrigo offered reluctant, albeit genuine smiles in return.

CHAPTER 12

MANY OF the boys in this Bear Springs Academy summer class had experience curling up to rest in the driest, safest place available to them under the circumstances, whether that was in a tent under an overpass, amid a nest of wrappers and trash in the back of an old van, or in a toolshed where a violent adult couldn't find them.

However, very few of the boys had ever spent a night in a tent as a recreational exercise. Let alone a tent with an ultralight sleeping pad and a zero-degree down sleeping bag, while wearing expensive thermal base layers—all of which had been provided to the boys by the benefactors of Bear Springs Academy.

Each of the boys had been given a small, one-person tent to take on the summer's expeditions, and shortly after arriving at the lake the counselors had the boys set up their tents and sleeping gear, then begin to run through a few "learning exercises." These included showing them how to use the water-purification pumps to make clean water from the small stream that trickled out of the rocks to feed the lake. Then one of the counselors—a ropey-limbed, beach-tanned dipshit named Mitchell—showed the boys how to fish for trout using a fly rod.

Ben found Mitchell as obnoxious as any other staff member at Bear Springs but couldn't deny how mesmerizing it was watching that asshole cast his fly rod out over the lake in the evening light. He thoroughly enjoyed watching the tiny little fly land on the water, where it came to rest before disappearing in a small explosion of nervous water when a deceived trout broke the surface at lightning speed to eat it.

Ben even shouldered his way into the group to get a look at the brightly colored, spotted fish. Mitchell said it was a species called a cutthroat trout, which attracted a chorus of chuckling and thoughtless, violent jokes from the boys. Mitchell rigged up several other fly rods and began instructing the boys interested in learning. Trent picked it up quickly, as he seemed to do with everything, and was the only one other than the counselor to have a trout rise to his fly that evening.

After that, some of the boys went off with Reid to set some traps and snares, which they'd been practicing at basecamp over the previous week. Trent, among them. Ben and Rodrigo stayed with the others at camp and helped start cooking dinner—a feast of simple hot dogs on fire-toasted buns, with an assortment of nuts and dried fruit on the side.

The group was properly exhausted by the time everyone gathered around the fire to eat. Ben could vaguely hear one of counselors giving some lecture on the star constellations becoming visible in the darkening sky. He made sure to follow the gestures with his eyes and engage in some properly timed nods and inquisitive head tilts, but he was only really paying attention to two things: Reid and Billy.

Reid appeared normal enough this night. He ate like the rest, and chimed in on conversations like the rest. There were no overt tells to pick up. Billy, likewise, maintained his usual stoic, removed disposition. Billy sat on a round stone away from the others, out at the farthest reaches of the dancing firelight. He leaned forward, head low, with elbows on his knees. The glimmer of the flames in his eyes showed his gaze toward the fire from under his large brows. He hadn't moved a muscle in an hour. Ben remembered some line from a movie where someone a bit like Billy was described as a *Philistine*. Ben didn't know what that word meant, but figured Billy would scare the shit out of ten *Philistines*.

The only interesting and peculiar thing afoot this evening—which Ben deemed worthy of his full attention—was the abnormal level of attention Reid was paying to Billy.

It was only a series of casual side glances to see if he was reacting to a joke or particularly interesting tidbit on the stars or animals of the area. Most wouldn't have noticed, but in the aggregate, it was more than enough for Ben to pick up on, and enough for him to come to the conclusion that Reid was uniquely interested in Billy this evening.

Ben was relieved Reid's attention wasn't on him, but nervous for Billy. Ben did not consider Billy to be well equipped enough to deal with Reid's adept level of mind gaming. He didn't think Billy would be able to either ignore or conversationally go toe-to-toe with an adult as smart and intuitive as Reid, if Reid chose to engage him. Ben thought it likely that, should Reid start prodding and prying at Billy as he had with Ben over the past weeks, Billy would react with violence.

So, Ben was waiting for Reid to trigger such an outcome, and thinking about how he could involve himself on Billy's behalf. Ben was still scared of Billy and was quite certain that if they'd met outside this environment, he'd avoid him at all costs. In fact, Ben figured he was worth avoiding even here. But they were in it together, they were in the same cabin, they were on the same team against the same adversaries, so far as Ben was concerned.

Above all, perhaps, Ben knew Billy was an important ally, or more honestly, an important *resource*.

Ben was confident that if any counselor or staff member tried to physically restrain Billy, Billy could, and likely would, beat them to death. Maybe even several of them. With the potential exception of Reid, he could see that Billy outclassed any one of the adults here, with specific respect to strength, bone-breaking ability, and general propensity toward violence.

Ben knew that Billy was the kind of dude who'd hit first, hit hard, and have no hesitation going for the nuts, the eyes, and the throat. Billy was the type who would engage in and maintain a jarring, terrifying level of violence from the very first second of altercation until he was either safe, or dead.

In this situation, Ben saw someone like Billy in the same way most other people would see a truck with the keys in the glove box and a full tank of gas, or a Glock 17 with a full mag in an unlocked desk drawer. A guy like Billy—to a guy like Ben—was a tool to keep in mind for use at the right time, if necessity arose.

As such, Ben carefully watched Reid carefully watching Billy, and when the moment had finally come, Ben knew it had before Reid even uttered the first word.

"Hey, Billy, you ever seen stars like this in Texas?"

A hush fell over the boys and counselors alike as all attention went to the large boy. Ben saw Rodrigo look over at him with his eyebrows raised. Ben shrugged, and Rodrigo punched his fist lightly into his other palm. Ben shrugged again. Rodrigo no doubt shared Ben's concern that a confrontation between Billy and a counselor was very unlikely to end *without* violence.

Billy did not react for several seconds, then he slowly lifted and turned his head toward Reid. He did not look up at the stars.

"No."

Not *nope* or *nah* or *I dunno.* Just a simple, deep *no.*

Billy's tone made it feel much less like an answer to Reid's question, and much more like a command—an order to foreclose any further attempt at conversation. That single word brought the entire group to silence. After a few seconds, Reid nodded, stirred the coals of the bonfire with one of the sticks they had used to cook the hot dogs, and finally responded with another question.

"Is this your first time camping, or did your family ever take you camping when you were growing up?"

Billy looked back to the fire with an expression one might see on the face of an exhausted parent. He slowly stood up and spoke as he turned toward the cluster of tents.

"I'm turnin in."

He only took a few steps before Reid called after him.

"Billy, hold up, buddy. Would it kill ya to just join the group, open up a bit? We're here together all summer, all these guys are in the same boat as you. This whole experience is much more enjoyable when you do it as a team."

Billy did not turn his body around to respond. He just looked off to his right, and spoke loudly.

"I'm tired. Fixin to sleep now."

Reid stood up. There was a playful exasperation in his smile.

"Billy, *please*, man. Just *one story*, one bit of *somethin* that tells us about who you are, tells us what you've been through. Everyone here has been through hard things. Opening up to people who want to learn more about who you, who want to learn more about what you've been through, do you feel that somehow makes you vulnerable or weak?"

Billy turned then. He took a few slow steps back into the firelight, where he stood, arms hanging at his sides, hands open. He looked up into Reid's face across the fire as he spoke.

"Not gettin enough sleep sure does."

A kid named Brooks spoke up then. Ben had chalked him up to be on the tougher and meaner side of the spectrum, even though Billy still made him look like a toddler in comparison. Billy *was* the far end of that side of the spectrum. Brooks's voice cut through the tension like one of the trout they'd watched earlier breaking the surface of the lake to feast on the evening hatch.

"What'd you do to end up here, bro? We all did some kinda bad shit to get sent here. What's yours?"

Everyone looked from Brooks to Billy, silently, even Reid. Billy didn't move or take his eyes away from Reid's face as he slowly spoke an answer to Brooks's question in his deep, Texas drawl.

"Jussa *long chain* a'misunderstandins is tha which'a why I'm here."

Reid scratched his forehead then ran his fingers through his somehow still perfectly tidy, side-swept coif of blond hair, then crossed his big arms as he took a deep breath. He forced some type of sympathy into his face as he spoke, so far as Ben could read it.

"People died that day, Billy. You took the lives of people who loved you . . . The judge believed it was an accident, but *do you* believe that, Billy?"

Reid only let the question hang for a moment before going on.

"The core of this program is about taking accountability for your past actions, being honest with yourself, *taking control* of yourself and your future, and moving forward in life as a better, stronger person."

Billy's expression didn't change at all as he responded. Ben couldn't understand how a teenager could look so worn, so carved out of wood. So tired.

"That's one a'them misunderstandins, see . . . Nobody who died that day had any love for me."

Reid's look of sympathetic concern didn't falter as he responded in a calm tone.

"What would your father and uncle have to say if they heard you say something like that?"

For the first time since anyone at Bear Springs had known Billy—he grinned. It was subtle, lips together, but it was a grin, a real one, from the mouth to the eyes.

"Not a damn thing, hoss. Them sons a'bitches is *dead*."

No one attempted to stop Billy as he turned and walked slowly into the darkness toward the tents. He whistled a tune that echoed off the dark alpine cathedral around them as he went, one Ben had heard before, but couldn't place. Besides a few excited whispers, no one spoke openly until after the sound of Billy's tent zipper faded. Ben, Rodrigo, and Trent exchanged wide-eyed looks.

Eventually, one of the counselors made a bumbling attempt to re-direct the attention of the group by launching into a story about some star he was pointing at.

Ben watched Reid, who stood there for a long time staring at the spot where Billy had faded into the darkness.

CHAPTER 13

BEN HAD a fitful night of sleep, at best. Sleep never came easily for Ben, and after what had happened around the campfire several hours earlier before they were all sent to their tents, and the cryptic message from the library playing itself over and over in his head, Ben was surprised he'd slept at all.

He woke up early and just lay there for what felt like hours trying to replay the events from the night before, but was too groggy, cold, and uncomfortable to remember it moment by moment, word for word. When the first gray wolf-light of dawn began to change the hue of his orange tent, Ben rubbed some warmth into his feet and hands, put on his jacket, gloves, and boots, then unzipped his tent flap as quietly as he could.

He was relieved to find he was the only one up. It was chilly, he could see his breath, and he could see where the sun would soon pierce over the rocky ridgeline to the east. He crept over to a boulder overlooking the lake, about sixty yards away from the array of tents, where he'd await the sunrise, and the warmth that accompanied it. The lake had a thin layer of mist above the mirrorlike surface. The reflection of the mountains on the other side of the lake shone in perfect detail on the water.

When atop the boulder, Ben sat down in a small crevice that obscured the view toward camp and began to run through the events from the evening before, chronologically, as carefully as he could, starting from the beginning. He found it hard not to linger on Billy. It was difficult to focus on recall when the mystery of that boy and what he'd been through was now so dramatized.

He sat there and ran through it all several times over, everything from the day before, trying to pick out any other important details. Long enough for the first rays of sunshine to creep over the mountains and hit him in the face and begin to warm his cheeks.

Ben, Rodrigo, and Trent all had separate tents, so they were deprived of their usual opportunity to bullshit and debrief the day's happenings. Ben looked forward to discussing this new information with them—this revelation that, as it would seem, Billy had something to do with the death of his own father and uncle. He also looked forward to investigating the locations mentioned in that message on the piece of wood, which he now stared at as he turned it over in his hands.

Ben took his gloves off and turned the back of his hands toward the sunrise to let them bake in the light. He was just beginning to feel the warmth sink into his skin when the piercing, shrill sounds of desperate screaming erupted from the rocky slope above the lake and camp. It sounded like a banshee's wailing.

Ben whipped around to scan the area where the noise came from, couldn't see anything, scrambled down off the boulder, and began running back toward his tent.

The boys began to shout profanity-laden inquiries about the shrieking from their sleeping bags. As Ben approached camp, he could see the morning dew shaking off the rainflies over dozens of tents as everyone began to stir simultaneously.

Ben caught sight of Reid, who was standing over one of the little portable gas stoves that hummed and burned under a French press of coffee. He was smiling up toward the rocks where the noise came from. Ben shouted the question at him before he'd even begun to slow down.

"Reid, what in the hell *is that?*"

A dozen of the boys who had emerged from their tents looked away from the screeching in the rocks and toward Reid, who answered Ben through a smile.

"That, Mr. Ben, is a *snowshoe hare.* A kind of rabbit. They sure do make a dreadful noise when snared, but it's the sound of success. One of you *fine young mountain men* just trapped your first animal! Come on, let's go check the trapline and get it ready for breakfast!"

Ben felt the shock of the terrible noise begin to fade. He saw Trent emerge from his tent with an excited smile on his face as he hopped around on one foot, stomping and pulling his boot on the other. Trent saw Ben and beamed a smile toward him.

"That's one of my traps, I know it!"

Trent and six or seven of the other boys began running up the rocky slope toward the noise, Reid and the counselor Mitchell power walking after them, laughing while urging them to calm and slow down before they twisted an ankle. Ben and some others followed the more excited group at a walking pace. Ben could see Trent ahead of the pack up the slope, deftly navigating the large rocks as he scrambled up toward some point where he must've set some of his traps. Trent rounded a larger rock, looked toward the ground, then turned toward the rest of the group smiling, pumping his fist in the air.

"It's my trap, I got one! Biggest rabbit I ever seen!"

The group formed a crescent around Trent's snare, which, indeed, was cinched tightly around the pelvis of a large gray-and-white rabbit. The creature was terrified, scrambling with the front legs that still worked fully, flipping over frantically in an effort to free itself. Reid stepped toward the trap and spoke to the group.

"*This*, fellas, is a snowshoe hare. In the autumn they actually begin to turn completely white to camouflage in the snow. Then, in the spring, they turn gray again. As you can see, this one is starting to change colors already. A little early for the color change, but I've seen it start this time of year before."

Trent spoke for the group.

"So what now? How do we get it out of the trap, what happens next?"

Reid pressed his lips in a tight smile and gave a slight shrug and nod.

"Well, now it's time to put the little guy out of his misery, then we skin it, dress it out, and eat it with eggs for breakfast!"

This elicited a burst of excited, anxious reactions from the boys. Reid knelt down near the animal, which was breathing so fast it looked like it could burst. Ben could see its eyes darting in every direction. Reid looked back up to the group.

"I'll do it this time so you can see how it's done. Guys, look away if you need to. I'm going to break its neck. It's painless, but if you don't want to watch, just turn away."

Some of the guys did, some didn't. Ben watched Reid's face as he grasped the frantic hare around its shoulders with one hand, then closed a fist around its head with the other. Ben could see the fast movement in his periphery and hear the hollow, wet crack. The animal went still immediately. Ben ignored the excited reactions of the boys and continued to watch Reid's face.

Reid then slackened the snare line and removed it from where it had cinched down into the rabbit's fur. Reid pulled out a knife from a sheath on his belt and began to explain what he was doing, but Ben couldn't hear, and didn't care, what he was actually saying.

Reid made a cut in the rabbit's fur near the shoulders, then gripped the rabbit's head and front legs in one hand and used the other to put two fingers into the hole he'd cut. He then pulled his hands in opposite directions, peeling the rabbit's skin and fur off and away from its body in one smooth movement until it flipped inside out and hung off its rear legs.

As Reid worked, he looked up at Ben, and smiled.

Ben heard something then. Felt it too. It was an unfortunately familiar sensation, but wasn't as shocking or terrifying as the first time. It started as a keening squeal deep in his ears, which popped like they did on the airplane. The sound grew louder and deeper until it was almost a roar. He couldn't move his body. At the same time, he felt as though he were heavier than the boulders around him, and as though he were falling. He could feel electricity dancing at the roots of his teeth. He felt like weeping and bursting into laughter.

All this sensation built and screamed in Ben's body while his eyes were locked on Reid. His hands worked adroitly, cutting the skin away from the legs, snapping the leg joints with his fingers then cutting them off entirely with the blade, sawing through the animal's neck to remove the head, cutting into the abdomen and scooping out its organs with his fingers.

Ben was pretty sure he appeared to be in a casual standing position but was actually on the verge of wetting and soiling himself, locked in completely, stuck in this hellish storm of sensation.

Reid gently ran his bloody fingers along the glistening, pink corpse of the skinned rabbit as he looked up at Ben. He was speaking to the other boys, but Ben knew—that Reid knew—Ben couldn't hear anything being said. In the moment they had locked eyes, when Reid smiled at Ben, Ben had felt again the hideous urge to both embrace Reid and weep within his strong arms, and to lean over to smash his face and skull into the jagged granite rocks above the snare.

As soon as Reid broke his gaze, the entire sensation dropped out of him, released its grip on him, the roaring and squealing went silent, and the normal sensations and sounds of the world flooded back into his body.

The transition was so extreme Ben started coughing and had to turn around to put his hands on a rock to keep from falling over. Ben could hear one of the other boys jeering about how the *softy is gonna puke.* Someone's hand went onto his shoulder to stabilize him. Looking over he saw it was Rodrigo.

Ben steadied himself and caught his breath. It was just like when he'd first met Reid back home in Lafitte, Ben realized. Same smile. Same bizarre, terrifying paralysis. Same shit. Reid's voice cut through and silenced the group.

"You okay there, Ben?"

Ben wiped his eyes with the backs of his hands and took a deep breath before turning back toward the group—who he knew would all be staring. He looked straight at Reid, whom he found smiling back at him. Ben saw a bit of challenge in the man's eyes. A *dare*, almost.

"Sorry, got a bit dizzy, probly that altitude sickness you told us about. Anyway, I read somewhere that real mountain men used to eat the raw nuts of the critters they'd trap. You a real mountain man, Reid? You gonna eat those nuts?"

All the other boys started laughing and whooping immediately. They all readily joined in a collective effort to urge Reid to ingest the rabbit's raw testicles, as Ben knew they would.

Reid's smile faltered briefly. Ben saw a twitch at the corner of his eye. Ben forced himself to smile back at Reid as he began a loud, slow chant, pounding a fist into an open palm with each iteration. "*Eat those nuts, eat those nuts, eat those nuts.*"

By the fourth chorus, all the boys had joined in, screaming in unison. Reid's eyes narrowed before he looked away from Ben and around the group, shaking his head. He stood, skinned rabbit in one hand, making an open-palmed calming gesture with the other, and shouted almost inaudibly over the chanting.

"Alright, alright, guys, easy, let's go cook up Trent's rabbit with some eggs for breakfast."

Reid walked out ahead of the boys, everyone still chanting, whooping, and laughing in his wake as they worked their way through the rocks back toward camp.

Ben stayed behind a moment. He felt scared. He'd chosen to engage in another of these strange, silent battles of wit with Reid, instead of backing down. He'd always enjoyed those moments with adults in the past, even violent, dangerous adults. But with Reid, something felt different. Something felt *very* dangerous. He just didn't know what the hell it was.

Rodrigo clapped his hand on Ben's back once they'd reached camp. "You all good, B?"

Ben felt embarrassed and just nodded as he avoided eye contact. "Yah, all good, just got dizzy, slept like shit."

Ben could feel Rodrigo's questioning gaze in response and would avoid meeting it at all costs. Rodrigo had the best internal bullshit detector Ben had ever encountered, and Ben knew it wasn't worth much effort to try, but had no idea how to explain what had happened.

Well, it seems as though Reid has the power to intentionally induce a paralytic panic attack by simply smiling at me was a batshit-crazy thing to say, let alone try to explain. Ben just meandered onward with the rest of the group and hoped Rodrigo wouldn't ask more questions.

The group spent the rest of the day fishing and exploring the area around the lake. One of the counselors brought some binoculars and passed them around as he pointed out some bighorn sheep on one mountain above the lake, and a small herd of mountain goats in a scree field on the other side. Ben tried to stay quiet and avoid Reid as much as he could. He wanted to look like a follower, not a leader.

He was reluctant to even admit to himself that Reid had, once again, paralyzed him with a simple smile. Even worse, having happened again, it was now even more difficult to rationalize as a panic attack or something of the like. Ben's mouth went dry and palms started to sweat whenever he thought of the knowing look in Reid's eye—Reid's apparent recognition of what he was doing to Ben in those moments. Although it was even more difficult to accept that this preppy fuck had some kind of mind control power. If he did, why wouldn't he use it all the time?

They ate more hot dogs around the fire that evening, the counselors told some shitty ghost stories, Billy kept his silence and distance, then they all climbed into their tents. After a half hour of the counselors hushing the boys' slap-happy shit-talking between the tents, the group began to drift off. The snoring, stirring, and farts of dozens of teenage boys filled the natural sounds of the alpine valley.

The next morning they packed camp, hoisted their bags, and began the ruck back to basecamp. As they crested the ridge and began to turn downhill and lose the alpine valley, Reid waited for all to pass so he could take up the rear. As Ben passed, the two locked eyes.

Ben, once again, was surprised by the casual sincerity and geniality in the man's face and tone of voice.

"Pretty amazing up here, isn't it, Ben? I'm really glad you got to see this place. It's very special."

Ben stopped and looked out over the valley, then back at Reid.

"Sure is pretty. Nothin like this in Louisiana."

Reid gently poked Ben in the breast pocket with one of his trekking poles and smiled.

"Well, everything we give you, teach you, and show you up here, you'll get to take home with you, Ben. It'll be a part of you forever, no matter *where* you are."

Ben, unusually, wasn't sure what to say, so he looked back at the valley, then nodded at Reid and kept hiking down the trail back toward Bear Springs. Back toward home.

CHAPTER 14

THE MOOD in the large dining hall was much more subdued than usual. Only the scraping of plastic utensils and quiet conversations could be heard. All the energy and enthusiasm left in the boys was directed toward the lasagna dinner they'd been served.

They had climbed a mountain that day. Shield Mountain, the summit of which something above 11,000 feet in elevation.

The beginning of the day's hike started as a long, increasingly steep slog through the pine-forested ridges above basecamp. While they were carrying much lighter packs than they did on the backpacking trek the week before, the first few hours felt similar to how that hike had started. Then the group came to a much rockier, open area where they followed a narrow trail that wound along up the mountain. The trail weaved ever upward through aspen glades, under towering granite cliffs, and crossed fast, cold mountain streams.

Toward the peak of the mountain, the group endured a miserable expanse of switchbacks that cut through a hot, unforgivingly steep scree slope. The obnoxious proclamations of encouragement and perseverance from Reid and the other counselors only made it more insufferable to Ben. Once atop the mountain, looking down at the large area they had covered, Ben did find himself warmed by a frustratingly enjoyable feeling of accomplishment. He even offered a begrudging grin in response to a friendly clap on the back and eerily sincere smile from Reid.

Throughout the week that had passed since the two-night backpacking trip to the alpine lake—since the revelation about Billy, and Ben's second moment of dreadful paralysis at Reid's smile—Ben had been focusing hard on keeping his head down around Reid. Playing the wiseass with Nicholas was a bad call, as well, as he imagined the man would bring that up to Reid eventually. But if he did, what would he really say, *that kid Ben can read a book?* Either way, Ben remained ever observant of Reid whenever around him, but did his best to keep out of the way and just go through the motions. He needed to play the unremarkable follower. Nothing Ben had seen from Reid served to corroborate the dread and danger that had wafted off him on the other notable occasions.

On the long hike down from the mountaintop, as well, Ben found himself actually paying attention and consideration to the casual, piece-meal lecture Reid offered along the way. Son of a bitch was giving good, constructive advice, and effectively packaging it in a way that young guys would actually be receptive to.

At one point in the hike home to basecamp, the group stopped to use the little hand-pump water purifiers to refill their CamelBak bladders from one of the many little glacial streams that trickled from the mountain.

Ben was standing over the small creek and pumping the water while Rodrigo was using the spout hose to fill a number of the boys' water bladders that they'd removed from their packs and lined up along the bank. There were several such groups doing the same up and down the bank— one of the time-efficient tactics they'd all picked up over the last several weeks in the mountains, especially on small streams moving through large rocks where there wasn't much surface access. The boys worked or milled around waiting for their water silently. This hike was the most arduous physical exertion they had been forced into so far this summer, and they were all exhausted.

Ben watched Billy remove the bladder from his pack, unscrew the lid, and dunk the entire thing into the cold, fast water, filling it up directly from the stream without bothering to use the purifier.

One of the counselors standing nearby, Freddie, saw this, and paced over toward Billy.

"Hey, Billy, you should definitely purify this water, dude. There are some beaver ponds upstream of us, and look at the moss and bug growth on the rocks in the stream, there's probably some bacteria in here you don't want in your gut."

Billy looked over at Freddie's midsection, not his face, slowly screwed the lid back onto his now-full water bladder, then looked away as he began putting it back into his backpack while taking a long gulp from the hose. Freddie's mouth worked to form words but didn't say anything else as he slowly turned and walked away.

One of the boys from another cabin, Joe—one of the bigger, grumpier, and more idiotic assholes out of the group—paced down the bank groaning about his *shitty, fucked-up shoulder straps*. As he did so, he kicked through a few of the water bladders Rodrigo had arranged along the stream, including the one he was actively filling up at that moment, spilling water all over his hands and boots. Trent and a few other boys who comprised this particular impromptu water-refilling team offered a simultaneous chorus of *watch it, man* and *come on, dude* exclamations.

Joe glanced down at the cluster of gear he'd waded through and offered a solitary *whoops*, and kept on strolling.

Rodrigo looked up at the bigger boy's back as he spoke.

"Pinche idiota torpe."

Rodrigo rarely spoke Spanish, so the boys who heard him stared at him, perplexed. Joe, who most of the boys knew was another Spanish speaker, whipped his head around to glare at Rodrigo, pointing at him as he spoke.

"Fuck did you just say?"

Rodrigo dropped the hose from the water purifier as he stood up straight.

"Me escuchaste, pendejo."

Joe's fists clenched and face went red as he offered some blistering, unintelligible response and started forward toward Rodrigo on heavy, plodding feet. A group of other boys backpedaled out of his way, someone shouting at Joe to chill.

Ben hadn't moved from where he'd been pumping water in the stream, he just watched Rodrigo.

Rodrigo's head didn't move at all as he turned his body clockwise a few degrees, orienting his left shoulder forward and shifting his weight onto his back foot. He bent his knees slightly and rolled his left shoulder as his left arm came to rest loosely several inches in front of his body, bent at the elbow.

Ben dropped the water purifier on the bank of the stream and crossed his arms. He looked Rodrigo up and down, then smiled and nodded in approval as he watched the boy fall quite casually into a proper boxing posture.

It would seem that his friend was a fighter, or at least had been trained to fight by someone who'd done quite a bit of it. Ben figured every kid at Bear Springs was tougher than average and considered a fighter by those they grew up with back home. Thus, he had been eager for tensions to boil to a point where he'd have the actual opportunity to evaluate who among them knew how to properly kick some ass.

"Stop right there!"

Reid's voice punched across the landscape and echoed off the crags and rocks around the whole drainage. Joe stopped in his tracks as every head whipped over to where Reid was jogging out of the trees into the center of the altercation. Reid put his hands on his hips when he reached a spot between the two boys.

"What the *hell* is going on here!?"

Joe started blathering about how Rodrigo started it. This triggered the group of boys who'd been filling their water bladders to launch back a series of overlapping declarations like *that's bullshit* and *that's not what happened*. Rodrigo remained silent, face calm, eyes on Joe.

Reid spoke with intensity, none of the usual levity in his voice.

"That's *enough!*"

There was sufficient volume and edge in his voice for even Rodrigo to look away from Joe and toward Reid, relaxing his fighter's stance as he did so.

"You guys are exhausted, and rightfully so. We pushed you hard today. You climbed a big mountain, and made it up there because we worked together *as a team.*"

Reid spoke with quick, precise hand gestures, the lines leaving his forehead and face relaxing slightly as he went on. He spoke to Rodrigo and Joe, but really to everyone.

"You will both encounter moments like this when you leave this place and get home. Moments that will test your temper, test your personal strength, test your discipline. Moments that will jeopardize your control over yourself. You have no control over the world around you, you cannot avoid moments like this, but you can *always* control yourself, you are *always* in control of your own temper."

Reid let his words echo around them until the babble and gulp of the small stream was all that could be heard. He cut through that natural stillness with his next words, shouted loudly, startling everyone.

"So *prove* it!"

Reid gestured toward both boys, then a spot on the ground in front of him.

"Come shake hands, and bury this hatchet *right* here and *right* now. It's not about *the other guy*, it's *never* about the other guy. Prove to yourselves, *right* here, *right* now, that you are actually the ones in control."

Both Joe's and Rodrigo's shoulders slumped in embarrassment and looked around their feet for a few seconds, but the effect of Reid's interjection was strong enough for them to eventually shuffle forward toward him. They begrudgingly extended arms and took one another's hands in a brief, limp handshake.

Reid maintained a serious expression as he nodded, turning to look both of them in the eye individually.

"Good. Good work, gentlemen."

He turned and shouted down the stream at the rest of the group.

"Now, fellas, let's get that water refilled and get the trail under our feet. It's lasagna night, and you all deserve a big dinner!"

The boys quietly went back to the chore at hand, deflated by the lecture, and by the deprivation of violence. Rodrigo picked up the hose and went about spinning the lid off another water bladder. Ben stepped in toward him, catching his eye, and gave him a sly grin.

"That would've been a helluva scrap. Looks like you know how to fight, but Joe's a big fucker, and probably used to taking a hard punch."

Rodrigo tilted his head from side to side as though considering the odds of the melee, then grinned in return.

"Yah, but big ol' Jose would've only had a couple seconds until it was outta my hands."

Rodrigo gestured with his head to Ben's right, to a spot that was behind where Joe had been facing during the little standoff. Ben followed Rodrigo's gaze and was surprised to find the imposing figure of Billy, leaning casually against a tree. As Ben and Rodrigo locked eyes on the large boy, he dropped a pair of round, grapefruit-sized river rocks, letting one fall out of each hand to thump into the soft bed of roots and pine needles at the base of the tree. He turned away and walked back toward the trail.

That afternoon they dumped their gear in their cabins and had an hour to kill before dinner. Most of the boys collapsed into their beds, but Ben went straight to the lodge. On the walls of the long hallway leading to the Great Hall were a dozen maps of the area under the numerous heads of moose, elk, and deer. Ben went from map to map, poring over each one that showed any ground to the west of basecamp, looking for the names in the message he found in the library. *Buckle Creek, Buckle Glacier*, and *Caravan Pass*. By the time the dinner bell was ringing, Ben had read the name of every creek, river, lake, mountain peak, glacier, and pass between basecamp and the Idaho state line. Not one of those places was mentioned. Ben walked to dinner feeling genuine relief that he had *not* found those places and was *not* getting worked up about what the implications of that, and the sinister message, would be for him.

As all the ravenous, exhausted boys sat in the dining hall, mumbling in pairs and quietly devouring their dinner, Ben ran through the mental catalog of the day's events as he always did, looking for any important details warranting deeper consideration. He glanced quickly up at Billy as he recalled the rocks he'd been holding.

He wondered whether Billy equipped himself with those rocks to act in Rodrigo's defense, or if he'd simply been preparing to take advantage of a moment of chaos for his own ends. He wondered whether Billy really would've crushed in the skull of a counselor or another boy on the bank of that beautiful, cold mountain stream. Ben supposed that he would have, indeed.

He heard loud footsteps coming down the aisle between the large wooden dining tables behind him and to his right, and looked up when Joe was already just a few feet away. By the time Ben had registered who it even was, Joe was already mid-crow-hop, winding up a giant punch aimed toward Rodrigo's head.

Rodrigo had only just begun to turn toward the sound and commotion when the large boy's fist smashed into his head.

The punch was a big one, and a bad one. It connected above Rodrigo's ear, slamming the smaller boy's skull into the space of wood between his own and Ben's plates of food, sending a shower of utensils, plates, and lasagna in a large halo around the table.

Joe was screaming *fuck you* over and over as he grabbed the back of Rodrigo's shirt collar, no doubt intending to pull his head up to land the next haymaker, which he'd already begun winding up. Trent jumped up from his seat across the large table and began scrambling over it toward Joe. Ben shot up and grasped Joe's wrist above where his soft, fat fist clenched a bundle of Rodrigo's shirt, and began to wind up his own punch with his other hand.

Before Trent could cross the table, and before Ben could throw his punch, Rodrigo moved his entire body with the speed of a snake.

Rodrigo twisted as Joe began to pull him up by the shirt, and with what appeared to be every muscle he had, threw a low left hook into Joe's solar plexus with such speed and force it made a smack that echoed across the entire dining hall. All the wind in Joe's lungs blasted out of his mouth and nose, bringing gobs and strings of spit and snot along with it.

Before Joe had even finished the exhalation, Rodrigo launched back off the bench and onto his feet, weaving smoothly under Joe's large arm and knocking Ben back into the aisle between tables. In one continuous motion as he came up from his weave under Joe's arm, he slammed a right uppercut into Joe's jaw, sending another audible snap of noise across the room.

Counselors were launching up from their table, knocking over benches, sprinting toward the fight, screaming at the boys to stop. Someone, Reid maybe, was blowing a whistle.

Rodrigo took a step away from the larger boy. Joe's head fell forward from the skygazing position it'd been rocked into by the hammer of an uppercut—and as he did, Rodrigo landed two jabs straight into Joe's nose at lightning speed. Those were enough to weaken Joe's knees, who began stagger-falling backward just as Rodrigo cranked his hips into a right cross that cracked into Joe's face right below his eye.

Before Joe could crumple or Rodrigo could get another punch in, counselors swarmed the area, bear-hugging Joe and Rodrigo and pulling Trent and Ben away from the combat as well. Ben watched Rodrigo's face as he was hauled down the aisle of the dining hall by Mitchell, one of the counselors.

He was screaming at Joe in Spanish and had a forced smile on his face, yet tears still poured down his cheeks from red eyes—in the way they do from young, angry boys who still experience fear, hurt, and rage as separate emotions.

Ben had pondered before about when a boy stopped doing that, and why most men, eventually, seem to start only using rage to express all their bad feelings.

Reid and the counselor Riley half guided and half carried Joe out of the room through the other door. A gaggle of other counselors did their best to chill the rest of the boys out and get them to finish eating, shouting over the excited postfight hum the conflict had stirred among the group.

Ben caught sight of the elder man Daniel, leaning his back and one old boot against the wall near the main doors to the mess hall, toothpick glued into the corner of his mouth where it always was. This was the first time Ben had seen one of the four elder men in the mess hall. He gave Rodrigo an amused, almost approving grin as the boy was hauled through the doors. Ben took note of this, because up until now, he'd chalked these four elder *interventionists* up as being the enforcers and musclemen of this institution. But here, to the contrary, it appeared as though the man only entered the hall to enjoy a good scrap, instead of breaking one up.

The boys went back to their cabins after dinner, walking through the rain, hearing thunder bang off the rocks high above on the mountains. When back at the cabin, Jimmy insisted they engage in their standard postmeal *bro-bro* conversation. Billy remained silent, as usual, but Ben and Trent sent a volley of questions at Jimmy about where Rodrigo had been taken, what was happening to him, what Reid would do to him. Jimmy couldn't handle the inquisition; he just flustered and blushed and became repetitive with assurances that Rodrigo would be fine.

After about a half hour, the door to the cabin opened and Rodrigo came through. He was with another counselor, whom Jimmy exchanged some words with as Ben and Trent began their interrogation about where he'd been taken and what had happened when he got there.

Rodrigo seemed angry and resigned. His answers were disappointing to Ben, only in that they lacked the level of detail he'd have preferred. Rodrigo explained how he'd been brought into the room they all went to for therapy and was then forced to talk through the events of the evening with his therapist. He said the staff was going to make him and Joe endure some terrible conflict resolution and anger management session together, as a pair. Eventually, Jimmy insisted the group get ready for bed, and the boys all went along with it much more easily than usual.

The rain on the roof and the cracking of lightning only helped lull them toward bed. Despite the excitement of the day, they were exhausted. Once Jimmy turned the lights off, the boys didn't even attempt to indulge in their usual, whispered review and debrief of the day's events.

Ben lay awake for longer than he'd wanted to. He could hear Billy and Rodrigo snoring, and the slow, paced cadence of Trent's breathing next to him, which Ben knew meant he was fast asleep. He was finally starting to feel some weight in his eyelids when he heard muffled shouting from outside. He almost dismissed it as a strange echo from one of the thunder blasts that were seeming to punch down from the sky directly above the camp. Then he heard it again, and it was unmistakable this time. It was definitely a person.

Ben sat up. Ten long seconds passed; two lightning flashes lit up the room, one after another. Then Ben heard another angry, but unintelligible, shout. He slipped quietly out of bed and tiptoed toward the window that looked toward the grounds between all the cabins and the lodge. He could see how hard it was raining within the orange, glowing arcs that surrounded the lanterns that lined the walkways. A motion on the porch of one of the cabins nearby caught his attention, and Ben strained his eyes.

Ben could see the cabin door was open, and a counselor was standing on the porch with his hands on the shoulders of one of the boys. It was Joe. Joe was shouting at the counselor, but all Ben could hear were the angry, urgent, muffled sounds of the boy's voice.

Suddenly, Joe checked the counselor—he slammed both hands into the man's chest and rocked him backward into the door of the cabin. Joe spun around and stalked into the rain, making a beeline directly toward Ben's cabin.

Ben's eyes went wide. *This crazy fucker is coming for Rodrigo.* He heard Joe's shouts more clearly then, perhaps just because he could see Joe's body strain with effort as he screamed.

"*Rodrigo!*" He was then screaming Rodrigo's name repeatedly out into the howling storm.

Ben began to suck in the air necessary to wake up his buddies with a shout when he saw Joe freeze. He went completely still, directly under one of the lanterns along a flagstone pathway. Ben could see the water soaking and pouring off the large boy, even in the dim orange light.

Every muscle in Joe's body was completely rigid. He looked like he was made of cement and rebar. Then Ben saw a large figure in the dark, behind Joe. Ben felt a jolt of fear and quickly stepped aside so that only one eye protruded from the darkness of his cabin to stare out the window.

The dark figure began moving forward toward the tent of light under the lantern where Joe was frozen in place. As it moved from the darkness toward the light, Ben could begin to see that it was a man, and eventually that it was a man wearing a dark rain poncho. The man walked casually, calmly, swinging his arms at his sides as though he were strolling through a park.

When the man entered the light, Ben could see that it was Reid. He was smiling at Joe as he talked to him casually, making subtle hand gestures as he spoke and walked in slow circles around the large boy.

Joe wasn't moving his head to look at him; he just remained frozen in place. A few seconds later, Joe suddenly dropped to his knees, but it looked more like he was wrenched downward by invisible hands, torn down to the earth. He remained there for a moment until his head ripped upward to stare up into Reid's face—it was as if Reid had yanked on a chain attached to a steel ring screwed into the large boy's jawbone.

Reid leaned down into Joe's face, putting his hands on his knees. Ben saw Reid break into an obscene smile then, his lips seeming to part from ear to ear. He could see Joe begin to shake in that same moment, his entire upper body and head gyrating violently under the big man's vicious grin.

Ben felt terror in that moment. He felt as he did when he was wedged under the grease trap behind the diner. He felt as he did when his aunt ripped little Wade away from him the day he was taken away. He felt his hands shaking, his teeth clattering. He stepped away from the window and pressed his back against the wall. He tried to control his breathing for a moment, then crept across the room and quietly slipped back into his bed. He thought about the message in the library and the dire suggestion that the reader hightail it to the west or kill themselves if they can't. He thought of the filthy-sounding name, *Silas*.

Eventually, Ben didn't ponder the circumstances he'd just witnessed, he didn't muse over potential explanations for what he'd just seen or anything else from the past weeks. He just pulled the covers up over his head, tucked his knees into his chest, and tried not to cry.

CHAPTER 15

A WEEK AFTER that long, sleepless night, the whole class sat before one of the counselors, Mitchell, who held up four fingers as he spoke. He paced slowly in front of where boys sat and sprawled out on the packed, bone-dry dirt, aglow in the rich orange light of early summer evenings. Mitchell maintained a contemplative, serious expression, nodding to himself as he spoke. This man's sham earnestness made Ben even more annoyed than he already was.

"There are four critical things to consider when setting a trap . . . that is to say, there are four essential elements behind any good trap. They're easy to remember as well. Just remember the acronym T-R-A-P."

Only a few weeks ago Ben would've already been chuckling aloud, ridiculing this adult's portrayal of the austere instructor. Instead, he looked down at his hands, took in a deep breath, then looked back at Mitchell. Reid could be watching, or would at least get word of any smart-assery.

Ben had continued to dedicate himself to the role of a quiet, contrite follower. It was not easy for him, especially in moments like this, but he'd stayed in character for a couple of weeks now and would remain disciplined. He watched Mitchell's hands, his ungainly body language, and concluded that he could likely have this man on the verge of tears within about thirty seconds. As Mitchell looked at the boys and began to speak again, Ben cocked his head a bit, and gazed up at his face with his best veneer of curious interest.

"The first element of a good trap is simple: it's an understanding of the *type* of trap that will be necessary, the design of the trap, the mechanics of the trap you will need to deploy. Whether it's a foothold, a conibear, a snare, a deadfall, a live trap like a cage, a feather spear trap, you've got to have a good understanding of how to assemble the trap itself, what materials to use, and how to bait and set it. And if you're going to use a snare or deadfall, what *type* of snare or deadfall is best for the situation?"

Mitchell nodded at the group and asked if there were any questions. No one had any. No one even said *no*, or shook their heads.

Mitchell ran his forehead along his shoulder and upper arm to wipe the sweat away. Ever since the big storm broke the morning after Rodrigo and Joe got into a fight, it had been oppressively hot. For over a week now, there hadn't been any clouds, any afternoon thunderstorms, or any of the mercifully cool mountain air that hangs close to the ground before sunrise. By 9:00 a.m. every day, heat waves shimmered off every surface.

Being from south Louisiana, Ben was used to heat, and one could escape this dry mountain heat in the shade. Ben couldn't do that back home, where there was no reprieve, where the weighted, humid heat clung to you like a wet blanket and crept into your clothes and lungs. Even so, this dry western heat was unique to Ben and frustrating in its own way—the sun was *hot* this high up in the mountains; it scalded, burned your scalp and shoulders, even through a shirt. There was no shroud of humid, polluted air to screen its broiling effect on the skin. It seemed to make the crickets scream louder, make the tree bark and rocks sharper, and keep dust hanging in the air longer.

"The second element of setting any good trap is the *range*. *Range* means the area where your prey will be; an animal's *range* is where they move, eat, hunt, live. Thinking about an animal's *range* helps you decide on a specific place to set a trap. If you're trying to catch beaver or muskrat, think about their *range*, and you'll know to set a trap along a riverbank. If you're going for squirrel, you'll know to set a trap along a log or branches they use to skitter around. For big game like deer or elk, think about *their range*, and you'll know to set a trap along a fresh game trail they've been using . . .'"

Despite the afternoon heat, despite having been outside all day, despite the exertion on the hike they'd done earlier to check their traps, the boys were at least *somewhat* interested. Trapping and fishing had definitely become the most popular activities among the group.

They were teenage boys, after all, and going through the process of skinning a small mammal and then using its brains and smoke from a small fire to tan the pelt was one of the most popular "skills sessions" the counselors could engage in. Spreading the animal's brains onto its skin before stretching the pelt on the tanning rack "was how the Native people of these mountains" used to do it, the counselors had explained. Whether that was true or not, the boys didn't know, but it was always entertaining, no matter how many times they'd huddled around the spectacle to watch it.

There was also some competitiveness in fishing and trapping, among this group at least. Trent had quickly become the reigning master angler and trapper of the group, and had amassed a nice, enviable collection of pelts on the tanning racks, which the counselors promised he could take home. Everyone wanted some pelts to take home. On top of that primal element of the practice that spoke to most of these boys, there was an undeniable satisfaction associated with catching a squirrel or a rabbit in a trap or a trout on a fly rod, then gutting and eating it. The cooks at the lodge would prepare the game or trout they'd catch for the group, and wild game soup or fish tacos had become the dinner favorites among the group.

Mitchell planted his feet and faced the group, holding up three fingers.

"Alright, the *third* element to any good trap is the *attitude*."

The man bunched his hand into a fist as he snarled out the last word. Ben bit down on the inside of his cheek to keep himself from laughing at the dramatic flourish.

"You only trap an animal that you're planning to eat, and that means you've got to be mentally prepared to take the life of a living creature. You do not trap for fun or for sport. You trap *for food*. Man set his first trap hundreds of thousands of years ago, when we were still part of the food chain, and *not* at the top of it. Man had to become a predator. No matter who you are, if you go back far enough, every single one of you is a direct descendant of someone who trapped their food. Wolves,

bears, and lions do not hurt living creatures for fun, enjoyment, or because they're bored. They *attack* their prey because that is how they eat,
that is how they survive, that is how they feed their family. You do not
hurt animals; you do not *maim* them or make them suffer. When you're
choosing to eat an animal, you're choosing to take its life. Quick and
clean. You're choosing to *attack*. This a mentality. This is an attitude."

Mitchell leaned forward and scanned the boys' faces with wide eyes
as he tapped his index finger into his temple.

"To *attack* is to make a decision as a man. It's a mindset. It's discipline. It's keeping your focus on the objective. Without those things,
without the predator's attitude, you will not succeed. So, remember, the
letter *A* is for *attitude,* because being a trapper is being a predator, and
what do predators have?"

Mitchell's pageantry actually worked on this occasion, as a large
number of boys actually shouted *attitude* in response, with notable
gusto. Ben was not one of them, but he did allow himself to grin a bit as
he felt a pang of reluctant approval for Mitchell wash over him. *At least
the son of a bitch is entertaining.*

"The fourth and final element of a good trap is the most important
one, gentlemen, and it's the one that takes the longest to master. The
fourth piece of every good trap can be remembered with the word . . ."

Mitchell turned and gestured toward the group with his hand as he
spoke the word, fingers and thumb in a pinch, as though he were holding an invisible feather.

"*Prey . . .*"

He scanned the faces of the boys for several seconds before he continued.

"A wolf understands the ways of the moose. An owl understands
the ways of the rabbit. A cougar understands the ways of the deer. You
must understand the ways of the *prey* you intend to trap. I'm not just
talking about their *range*, which is element number two. I'm talking
about putting yourself into the minds of the *prey* animal you are trying
to deceive. Understanding your prey is understanding how they think,
where they sleep, *when* they sleep, what they eat, *where* and *when* they
eat, do they have *their own* living *prey*, what else is hunting them, what

scares them, where will they go to hide, what're they watching for, what smells frighten them, *what is it that motivates this animal* to go from point A to point B. Understanding your *prey* is how you truly become a proficient trapper."

Mitchell put his hands on his hips and smiled, apparently deciding the time was right to drop the vibe of stern sobriety.

"Alright, boys, let's go through the four elements, alright? T-R-A-P. What's the *T* stand for?"

Ben did not respond or look around, but wondered how many of the boys would remember the word *type* given the length of time that'd passed—sitting hungry, baking in this dusty sun—since this little lecture began. Four or five of the boys mumbled the word *type*, Trent being the loudest.

Mitchell nodded and smiled. "That's right, *T* is for *type*, the type of trap most appropriate for the circumstances. Now how about the second element of a good trap?"

It seemed about twice as many boys decided to participate for this one, shouting out *range* in response. When Mitchell prompted the third element, almost all the boys shouted *attitude* with jovial enthusiasm.

A portion of Mitchell's previous seriousness flushed back into his expression before he spoke again.

"Remember, gentlemen, the fourth element is the most important one. It stands for the most critical element in being a trapper, a hunter, a *predator*. What does the *P* stand for?"

Most of the boys participated again, with one of the boys off to Ben's right shouting out *punk-ass bitch* shortly after the chorus of *prey* had ended. This sent a bolt of cackling and laughter through the group.

Mitchell let his head hang as he sported a reluctant, resigned smile.

"Alright, fellas, *clearly* you're ready for dinner. Let's get into formation and head down toward the dining hall."

Mitchell shouted out the *fire circle* colors and sides of the formation, and *green* was called to the front. Trent popped up from where he'd been sitting while Rodrigo stood slowly, wiping dust from his pants as he rose. Ben, Trent, and Rodrigo all exchanged deflated, challenging looks.

Usually this was a contentious moment, deciding who among the *fire circle* groups at the head of the formation would carry the flag. Several fights had almost broken out about it. The flag and the flagpole itself was heavy as shit, heavier than the mount that the other dude on point would have to carry, so there was a complete lack of enthusiasm for this particular chore. The unwillingness to volunteer meant that—nine times out of ten—a counselor would just have to pick someone from one of the front groups to carry the flag, resulting in a groan from the victim and jeers from the rest of the guys. *"There's our little Girl Scout!"* was one of the favorites.

"Oh, I'll do it! I call flag duty!"

All three boys turned toward the shouted declaration. It was Joe. His *fire circle* color was also called to be at the head of the formation, and Joe was skipping toward where the Bear Springs summer class flagpole hung limp in the hot air. His face wasn't as swollen as it had been, but there were still dark scabs nestled among blue, purple, and yellow blotches where Rodrigo had landed punches the week before. The boys watched silently as Joe lifted the flag out of the mount, turned on his heel, and jogged back to the head of the formation, laughing and whooping as he went.

Trent smiled at Rodrigo as he slapped him on the shoulder.

"You really beat the manners into that one, Rod!"

Rodrigo chuckled and shook his head.

"What a goofy motherfucker."

Ben did not smile or follow his two friends as they walked toward the assembling group. His skin crawled as he watched Joe, and he shrugged to suppress the shudder he felt coming on. He turned to look for Billy, whom he found standing behind the group, staring through narrowed eyes at Joe's flamboyant march toward the head of the line. Billy's expression didn't change as he turned his head to meet Ben's eyes.

He held Ben's gaze for a moment before he turned and took his long, slow strides into the group, the boys anxiously parting around him as he went.

Ben hadn't told the others about what he saw that night of the storm, a week earlier, after Joe and Rodrigo's fight. He hadn't told them about the large boy falling to his knees before Reid. He hadn't told them about how the boy shook, how Reid smiled. He wasn't sure what the hell he'd even say.

He'd just filed it away like one would a nightmare.

The week before, the morning after that terrifying moment, Joe was waiting outside their cabin with his cabin counselor. Jimmy went out to greet them, then invited both Joe and the counselor inside. Trent, Rodrigo, and Ben all stiffened when they realized who'd entered their room. All three subconsciously puffed out their chests, lifted their chins, and clenched their hands into fists. Billy was sitting on his bed, and did none of those things. The only thing that changed about him was his facial expression. Ben watched his face as his resting expression of menacing distance faded into a look of subtle curiosity, Billy's version of it, at least. Billy cocked his head a bit and looked Joe up and down as though he were one of the more boring animals at a zoo. When Jimmy started talking, Billy stood and walked into the bathroom.

"Fellas, Joe here wanted to come by and say a few things."

Joe's face was swollen, with deep cuts on his nose and cheek that peeked out from behind butterfly bandages. A harsh shade of red covered his eye, cheek, and jaw. Ben knew that hue of red. When on the face of a woman or a child, Ben knew it was the kind of red that promised to blossom into a sickening mélange of blue, brown, and yellow.

Joe clasped his hands together in front of him and, despite the damage, a sincere, embarrassed smile spread visibly across his face. He looked up into Rodrigo's eyes.

"Rodrigo, I've come here this morning to say I'm sorry. I am so sorry for attacking you, for expressing my feelings with violence. I do not expect you to accept my apology right now, but I hope that, eventually, you feel as though you can."

Joe slowly nodded at Rodrigo once, then looked over and spoke as he glanced between Trent and Ben.

"I also wanna say I'm also sorry to you two for my behavior at the creek yesterday, when we were filling up our water, and for putting both of you in danger with my outburst later at dinner. I'm really, really sorry."

Joe hung his head and stared at his clasped hands. Jimmy broke the awkward silence that followed, walking up to Joe and grasping his shoulder amicably.

"It takes a big man to apologize like that, Joe. I'm proud of you."

Jimmy lightly thumped his fist on Joe's shoulder a few times as he looked back at the other three boys.

"I don't expect you all to bury the hatchet this very moment, but I hope you remember this moment. This is what courage looks like. This is what accountability looks like."

Joe and his counselor left the cabin. When the screen door clanged loudly behind them, Trent and Ben glanced at one another, while Rodrigo just stared out the door into the morning light.

Jimmy walked up to Rodrigo and put his hand on his shoulder. He bent his head down to try to catch Rodrigo's gaze, smiling at the boy as he did. Just as he began to say something, Rodrigo looked up at Jimmy and cut him off.

"Nah, *fuck* that, dude."

He shrugged Jimmy's hand away, grabbed a towel and some clothes out of his dresser, and stalked into the bathroom. Trent let out a long breath through pursed lips, shook his head, then grabbed a towel and headed in to catch a shower as well.

Ben sat down slowly on Trent's bed, resting his elbows on his knees, wishing he could stop time or teleport somewhere else to digest what he'd just witnessed.

Jimmy sat down across from him, letting out an intentionally audible exhale. Ben heard at least two of the showers going, so knew he had a minute without an audience of peers to "be himself" as he dealt with Jimmy. It had been a few weeks now since he'd really let his hair down, and an abrupt return to his true character at this point could serve to alienate his friends. It certainly had in the past. Ben waited until Jimmy was about to speak, then cut him off abruptly as he locked eyes with the man, amplifying the volume of his first couple of words.

"*I think*, Jimmy . . . if there's a *lesson* from that little interaction worthy of further reflection, my grasp of it could actually *suffer* from your attempt at clarification. Surely the lesson's lasting value lies in my ability to reach it independently, alone, in *silence*. Wouldn't you agree?"

Jimmy blinked at Ben as he opened and closed his mouth a few times. Ben smiled.

"I knew you'd understand, man. You always do. We'll be out there soon."

A dumb smile slowly spread across Jimmy's face. Ben kept smiling and nodding slowly at the man as he stood, looking satisfied, almost proud of himself.

"Right on, bro, well . . . get those other guys moving, alright? Meeting at the Lodge Pole in fifteen minutes!"

Ben watched Jimmy trot out of the cabin and down the porch, then heard him shout some shrill, silly greeting at another counselor that included the word *bro*, a word that Jimmy, somehow, stretched into multiple syllables.

Ben jumped a bit when he heard an unexpected snort over his shoulder. He turned to see Billy staring down at him, leaning on the ornate trim around the opening of the hallway to the bathroom. Ben felt a jolt of mild panic. He'd decided early on that it would be safer for him to avoid "talkin all smart" in front of the guys at this program. The feeling faded almost immediately, as he connected the sound of Billy's nasal snort to the faint grin he now saw on Billy's face. Billy, for the first time Ben had seen it, actually looked amused.

Ben looked down between his feet, then back at Billy. Unsure what to say, Ben just shrugged. Billy looked away, gazing out the front door of the cabin, and spoke.

"Stupid-ass thang to do, lettin these bastards see who you really is, bess keep that kinda fancy lip to y'self."

To Ben, the comment didn't sound like a suggestion; it didn't have the tone or feel of a warning or cautionary note. It sounded more like a demand. An order, almost.

Ben felt a hot surge of anger, or maybe just defensiveness. He'd never let someone near his own age question his intelligence without going toe-to-toe. It's the only thing he'd ever had. He might get his ass kicked, as he had before, but Ben would guarantee that ass kicker would walk away with a deep insecurity and feeling like a proper idiot. Maybe it was just talking to someone else with a southern drawl that served to spark some fire and nerve. Ben could hear his Cajun accent coming out—just like it always did when he was pissed—before he realized he'd even started talking.

"Ooo mais, that's some truly excellent advice there, Axe. Please *di-vulge* how *you* go bout not lettin these bastards see who *you* really is. If your whole daddy-battered, foster-reared, *bruised fruit* persona is just the angry facade you're strategically *lettin them see*, as you put it, who is the *real* Billy behind this brilliant performance? Other than a legendary thespian, of course."

Billy snapped his eyes back on Ben's with an expression on his face that was somehow half surprise, half murder. No other part of Billy's body moved as he spoke, seemingly even his lips.

"That's y'one strike with me."

Ben held the gaze for longer than he knew Billy expected him to, then broke his eyes away from Billy's to look at the floor. He groaned as he rubbed both palms on his eyes, then stood up, cocked his head, and pointed toward the armoire at the far end of the room.

Both boys stared at the armoire that Billy had yanked the kid Michael out of. The kid who'd been so desperate, feral, and terrified. The kid who'd changed into a different person overnight.

Ben heard the creaking wail of the rusty knob in one of the showers as it was turned, then heard the hum of running water in the pipes reduced by half. He looked back at Billy, who was staring at him, and gestured toward the front door of the cabin.

"Joe remind you of anyone this mornin?"

Billy raised his eyes to look back across the room toward the armoire, then nodded slowly before speaking.

"Joe dun got broke las' night. Just like that Mike fella. Like a switch got flipped."

Ben watched Billy's face for a long moment. He heard the other shower turn off and could hear Trent's and Rodrigo's muffled voices and laughter as they joked with one another.

Ben walked toward the middle of the room, where he stood for a moment before following Billy's gaze back to the armoire.

"*Mais*, dis shit's startin to g'me *d'frissons*."

Billy looked over at Ben.

"Fuck you juss say? I don't speak swamp rat."

Ben took a breath that he held in for a long moment. He almost mentioned what he'd seen happen in the darkness the night before, the confrontation between Reid and Joe in the rain, he wanted to bring it up, but wasn't sure how to even describe it. Not to Billy.

"I just said that this is gettin pretty creepy."

Billy responded by furrowing his brow in a way that suggested he was disappointed, disgusted, and bored by Ben's translation. He shook his head slowly as he pushed himself off the trim he'd been leaning on, then paced toward the front door, forcing Ben to scurry aside so as to avoid getting bowled over.

As he wrenched open the screen door with his massive hand, Billy stopped. Without turning around, he spoke just loud enough for Ben to make out his words.

"You ever call me Axe again, I'll hold you down n' take y'eyes out, thass a promise."

Ben ran through the memory of that morning in his head as they walked toward the lodge from this *T.R.A.P.* lecture and lesson. Although a week had passed, plenty of fine detail still remained; how Joe had fallen to his knees before Reid in the storm that night, how Joe had seemed to be an entirely different person the next morning, and how hard Ben had blinked as the screen door slammed shut behind Billy.

CHAPTER 16

THE BOYS shuffled out into the darkness of the predawn morning, flinching visibly at the counselors' enthusiastic backslaps and loud greetings that pierced the quiet mountain air.

The night before, they'd stuffed everything on their river expedition packing lists into big, rubber bags that Jimmy called "dry bags." The procession of half-awake boys dragged their dry bags behind them as they squinted into the darkness and zombie-shuffled toward the light and engine hum from all the idling Bear Springs vans in front of the lodge.

About a dozen counselors herded all twenty-eight boys into the vehicles for a several-hour drive toward Glacier National Park, with the objective of embarking on the three-day, two-night float on Middle Fork of the Flathead River. This was the big river expedition the counselors had been trying to get all the boys hyped about all summer. *It's always a top-three experience for Bear Springs graduates,* they repeatedly promised.

The large double doors to the lodge were open, spilling warm light into the darkness. Ben squinted up to see Reid facing his four goons—Gordon and Javier, who had come to take Ben from his aunt's trailer, and the other two, Daniel and Nicholas. They formed a crescent around the younger and larger Reid, nodding at his words with grave, serious expressions. Ben lost sight of them as he climbed into one of the vans, and lost interest in them once the drive began.

The boys were asleep for most of the drive, until they got to West Glacier, Montana, where they stared out the windows of the van, slack-jawed, at the mountains that surged up into the sky above sky-blue lakes and endless, sprawling forest. They'd all grown fairly well accustomed to the landscape of the Northern Rockies and were certainly no strangers at this point to big mountains and alpine country, but this scenery was a whole different level of stunning.

They wound their way up a highway that ran along the river, giant mountain ranges screaming up on both sides of them. They began to see groups of rafters and kayakers crashing through the rapids in the river below the road, which only served to amplify the angst, excitement, and bravado of the boys.

They eventually reached a pullout along where a large oxbow in the river had made a huge sandy beach along the bank. Here they found the outfitter company that Bear Springs was using for all the rafting gear. There was a fleet of white-water rafts and a few kayaks set up on the large beach, with a handful of mostly twentysomething-year-olds stacking oars, pulling gear off trailers, and strapping things onto the rafts.

The boys clambered out of the vehicles and scattered about the area, shouting, joking, and pissing. They were ushered into an area along the beach where they all sat in the sand to go through a final safety presentation by the counselors as well as some of the guides from the rafting outfitter. They talked about the difference between a draw stroke and a sweep stroke, how they'd be arranged in the rafts, what to do if you fell out, helmets, personal floatation devices, that kind of shit. Most of the stuff they'd discussed back at basecamp over the last several days, even watching a few short safety films about white-water rafting.

The guy who gave the safety briefing to the boys was the head of the rafting outfitter company, and other than the four older *intervention* specialists, was the only man Ben had seen in weeks who could be described as middle-aged. His name was Carl. He was at least fifteen to twenty years older than the other rafting outfitter employees, as well as all the camp counselors. Ben could hear the last ghost of an accent in the man's voice that betrayed his having spent at least a few formative years along the Gulf Coast. It was too faint for Ben to say exactly where, but he heard enough to know it was somewhere between Lake Charles, Louisiana, and Tallahassee, Florida.

He had a shaved head, a large unkempt beard, and kind eyes trimmed by those lines that only form after decades of either staring into harsh sun or screaming, salty wind. He was well over six feet tall and sported a large beer gut that Ben could see would not actually slow the man down much if he really wanted to move fast. His calves were massive, one covered in a large tattoo of a sea turtle, his forearms huge, where another long-weathered tattoo could be seen that Ben recognized as the *eagle, globe, and anchor* of the Marine Corps.

Ben was fascinated by him. He did not trust any adult really, almost as a rule, but he certainly wished *this* dude was in charge of Bear Springs Academy.

The rest of the rafting company employees fell comfortably within the stereotype that Ben had begun to grasp since leaving Louisiana—that of the seasonal mountain recreation professional. Expensive outdoor clothing, tattoos of fishing flies and mountains, flip-flops, stickers all over their Toyotas or Subarus, and those goofy fucking lanyards on their sunglasses.

The counselors and outfitters spent a half hour or so loading up all the rafts, as well as one raft loaded only with food and supplies that one of the counselors would pilot, called the "baggage boat." Most of the other boys fucked around near the water, or engaged in antics in a throng that shadowed the several beautiful young women among the rafting outfitter crew, who giggled and seemed amused by the ill-concealed attention they were getting from the boys.

Ben wanted to talk to the boss man, Carl. He slowly walked over to where the large man was standing near the open rear driver-side door of his Toyota T100, fiddling with something in his hands.

He looked over as Ben walked up and saw the boy looking at his truck. "Pretty cool truck, eh, bud?"

Ben squinted down at the tires for a long moment, then up at the large man, grinning just a bit as he began to speak—without any of the practiced constraint on his southern accent.

"Mais, I don't fuck with gas trucks. Somethin dis big, runnin on anythin but *diesel*, just seems a bit, well . . . flimsy, y'know?"

A large, immediately contagious smile spread across the man's face, which cracked into a real-deal belly laugh when Ben smiled back. Ben approached the man and looked up into his face as he extended his hand, which the man buried into his own.

"Carl, I'm Ben."

After the brief shake, Ben put his hands in his pockets and leaned back onto the wheel well of the truck, a few feet from the large man. Carl watched Ben with curiosity as he dropped whatever he'd been working on into the back of the truck, then leaned on the open door.

"Pleasure to meet you. You got a bit a'that bayou sound, Ben."

Ben nodded.

"From Lafitte, bout a half hour south a' *Nwaluns*. Sounds like you spent a few of your early years somewhere within a few hours of there as well, I reckon."

Carl let out a deep snort through his nose.

"You got an ear on ya. From Daphne, Mobile, basically, just across the bay, but was only there till I was about twelve."

Ben nodded again.

"Hear there's some good red and speck fishin round there."

Carl smiled.

"Yah, all my cousins still down there spend a lot of time chasin reds, speckled trout, snook, they're real into all that inshore stuff . . . Not much else to do around there, after all."

Ben stared out toward the river and commotion around the rafts, letting the silence inflate until Carl broke it.

"How you liking it out west, compared to home? Having a good time at summer camp?"

Ben felt some genuine disappointment at this question. He'd figured this man to be smarter than someone who'd ask *that*, unless he truly was clueless as to what kind of camp this was, which was pretty damn hard to believe. He glanced over at Carl with a raised eyebrow, hoping this man was capable of recognizing that gesture as a sufficient response.

Carl pursed his lips, then looked away from the boy as he turned to lean his butt against the back bench of the truck, staring out at the river. *Thank God*, Ben thought.

"Yah, well, I suppose this ain't really a *normal* summer camp, now is it . . . So, what'd you do to land yourself in this kinda program?"

Ben let out a long exhale before responding.

"Heisted a leaky ol' johnboat, knocked over a gas station with a fake gun, handful of other stupid-ass things in between."

Carl couldn't help but start to belly laugh again, and talked through it.

"Well, kid, you can steal shit, or you can get arrested. Gotta pick one though, can't do both."

Ben laughed at that; it was a real laugh too.

"*Don't I know it*, Carl."

Ben stared down at the counselors, the other boys, at Reid, all bustling around the rafts and along the riverbank. Coast was clear, for now at least, and if he was going to get any real information out of this guy, he had to set the stage, and the time was now.

"But y'see, Carl, I gotta kid brother to look out for, no parents, judge gave our momma's sister full say and control over us till we're eighteen—and lemme tell ya, man, adjectives like *maternal, amicable, sober, nonviolent*, those ain't the kind you'd use to describe this woman. Last few years, started to see a real decent chance exists that one or both of us ain't gonna make it to the end of that custody sentence. And say we somehow do both make it to eighteen under those . . . *conditions*, we'd be stuck with that special kinda mental baggage you just can't ever off-load. That kinda baggage you gotta clean outta your head with a bullet before it turns you into the person who put it there. Not knowin which was worse, I had to try *somethin* to get my little bro outta that smoky little shit den. Didn't plan or execute that little scheme well enough, *obviously*, but figured I had to try."

When Carl finally asked the question, without looking at his face, Ben still would've bet good folding money that lines of puzzlement or surprise had carved into the man's big forehead. It was a benchmark for Ben, that sound in a person's voice—that vocal inflection of astonishment and curiosity that adults would often unintentionally dash onto the edges of this question.

"H . . . how old are you?"

"I'm thirteen, Carl. Thirteen goin on fifty-five, it would seem."

Ben let his words float away, then finally glanced up at Carl, having decided it was time to give him *the look*.

There wasn't anything real special or technical about this look. In moments like this, Ben had no need to employ any of the expressions, gestures, or corresponding body language he had cataloged, no need to get fussy, to overcomplicate things. It was simple, yet one of the most powerful things Ben could send an adult's way. It's a hard thing to describe with words, beyond it simply being the look a hard man gives another man when it's finally time to cut the shit and be honest. Coming from this thirteen-year-old boy, when Ben made sure it was properly timed, it never failed to floor the recipient. Carl was no exception.

"What do you know about this Bear Springs Academy program, Carl? I ain't talkin about the bullshit you'd read in the brochure. I'm talkin about the scuttlebutt, the shit you've heard whispered on the river, in the bars, maybe even seen yourself and didn't feel right about. Give it to me straight."

Carl's mouth hung ajar as he stared at Ben through squinted eyes. He looked away eventually, shaking his head almost imperceptibly, then back into Ben's face. He started to form a word with his mouth, abandoned it with a humorless chuckle from his big chest, then started over and did the same thing again.

Ben pointed at Carl with an open hand, fingers together and thumb to the sky, and spoke as clearly as he could.

"Carl, what's important right now is that you *stop thinking about the circumstances of this situation*, pretend I don't exist, do whatever you've gotta do to focus entirely on providing an honest answer to my question. If they look up here to see you all flustered, I'm fucked, so take a deep breath, alright? Look, I got a *bad feelin* about this place and the people in charge, and *no fuckin time* to explain that to you. I just need an honest, outside perspective on this program and these counselors. If you truly have no idea what I'm talkin about, that's fine, just say so. But if you *do know what I'm talkin* about—even if it's just a feelin, an instinct—please, man, you gotta just gimme what you got, and quickly."

Ben looked back toward the river to find everyone of concern still busily occupied. As he did this, he made sure to look concerned, even a bit scared, before looking back at Carl.

Carl looked down at the crowd on the bank and appeared to calm down considerably as he did so. Carl began to speak without looking over at Ben.

"Bear Springs ain't considered local around here, y'all are out kinda near Libby, right, in that Kootenai country, so I don't know much about em other than the place has been around forever, and the fact that I've run this trip for em for the last decade or so, alright?"

Ben just nodded, knowing this was not the time to interrupt a flow.

"I run rafting certification courses through my outfitter, skills assessments and shit like that. Back in '94 I think, Bear Springs sent three counselors to an advanced white-water assessment course I was running. It was those three plus a half dozen other folks in my class. Spent the morning making sure they knew how to hold the raft to what's called a *ferry angle* in order to cross a river, manage their oars, back row, deal with an eddy, stuff like that. Basically, just running through a skills checklist and making sure they knew what to do. Lunchtime came around and we were all eating on the bank, those folks in the class plus a few folks who worked for me. I was making small talk with the Bear Springs trio, asked them about the program, eventually asked if any of the counselors had ever actually been a graduate themselves. They said *actually, all of us are graduates*. That was news to me. Few minutes later I asked em a version of a question I used all the time back in the sandbox with shook-up marines—a question that always seems to ground people who are in a tough spot far from home. I asked em *what was the last thing your parents said to y'all before you got sent off to Bear Springs . . .*"

Carl ran his big thumb across the side of his nose a few times, glanced at Ben for a second, then looked ahead and went on.

"They all got real quiet and still. It was weird. Just kinda frozen there, holding their sandwiches. I was about to change the subject when one of em, dude named Jason, said something like *we don't talk about our personal circumstances to Bear Springs students until after your graduation.* When he spoke, all three kinda just reactivated, came back to life, started eating their lunch again. I was confused and said somethin like, *well, I ain't a student, so you're cleared hot to answer, what did your parents say to you before you left?* They froze again, for even longer this time. I was about to shake one of the bastards when one of the other counselors,

Mike or some shit, can't remember, said the exact same thing again: *don't talk about personal circumstances to students until after you graduate* blah blah blah. Then they all unfroze and went back to normal. It was fuckin creepy, man. I was speechless."

One of the ladies on Carl's staff yelled some question up to him. Ben didn't hear what she'd said, but Carl shouted back that *it* was already packed up on the baggage boat. The interruption prompted both Ben and Carl to scan the group to make sure no one was coming up toward them, then Carl cleared his throat and went on.

"So, at this point I figured they were either just fuckin with me or being real damn rude, so I leaned into it, that's just my nature, for better or worse. I said somethin like *oh come on, I ain't a student, and I ain't judging you guys, I told you what my parents said to me before I got on the bus and went off to bootcamp, what's the last thing your momma said before y'all got sent to Bear Springs.* That's when it got all fucked-up. They all froze again, but were *shakin* this time, like they were hypothermic, one of em so bad I started hearing his teeth smashing together like a typewriter. The other folks eating lunch on the bank noticed their shaking now, too, one of em pointing all frantically at one of the counselor's heads. I stood up and saw blood running out of all their ears. At this point me and one of my other instructors, we're both EMTs, each had one of em by the shoulders, figured they were seizing or some shit, until . . ."

Carl rubbed his palms in his eyes and took a deep breath before going on.

"Until one of these bastards stands up, walks over to a boulder like some hypothermic fuckin zombie, and starts *smashing his face into the goddamn rock.* I shit you not, man, it took three of us to restrain him, and he'd already shattered his nose, orbital bone, most of his front teeth, it was fuckin insane . . . Within a minute or so they all kinda just fell asleep, or went into a coma, I dunno. No cell service in the canyon so we piled them into the trucks and started ripping down the road. Closest hospital of any kind back then was in Kalispell. They all came to just a few minutes into the drive and had no memory of what had happened. We got em there to the ER and I used the landline there to call up Bear Springs to get em up to speed . . . Never saw any of those three dudes again, they're never on these trips we do every summer, I guess some other counselors came and scooped em up once they got released."

Carl let a long moment pass before continuing, only doing so after a subtle headshake, as though he were, once again, brushing aside the creepiness of that experience and surrendering the significance of his suspicions. It was a defense mechanism, Ben knew. It made sleeping at night easier.

"I've asked after em with other Bear Springs folks, whenever I saw one, and they always said the same shit, somethin about them all having encephalitis, which can cause seizures. Eventually I just stopped asking about it. I've wondered if it's some kinda cult, fuckers were brainwashed or somethin, but I've also wondered . . . Maybe it really was encephalitis, I ain't a doctor. I've known Reid, Mitchell, and a few other Bear Springs staffers for years and they've always seemed normal enough, and the kids have all seemed happy enough, they write me a fat check every summer to organize this trip. They've got a good reputation throughout Montana, too, always braggin about the success of their graduates. So, I've kinda just shrugged the whole thing off into the crazy-ass-shit category. Until now, at least. But that's it, kid. That's my *honest answer* to your question, without anything left out."

Ben stared blankly at the gravel in front of him, but his mind was racing through all the interactions he'd ever had with Jimmy, his therapist Jessie, other counselors, and connecting kernels of memories to what he'd just learned from this man. His attention was ripped back to the present when Carl planted his shoulder.

"Kid, you've gotta be honest with *me* now, alright? Have you seen or heard anything specific to make you feel like you're in real danger, or have these counselors *already* done anything that's inappropriate, or anything that just, well . . . feels fucked-up? If so, you've gotta tell me right now."

A lot of things careened through Ben's mind in the following five seconds. The two moments when Reid sent him into a state of terrifying, pants-shitting paralysis by just smiling at him, first in his aunt's trailer back in Louisiana, then again in the boulder field above the alpine lake. The wild-eyed kid Michael hiding in their armoire, hearing the wolves howl as he was dragged, shrieking, into the lodge. The moment when Reid confronted Joe the night of the storm, the way Joe fell to his knees and began to shake. The overnight transformation of Michael and Joe. Those subtle, brief moments when it seemed Jimmy and Jessie were glitching out.

Ben looked up at Carl.

"Nah, I ain't really got any specifics, Carl. *They ain't fuckin us*, if that's what you're thinking, no real violence either. They've restrained a couple who were fighting or trying to split—shit, they restrained *me* in Louisiana and forced me onto a damned plane—but I spose that's in their job description, and somethin a cop or a judge would only applaud. When it comes to things that just *seem fucked-up*, as you put it, well, yah, I got a trove a'that kinda shit, but it's all stuff you kinda had to see, had to feel, nothin that'd be easy to describe in a way that makes any damn sense. I'll tell you one thing though . . ."

Ben stood and turned to face Carl, putting his hands into his pockets as he did so, slipping out the piece of paper he'd prepared the night before as he did.

"Not a damn thing you just said comes as any kinda surprise to me. Almost makes sense, truth be told. Fits in with some other shit I've seen over the last five weeks."

Carl looked worried, like he was torn about what to do or say next. Ben glanced toward the group, where movement and business had slowed, a few of the counselors starting to idle around, suggesting the pre-trip work was about wrapped up and that they'd be getting underway soon. Carl grabbed his attention when he started to speak with a bit of renewed urgency in his face.

"Look, Ben, if you really don't feel safe . . . if you really feel like you're in danger, I mean . . . I can't just stand by like a dipshit, I can't just let you—"

"Stop."

Ben patted once toward the ground with an open palm as he spoke the single word. Carl shut up immediately. He'd seen Reid beginning to look around for the other counselors in the way he often did while preparing to conduct his little head count. Ben's time was almost up.

"My guardian signed me over to them, judge signed a court order for me to be here, ain't no way I'm gettin outta this program in the light of day, you can't do a damn thing for me right now, alright? In about fifteen seconds they're gonna see us talking then come up here to collect me and to thank you, and—*if I ain't* dead-ass wrong about all this—they're gonna be assessing *you* as much as they're assessing *me* when they get here. I need you to smile, put on an act, look like a dude who's just been pleasantly bullshitting with a teenager for the last ten minutes, alright?"

Ben was pleased with Carl's efforts. Carl forced a casual smile across his face. He watched the tension release from the large man's shoulders, and his hands slacken. He watched the man's breathing slow and his posture slouch as he crossed his arms and leaned back into the side of his truck. Most importantly, Carl *did not* look over at the counselors, who'd by now certainly seen them talking, and might even be walking over. Ben spoke fast, and smiled as he did.

"Need you to do something for me, Carl. There's a folded piece of paper on the ground behind your back left tire with my aunt Nicki's address, phone number, her and my brother's full names, a half dozen of my neighbors' names, and the number for the Jefferson Parish Sheriff's Office. Today, if you can, call in a report of child endangerment and abuse on my aunt Nicki, tell em you heard crashin and the boy screamin for help. Give em a neighbor's name if they ask. Do it again next week as a different neighbor. If there's some heat from the cops on her she won't leave burns or bruises on him for a while, but *she fuckin will* if there ain't any. Do this for me, Carl, if nothin else, *do this*."

Ben snarled the last words through his fake smile. He heard one of the counselors shout at the group, mustering them toward the rafts, reminding them to make sure they had their oars, their life jackets, and their helmets.

Ben was about to start speaking again, but stopped himself as soon as he saw Carl's eyes flick past Ben. Carl let his fake smile grow just slightly into something more sincere as he cocked his chin up to greet someone Ben could now hear crunching through the gravel toward the two conspirators.

This big fucker puts on a half-decent performance, Ben thought.

"There you are, Ben. We've been yellin for ya, bud. It's time to go."

Ben turned to Reid, making sure his smile was maintained as he did, then slumped his shoulders as he looked back to Carl.

"Alright, we gotta go. Grand Isle though, seriously, for all the inshore species, it blows any part of the Bama coast outta the water. It's not even *close*, man, *not even close*."

Carl chuckled and rocked on his heels as Ben turned away toward Reid, then shouted a rebuttal at Ben's back.

"Kid, there are more snook in Mobile Bay alone than you could find along any hundred-mile stretch of that dirty Louisiana water."

Ben smiled and waved at the air near the side of his head as though shooing the retort away. As he approached Reid he pointed back over his shoulder toward Carl with his thumb.

"I hope this guy knows more about renting out good rafts than he does about finding redfish and speckled trout in the Gulf."

Carl laughed heartily at that one, and Ben watched Reid look up at Carl, appearing at least somewhat amused by the banter and laughter, then look back at Ben as he passed by.

Ben wasn't sure if he actually did see suspicion in Reid's face in that moment, or if he'd imagined it, but he fought hard not to react either way.

Perhaps Carl saw it though—or something that motivated him to add one more bit of padding on to their little ruse—because right then he shouted down the slope, causing both Ben and Reid to look back up at where the large man stood, pointing down at Ben and side-eyeing him with a humorous challenge.

"Hey, kid, don't forget, what do you need to do with your raft in order to cross a river?"

This son of a bitch really is good, Ben thought. Reid looked back at Ben as the boy ran his hand across his scalp and stared down at the ground in his best iteration of deep, anxious contemplation. Ben knew the answer immediately, but let a moment pass before widening his eyes, saying the answer uncertainly, just loud enough for Reid to hear, then standing up straight and pointing back at the large man with triumph and excitement in his eyes.

"Ferry angle, it's a ferry angle!"

Carl smiled and nodded as he pumped his fist a few times at the boy. Ben glanced at Reid and saw him smiling easily now, then began jogging toward the group along the riverbank.

Every raft had one counselor in the back and five or six of the boys, while several additional counselors were on kayaks, ferrying between the rafts, checking on everything. Ben had not known that two of the counselors who drove down with the group were actually staying behind with the vehicles and doing a few errands while the others were on the river.

All the boys were loaded into their positions with their matching PFD and helmets, hooting and hollering challenges at one another as the counselors held their rafts in the eddy, waiting for the last stragglers to get into the kayaks. Reid was one of them. He'd walked down to the water with Carl, appearing to chat amicably as they went. Ben watched Reid give a sincere smile to Carl and a firm handshake before he clambered down and got into his own kayak.

Reid paddled out between the rafts toward the front of the regatta, shouting out final instructions to the other counselors as he went. Ben looked back at the bank at Carl, who stared back at him with his arms crossed. Carl's smile slowly faded. Ben felt bad for him, he felt guilt for what he'd just done, he'd properly freaked that guy out and really put him on the spot. Now Carl was watching this strange, sharp boy set off into the wilderness under the wing of adults whom Carl had spent years trying very hard not to be unreasonably suspicious about. He'd been mostly successful in that effort, until today.

Carl nodded once at the boy. Ben nodded once back, then looked ahead as they started to float downstream.

Trent clapped his hand on the back of Ben's life jacket, grabbing on to the straps for a moment and giving him a friendly shake from side to side.

"You excited, B?! Don't tell me you're scared. Hey yo, what were you talking to that old rafter guy about?"

Ben smiled, then looked over at Trent.

"Reds and specks, pal. Talked about fishin for reds and specks."

CHAPTER 17

OME ON, Rod, just jump, bro, just plug your nose and jump!"
Ben, a dozen other boys, and a few counselors—all also tread-
ing water in the deep river eddy—joined Trent in shouting encouragement up at Rodrigo, who stood fifteen feet above them on a basalt cliff
above the cool water.

A few of the other guys sent *pussy* and *chickenshit* at Rodrigo, which
appeared to be the last bit of motivation he needed. He took a deep
breath, plugged his nose, and jumped, legs flailing a bit awkwardly as
he fell, but ultimately crashing through the surface of the river mostly
feetfirst.

He shot back above the surface, gasping and smiling, looking a bit
embarrassed as he was greeted by a chorus of cheers. As he side-stroked
past Ben and Trent toward the shoreline, he offered a single "that wasn't
so bad."

Almost all the boys and the counselors had done the cliff jump, and
had been at it for an hour now. Billy had not. Once they'd reached the
first sandy beach that the counselors had preselected as their first night's
camping spot, Billy heaved one of the rafts all the way onto the sand,
removed the massive cooler, then lay down in it and fell fast asleep.

The first two days of the trip had been really fun. Even Ben was enjoying himself, despite his worries about what was really going on at this
program. There was so much to consider; Ben felt as though so much
had happened so fast.

Something about the days leading up to the river trip had actually
begun to palliate Ben's concerns a bit. He figured, in passing at least,

that if these creeps were going to do something evil to them, why were they spending so much time briefing them on safety? Furthermore, why would they have let themselves be seen with the boys in public, in front of so many other seemingly normal adults at the gas stations they'd stopped at, as well as the folks working for the river outfitter?

Then he met Carl. Carl's anecdote of bizarre behavior was concerning, to be sure, and weighed heavily on Ben's mind. He was not sure what it meant, or what he could possibly do with that information, but it rendered his understanding of Bear Springs back into a state of creepy, unstable flux. And there was Carl himself. Ben got a good feeling about him, and wanted to trust him, but maybe he remembered the details wrong? Maybe he exaggerated or didn't relay the memory accurately. How could any sane person have witnessed what he did and gone on to accept the explanation that the counselor's bizarre seizures and self-mutilation were caused by some infection? Are there even infections that can make someone behave that way?

Every time Ben tried to reason through one question, ten more sprouted up. If he were back home, or back at basecamp, this would be dominating his mental existence. As it was, he was not focusing on it. He was enjoying every minute outside in one of the most beautiful places he'd ever imagined could exist.

The first day when they left the outfitters behind, they only floated for a few hours through some pretty calm water until they reached the big sandy beach near the cliff-jumping spot. They made a fire and ate a big meal. They pitched their tents and went to war with mosquitos. Most of them slept pretty well. Nothing out of the ordinary.

The second morning they loaded back up and got going after a light breakfast. Within a few hours, they were in *real* white water for the first time. Ben, Trent, and Rodrigo had never experienced anything like that in their lives. It was, undeniably, some of the best fun any of them had ever had, and none of them were trying to conceal that reality. It seemed all the boys were loving it just as much, whooping and hollering after every big rapid. All the boys except for Billy, at least.

Billy did not seem notably *unhappy* about the experience, just unamused. Although, on one particularly long run of category III and IV rapids, the raft went into one at a strange angle, and the counselor in their raft roared an instruction for the boys on the left to *paddle paddle paddle*. Billy flew into action and Ben was confident that he could feel the force of Billy's oar clearly on every stroke, holding back the rage of a river. As they went through the rapid, a kid from a different *fire circle* named Andy who was in their raft got pitched up and almost went over the side. Billy launched up and grabbed the kid seemingly out of midair by the life jacket straps, slammed him back down into his seat, then went back to his own, without his facial expression changing much at all. Watching him in this situation was entertaining from an athletic perspective, but it was also particularly enjoyable for Trent, Rodrigo, and Ben to see Billy thrown into an activity where he couldn't *not* participate.

That night the counselors busted out the big gas camping stoves and made burritos. The boys ate ravenously. They did the usual campfire time, counselors lecturing on nature, manhood, self-control, *autonomy*, that kind of shit.

During a lull when everyone was speaking freely and making s'mores, Reid came and sat next to Ben. Ben was pretty pleased with his performance over the previous weeks. He'd kept his head down, he'd been obedient, he'd been a good listener, he'd divulged more than enough material and masterfully feigned emotion to his therapist Jessie to cover that end of things. Also, he was pretty sure he and Carl had effectively convinced Reid they'd simply been having some benign conversation about fishing and rafting. Even so, no matter when Reid singled him out, Ben's asshole puckered and he had to muster all his focus to keep the contrite-good-boy performance alive.

Reid clapped Ben on the shoulder as he sat down in the sand next to him.

"Pretty nice being able to swim without having to deal with alligators and poisonous snakes, right, B?"

Ben planned out the elements of his response in less than a second. *A little comedy, a little sincerity, a dash of my old persona.* It had to be perfect to convince this man. Ben looked over at Reid with his best combination of amusement and exasperation.

"Dude, like two weeks ago you made us watch that long friggin video about rattlesnakes and how dangerous they are, what do you mean *no poisonous snakes*, I've been out here checkin under rocks for em this whole time, you tellin me that's all been for nothin!?"

Reid chuckled and looked down between his knees, as did a number of other boys around them. Ben made sure to join in.

"Well, shucks, you're right, I guess there are actually some poisonous snakes around here . . . but the lack of alligators makes taking a swim a bit more casual, right?"

Ben giggled in response, making it sound as though the laughter surprised him. He nodded as he took a bite of s'more.

"Yah, I can't deny that, sure is nice swimmin in water without man-eatin dinosaurs, and water that won't give you cancer."

Reid grinned and nodded, then looked up at the stars, where he held his gaze as he spoke more quietly.

"You've come a long way since you've arrived here, Ben. I can see it, Jessie can see it, Jimmy can see it. The other guys, they look up to you. Carl, the rafting guide, said some very nice things about you after y'all spoke. It's impressive to see, man, it really is, I mean that."

These were the moments that made Ben wonder if his fear of this man, of this place, was all just unfounded paranoia. Sometimes this bastard just seemed so *real* to Ben, so normal. *Kind* even. It made responding in a passable way that wouldn't set off any of Reid's bullshit alarms quite a bit easier, as well.

"Yah, well . . . I . . . I dunno, I miss my little brother. I'm just worried about him."

Ben forced himself to look up into Reid's face, who was already looking into his, nodding with a solemn expression.

"My aunt Nicki ain't a kind person, Reid. When I'm not there, she takes it out on Wade. I just . . . I just wanna get home to him. I ain't gonna deny that I've been havin a good time, but it's really hard to take my mind off my brother. I just wish he was here, where I could take care of him. I wish he was doin all this stuff, seein all these places."

Genius, Ben thought. *I wish my brother was here*, what a golden fuckin line, how had he not dropped that one yet. Ben maintained a distant gaze into the fire and hoped Reid would eat that shit up. He looked over at Reid when he patted him gently on the knee, and was pleased to find that the man, indeed, had.

"Ben, that sure means a lot to me, hearing you say that. If you think this place, this experience, is good enough for your brother to enjoy, and safe enough for him to be here, after what you've been through, well . . . I take that as a pretty huge compliment."

Ben looked at the fire, then reluctantly back at Reid, and decided some well-timed silence would work well for this moment. He just shrugged, then went back to nibbling at his s'more. Reid went on.

"You're right to worry about your brother, but he is going to be fine, and you'll be home to him next month, and will be there for him as an entirely better person, you can share the things with him you learned here, and that'll make him stronger as well."

Ben decided to play the kid. He shrugged.

"Yeah, I guess."

Reid smiled and nodded, then pushed himself up to his feet. He began telling the group to finish up their s'mores and start thinking about brushing teeth and getting their sleeping arrangements made.

As he walked away, Ben let out a shuddering exhale. He stared at Reid's back and really wasn't sure if he was still genuinely creeped out by that man, or if he was just upset that he'd finally encountered an adult he felt intimidated by. It was certainly one or the other. Either way, he'd keep this act up, until he couldn't any longer.

The bugs weren't as bad at the second camp as they were the night before, so lots of the boys slept out, under the stars, with just their sleeping pads and bags. Ben lay awake for a long time looking up at the stars, conducting something of an after-action report on the events of the days prior.

He wondered if Carl really would call in a wellness check to his aunt's house for his brother. He knew that could easily result in Wade catching some hell, some kinda beating, the thought of which made him squeeze his eyes shut. That said, Ben knew the beating wouldn't be *that* bad. Nothing compared to what she used to do to him, at least, before the cops came by the first time. No getting woken up by her using his little back and shoulders as an ashtray, none of the horrible infections that followed, no holding his face into the dirty floor of the trailer with her shoes. If the cops were snooping around, Nicki couldn't afford to have Wade showing any visible bruises, cuts, or burns.

Aunt Nicki's worst nightmare was prison, and her only reliable income was the meager child support she'd started earning from the state once she agreed to take them in. Ben just hoped Carl really reported the complaint.

He wondered if he'd rushed that play. He'd written all that stuff down the night before, assuming it *might* be his only chance to get it to someone in the outside world for the rest of his time here. He'd been imagining pitching that request to a gas station attendant or some random fly fisherman or kayaker they'd passed by. None of that would've worked, not a chance in hell. He was *lucky* to have met Carl, he tried to convince himself.

The next morning the counselors made a big, proper breakfast with bacon and eggs. They only had a few hours left on the river before getting to the takeout where the rafting outfitter had shuttled all their vans.

The counselors let the boys go explore around a bit, telling them to take their emergency whistles, and not go any farther into the woods or up the ridge above camp than earshot. They'd be leaving at noon, so all the boys had to be back by then, without exceptions.

Rodrigo, Trent, and Ben found a small stream that trickled out of the forest onto the beach, and decided to trek up it. The water was icy cold, and full of tiny little flakes of gold in the sandy bed. Rodrigo said it was *fool's gold.* They scrambled up the steep drainage until they entered a flat, open meadow—a large glade where wildflowers carpeted the area between small clusters of aspen trees. The boys wouldn't have described it this way, at that time in their lives, but it was beautiful. So much so that they all stood for a long moment, taking in the scenery.

"Yo, what's that?"

Trent was already walking over toward what looked like an old section of wall from a log cabin. It was barely visible in the tall grass, but once they reached it, they saw that it was certainly the foundation and remnants of an old, large cabin that had burned down. They found a stone hearth and parts of the long-collapsed chimney.

After a few moments, they came upon more burned remains of old log and stone buildings, a half dozen or so of them. They spent a while kicking around the overgrown ruins, finding half-buried bottles, bedsprings, rusty tool parts, and the like. Within a few moments they'd decided they really wanted to find a pistol, or a hunk of gold, and that's what filled their minds over the next thirty minutes.

Ben was sifting through the tin, wood, and glass detritus at the base of a fireplace when he found what looked like a pile of a dozen brass picture frames.

He picked them all up and moved over to a large stone, where he sat and began inspecting the first one. The frame was in decent condition, but there was only a small, charred remnant behind the shattered glass that, Ben assumed, had once been a picture.

Before long, Trent and Rodrigo were leaning over his shoulder, watching as he sifted through each of the frames. The fifth or sixth one had a discernible portion of a tintype picture surviving within it. It was terribly sun-bleached, but one could clearly see a group of three young men standing next to a horse, in front of a large wooden cabin.

"Damn, how old do you think this is?"

Ben shrugged.

"I dunno . . . I know there were pictures from the Civil War, in the 1860s, ain't never seen pictures from times much older than that, so I reckon sometime between the mid-1800s and early 1900s. So . . . *old as shit*, basically."

They got to the last one and found a layer of dirt and dried ash caked on the glass of the frame, but could clearly see several details betraying the existence of a photograph within, so Ben flipped the frame over, cracked into the back of it as carefully as he could, and removed the small panel. What they were looking at was the cream-colored backside of an almost-intact photograph, with faded script handwritten in cursive. Trent leaned in to read it.

"Shit, it says . . . *something, something*, Summer, 1894."

Ben used his fingers gently to extricate the photograph from the crumbling frame. He got it out, then dropped the frame into the grass at their feet as he began to flip it over.

What they saw was another tintype photograph of a group of a few dozen boys, boys around their age. They all posed facing the camera, some smiling, some not.

"What tha fuck . . ."

Rodrigo uttered the inquiry, which is what they all were thinking. Ben and Trent were scanning the features of the boys' faces when Rodrigo spoke again.

"Yo, yo . . . wait . . ."

He snatched the photo from Ben, taking it in both hands and holding it very closely up to his face. Trent looked at Rod as though he'd just cut him in line.

"Easy, Rod, Jesus Christ, relax."

Ben and Trent stared at Rodrigo, watching his face take on the features of true, real confusion, and then true, real fear. He glanced up from the photo to the other two boys, then back down again, and then back into their faces, looking exasperated. Ben gestured to the photo, growing impatient.

"Well, what the fuck is it, Rod, don't just stand there lookin at us like a dipshit."

Rodrigo looked down at the photograph one more time, then slowly turned it around, pointing with his other hand, his finger shaking, at one specific person in the group who was standing at the top left corner.

"Wh . . . who *the fuck* is that guy?"

When Ben got a good look at the person in the photo, it felt like his gut jumped up into his throat. Adrenaline made his heart race. Ben heard Trent utter something along the lines of *holy shit* as he snatched the photo back from Rodrigo. He flipped it over, reading the handwritten date that clearly said *Summer, 1894*, then looked back at the photo again.

Ben could feel his heart pounding in his neck and ears as he leaned over to look into the face of the man in the photograph in Trent's hands. The vibration of the tintype showcased how badly Trent's hands were also shaking as he slowly looked back up into his friends' bewildered faces.

Trent looked between the two other boys and the photograph, then swallowed loudly as he began to speak.

"That's . . . *that's fucking Reid.*"

CHAPTER 18

THE TEARS were real. Real enough, at least. He'd certainly worked himself up intentionally, but Ben didn't need to engage in a whole-cloth fabrication when talking about his little brother, Wade. He'd told Jessie about how worried he was for Wade without him there to take care of him. He'd told him about how Wade called him *Pee-Pan*, and about how that old nickname their mother had given Ben was the only thing left in the world that the boys and their mother shared. He'd told him about scolding Wade for calling him that in front of other people, the look on Wade's face when he did so, and the broiling guilt that churned through his guts whenever he thought of those moments.

Jessie had gotten up from his own chair and sat down next to Ben a few moments after the boy had pinched the bridge of his nose, squeezed his eyes shut, and begun to softly cry. The therapist put a comforting hand on Ben's shoulder and offered several soothing comments, as well as a reiteration of his earlier directive that crying was actually a healthy, constructive thing.

Ben deemed it sufficient, the length of this first "real" cry during one of his therapy sessions, and took one of the tissues Jessie had been holding toward him for the last several seconds. After wiping his eyes and nose, but before looking up at the man, Ben steeled himself to confront the flickers of triumph and self-pride he expected to find in the therapist's face. Ben did not want to spoil this *breakthrough moment* he was certain Jessie was enjoying—and would certainly report back to Reid about—by falling out of character. He knew he could be easily triggered by any wisps of gratification swimming behind this therapist's veil of empathy. He knew that seeing such a thing could launch him into a vicious and detailed assault on this weak man's character, personality, and profession that would leave him speechless. But Ben couldn't allow that to happen. Not yet, at least.

Ben finally looked up at the man. There they were, those flickers and wisps, and not very well concealed either. Ben swallowed, looked back down at the tissue clutched in his hands, and mumbled an apology for crying.

"Ben, buddy, you *never* need to apologize to me. You *never* need to feel guilt for expressing your emotions. You *never* need to hold back how you really feel."

Oh just you wait, buddy, Ben thought, but he just nodded his acknowledgment to this bland therapeutic talking point.

Ben felt some hesitation, like before he jumped off the cliff into the Flathead River on the rafting trip the week before, but knew he had to do *a little* testing, and wasn't sure when he'd get another chance. He thought of what Carl had told him, he thought of the 130-year-old picture of what appeared to be Reid and a group of boys, and swallowed before looking up at Jessie.

"Jessie, what Bear Springs class were you in? What year, I mean?"

Ben saw the man's eye twitch, and the warm smile fade from his eyes though not from the rest of his face. He did not look surprised by the question, despite never having told Ben he'd been a Bear Springs graduate, nor did he look anxious about having to provide an answer.

"I was in the 2009 summer class."

Now was the moment, the chance to test what Carl had told him before the rafting trip. Ben had given this lots of thought, and he'd come to the conclusion that he needed to see it work to corroborate the narrative provided to him by the large rafting guide—fully substantiate the reality that this *was not* in his head, and that something seriously fucked-up was going on.

"What was the last thing your parents said to you before you got sent to Bear Springs, Jessie?"

Ben's heart seemed to freeze, just as he watched Jessie's entire body do the same. It's hard to notice all the tiny little movements a person makes, even when they're sitting still, until seeing a person actually *freeze*. That is when one can really notice—when you see the entire medley of tiny little movements just stop. It was a preternatural stillness. It was like the man's interior turned into hardened steel in a split second. Ben sat up straight and then moved his upper body and head around to the side, seeing if Jessie's eyes would follow his. They did not. Jessie just kept staring into the space where Ben's face had been seconds before, completely unmoving.

Ben's heart was pounding as he moved himself back into his original position and waited. When it finally came, when Jessie finally spoke the words, Ben was surprised to find that his heart could beat even harder as it thundered in his ears.

"We do not talk about our personal circumstances to Bear Springs students until after your graduation."

Ben had played this moment over in his mind a hundred times over the last week. He did not need to strain at all to confirm that Jessie had just said *exactly* what Carl remembered those other counselors saying almost a decade earlier when asked the *exact* same question. He wanted to keep going, he wanted to keep asking that same question until the man started having a seizure or smashing his nose and teeth into the large, oak desk in the center of the room. Carl recalled to Ben that he'd been told the counselors had encepha—*whatever the fuck*, some kind of disease or infection that caused seizures. Ben could find out once and for all right now, but he knew he needed to wait. He knew that if he were alone with Jessie while the man fell into that state, Reid would know that *Ben* knew. All of Ben's hard-earned good graces with the man in charge would dissolve immediately.

He took some deep breaths, prepared himself, and when Jessie seemed to reanimate, when he seemed to snap out of whatever frozen trance he was in and fall back into his relaxed state with his warm, comforting smile, Ben was smiling and nodding at the man.

"I understand, Jessie. I'll try to remember to ask you about that again after my graduation."

Jessie cocked his head and furrowed his brow slightly, as though he was a bit confused by what Ben had just said.

Ben gestured toward the door by pointing his thumb over his shoulder. "I should probably get going, want to try and catch a shower before lunch."

Jessie walked Ben out of his office, walking with him outside where the morning sun engulfed them both, congratulating him all the while on his progress—*his increased familiarity with his emotions, which would turn into increased control over those same emotions.* He clapped Ben on the back and congratulated him on getting to the halfway point, as they had been in camp for six weeks now and would be heading home after six more. Ben nodded along, then thanked the man shyly as they parted ways.

Ben walked back in the general direction of his cabin, saying *what up* to a few guys from a different cabin heading in the other direction. It seemed as though the calendar of activities and time away from Bear Springs basecamp had increased significantly as the summer had cranked on toward graduation. Thus, this was one of the increasingly rare several-hour periods when the boys got to do their own thing around basecamp between scheduled outings or lessons.

Over the past week, Ben, Trent, and Rodrigo had debated the significance of the old photograph they'd found, in great detail and at great length. Over that time, Trent and Rodrigo had begun to shrug away the significance, eventually falling into the general unified conclusion that it was just someone who *looked like* Reid, and that it would be *impossible* for it to in fact be Reid, "unless you believe in fuckin magic," as Rodrigo had put it. Reid was a "pretty normal-looking motherfucker" who probably bore significant resemblance to "a lot like those old-timey motherfuckers," as Trent had put it.

Ben saw the direction they were going in their own minds early in protracted discussion about the photograph and did not bother trying to connect the significance of Reid's likeness in the old tintype to the other bizarre occurrences they'd witnessed, like the runaway Michael and Joe becoming completely different people overnight. He also did not inform the other two about what the large man Carl had told him before the rafting trip.

Trent and Rodrigo included Ben in everything, but they were

closer than any other two boys at the program, and to convince one, he'd need to convince both. Ben figured that if he wanted to—*when he needed to*—he could effectively convince these two that something sinister or unexplainable was going on. There was still one more thing, one last step he needed to take to successfully remove all remaining doubt from the minds of Trent and Rodrigo, with respect to the element of supernatural or impossibility simmering beneath the ground of this place and skin of these counselors. In a moment of candor, Ben knew that same last step was actually that *he himself* needed to also fully accept there was something unexplainable going on, as well.

Until the time came for that, getting Trent and Rodrigo all worked up or freaked out only served to create more variables outside his control. As such, Ben had decided to forgo offering Trent and Rodrigo a retelling of Carl's recollection from the decade before. All the boys had also kept the photograph and associated debate away from Billy's attention.

In the days that had passed since Ben and Billy had their first honest exchange in the cabin after Joe had stopped by to apologize, the frightening boy had fallen back into his disdainful, distant, dangerous character—completely ignoring the other three. This angered Ben, and confused him. Billy was the only other boy there who seemed to grasp the sinister nature of what was going on. Because of that, Billy's reversion back to such a cold, dismissive attitude toward Ben undermined any allegiance Ben felt toward Billy. *Fuck'm*, Ben figured. If he wanted to be on his own, he damn well could be.

For now, Ben would just continue to play the role of the obedient student, maintain his facade as the reluctantly yet increasingly happy camper. He felt the effect of having kept a disciplined front on for so long, too, in a good way, a way that he could not have explained if he wanted to. The longer and more sincerely he carried on with this persona, the more buy-in he pretended to expend, Ben could *feel* Reid's attention and watchful gaze lessen more and more.

That humid stench, that static electricity of suspicion that seemed to emanate from the man so fiercely in the first days of the Ben's time here, had extinguished itself almost completely. Now, by Ben's closest estimation, whenever he'd cross paths with Reid throughout the day, the man looked at him with an expression somewhere between casual friendliness and genuine pride.

Over the next few days, with the exception of a few big day trips up into the mountains, the boys slept in their own beds in their own cabins every night. All things considered, it was as relaxed and as routine a week as the group had enjoyed since the first week of the summer, when the novelty of the whole experience undermined any such effect it might've otherwise carried. They hiked, they fished in the nearest lake and in the two trout streams within day-trip distance, and they set their snares for rabbit and squirrels and their foothold traps for coyotes. They did their individual and their group therapy sessions, they endured the lectures from Reid and the other counselors. It was a predictable few days and, thereby, ultimately a calming few days.

Ben wondered if this was part of the design—give the group a week of stability to increase their familiarity and ease, while draining away the suspicion and discontent. They were doing their first six-day, five-night expedition at the end of the week, so Ben used this time to continue his corroboration of Carl's recollection.

After lunch one afternoon, when the boys had a couple of hours of free time, Ben saw one of the other cabin's counselors—a smiley douche-bag named Pete—head into one of the barns that stood on the grounds of basecamp where they stored a lot of the fishing, trapping, and other recreational gear. He heard the man say he wanted to rig up a dozen fly rods for the planned afternoon of hiking to and fishing at one of the lakes only an hour away.

Ben told Jimmy and the other boys he was going to his reading spot, a gnarled old ponderosa tree on a grassy rise above basecamp that enjoyed a commanding view of the area, where he often took a book and, most of the time, pretended to read. He sat at his tree for a moment, then when the time was right and there were no eyes on him, he made his way around the back of the barn where Pete was working, going slow and taking great care to be certain he was not noticed.

He squeezed himself in between the two large barn doors, so as to not alert Pete by heaving against one of the old slabs to widen his only point of entry. Ben actually liked the numerous old barns at basecamp, never failing to notice how well attended and lived-in they felt.

When Ben entered the barn the breezy, hot summer weather outside immediately fell away, replaced by the still, cool air of a rustic structure. There was an old radio in this one that was always on, quietly playing an old country swing station, even through the night. He could see Pete at the other end, standing under several lamps at a long bench where the fishing gear was stored, cleaned, and worked on. Ben made his way through the beam of yellow light cutting through the slit in the barn doors, which seemed to almost have a tangible substance of its own due to the ambient dust that hung and danced inside the building.

Ben could hear the *click-click-click* of a fly reel as he approached the man from behind. He did not want to startle Pete, but he did not want to give him much time to adjust to his presence either. Ben began to whistle a tune just a second before he lifted up a large tarpaulin covering a trailer that they had used to haul all the gear to and from the river the week prior. He could hear the man's feet turn fast in the hard-packed floor before he spoke.

"Hey, is that you, Ben?"

Ben acted as though he were the startled one, putting his hand on his chest and pulling his upper body away from the noise of the man's voice as though he were weaving away from a punch.

"*Jesus Christ*, Pete, hey, sorry. Y'scared the heck outta me."

Pete smiled at the boy, with a bit of curiosity in his face.

"Sorry, buddy, didn't mean to. What're you lookin around in here for?"

Ben turned back to the trailer and went about rummaging around under the tarp as though he had all the right in the world to do it.

"Lookin for my raincoat, haven't seen it since the river trip, figured it might be in the trailer we hauled all our gear back with . . ."

Ben watched the young man from the corner of his eye wrap the fly line once around the reel, then hook the fly onto one of the lowest eyelets on the rod. Pete emitted an inquisitive *hmmm* as he set the fly rod back into the rack where several dozen others stood vertically. He turned toward Ben as he began to speak.

"Where's the last place you saw it? You sure you didn't leave it on the riv—"

Ben cut him off before he could finish his question, turning toward the man and speaking in as direct and phonetic a voice as he could.

"What was the last thing your parents said to you before you got sent to Bear Springs Academy, Pete?"

Even though he'd already seen this once before, his heart seemed to freeze, just as Pete's body did. The man had begun to gesture toward Ben as he asked the question and his hand froze in front of him, his mouth ajar. Ben took several slow paces to one side, checking to see if the adult's eyes would follow him, as he had done with Jessie. The eyes remained fixed on the spot he'd been standing when he asked the question.

Ben had begun to count as soon as he saw the man freeze. He got to around nine-Mississippi before the man said what Ben was hoping he would not say, but felt very confident he would.

"We do not talk about our personal circumstances to Bear Springs students until after your graduation."

As soon as he saw vitality flow back into Pete's muscles, Ben responded from his new position several feet to Pete's right of where he had been before the man had turned to stone. Ben held up the book in his left hand as he did so.

"Well, I'm gonna try to finish my book before we hike to the lake. If you happen to see my raincoat anywhere, will you drop it off at my cabin, or maybe just tell me or Jimmy where it is, and I'll come grab it?"

Pete looked a bit confused as he turned to face Ben, but it faded within a second and his normal, goofy smile returned.

"You bet, man. Hopefully you didn't leave it on the river! But no biggie if you did, we can just get you a new one, got plenty of those lying around."

Ben returned the smile as he made to leave and felt relief as the man also turned back toward the rack of fly rods and took another down to rig it up. Ben whistled a bit as he strode back toward the large barn doors, this time hauling one of them outward a foot or so to pass through more easily.

Ben opened his book as he slowly walked up the grassy slope toward his reading tree, trying to appear as though he were reading as he went, in case he was being watched leaving the barn. He saw how badly his hands were shaking as he did this, the dog-eared old pages shaking like leaves on a tree. If he *was* being watched, he hoped that would not be visible to anyone else.

Up until this point, Ben realized as he walked that he had still been holding out hope that this was all just in his head. He realized he had subconsciously been willing to concede all the bizarre shit he'd encountered; the two panic attacks brought on by Reid's smile, Reid cornering Joe in the storm, Michael's and Joe's entire personalities changing overnight, Carl's recollection, the cryptic message in the library, even Jessie turning into a statue and his comment matching Carl's story perfectly. In that moment, walking slowly up the breezy slope toward the large ponderosa tree trying to keep his hands from shaking in dread, Ben realized he'd been deeply hoping for an opportunity to write it all off as coincidence, regardless of that profound improbability.

He had not drafted out some logical chart on everything that had consumed his thoughts all summer long. He didn't have some well-developed case file jotted down on paper. That's not how Ben operated. His mind could make these connections on its own. Ben had always needed to see something for himself to believe it. He would never allow a hole to be filled by someone else's story, assurances, or evidence, and in that moment, he was not sure what else he needed to see to accept that something was very, very fucking wrong here. He now had personally acquired several critical, world-shaking pieces of information.

One of these pieces of information was that he had now frozen two grown men into statues by asking them a single question, and both had not even remembered being asked the question or mumbling out their identical responses. Another piece of information was that this was *exactly* what another man had seen almost a decade earlier, when asking *different* counselors—*different* Bear Springs graduates—the exact *same* question.

Ben's head spun as he approached his large tree and sat slowly against the trunk, not bothering to check for and kick away the two or three scouting ants he usually found in the gravelly dirt apron that surrounded the trunk. Ben repeatedly scanned his eyes across the same line of text in the tattered old Louis L'Amour novel he'd pulled off one of the shelves in the Great Hall in an effort to appear enthralled with the old Western.

Being in full view of basecamp now and wanting to maintain the illusion in case he was being watched by Reid or anyone else, he turned a page. He fake-read the next several pages as he peeled through the situation several times over in his head, hoping to find any last shred or hole that would support the conclusion that these counselors *were not* brainwashed or possessed and all the other horrifying shit and consequences that naturally spun out of that situation. That *reality*.

After several minutes Ben leaned back against the tree to scan the camp below him. He saw several counselors, Reid included, playing Frisbee with some of the other boys on the lawn between several of the cabins. He saw Billy lounging in the sun on the porch of their cabin. He saw Rodrigo walking from the lodge, having just finished his therapy session. He saw Pete beginning to stack a row of fly rods on the outside of the barn. He saw Trent and a few guys from other cabins hunched over tanning racks at the other barn where the pelts of the rabbits and squirrels they had trapped over the summer were stretched and treated.

Ben's heart was still racing, his mouth was dry as sand, and he could feel tears throbbing up behind his eyes as he looked over the scene. *None of these poor sons of bitches know what's going on here*, he thought. No one except for Reid, at least. Ben felt deep down that if he were to ask Reid that terrible, sinister, triggering question—ask Reid what *his parents* said to him before he got sent to Bear Springs—the man would *not* freeze, he would *not* regurgitate some canned response, he would *not* go into a robotic trance like the others. He'd known all along that Reid was different than the other counselors. *Something* was different about him, at least, and it wasn't just the fact that he was the leader. It was something that danced behind the man's eyes and smile. It was something formless that pulsed and coursed beneath his skin.

Ben was overwhelmed most in that moment by the monumental, potentially impossible task of trying to convince any of the other boys of what was going on and articulate for them what he'd learned. Even if he were to stroll down there right now and ask the group of counselors playing Frisbee *what the last thing their parents said to them was before they got sent to Bear Springs* and then screamed out a demand that all the other boys watch how they froze up in response, what would that really accomplish? He was virtually positive Reid would just haul him off like he had Michael and Joe, then justify the counselors' behavior somehow. He'd be lucky even if he managed to convince just Trent and Rodrigo of what was going on, let alone dozens of hardheaded guys like himself.

He felt a deep urge to run as he considered this. It felt as though some magnetic force were pulling his shoulders back into the sprawling forest behind him, activating the muscles in his legs to prepare him to sprint. But an even stronger force kept him in place. The shame of leaving Trent and Rodrigo behind outweighed the urge. He couldn't just bolt. *That's why I'm in these goddamned fucking mountains in the first place*, Ben thought, *splitting off by myself without a proper plan, leaving my brother behind*. He knew he wouldn't get far anyway.

Ben leaned his head back against the trunk of the tree and looked up into its tangled branches. He felt a strange resentment or frustration toward the tree. This great, old thing—this massive living organism—had been rooted here, standing sentinel over this place certainly for as long as Bear Springs had existed. Ben wondered if it was evil, too, or if it would've done something to stop all this, whatever the hell it all was, if it could've. He thought of the feral, terrified look in the boy Michael's eyes when they pulled him out of the armoire, he wondered what he'd seen, what pushed him to finally run. He thought of his little brother. He needed to get out of here, and he needed to do it right.

CHAPTER 19

---

*C*OME ON, Louisiana. We're supposed to have finished a shelter good enough to use during a rainstorm by the time the counselors do their rounds."

Ben heard the growing exasperation in the boy Charlie's voice from where he sat, reclined on what ended up being a surprisingly comfortable chair made of stones he'd constructed at the base of a stout fir tree. The forested area where they were conducting today's "lesson" was just beyond the archery range above basecamp, and Ben decided this would be a nice place to sneak off for a nap during downtime.

Thick branches extended away from one another out of two gnarled knots in the trunk, each one a few feet above Ben's shoulders. He'd used a bit of paracord to run a tight lattice of sticks outward over those two branches, then covered it in a carpet of thick, green moss he'd collected near the stream a short distance away. All the pine needles and rocks around the chair had been swept away, leaving a tidy floor of hard-packed dirt and a few thick, gnarled elbows of exposed roots. To Ben's right and left, below the two ends of the wood and moss awning above his head, he'd quickly dug two long gouges in the earth running down away from the base of the tree, four inches deep and across. Drainage, Ben had thought, would surely be a convenient feature.

Shelter building, the counselors had called today's lesson.

Ben had been paired with Charlie for this exercise, which had begun several hours earlier. Ben had grown weary several days earlier of Charlie's flagrant desire to please and even befriend the counselors. Charlie wasn't the only boy at Bear Springs who did this. Ben figured that, through this

Bear Springs program, quite a few of his classmates were actually making first contact with a deeply mysterious, intimidating, alien species; men who are generally kind, interested in what they feel and think, and who make eye contact while they listen. Truth be told, Ben was also making first contact with their kind. The difference, perhaps, was that Ben found the idea of even quietly befriending or trusting these men to be preposterous. Openly doing so, for others to see, with eagerness, no less, was just ridiculous and undignified.

Even so, Ben had still hoped that, once alone together, he'd find some characteristic of Charlie's to be useful, or even just mildly interesting. Ben abandoned the effort of fleshing out some glimmer of quality from Charlie within a few minutes of conversation. Ben wondered if *this* was the by-product of suburbia, not having much experience with that type of person. He knew many very stupid people, but where he grew up, even those had at least *some* kind of keen edge. *Something* that had kept them alive. This boy, however, was a legitimate, full-blooded simpleton. Catastrophically underwhelming and forgettable. A real vanilla paperweight.

Ben opened one eye and squinted up at where Charlie still stood staring down at him, awaiting some kind of verbal response, using a finger to impatiently twirl one of the absurd wide-brimmed sun hats they were all given the first day here. The breeze maintained a steady whisper through the canopy of the forest that waved and danced above them.

Ben mentally noted what an unusually windy day it was as he slowly pointed above his head to the tidy little roof he'd fashioned over his rock throne.

"We're all finished, Charlie. Pull up a chair."

Charlie rolled his eyes and huffed through his nose. As he spoke, he gestured between the bushcraft awning above Ben's head and the unruly mass of sticks behind him he'd spent the last hours assembling.

"We need to build a *real* shelter, dude, something that would *actually* keep us safe and dry during a rainstorm, like Mitchell said. You basically just built a stupid friggin umbrella. Seriously, come on, help me finish this *real* shelter."

Ben looked past Charlie at the messy four-foot walls of sticks and branches that vaguely formed a sad, flaccid rectangle on terribly uneven ground. He exhaled for several long moments, adjusted his butt, then leaned his head back and closed his eyes again as he responded.

"Chuck, that pile a'slash wouldn't keep a cat dry from a piss trickle. Come on now, slap a chair down here next to mine. You can tell the counselors you built the whole thing."

Real exasperation could be heard in Charlie's voice as he responded.

"Dude, *come on*, seriously, Mitchell is gonna come by soon and inspect our shelter. He's gonna judge whether it's good or not, he's gonna tell you how dumb yours is, you're gonna make me look like an idiot."

A fatigued grin spread across Ben's face as he pointed in a slow circle around a section of the bare, empty dirt to the right of his stone chair.

"Behold, *dear Charlie*, my garden of shits to give. *Alas*, it is barren . . ."

Charlie shifted his weight from foot to foot while his face betrayed some mixture of confusion and offense as he fumbled out a response.

"Your shelter *sucks ass*. You'd get, like, absolutely friggin *soaked* sitting there in a rainstorm, you don't even know, dude, you'd be so freezing you'd probably start *crying*, then you'd be *begging* for a better one."

Despite the childish idiocy of Charlie's comment, it still served to activate a drum wheel of snapshots in Ben's memory. These were all some iteration of the many nights Aunt Nikki locked him and his little brother, Wade, outside the trailer until morning; huddling under a tarp in the back seat of the old windowless Chrysler in the empty lot across the street, rubbing Wade's chest and back with both hands until the little boy's teeth stopped chattering, covering Wade's body with his own under their rotten little front porch for hours as hurricane wind lashed the trailer park. The memory of that hurricane was so vivid he could almost feel his little brother's terrified sobs racking into his body. A deep rage came on that blocked out the recollections like a curtain.

Ben let his head slowly fall forward until he locked eyes with Charlie, who had never actually seen that kind of look on anyone's face before, let alone someone his own age.

"You finna getch y'self learnt up on cryin n' beggin, *Charles*."

The hat slipped from his hands to the ground as he involuntarily recoiled a step away from where Ben sat. He couldn't break eye contact.

It was as if steel wires ran from Ben's pupils to his own. The pounding heartbeat in his ears drowned out the roar of the wind in the treetops above. For the next several nights, after everyone else in his dark cabin had fallen asleep, goose bumps crept over Charlie's body as he checked all the windows he could see from his bed, just to make sure that Louisiana boy wasn't outside, staring back at him with those cold, vicious eyes.

A jarring sound pierced through the forest, pulling both boys' attention away from one another. The sound was somehow both a groan and a whine before turning into a prolonged splintering crack, followed by a massive, deep crash. Both Charlie and Ben were standing now, staring into the woods toward the noise and commotion of running boys, visible only in flashes between the tree trunks. Several long seconds passed before the screaming started.

Several boys were screaming, but one of them was the jittery, panicked scream of reality-shattering pain. Charlie, Ben, and all the others were now bounding through the trees toward the commotion. Ben could see now that a large tree had started to blow over, and while the root ball had held firm to the earth, the weight of the falling tree and gravity took the rest—ripping apart at its base and crashing to the ground, leaving behind only a few feet of trunk, crowned by a sharp mess of fresh, ivory-colored bark blades. A similar shark's mouth of splintered wood formed the end of the large tree that had separated from the trunk and crashed down onto the forest floor. Dark, wet mulch covered the ground between the trunk and tree, belched out of the core, which was almost entirely hollow with rot.

Halfway up the length of the fallen tree, one boy jumped up and down and shouted incoherently, pointing frantically at something Ben could not see. He and several other boys vaulted over the trunk to see what had the kid all freaked out, just as a clutch of counselors swarmed in from the other side.

Danny, one of the boys who, like Charlie, Ben had also lumped into the insufferable-blowhard category, was lying on his back. It took a few moments for them to process what they were seeing, but when they did, a collective groan emanated from the group as they all took several steps back. Freddie, Pete, and a few other counselors put hands on their chests, pushing them back as they screamed *back up, back up*.

Danny's legs were both crushed. Only his pelvis and a bit of his upper thighs could be seen, which had been smashed into a deep indentation in the hard-packed dirt, but everything from the crotch down was concealed under the gnarled trunk of the old tree. His left arm was also pinned to the ground by a thick sword of a branch that had skewered it, shattering his arm near the elbow before driving through it entirely and continuing deep into the earth. Only skin and a few tendons held his lower arm to his upper, where splintered bone could be seen amid the bright red blood pumping down the branch to pool below him.

Ben scanned the faces and then the hands of the counselors, knowing that anyone with EMT, wilderness first responder, or even some basic first aid training should have seen everything they needed to begin immediately preparing a tourniquet.

Ben's attention went up to Danny's face when he vomited and appeared to begin seizing. His eyes went wide and rolled back into his head. Just then the counselors began grabbing and pushing the boys away from the carnage with more force.

Ben checked his watch.

Several of the counselors were roaring at them to get moving down the hill back toward camp with enough urgency in their voices to motivate action from the boys. Ben glanced back to see a few counselors kneeling around Danny, but within a few seconds the entire group was being driven like steers through the forest almost at full jogging speed. None of the counselors would answer questions, or even acknowledge them; they only continued shouting *let's go* and *move* and *back to camp* over one another. The group did not slow its momentum at all as Reid and two of the camp's elder interventionists, Javier and Daniel, sprinted past them, up the slope toward the fallen tree.

The urgent procession did not stop until the group had reached the lodge, where counselors ushered them into the Great Hall and began giving out bottles of water. After a few minutes of relatively quiet hydration and catching of breath, the boys initiated their inquisition anew, shouting questions at the counselors about what the hell had happened, whether Danny would live, how they would treat him, where they would take him for treatment, and when the ambulance would be here.

The counselors did not try to answer specific questions. They just engaged in open-palmed calming gestures and repeated assurances that medical first responders were on the way, and that Danny would be alright.

Ben *highly doubted that.*

He checked his watch again, and instead of taking part in the exchange, he grabbed another bottle of water and made his way over to one of the windows between the bookshelves that looked out onto the well-manicured grounds outside. He glanced across the lawns and cabins that comprised the largest footprint of basecamp, where, as he knew well, the tall, bronze lanterns that lined walkways and the imposing old-growth ponderosa and fir trees punched into the sky just about everywhere. What he couldn't recall at the moment was the specific extent of open lawn where the guys would often play Frisbee or football during downtime, out near the barns where fishing, rafting, and camping gear was stored. Giving it a quick scan, he confirmed his recollection; quite a few more of the large trees jutted from the lawn in that area as well.

He strolled over to another window across the room as the exchange between the boys and counselors lost some of its animation and began to quiet. He quickly scanned the area behind the massive lodge.

The archery range then, he concluded. *It would have to be the archery range.* Only possible option he could imagine.

Ben walked back into the center of the large room and dropped into one of the leather chairs that he made sure had a view through one window toward the long driveway leading up to the camp from the county road, and another window toward the big, forested slope to the west—the forested slope where poor Danny was crushed, and where Ben could see a break in the canopy under which sat the archery range.

Ben recalled a medical diagram he once saw of the human body, as he had several times since seeing Danny's wounds. He recalled the bold, red lines that portrayed the brachial artery, then the ulnar and radial arteries below the elbow. The gladius blade of a branch that had smashed through Danny's arm had certainly caused an arterial bleed.

Ben had to assume that simply based on how the blood pumped and spurted from the wound. Perhaps all three arteries had been destroyed, Ben wondered.

He checked his watch yet again and assumed, at this point, the poor lad was *thoroughly* fucking dead. Unless, of course, one of the dipshit counselors had had a moment of competence and applied a tourniquet, which Ben figured would've needed to be cranked down *immediately* after they'd been shooed away if there were any hope for the boy. That didn't really matter, though. There was only one reasonable course of action for this staff, and he had yet to see any sign of it being taken.

Trent and Rodrigo broke away from the larger group to come and join him in other chairs nearby. Rodrigo shook his head as he spoke.

"What an unlucky son of a bitch, man."

Trent nodded, staring at a spot on his hand that he massaged with the other.

"No doubt. Did you see his arm? That was . . . That was fuckin bad, bro."

Ben made a tight-lipped expression in response and shook his head slowly in what he thought was a sufficiently solemn, contemplative gesture, then glanced back out the window toward the slope to the west. Toward the archery range.

A full hour passed as the antsy boys were kept in the Great Hall. Some read books, some played cards. Billy, Trent, and a few others just slept on the large couches. Rodrigo found a magazine and read it in the chair next to Ben. Ben watched the counselors talk into their radios from time to time. He scolded himself internally for not having stolen one yet. He couldn't put that chore off any longer; that had to be top priority after today.

Eventually, Ben saw the massive counselor Freddie pull his radio up to his mouth, issue a few one-word responses, nod a few times, then clip it back onto his belt. He raised his muscular arms as he addressed the room in a loud voice.

"Alright, fellas, we just got word that Danny made it to the emergency room in Libby, and that he's in stable condition, and while it'll take a few months, he's expected to make a *full recovery*."

The counselors all cheered and began to clap, as did some of the boys. The counselor Devin went boy to boy giving them high fives. Trent sat up from his reclined position and nodded in approval. Rodrigo appeared to let out a deep, long-held breath of relief.

Ben checked his watch.

CHAPTER 20

THE BOYS had a bit of time to kill before dinner, so Ben, as usual, went toward the library. He found the elder man Daniel leaning against one of the huge, live-edge pillars that flanked the front doors to the lodge. They exchanged nods, and Ben began scheming immediately.

Ben had one very important question he needed some kind of answer to, and he traced the outline of the wooden note card in his pocket as he considered the best way to approach this. Ben had done enough due diligence to support the conclusion that the thing in his pocket was, indeed, just an old bookmark with some random scribbling upon it. But if that was *not* what it was, then Ben had to assume that it really was a dire warning left behind by a former student. He felt strongly that it had to be one or the other, and nothing else.

Ben spent fifteen minutes going down the long hallway to the Great Hall, triple-checking all the maps on the wall. He'd done this several times and was certain he'd not missed any references to any landmarks to the west of basecamp. Ben made his way back to the doors to the lodge and found Daniel hadn't moved, and no one else stood within earshot. He felt a chill pass over him as he wondered why, and for what purpose, this large, frightening man had *run* up the mountain slope toward where Ben had last seen Danny, seizing, vomiting, and bleeding to death. He knew approaching this man with this particular question was a risk, but he figured, or at least he hoped, it was a risk worth taking.

"Hey there, Mr. Daniel."

The man glanced over as he spun the toothpick in the corner of his mouth, then touched the wide brim of his hat with his thick, scarred index finger.

"Mr. Ben . . ."

Ben took a step closer to the man.

"Sir, you spend much time in those mountains?"

Daniel glanced up at the range to the west and nodded.

"More'n most, I reckon."

Ben looked down at his hands, then back into the man's face.

"So, last week when we were up there we came up on this real old, rotten sign with an arrow on it, seemed to suggest that something called *Buckle Creek* and *Caravan Pass* were off yonder, in the direction of the arrow. Sign was knocked over so I couldn't tell which way it was pointing, but I like maps, and have looked over all those I can find, and I can't find nothin in em that mentions any *Buckle Creek* or *Caravan Pass*, just wonderin why that would be up there."

The man chuckled softly as he smiled into the distant mountains. He looked like he was recalling a pleasant memory as he began to speak.

"Yah, welp, there *used to be* a Buckle Crick and Caravan Pass up there, but when the feds started gettin all friendly with the Indians, they went about renaming all kinds of places on federal land back to what the Indians called em, I guess. It was a whole fuss. What was called *Buckle Crick* is now *Kaniksu Crick*, and *Caravan Pass* is now *d'Oreilles Pass*. Or, I reckon they've *always been* Kaniksu Crick and d'Oreilles Pass to some folks, but it's sure given me a headache over the years tryin to keep up with all the changes."

Ben's breath left his lungs, and his heart was thundering in his ears. Ben did not need to look at another map to make sense of what he'd just learned. He'd never laid eyes on them, but he knew *exactly* where d'Oreilles Pass and Kaniksu Creek were and thus had a pretty good idea where *Kaniksu Glacier* was, nestled somewhere up in the rocks where it trickled out braids of water to form this stream of freedom and emancipation that he'd thought so much about over the last weeks. These features of the landscape were, indeed, to the west of basecamp, as the ominous warning from some former Bear Springs student suggested. He forced himself to nod and clear his throat before responding.

"Well, I spose that sign makes sense now, thanks."

Daniel spoke Ben's name as he'd begun turning away from the man, freezing him in place.

"If you pass by that sign again, and it ain't too much trouble, would you mind fetchin it for me? Reckon I'd like to hang that in the lodge here. If it works out, I'll pay for your labor and freight in candy and soda."

The man smiled with some genuine warmth, and Ben did his best to return the same.

"You bet, Mr. Daniel."

Ben walked into the grounds, not knowing where he was headed. He flipped the wooden note card over and over inside his pocket as he went. His mouth went dry as he reasoned through this new information. The dire message and warning was written about this place, by someone suggesting the reader try to escape at all costs, or kill themselves. *A former student wrote this*, Ben finally accepted, then hid the message in hopes that a later student would find it and heed its warning before it was too late.

Ben meandered around until dinner began a short time later. In the mess hall, Reid offered a more detailed accounting of the rescue operation. Apparently, the counselors had been able to stop Danny's bleeding and get him out from under the tree just in time for the medevac team who showed up *in a small helicopter* that set down *in the archery range*. They put the boy on a stretcher, then airlifted him out to the nearest emergency room.

Ben heard one boy inquire about how they didn't hear any helicopter, but then even more comments about how thick those lodge walls are, and how hard it is to even hear the assembly bell and the noise of basecamp from the woods.

There wasn't much chatter that night in the cabin after lights-out, and everyone fell asleep quickly. Except for Ben, who stared out the window toward the shadow-cloaked slope to the west. Ben wondered if the boy who'd left the 1917 warning had made it out. He wondered whether he'd taken Buckle Creek to Buckle Glacier, then finally crossed over Caravan Pass. *d'Oreilles Pass*. Ben's heart rate increased as he considered everything he'd learned this day.

In the time that elapsed between the forced march from the carnage of Danny's accident and the news of Danny's arrival at the hospital from Freddie, Ben had been able to get his eyes on the slope to the west and the area above the archery range *at least* once every ninety seconds.

There was no fucking helicopter landing on that slope this afternoon. Danny was not airlifted anywhere.

Ben did feel some pride in, once again, seeing through a group of adults' clumsy narrative, but in that dark room, it faded into dread at what terrible things that could mean.

CHAPTER 21

"Y OU GETTING all packed up, fellas, you getting *set to jet and rigged to flip?*"

None of the four boys responded to Jimmy's inquiry; they just kept silently packing all their well-worn gear into their large backpacks. They did this with real knowledge now, a real sense of necessity and convenience and ground truth guiding their processes—field craft they'd learned over the weeks and weeks of rucking around in the Northern Rockies and living out of these large, heavy packs.

They would be leaving early the next morning for a five-night expedition into the mountains, the longest backpacking trip they had taken so far, and the longest they would be taking this summer, with one more of these long trips slated to take place a week later. They would spend the first night at the alpine lake where Trent had trapped his first snowshoe hare, where Reid had confronted Billy and sent Ben into a jittery paralysis with that loaded, lightning smile. Then they would hike up over the pass above that lake and continue on into what was, for the boys, uncharted alpine territory.

Ben had been more quiet than normal since the previous day, since his encounter with Pete and the associated realization it brought kicking and screaming into Ben's mind. He had not come any closer to a plan on what to do on any level, but had moved farther along the path of acceptance, even if Ben could not describe *what* he was accepting with any clarity or sense. He did notice, almost with some surprise, that he was packing his bag more carefully now. He was not just thinking about what he would need for *this* particular five-day trip, but what he would need for a considerably longer stint in the mountains, if he were to decide—or have the balls—to make one at some point along this expedition. He remembered the kid Michael's thrashed boots and clothing and packed extra shoelaces and a roll of duct tape.

"Alright, fellas, I'm gonna brush my teeth, let's start getting ready for bed, big day tomorrow, so lights-out in fifteen!"

Again, none of the boys responded to him as he sauntered down the hallway to the bathroom. Ben waited a minute or so until he figured Jimmy was getting close to finished, then he cinched down the brain on his large pack and turned to the other three boys. He scanned each of their three faces before he began to speak.

"I need to show you guys something. When Jimmy comes out of the bathroom, I'm going to ask him a few questions. Nothing more. If you respect me at all, if you trust me at all, please do not interrupt, or speak at all while I'm doing this. *Just watch Jimmy*. Watch his face and his body. After it's over, we can discuss it, but what you're about to see *cannot* leave this cabin. It's imperative that we keep it between us, and don't tell another soul about this. I can't answer any questions right now, wait until it's over, it won't take long."

Both Rodrigo and Trent looked as though they were about to speak, lips just beginning to form words. Ben used one hand to pat once downward toward the floor as he spoke, cutting them off.

"Stop . . ."

They did. It would be a long time until Trent and Rodrigo understood why, or how, Ben could get them to listen when he used that strange tone of voice with its surprising clarity and maturity. None of his usual Cajun accent, none of the usual rounded consonants or inflection he naturally spoke with. To them, it sounded as though an entirely different person was speaking.

Ben gestured toward the bathroom with his head as they heard Jimmy turn off the faucet and smack his plastic toothbrush against the old, scuffed porcelain sink. Billy hadn't moved from where he sat on the edge of his bed with his large pack on the ground between his legs. Trent and Rodrigo each whipped their gaze from the hallway on to Ben, then back again, wide-eyed as though they expected violence or something equally jarring. But they did not speak, and eventually took a step away from Ben, back toward their respective beds.

Jimmy entered the room shirtless, holding each end of the towel that hung around his neck. He looked at the three boys near their beds, with his ridiculous smile, then at Ben, who stood in front of him but was facing the other boys.

Ben crossed his arms and took a deep breath as Jimmy came to a stop and looked between the group. Just as the man began to emit the first sound of the first syllable of whatever stupid fucking thing he'd thought to say, Ben turned to face him and interrupted him. He spoke in a firm tone devoid of any emotion or the inquisitive inflection that would usually garnish the end of a spoken question.

"Jimmy, what was the last thing your parents said to you before you got sent to Bear Springs Academy?"

As Ben knew he would, the man froze, mouth ajar and slightly rounded. Ben took a few steps to Jimmy's side, then held out his open palm in front of the man's face. Ben looked at the other three boys one at a time as he waved it up and down just inches from the man's eyes. Ben could see confusion leaving the features of Trent, Rodrigo, and even Billy, as it was slowly replaced by wonder and disbelief.

Ben walked back in front of the man, and looked at the other boys as he quickly said the last few words of the sinister pronouncement just a second before Jimmy began to speak.

"Not until after your graduation, fellas."

"We do not talk about our personal circumstances to Bear Springs students until after your graduation."

Ben looked back at the man just as the concrete affect broke and the life and movement returned to his body. Trent and Rodrigo couldn't decide who to cast their disbelieving faces on, Ben or Jimmy. Billy just narrowed his eyes as he slowly sat up straight.

Ben was going to push it this time. Not all the way, but he knew Carl had gotten away with asking the question twice before the other counselors started seizing or smashing themselves against rocks. He felt the overwhelming importance and need to drive the reality home for these other three boys.

Jimmy had begun to look at the boys' faces. He had an extra dash of puzzlement in his face, on top of the jovial, ambient befuddlement he usually walked around the world with.

"Jimmy, what was the last thing your parents said to you before you got sent to Bear Springs Academy?"

This time, the abrupt end to all movement through the man's body stood out with even more definition.

Trent and Rodrigo couldn't hold back their disbelief on this second round. One whispered *what the fuck* as the other let out a sharp *holy shit*.

Ben snatched a sock hanging off the end of Rodrigo's bed and tossed it toward the man's hands.

"Catch, Jimmy . . ."

The sock brushed against the man's fingers and fell onto the old, scuffed wooden floor between his bare feet. Jimmy neither looked nor made any responsive movement whatsoever. Ben locked eyes with each of the other boys, making sure they'd seen what he wanted them to see this evening. Making sure the import of this impossible spectacle was not lost on them. As he did this, he whispered the full statement just loud enough for the others to hear—*we do not talk about our personal circumstances to Bear Springs students until after your graduation.*

Ben looked back at Jimmy, taking note of the extra five or six seconds longer the man was motionless compared to the first time he'd asked this question to all three adults he'd tried it on thus far.

"We do not talk about our personal circumstances to Bear Springs students until after your graduation."

The man's body revitalized toward the end of the sentence. This was obvious on its own, but even more so this time because he shuddered, as though a cold breeze had run up his spine, then cast his eyes down for a moment at Ben's midsection as he blinked rapidly and rubbed his eyes.

"You heard Jimmy, fellas. We start a big expedition tomorrow, we needa turn in and get some good sleep."

Jimmy looked at Ben, still a bit confused, but his resting stoner face and goofy smile returned as he began to nod. He pointed between the boys as he walked toward and then into his bedroom at the other end of the cabin.

"*Attaboy*, Ben. You guys heard the man, an epic adventure kicks off tomorrow first thing in the a.m., so I wanna see lights-out in ten, alright?"

As usual, Jimmy failed to register the glowers of disbelief that followed him out of the room—even these more amplified versions of disbelief aimed at more than his mere tone-deaf stupidity. As they heard the old, creaky hinges and door of the bedroom close, Trent, Rodrigo, and Billy all slowly turned back to face Ben, who could see, and almost *feel*, the building onslaught of questions that were about to come his way. Ben walked to his bed, where he sat and spoke as quietly as he could.

"They all do it, just like that. All the counselors are graduates of Bear Springs, and they respond to that particular question with that *exact same answer* you just heard, word for word. I've tried it on three of them so far: Jessie, Pete, and now Jimmy. It could be that it's not all the counselors who respond that way. Maybe I've just gotten lucky with those three, but I think it's likely the same for all or at least most of them, except for Reid. I have no goddamn clue why, how, or what the reason for this is. I don't think it does us any good to speculate on that kinda shit."

Ben took a deep breath and slowly pointed toward the door of Jimmy's room, hoping it would ward off interruption.

"I don't know if these motherfuckers are programmed, brainwashed, or possessed. I don't even *really* know the difference between those things. All I know is what you just saw, and that is some very, *very* abnormal shit. On top of that, I have a strong feeling that after our *solo night*, or after that special one-on-one session with Reid like that kid Michael had the night he tried to escape, and Joe had the night after he attacked Rod . . . *that's* what fuckin happens. You end up like *that*."

Ben watched the other boys and thought Trent and Rodrigo looked younger than they were. For the first time, they looked truly scared. Billy looked dangerous.

"Guys, we *cannot* tell anyone else about this. We *cannot* risk the counselors finding out that we know something is going on until we have some kinda fuckin plan, alright? I know it'll be difficult, but we need to keep our shit locked up until we get ourselves a plan together—a plan to get the *fuck* out of here. Do you understand how important that is?"

Rodrigo's swallow seemed to echo around the quiet, tense room. Both he and Trent nodded, Trent mumbling a quick *for sure*. Ben looked at Billy, who was staring back at him.

"Billy?"

The large boy stood slowly, holding Ben's gaze for a long moment once on his feet, then wrenched his head to one side, emitting a startling crackle of pops from his neck. Billy finally spoke as he slowly turned and made his way toward the bathroom.

"That little show you just put on don't change nothin. I've known the counselors was wrong in tha head since before I even got here, *and I still* ain't got no reason to go chattin with any of you stupid-ass dipshits. Ain't a damn thing's changed."

That was good enough for Ben, for now at least.

The other three boys sat propped on their elbows on their beds in the dark for well over an hour discussing everything that was now on the table, while Billy was asleep and snoring. Ben told them about how he'd spoken to Carl before the river trip, and about how the other counselors started seizing and smashing their faces into rocks once the large man had pressed them on that question for a third time. He told them about how he'd watched from the window of their cabin as Reid confronted Joe the night of the storm after his and Rodrigo's fight. The discussion took many curves and turns but did not evolve into actually planning an escape. That, they agreed, they'd need to put some *real* smart thinking into.

Before he drifted off to sleep, Ben felt some measure of increased calm now that these other guys were *in the know*. It was one thing to simply be buddies with them. Ben had buddies back home, shallow connections with people he never actually, sincerely connected with on any deeper level than the flimsy bonds of shared childhood experience and custom. This was something different.

Ben still recognized that Trent and Rodrigo had a special bond, the kind that usually only grows after a lifetime of friendship, or between twin brothers. But even so, he never felt *left out*, as some people their age easily can. This bond between the three of them went beyond trivialities. It was created by something dark and dangerous they faced together, something no one else in the world would believe if they tried to convince them. The basis of this particular bond was the collectively shared reality that their lives or their minds, potentially both, depended on what they did next.

As he lay there staring up at the ceiling, Ben realized that for the first time in his life he was really, truly part of a team. *That's all well and good*, Ben thought, and it surely was, but all that really meant now was that he needed to come up with a plan. A *good* plan.

CHAPTER 22

THE ALPINE lake that the boys had all been so smitten with several weeks earlier—the location of their first night sleeping in the wild—had not lost any of its sheen, or become any less beautiful. They had spent most days hiking around these mountains since that first night, fishing and trapping and sitting cross-legged on the ground as the counselors lectured them on self-control and discipline. However, they had not recently been this high up in altitude, above the tree line.

The landscape had changed a bit. There were no more snowdrifts on the far end of the lakeshore, or any more ice runs along the edges of the boulder and scree fields. The heat of the summer sun and the afternoon rainstorms had seen to the demise of any vestiges of winter in the high country that happened to survive into the late spring, with the exception of a few ancient glaciers here and there. Wildflowers had started to pock the landscape as well. None of the twenty-eight boys in the summer class of Bear Springs Academy ever thought they would be awestruck by flowers. Yet here they were, most of them in a teenage-boy version of silent reverence as they gazed across the alpine meadows filled with bluebells, lupine, and Indian paintbrush.

Several of the counselors pointed out these differences in the natural world to the boys. Ben ingested their remarks and cataloged them away, as he had with every word spoken by every person within earshot throughout this summer, but he was seeing something else. Something different, in addition to the organic benchmarks of a season's high time.

He was judging the steepness in different draws and drainages, taking note of how they looked from afar on their approach and then comparing them to what he saw when right up close. He was thinking about water sources, passable saddles in ridgelines, making mental notes about which kind of ground cover was the loudest and which the quietest to walk upon.

Ben was thinking about his escape.

The boys were encouraged by the camp staff to maintain a journal and had been given nice leather-bound journals upon their arrival, as well as a stick of glue to add in pictures and packing lists and other mementos of their summer in this place.

The afternoon before the group set off on this six-day backpacking trip—shortly before pushing Jimmy into the strange glitch mode so as to showcase the freakish nature of the situation to his friends—Ben had snuck into one of the offices in the lodge. He did not find anything hugely substantial with respect to the odd nature of the place, like a phone or a gun, but he did find a large topographical backpacking map of the area, several folding knives, a bag of road flares, and a big can of bear spray with its belt holster, all of which he'd hidden away within his gear. He'd also snuck up the massive stairs in the entrance of the lodge and tried the large double doors at the top, finding them so securely locked that neither even gave a millimeter of ground.

Ben had cut the topographical map into smaller sections that fit into the pages of his journal, which he'd glued in meticulously the afternoon before.

Now, lying in his small one-man tent on the side of that lake, as a dozen other boys were using their headlamps to journal their experiences or read one of the paperbacks taken from the library in the Great Hall, Ben studied the map closely, marking routes and locations from memory that he could be certain were correct, all of which led toward Kaniksu Creek, which tumbled down from the monstrous causeway that led up, and ever up, toward d'Oreilles Pass and the freedom beyond. By the time he fell asleep, he had also identified four different downhill routes from Bear Springs basecamp, if that ended up being where he'd need to make his escape from. Ben made sure that each of these routes would lead him to the state highway that was several miles away, and that they kept a wide berth from the desolate county road that ran through the densely timbered landscape on its way to camp, where counselors likely would be patrolling in vehicles once his absence was noticed.

There were around five more weeks before the boys would be going home. But before going home, each of the boys was expected to go on a *solo night*, which represented the final step—the final, therapeutic threshold to cross—of this entire program of self-mastery and discipline. Ben felt confident that this *solo night* was when something would happen to him, to all the boys here, like all the boys who'd ever graduated from Bear Springs. Like Jimmy, Jessie, Pete, Michael, and the rest. It was the only thing that made sense, the only time in the entire summer when an individual boy was alone, completely separated from the larger group.

The counselors had started talking more often about this *solo night* during hikes and dinners, and across the campfires. They spoke of this experience with a level of piety and veneration that made Ben's skin crawl. They talked about how during the last two to three weeks of the program, boys would start being selected to carry out their *solo nights*, once the counselors deemed the individual boy fit, ready, and finally able to approach this last gauntlet of temperance and maturation. Sometimes, if someone was *really special*, they got selected for their *solo nights* even earlier than that. This factoid was divulged by the counselor Riley to the exhausted, grunting group of boys during the last mile of a particularly arduous day hike the week before, as though he were a parent coaxing good behavior from a child to avoid receiving a lump of coal from Santa.

Ben packed his bag the next morning with eyes groggy from an erratic night of sleep. The boys were made a breakfast of oatmeal and dried fruit, and then set off toward the pass above the alpine lake, officially casting off into uncharted mountain territory they had yet to explore. By late morning, most of them were dragging their feet and sporting dark sweat stains under their arms with T-shirts that sucked into the skin at each point of contact with their large packs.

The counselors had selected a spot for lunch on the other side of the pass—another stunning alpine lake that looked almost as if it were dyed a rich baby blue. When they arrived, the boys dumped their packs and collapsed like bags of bricks into the fine gravel and tall grass that made

up the lakeshore. Some of the boys were only down for a few minutes before springing into action when Mitchell shouted out to the group that
this was a great lake to catch brook trout in. The information triggered
a frenzy of action from those in the group who'd become enthusiastic
anglers, Trent being one of them. The dozen or so boys among this demographic raced one another to see who could put their rods together,
set up their reel and line, and tie a fly on the fastest. Ben and Rodrigo
remained on the bank with the rest and watched.

Ben, Trent, and Rodrigo had not discussed what they'd witnessed
in their cabin the night before they left, nor had they carried on any
discussion of their escape. Ben had been watching both boys closely
since then, and figured it was best to give them some time to digest and
ponder the new reality they faced. The new reality that fought against
that little bit they held on to as natural law in this world. Brainwashing
or human programming was a largely foreign concept to thirteen-year-
old boys, with the extent of exposure to such subject matter in movies
or television shows. It was a whole lot to take in.

A good number of brook trout were indeed caught in that blue lake,
and Mitchell used a small measuring tape to determine the dozen or
so that were legal to keep and eat for dinner that night. The boys had
become rather adept at gutting trout at this point, which they did under
the watchful eye of a counselor who lent them a small pocketknife to
complete the task, before wrapping them in cellophane and putting
them in a cool, dark part of their packs for later.

The group devoured a meal of freeze-dried macaroni and cheese as
Reid and one of the other counselors rapped on about the first leg of a
journey being important because of something having to do with *laying
a foundation for yourself*, and before any of the boys were truly ready,
they hoisted their massive packs and continued their slog into the sharp,
granite mountain range.

That night they camped in a large meadow, within a ring of gnarled,
old lodgepole pines that were considerably stunted because of the re-
lentless environment at this high altitude. This was explained to the
exhausted group by the counselors as they shoveled a meal of small
chunks of grilled trout fillet over more freeze-dried food into their

mouths around a large campfire with the feeble backpacking sporks they had been equipped with.

In his little tent that night, Ben again studied the map he had glued into his journal, marking their progress on this trip thus far and then surveying their potential route for the upcoming day—something none of the counselors had readily divulged, nor any of the boys asked about. To them, it was just another steep ruck, another trudge in the mountains in a summer filled with the same. Ben wanted to know, and he wanted to keep track of the various routes that led away from the trail he supposed they would most likely be taking, and their relation to the creek, glacier, and pass the old Bear Springs student advised he use for escape. Ben was not sure why he trusted the navigational suggestions of a boy who'd given them over one hundred years ago, but he did, wholeheartedly. This guy left a warning for another boy he knew would be reading those long-neglected books. This guy left a warning *for Ben.*

The next morning they encountered their first group of other backpackers. Three women, clad in similar trendy outdoor gear to their own. These ladies stepped to the side of the path and smiled at the group as the boys passed them by, the counselors exchanging pleasantries with them as they went. Ben looked at their faces closely as he passed them. Their smiles were so genuine. He felt something close to awe as he considered the fact that they *chose* to do this, they *chose* to traverse these steep mountains as a recreational activity. He thought about how crazy it was to *actually plan* something like this out, volitionally. He wondered if these women actually paid real money for childcare or dog sitters so that they could do this of their own free will. It was mind-boggling to him. Ben knew this place was beautiful, he knew the scenery was nice, but after almost two months, he couldn't fathom ever wanting to do it again.

That afternoon the group saw their first grizzly bear.

It was hundreds of yards away, halfway up a large ridge that shot up to the left of the trail they were on. Despite the distance it was still exciting for all of them. On their various outings accomplished thus far in the summer, the groups had seen deer, elk, mountain goats, bighorn sheep, two large bull moose with bulbous antlers covered in summer velvet, and one small black bear about the size of a large dog. *This* one was different. They'd long been eager for an encounter with this beast of a predator they'd heard so much about.

They all took turns passing around several pairs of binoculars the counselors carried in their packs. When Ben got a look at the animal through the optics, what he first noticed was the massive size of the bear's shoulders as it flipped over rocks larger than him with ease. The bear did this with a dozen large rocks in a row, licking at the bugs and larvae underneath. Ben could picture the worms, grubs, and ants going about their business in what had always been their safe, cool, dark little haven before having their sky torn open. He could imagine them as they fell into a state of terrified chaos and tried to rescue their eggs or writhed and skittered to escape the tongue of the giant beast.

An hour or so later they were working their way up a mercifully relaxed grade in a massive, wide valley. A babbling stream trimmed with blueberry and coniferous bushes flowed down to the left of the trail. Several boys chirped back and forth at one another whenever a small cutthroat trout was spotted. Flat glades and meadows filled with wildflowers terraced both sides of the large drainage all the way up to where the grass gave away to rocks that surged up to form the boundaries of the natural stadium. The light of the late afternoon cast a warmth on everything around them, turning even the most mundane gray lichen on rocks into a pleasing color.

The counselors began pointing up toward a spot maybe a half mile ahead in the massive expanse where the ground leveled out into a large meadow next to a stream where small groves of oxygen-starved aspen trees grew. They announced that it was the camping spot for the evening before offering a smattering of encouragement. *This is the last leg, fellas,* and *come on guys, last push of the day.* It was so fucking unnecessary, Ben thought.

He was staring at the trail a few feet in front of him, subconsciously planning out the best place to plant his aching, sweaty boot for each step. His attention was pulled up when he heard one of the boys ahead in the single-file marching line shout a question he could not discern. A few seconds later, one of the guys a couple of people behind him asked loudly, "Yeah, who is *that* guy?"

Ben looked up ahead and, at first, wasn't sure what he was seeing. The group came to a natural stop on the trail as more inquiries were shouted, and Ben could see what it was now. There were four horses, or mules. Ben could not tell the difference. They were tethered together, heading down a section of trail toward them that bowed away from their line so that the surprising procession was all in broadside view to the group. The three horses in the back appeared to have large bundles of gear strapped to their back, while a man rode on the horse at the front of the line.

The counselors ushered the group off to one side of the trail so that the man and his mule train could pass. Reid stood up on a grassy knoll on the other side of the trail from the boys, around the midpoint of the line of boys and counselors, and addressed the group in his flowery, didactic manner.

"That, gentlemen, is Mr. Rickert. He is a Montana state game warden who has worked in these mountains for a very long time, longer than any of you have been alive! Game wardens are like police officers, but they have a very specific mission, which is to protect the fish and game throughout this beautiful state. They make sure there aren't any poachers out here illegally killing the animals, and that people are following the hunting, trapping, and fishing regulations. Also, if a bear or wolf or mountain lion attacks or kills a person, Mr. Rickert up there is the one they call upon to track it down to trap and relocate it, or kill it if necessary. If any true mountain men are left in this world, Mr. Rickert is certainly one of em!"

Ben could see the man more clearly now. He had a beige wide-brimmed cowboy hat. A badge was pinned to the breast of his long-sleeved button-down shirt that was once perhaps a vibrant red but now something much flatter and duller, the color having been tortured away by years of sweat, salt, and the power of the sun itself. This shirt was tucked into pants covered by battered leather chaps, the color and consistency of which almost matched the skin of his face perfectly. He had a large mustache that hung down well below the edges of his mouth, and short salt-and-pepper hair barely visible under the hat.

He was not a particularly large man, smaller than Reid, and he was wiry and ropey. He looked strong. His forearms exited the folded cuffs of his shirt below the elbow and looked like they were carved out of wood. His fists were gripped around his horse's reins and saddle horn with knuckles the size of walnuts. He could have been thirty, or sixty, Ben really was not sure.

None of these features stood out to Ben, however. He took them all in at a glance. What caught Ben's full attention, once the man was close enough, was his eyes.

Long before Ben started to become aware that his aptitude to read, predict, and manipulate adults far exceeded that of his peers—or anyone he'd ever met, really—he had concluded that an adult's eyes were the most fundamental vector for evaluation.

Other information could certainly be gleaned from a grown-up's attire, the way they held their shoulders or spoke, an old injury perhaps, but most of these differentiae were superficial. They could be faked or fronted. These cosmetic elements of an adult's appearance sometimes helped Ben establish a color palette but were, taken individually, of no real use in frisking someone for their invisible blades—their true nature.

The eyes were where the *real* prospecting went down. Someone who is scared, lying, fucked-up, traumatized, someone who wants something from you, someone who wants *to do something to you*—each kind had a look in their eyes that Ben had categorized over the years. Doing so had been natural for the boy. It had been a defense mechanism, and he'd often, very often indeed, been right about what kind of person the eyes revealed.

But Ben had never seen eyes like this man's before. He was not sure where to even begin as his brain starting churning through different potential categorizations.

Maybe he had the eyes of someone who carried a horrifying piece of information that could only be shared in a language no one spoke anymore. It could be that they were the eyes of someone being punished with life—someone whose ability to die wasn't just stolen, but destroyed. Perhaps these were the eyes of a man who had met God but found the experience tragically disappointing.

Ben was overwhelmed by his own imagination, and shook his head as though he were clearing the scribbles from an Etch A Sketch. He wasn't sure what category of man had these eyes. He did come to one conclusion, though. He was confident these were the eyes you'd see on a man who—after weighing and rejecting all possible alternatives—had finally realized that killing you was not just the best option for him, but also the *right thing to do.*

And his eyes were locked on Reid.

Reid smiled back at him. It was that same smile, the one that had sent Ben into a fit of howling, biting panic twice before.

"Say hello to Mr. Rickert, gentlemen! Mr. Rickert, meet the Bear Springs Academy summer class of 2023!"

Reid did not take his eyes off Rickert's face as he used both arms to gesture toward the group on the other side of the trail from where he stood with his mocking, theatrical manner. The man did not even glance at the row of boys and counselors on the other side of the trail as he began to pass them. He just stared ahead at where Reid stood on the little knoll on the other side of the trail. Ben looked up the row and watched as all the boys stared up at Rickert with awe, wonder, and even some surprise. Even Billy stared up at the man with round eyes and a mouth slightly ajar. Several boys shouted questions at him, *what's the biggest bear you've killed,* Ben heard. A few others asked questions or shouted dumbass comments about the large revolver the man wore on his belt and the lever-action rifle holstered in a leather sheath on the right side of his saddle.

At the same time, Ben watched the six or seven other counselors ahead of where he stood in the line not only look away from the man as he passed, but something more than that. Riley stared at his feet and squeezed his eyes shut. One of the counselors, Devin, recoiled a few steps as Rickert's large horse passed him. Pete took a step away from him as he passed and began to raise his hand to his face, as one might when standing too close to a burning car finally beginning to flare up, or a loudspeaker bursting a teakettle shrill of interference.

Mitchell was only a few people ahead of Ben, but unlike the rest, he held his gaze up at Rickert's face as he rode down the line. Like he was playing chicken with a man who didn't even acknowledge his existence.

Ben watched as Mitchell's shoulders tensed and hands squeezed into white-knuckled fists. His entire body appeared to begin shaking. As Rickert's horse got to within ten yards of Mitchell, the counselor turned away from him abruptly and took several steps on shaky legs toward the creek, stifling a coughing fit with his fist. None of the other boys—too enamored with this magnificent cowboy, this real-life lion hunter—noticed, or the way Mitchell let out a long, jittery exhale through clenched teeth with drool running down his chin.

Ben looked back up at Rickert, whose expression had not changed at all, and who had yet to look away from Reid's smiling face. Reid had no such reaction to the man's presence. He did not change his attitude at all as he told several of the boys shouting questions about predators and guns to *pipe down* in a friendly voice, then spoke to Rickert loud enough for all to hear.

"Mr. Rickert, can you tell the guys a bit about what you're doing up here this time of the year? Are you monitoring the elk herd in their summer range as hunting season approaches? They'd love to hear a bit about your work!"

Rickert reached the elevated position on the side of the trail where Reid stood. They were almost eye to eye. Instead of turning his head to hold Reid's smiling gaze and carry on this bizarre staring contest as he passed by, he looked down and spit a small, white dart of phlegm into the trail below Reid's feet, then glanced back into the counselor's eyes briefly before staring ahead again, gazing down the trail.

Rickert reached out to his right, taking up the slack in the leather strap that ran between somewhere on his horse's saddle to the mules following behind. Ben was wondering why the man had done this just as the first mule passed by where Reid stood. When it did, it let out a piercing whine and jumped forward a pace, kicking its back legs out behind it, causing the other two mules behind to do the same. Ben could see the eyes of the mules go wide, white, and wild in that moment. The canvas-covered cargo loaded on the backs of the three animals jostled loudly, and the commotion sent a clutch of the nearest boys scampering backward a few spaces, a few even yelping in surprise.

It seemed Rickert had anticipated the animal's fright—just as the mule screamed and jumped, he hauled on the line he had taken up the slack of a second earlier. He made a few loud clicks with his tongue that seemed to echo around the valley, calming the animals down back into their original cantering pace. When they did, he let the line fall from his hand again.

Rickert's voice was like hot gravel. It was like one of the rockslides the boys had traversed over the last several days—the rockslides that ground, cracked, and smashed together in the violent winters this high up when no humans were ever actually within earshot.

"Wilderness boundary's a few hun'rd yards up. I find any traps or snares in there I'm comin for ya."

Reid's chummy smile broadened even more. He put one hand on his hip and waved a finger at Rickert's back with his other as he responded.

"Don't you worry about that, Mr. Rickert. We always follow the trapping rules and regulations, and know it isn't allowed within the wilderness area. *Isn't that right, fellas?*"

This elicited a number of dejected, drawn-out *yeahs* from a large portion of the boys. The counselors had indeed already told the group that they'd be spending several days of this expedition in a federally desig-nated wilderness area where there was a prohibition on trapping, which came as a great disappointment to many in the group who'd grown fond of the pastime, and even more fond of the rabbit and squirrel pelts they sought to take home as trophies.

Reid looked down the row behind him and shouted again for all to hear, waving his arm above his head as he did.

"Alright, guys, everyone say *thank you for your service, Warden Rickert!*"

Most of the boys did so, in a mixed chorus composed of both mumbles and shouts. Ben saw Reid hop down back onto the trail in his periphery and could hear him clap a few times and shout some directive to the other counselors and boys about getting back into line on the trail once the man had passed. He could see the group begin filing back onto the trail behind the last mule and hear excited chatter among the boys.

Ben just stood there motionless in his spot toward the back of the row, thumbs hooked into the shoulder straps of his massive pack, leaning forward a bit to balance its weight onto his trunk, his full attention again harnessed by Rickert's face, and his eyes still staring down the trail.

As Rickert was only a few feet from Ben, he glanced quickly into the boy's eyes, then began to look away for only a fraction of a second before doing a double take. As their gaze locked, the man's eyes narrowed slightly as the boy's went wide. Ben felt something immense as they locked eyes. Something new. Competing feelings blended into a strange emotional surge.

It felt like fitting the correct Allen wrench into the drive cap of a screw after trying several that were too large or too small. It felt like spinning a T-shirt around that you'd accidentally put on backward. Ben also felt the surprising urge to scream, to shriek a thousand questions, to demand he tell the boy what he knew about Reid and about this program. Perhaps the man with those killer's eyes read these feelings in the boy. Ben could not be certain of that. However, Ben was certain that he saw him issue a single, almost imperceptible shake of his head just as he looked down over his right shoulder at the wide-eyed, exhausted boy.

Then Rickert lifted his head and stared back down the trail. As he did this, he reached up and pulled the brim of his hat down a bit over his eyes without dropping the reins he held in the same hand. Ben watched him go until one of the counselors clapped his hand on his back and said something to the effect of *let's go, buddy, just a few more minutes until we reach camp.*

A short time later the group was setting up their tents among the altitude-stunted aspen trees in the large meadow along the stream they had seen earlier from down the valley. Ben made sure to wait until the others had claimed spots so that he could pick one on the outskirts of the group, as he usually did. The group assailed the counselors with a torrent of questions about Mr. Rickert as they did this; what kinds of animals he'd hunted, details of the gunfights he'd been in with poachers, what kind of gear he was carrying, that kind of stuff.

Reid said he figured Mr. Rickert would be setting up camp in some area a couple of days away, where the elk live this time of the year, and where he'd seen Mr. Rickert camped before. He explained that game wardens in several different parts of Montana would set out this time of the summer to spend a few weeks watching the elk herds while they were still in their summer ranges above tree line, shortly before they'd start breeding. He explained that hunting guides and individual elk hunters would often do the same, heading up in the mid to late summer to scout their hunting unit and find the biggest herd bulls to target during the upcoming hunting season that would open in September. Mitchell added a comment to that end, something about how *when hunting season is getting close and hunters start watching the animals, game wardens need to already be a step ahead.*

By the time the counselors were cooking dinner it seemed like at least half of the boys had openly proclaimed that they intended to become game wardens when *they* grew up.

That evening they actually ate quite well. Steaks, potatoes, veggies, and a salad. Several of the counselors had hiked up here a few days ahead of the group and hung a large cache of fresh food cooled by dry ice in the only tree in the area tall enough to do so—one of the aspen trees that lined the glade and boasted one strong branch fifteen feet or so off the ground.

The boys went about their usual work of dragging rocks, stumps, and root balls around the *fire circle* for chairs and places to eat. One of the boys who'd become one of the most popular among the counselors and kids alike—a kid named Greyson, from somewhere in New Jersey where the accents still grew strong—always put a great deal of effort into this project, expending completely unnecessary energy to construct a throne of a chair with armrests, a large back, and often even a footrest. Goading him on through this process was always a source of entertainment for many of the boys.

When Greyson finally sat back into his stone-and-aspen-branch throne with his plastic plate of food, the counselor Devin chided him for the whole group to hear.

"Greyson, you didn't get any veggies at all, man. You make this whole dinner throne, and only enjoy one part of the dinner!"

Greyson looked down at his plate and poked at the single quarter of baked potato that sat next to his steak.

"You gonna tell me this spud ain't a veggie, Dev? Eh? You gonna sit theh with a straight face n'tell me it had a family and a motha a'somethin?"

The boys and counselors alike all erupted in laughter at both the boy's joke, and his strong New Jersey accent, which always helped amplify the value of the former. A truly happy air hung above the group this evening as they dined in the mountain summer twilight. This was Ben's favorite time of day in the mountains, his favorite light. It turned all the granite spires, faces, and peaks of the mountains that hugged all sides of the valley from their usual slate gray into purple and deep pink colossi.

"Is it another bear!?"

All the boys looked up at that question, unsure who asked it, or why, but all saw Reid standing a few yards from the fire staring through binoculars down the valley they'd hiked up that afternoon. A few boys even set their food down and jumped up toward Reid, asking to use the binoculars to see it. Ben followed the counselor's line of sight and saw a small, orange flicker cutting through the evening's dying light. Reid patted the air as he shook his head, smiling.

"No, no bear, fellas, just a campfire. Looks like Mr. Rickert decided to set up camp for the night just down the valley a bit."

Ben's heart rate quickened. Many of the boys seemed even more eager to get a look at this through the binoculars than they had been for the bear. This brought another onslaught of questions and enthusiastic declarations from many of the boys about what *they* would do once they were game wardens.

Ben made a conscious effort *not* to express much interest in Mr. Rickert. Instead he focused on finishing his meal, and on the gleam of the game warden's small campfire. It looked as though it was in an area only a few hundred yards from where they'd run into him, in a small meadow on the other side of the trail from the stream. Ben could just barely make out the four dark masses he assumed must be the man's horse and mules. Ben finished his meal, wiped his plate clean in the stream with a clump of dead grass, stashed it into his pack, and went back to the fire. He sat on the dirt in front of the large rock he'd lugged over, stretching his legs out in front of him and leaning his back on the stone.

Physiologically, Ben was truly exhausted.

This was abnormal, at least in the eyes of all the others. While Billy was usually the first one to go to sleep as soon as he was done eating,

Ben was always in the last group of nine or ten boys sitting around a campfire. These were the guys who would willingly stay there feeding the fire and bullshitting until morning if the counselors didn't eventually have to command this group to go to their tents to get some rest. Not this evening, though.

During lulls in conversations with the other boys, he would stare past the fire down the slope toward Mr. Rickert's camp, then after a minute or so his eyes would drift closed, his arms would go limp, and his head would sink forward. He'd yank it back up a second later, sniffing and blinking, then laugh at bit at his own expense when two or three of the boys would tease him for the head fake, asking if he was a *sleepy little boy*. On the third time he did this, even Reid joined in with some good-natured teasing, as he often had done with other boys displaying signs of exhaustion throughout the summer.

"B, I know you don't like to miss out on campfire time, but maybe tonight you turn in a bit early, my friend. Tomorrow's another long day, and you've got a comfy bed just waiting for ya."

Ben rubbed his eyes with his palms as he nodded.

"Yeah . . . yeah, I'm callin it."

Several of the counselors and boys said good night to Ben as he stood. Ben gave a lazy, mock salute in response. He caught Rodrigo looking at him from several spots down to his right. Rodrigo had one eyebrow raised and a small ghost of a grin. Ben did not return the grin; he just turned and yelled back at the group as he walked toward his tent.

"Don't piss on my tent again, Marcus."

The group erupted in laughter at this throwback reference to a camping expedition earlier in the summer when the gangly, car-thieving kid from California had mistakenly pissed onto the rain fly of Ben's tent in the middle of the night.

Ben climbed into his tent, leaving his boots on, and turned on his headlamp as he did every night he slept in a tent in order to read. He turned it off only four minutes later and lay back on top of his sleeping bag with his hands under his head.

Physiologically, Ben was truly exhausted.

But Ben had walked through most days of his life dealing with some

combination of sleep deprivation, hunger, low blood sugar, or dehydra-
tion. Often enough, all four. Ben was exhausted, but he was not actually
ready to sleep. Not by a damn sight.

With the game warden camped just down the valley, just a short hike
away, Ben's mind and body buzzed with electricity and adrenaline. He
wasn't sleeping at all tonight. No, sir. After he heard the last counselors'
tent zippers zip, once he heard the cadence of teenage boys' snoring and
farts begin to hum steadily into the mountain air, Ben was going to pay
that man a visit.

CHAPTER 23

I T TOOK him around seventy minutes to get from his tent to where he now sat, crouched behind a large, flat boulder covered in lichen. He rested his palms against the stone, feeling the heat of the day still cooking off the rock despite it being well after midnight. He lifted his head over the top just far enough to see the small campfire crackling seventy yards ahead of him.

Ben had seen the game warden a half hour earlier sitting on one of the cargo bails he'd stacked along with his horse's saddle in a kind of horseshoe around the fire—all of which he'd relieved from the animals much earlier in order to turn them out to graze unencumbered overnight. Since then, Ben had not seen the man. He could not constantly keep his eyes on the game warden's camp as he traversed the alpine landscape between his tent and where he now crouched, but he had still grown a bit worried about Rickert's disappearance. Ben did not want to wake a man like this up.

Ben had thought it would only take him about forty-five minutes to creep down here through the grass along the trail, which he would need to do to avoid making any noise that would betray his little field trip. Getting out of his tent and away from camp was the easy part. There were twenty-eight boys and ten adults who'd been chugging water all evening sleeping up there. It was often the case on these nights out camping as a group that there was someone leaving their tent to take a piss every few minutes. However, even with the conveniently significant light of this night's near-full moon, it was slow going to ensure keeping quiet. Once he was closer to the man's camp, he also had to take fifteen

minutes to traverse around to one side so as to avoid passing through
the area where the horse and mules grazed. Ben was sure these kinds of
animals would act as sentries for their master in wild places like this.
He'd be truly disappointed if they didn't.

Ben wondered if the man had laid out a bedroll somewhere away
from the fire and gone to bed. The fire looked pretty well fed and lively,
so he doubted this, but he had read in one of those Louis L'Amour
novels something about *real cowboys* never sleeping that close to their
cooking fires, so as to either avoid or get the jump on any unwanted
company.

It was mostly open ground between the boy and the camp. Even with
the handful of other boulders and bushes that could be used as potential
hiding spots by someone Ben's size, he knew that he would be almost
entirely exposed on this last leg of the approach. Ben had already been
trying to psych himself up to close the distance for the last ten minutes
when he finally found the nerve to creep around the boulder and start
working his way toward the fire very, *very* slowly.

He had already gone over the monologue he'd open with, the case
he'd make for being down there and creeping into this man's camp, but
the adrenaline that ramped up now as he was so close made him forget it
all. The only thing occupying space in Ben's mind was every soft crinkle
or crack of dry blades of grass or disturbed pebble under his deliberate,
careful steps.

After what felt like an hour, but was actually only about two minutes, Ben crouched low behind a bush only twenty paces from the
fire, and about one pace from where the farthest fingers of its light
reached out into the darkness. His heartbeat thundered in his ears as
he frantically scanned the foreground and area around the fire, willing
the flames to blaze and surge just for a small bit of extra light to try to
find where the man was lying down. Ben's breathing stopped without
need of cognitive command when he saw the faint outline of one of the
mules or the horse beyond the fire snap its large head up from where
it was gnashing on the last dregs of a grass clump. It looked in his direction, straight at him, and froze. Its eyes glowed lightning-yellow in
the firelight.

Two or three very long seconds later, the other three animals' heads snapped up and locked on to him. Ben was no longer looking for the game warden. He was not even *thinking* about him. He was just frozen in place by the four pairs of eyes floating in the darkness beyond the fire, challenging him to come any closer.

"Chu want, boy?"

The first instant of the first syllable spoken by the game warden scared Ben so badly he whipped his entire body around *and* fell over the bush he'd been hiding behind in the same second. As he fell hard onto his ass and palms within the arc of firelight, the one graceful thing Ben did was to successfully prevent activation of his larynx. Even so, through clenched teeth, Ben blasted out all the air from his lungs that should have carried the scream into the darkness until it smacked into the dark rock Goliaths towering over both sides of the valley. He might've avoided the scream that would've awoken Reid and the other counselors, but the sound he replaced it with was no more dignified for the man standing only fifteen paces away from him.

Ben, his back now to the campfire, was staring at the dark outline of game warden Rickert. Fire danced in his eyes and off the badge on his breast. Ben put one palm up toward the man in a pleading gesture as he groped for words. A dread gripped Ben in that moment, one he hadn't actually considered until now as he watched the flames illuminate that badge. *This is a fucking cop*, Ben realized, *the ones who sent me here in the first place.*

The man stood in the center of the exact path Ben had taken into the camp, one boot on a cooler-sized rock that Ben remembered stepping over just a minute earlier. *Fucking ninja and a cowboy*, Ben thought.

He had what Ben assumed to be his lever-action rifle resting over one shoulder, which he lowered to where he held it casually at his side, then began walking slowly forward, coming into focus more as he approached the light. Ben did not get to his feet but pushed himself backward toward the fire with his heels and one palm, the other still raised in placation toward the man coming out of the darkness with fire in his eyes, his startled brain still raking itself over for the right words.

"S-sir, I'm sorry, sir. I-I needed to ask y . . . I needa talk t'ya, then I'll leave, aight? I ain't tryin nothin, I just needa to ask you somethin, then I'll leave, I swear t' tha lord.'"

Ben cringed inwardly as he heard the bayou accent on his words in full flush, ushered in by panic and fear as it often was. When the man reached where the boy was sprawled out, he did not slow at all, but just continued his casual stride past him toward the fire. Ben let his extended, pleading hand drop as the game warden passed him, and turned his body to watch Rickert lean his rifle against one of the large, canvas-covered loads he'd removed from one of the mules and set near the small fire. The man took a small piece of firewood from a neat stack he had set on the far side of the fire and sat down on the load where his rifle also rested. He leaned forward to place the small log into the flames, but before he did, he used it to point as he spoke without looking over at the boy.

"Go on n'set y'self in the dirt next to that pannier, but *not on it*, incase y'boss man gets inclined t'glass us fore we wrap up."

Ben understood enough of that to gather that he'd been instructed to sit beside the canvas-wrapped load of gear adjacent to where the man sat, in order to avoid being seen should Reid decide to look down here through his binoculars. Ben did this, and he did it very slowly. As he lowered himself into place, Ben froze and suppressed a shudder when he saw that the horse and three mules had moved toward the fire, crossing a large expanse of ground silently, without him noticing. They appeared massive where they stood side by side just outside its glow, all motionless, staring at him with their burning eyes.

Ben sat and wiped his hands off on his pants, plucking a piece of gravel that had become stuck in the calloused palm of one. He watched the man as he did this and arranged the opening of his monologue. He was about to speak when Mr. Rickert did, without looking over at him.

"What was it ya did to get y'self sent here? Don't bother fixin to lie now, cause I'll know if'n y'do."

The man set his eyes on to Ben's as he spoke those last words. Ben let a second pass, but only one.

"I ran off, stole a johnboat, took it out into the bayou. I hopped between fishin camps, kinda like what you'd call a cabin up here. Private getaways in the swamp folks use for fishin and huntin n'whatnot. Busted into em, lived in em for a day or two, n'went to the next. Finally ran outta food and camps to raid so headed back in n'knocked over a gas station with a fake gun, got picked up few minutes later. Didn't hurt nobody."

Ben didn't bother trying to justify his actions. He didn't think this guy would care to learn that Ben was trying to find somewhere safe to take his little brother, Wade, somewhere their aunt Nicki couldn't find them. Ben still didn't know how to read this man's eyes, but based on what he did have to work with, he figured straight shooting was his best course. For now, at least.

Rickert looked away from Ben after a long moment and back into the fire, where he continued to gaze as he spoke.

"Them scars on y'right arm there, up near y'elbow, y'daddy put them cigarettes out on ye?"

Ben was impressed by Rickert's power of observation and wondered for a second about where or how he'd acquired the unfortunate ability to identify this particular type of scar, but did not miss a beat in responding.

"Never met my daddy, sir. Momma said she didn't even know the names a'several fellas it coulda been that knocked her up. In the eight-odd years I knew her, she ain't never give me no reason to doubt that. Thems from my aunt Nicki, most of em at least, spose her boyfriends gave me a few as well. I got a whole bunch more in my collection under this shirt though, sir. Even a couple cigar burns up on the ol' shoulder blade. But as far as puttin a hard name on which came from who, well, sir . . . I lack sufficient information to do so, having acquired them during what I can only think to describe as a *hazy period* in my life. So, best I can do is say most these scars come from Aunt Nicki."

The man looked over at Ben, appearing at least somewhat amused.

That was good, Ben thought. He knew he was pushing it a bit, straying well into the realm of smart-assery was a bold play to start off with, but he needed to get down to brass tacks with this guy, get on the same level, and he figured he was talking with someone who liked to bullshit, or for whom the practice was at least not something foreign. Rickert had barely begun to form the sound of the letter *h* when Ben spoke over him, answering the question he knew was coming.

"I'm thirteen years old, sir. Born in New Orleans, February tenth.

Now, I can provide all the biographical information you'd like, and I'm more'n happy t'let this whole flirty repartee run its natural course, but I honestly believe that this here disciplinary program I've been roped into ain't what it seems and that I'm actually in danger, sir. In danger of what, I *cannot* really say, not in a way that makes any sense, at least. But I came down here this fine evenin to have a chat cause I reckon *you just might know* what kinda danger that is, sir. Or you might at least have some insight that could be helpful to me."

The amusement melted out of the man's features. Ben felt nervous, but the man didn't scold the boy, he just stared back at him with his haunting, stalker's eyes. Ben could hear himself swallow and was pretty sure this Mr. Rickert could as well.

"Sir, I seent the devil in your eyes when you stared down that man Reid. I seent the way those other counselors got all flinchy and vexed when you got near em, like they was mosquitas buzzin away from a citronella candle. Ain't never seen nothin like that before. I don't have much time to spare down here, sir. I ain't askin for you to give me a novel, I ain't askin you to share anything about yourself, I just think it's very probable that you have some kinda information that would be incredibly important to a shit-heel like myself in my particular situation in *this program* under the control of *that man*. So please, sir, just give me somethin I can work with."

Ben had laid his hand down, and he knew he had. This man was a law enforcement officer, one he'd never met, never even spoken a word to, and he'd just laid it all down. Ben knew this was risky, he knew it was bold, downright *fucking insane* really. But he also knew they shared that look on the trail. Something lived in that look, something nameless, but something real. Ben wasn't sure how, or why, but he was actually fairly confident Rickert had decided to set his camp up here in this spot because *he knew* Ben would come down to talk to him. Nothing he'd seen thus far undermined the broiling feeling in his gut that Rickert could help him, that he *wanted* to help him, which kept his nerves from fraying entirely under his icy gaze.

Rickert stared at him for a long time without speaking, then looked into the fire. He produced a paper and plastic bag Ben recognized as a pouch of tobacco and began rolling a cigarette without taking his eyes from the flames. The silence stretched out so long and birthed so much tension that Ben had to look away from him, staring back into the flames as well, letting the mood idle as the man considered the situation and what words to choose.

Ben watched as Rickert seemingly produced a match out of thin air that he struck on something Ben also could not see. The match fizzed loudly as he lit the cigarette. A thin braid of fine, coiled smoke marked the course of the spent match the man flicked into the fire. The man took a short drag of the cigarette but exhaled a jet of smoke from the side of his mouth that lasted so long it seemed impossible to Ben for human lungs to accommodate such a thing. Finally, the man spoke, and his voice was barely more than a whisper, but it still felt like Ben could feel its timbre in his guts and at the back of his eyes.

"Flinchy and vexed . . . as you put it. Them other counselors get all *flinchy and vexed* near me because . . ."

Ben was patient, but Rickert paused for so long that he almost prodded the man to continue, but stopped when he reached up and removed his hat, ran his forearm across his forehead, slowly placed the hat back over his thick shock of short graying hair, looked over at the boy, and spoke.

"They *know* that *I know* . . . what they really are. And lemme tell you somethin, boy, as soon as you know, as soon as you've seen them sons a'bitches for what they really are . . . *they'll smell it on ya forever.* You won't be able to hide it neither. It'll come offa you like heat offa wood burner, like stink offa shit. As soon as you've seen what they really are, you're as good as dead, bucko. They'll root you out n'tree ya like a pack a'lion hounds . . . and like a pack a'bay hounds, they'll keep ya tree'd until the houndsman comes to collect em, and *collect you.*"

Ben embraced the long pause between comments this time, trying to work out what he'd just been told, jostling it around his mind to make sense of it. The man's accent was new to Ben. It felt old, *very* old. Like some mixture of West Texan and Canadian, but neither at all.

"So, can you at least tell me what they are? I mean, are you tellin me th—"

This time Ben was the one to be interrupted.

"No. What I'm tellin you, boy, is this . . . soon as you see what those *counselors* really are, they'll know you've truly learned their little secret, no matter how hard you try n'pretend you haven't. That stink of knowledge'll waft right offa ya. The fact that you're down here rappin with me at all means you ain't seen em yet, it means you still have some doubts, some holes in your knowledge, all you gots is a theory on em that ain't all the way cobbled together yet. Now . . . *that's a good thing*, boy. You go and *keep it that way* as long as you damn well can. You don't need me tellin you nothin about em, don't go pushin the boundaries here. Seems your instincts already know something ain't right, and instincts are somethin a man outta just trust."

Adrenaline pumping, Ben could feel his heart pounding at the top of his throat. The weight of what he was being told, and the power of the man's voice, made the world feel like it was curling around the little campfire—like the whole planet was flipping inside out to form a little tent around where they sat, bathed in the light of only fire and the moon. Ben looked over at the warden again.

"How come you're still here then, if you've seen them? How can you know what they really are and not have em go after you?"

The man issued a humorless snort before answering.

"They have, son, oh . . . *they Goddamn well have*. But I ain't never been one a'their wards, and this is big country, this here's *my country*. They can't do nothin to me no more, or they juss gave up tryin, for now at least. I learnt em well on what happens when they go toe-to-toe with me, that ol' houndsman lost a *lotta dogs* fore he got learnt, too. But *you* . . . *you* ain't got time on y'side, son."

Ben sifted through the implications of what the man had just said, trying to home in on a single question among the hundred that roiled through his mind. Ben abandoned the effort when the man's voice cut through the air.

"What I can tell you is this, boy . . ."

The man produced a tarnished old flask seemingly from out of nowhere. He removed the cap and took a long, six- or seven-bubble swill. He placed the cap back on as he stared into the fire, tucked it away to his far side, then looked back at Ben.

"You get your shit in order to split, and when you do, you don't stop runnin till you're a *long ways off*. Get to a highway and rob a car, knock over another gas station, *get sent to prison* if you have to. The slammer'll be a damn sight better'n what they've got in store for you here. You do *whatever it takes* to make sure you ain't nowhere near this place when your number's called for the *solo night*. Steer well and fuckin clear a'this place before then. And *don't you go askin for my help*, because it would just be the opposite. I've gone down that road before, trust me, *you don't want it*. Like I said, I've seen what that ol' houndsman *really is* with my own eyes, so that piece a'shit dry-gulcher can smell me from *miles* away. Son of a bitch is teed up and revvin in tha red whenever I'm nearby, so don't go lightin off tomorrow, or even the next day. But next week, week after maybe, pack a bag, time it right, and *you skedaddle*, boy."

Ben felt like breaking down into sobs and laughing at the same time. He'd just been fed the most inane, cryptic diatribe of his life, but he didn't doubt a single word of it. Ben thought of what he already knew, of what he already had figured out. He thought of Carl and how he'd made Jessie, Pete, and Jimmy glitch out by asking about their parents. He pinched the bridge of his nose and squeezed his eyes shut for a moment before responding.

"Might already be too late, sir. I've already figured some of it out, I've already been pushin the counselors' little buttons, I know they're programmed or brainwashed or some shit, I figured out how to trigger em in a way. So, maybe it's already too late, maybe *they already know* that I know."

Game warden Rickert smiled then for the first time. It was not a kind smile. There was darkness in it. It reeked of condescension.

"Boy, trust me, if you're still here, if you hadn't beat cheeks yet, ain't no way you've seen what they really are. Believe me, till you seen em, the *real* them, you don't know *shit from Shinola*. You go and keep it that way too. Quitch your diggin around. You go on back up to camp and try to catch some z's before sunrise. You *can* get away, it's within your doin, but when you scoot you bess not stop scootin till you *know* you're outta the houndsman's reach. He can't do nothin to you permanent-like once you're outside a'his domain."

There was a conclusory tone in the man's statement. Something about it precluded any potential for further questions or conversation. Ben picked up on that, then stood on wobbly legs. Time bent back around him as he did this. It felt like he'd been sitting at that campfire looking into that man's eyes for weeks. The dark, moonlit valley whirled and snapped back into focus around him. Ben mumbled thanks to Rickert and started back the way he'd come. When he was at the edge of the firelight Rickert's voice pulled him around like a lanyard tied to his shoulder.

"You know the way back t'yer tent, boy? Can you get back in there undercover?"

Ben looked up the dark slope toward his camp, then back at the man.

"Yah, I'll get back in without gettin caught."

Rickert nodded from where he sat. Ben turned, and the man's voice brought his attention back once more. He stood as he spoke. He took a final drag from his cigarette before flicking it into the flames, hooking his thumbs in his belt loops, and planting one boot onto the spot his ass had just vacated.

"Boy . . . I gone and put a whole mess a'that houndsman's dogs in the dirt over the years as he sent em after me. Couldn't even put a figure to how many. Enough so that he juss finally laid off a few years back. Threw his towel in the ring, I spose. That bein said . . . I reckon he'll try again, ventually at least. And when that time finally comes, *I don't wanna see you in his pack, boy.* You hear me? Ain't got no prollem killin his hounds, just ain't fond a'puttin those down I knew fore they got broke. N'boy, *I know you now,* so don't make me do that."

Ben let a long breath out of his nose as he stared back at the strange man and the silver-rimmed outline of the mountains behind him. As Ben felt the mountain air, heard the distant breeze wheeze off the rocks on the mountains above, the gurgle of the mountain stream, the crickets, he also felt something very foreign to him. Ben felt a pride for where he was from. He was hit with longing passion for *home* that almost took his breath away. Longing for the cypress trees, the black-water swamps, the humid, heavy air, the deep, tragic, beautiful history that soggy, poisonous land had broiled into his blood. He let the Acadian accent flow and writhe into his voice now. For the first time, it was beautiful to hear it go unrestrained in his own voice. Every word he cooked the Cajun sound of his kith and kin into was empowering.

"*Game wah-den Rickert* . . . if I end up one a'his dogs, you do me a favor n'put me down. Strange thing to hear, you know . . . a savvy, keen, *dangerous* man like y'self, *in his own home*, walkin tru life with his back on tha ropes all these years? Standin by n'juss *watchin*, so long as it don't mess with y'own biness? Sounds to me like you been on defense a whole long while now, *wah-den Rickert*. Sounds to me like times come for a little *offense*. I'm juss startin t'see now though, *game wah-den*, it's big, *young* country like this . . ."

Ben gestured with both arms up toward the looming, dark mountains around him. He didn't care if anyone heard him now. His anger at this place, this program, these mountains, this cryptic cowboy motherfucker, it was boiling now, and he had to just let it dance and let his rage snarl into his words.

"Spose afta while, big, young country like this'll juss do that to a man. You can *ride away* in big open country like dis, you can *scampuh off* to better ground n'pick anotha day to fight. *Where I'm from*, that traipsin' off don't fly, not in *old country*. No suh. Where *I'm from*, y'backs *always against tha wall*, the sea eats the land away, tha trees n'swamps don't letcha run from tha fray, you gots t'face it. Only ground you got *you make a stand on*. Big country like this here, all this space, all these options, I'll be damned . . . it makes a man soft, *game wah-den*. It makes a man *yelluh*. The *majestic western cowboy*, it's all a farce. It's a sad, *sad* ting to see."

Ben let the words hang for a moment, then turned and started making his way up valley. Mr. Rickert did not say anything else to the boy.

It took Ben almost two hours and was close to 4:00 a.m. when he finally got back into his tent. He had to wait for a window between groggy, pissing boys to make his final move. Once he lay on his sleeping pad, after listening for signs of counselors alerted to his absence and return, Ben stared up at the orb that was the moon piercing through the yellow rain fly of his tent and let himself relax a bit. After a short while, sleep, and its nightmares, finally took him.

CHAPTER 24

BEN AWOKE after only a couple of hours of fitful sleep with a burning in his bladder that almost brought him to his feet all on its own. As was often the case when he awoke in a tent on some fucking mountainside in Montana, it took him a moment to realize where he was.

When that clarity came, Ben groaned, stuffed his feet into his boots, didn't bother lacing them, and unzipped his tent. He didn't check his watch, but the sun hadn't reached over the rocks of the ridge to their east yet. The gray wolf-light of predawn hung around the valley. Ben squinted around to see if anyone else was up, but it appeared as though everyone was still crashed out.

He plodded over to the stream and looked down the valley to where the game warden's camp had been just hours before, to find that it was gone. Horse, mules, all his gear, it was all gone, it was just an empty mountain meadow like all the rest that filled the valley. Ben wondered for a moment if he had dreamed the whole encounter. He couldn't hear his own piss cascading into the running water over the noise. It was also loud enough to drown out the clanking of flatware against the large cast iron pot that was being cleaned upstream.

Ben was about to turn around and head back to his tent to sleep until he was mustered up with the rest of the guys to continue on their death march, when he saw Reid, about fifty yards upstream from him. The man was kneeling over a cast-iron pot, half-submerged in the stream, scrubbing it with a small camping sponge. A halo of suds formed around the pot before being caught in the current and pulled down the valley. Ben knew it was Dr. Bronner's soap. He could gin up the smell of the stuff somewhere behind his eyes without actually smelling it. After months of it hanging on to everything in Ben's life, it had become an unwelcome aroma. It was made for backpacking, the counselors had told them all, and each of them was given a small bottle of it and told to use it to wash their hands, faces, bodies, and their dishes. It was good for everything, and *not bad for the environment*, they'd promised and repeated.

Ben was about to turn around, again, uninterested in interacting with Reid, with the *houndsman*. Movement cut Ben's turn short as something off to Reid's right caught his eye in the open ground on the other side of the stream from the man.

Ben's heart stopped when he saw what it was.

A grizzly bear plodded through the bushes into the glade across from Reid with its snout in the grass. It was larger than Ben had thought these creatures could ever be. It appeared bigger than the old Mastercraft motorboat that sat decaying on dirty cinder blocks in front of the trailer a few doors down from Aunt Nicki's. Jiggling shock waves flowed through its fat and skin every time it planted one of its drink-tray-sized paws into the soft earth. Ben could hear its snorting and snuffling even over the babble of the stream. The fur on its mammoth skull, shoulders, spine, and rump was the color of the old wooden floorboards in Ben's cabin. Its legs and belly were sodden and darker—soaking wet from what must have been gallons of dew it had picked up off the tall mountain grass it had trampled through this morning as it made its way into Ben's life.

The boy froze in place, wrenching his gaze back and forth between the beast and Reid, whom the bear was walking directly toward. Ben's first attempt to suck in the air necessary to scream a warning at Reid was hindered by a quivering bottom lip. This automatic, protective instinct to warn the man would bewilder Ben in the days to come, and the effort was quickly abandoned as he saw Reid's head jerk up and his eyes lock on to the bear.

The man and the bear were maybe thirty paces away from one another, with only grass, a few bushes, and the twelve-inch-deep stream between them. The counselors had made the boys watch a safety video at the beginning of the summer that mentioned the grizzly's ability to explode into a 35-mile-per-hour sprint. The bear could cover the distance between where he now stood and the man scrubbing the pot in two or three seconds.

The grizzly seemed to feel the man's presence before seeing him as it appeared to roll to a full stop like an old, manual-transmission jeep. It did not lift its head up. It did not open its mouth. Its snout and nose remained just a few inches above the grass it had been sniffing a moment before. Only its small, dark eyes rose under its heavy brows as they peered up and ahead to lock on to Reid's own. The bear did not actually move anything but its eyes, but Ben could see the animal slowly begin to tense. Muscle and bone definition appeared on the bear's shoulder blades. Between those two massive slabs standing five feet above its front paws, toast-colored fur rose straight up into the air.

After several long, tense seconds, the bear's bottom lip slackened from its jaw and slowly extended forward.

This simple gesture—the small protrusion of the grizzly's bottom lip under its dark, focused butcher's eyes—hit Ben somewhere deep in the gut. It sent a boiling-hot warning into some old, primal, nameless part of Ben's anatomy. Some tiny vestige of an ancient ancestor's trauma or hard-learned lesson that the DNA deemed worthy of bundling up and passing down through the progeny.

Ben had never seen a grizzly bear's face in real life, not once, but deep down he somehow already knew what that extended bottom lip meant.

It was a promise of forthcoming violence. It was a pledge to tear flesh and crack bones. It was an assurance of the beast's incapacity for mercy. The bear could've bared its teeth and bellowed an earsplitting roar, and that would not have been nearly as heinous or dire a warning.

In the same moment, Ben felt *and* heard the soft thunder and reverb of the growl that came from somewhere deep in the bear's massive chest.

This was it. Ben was about to watch Reid die. He didn't have to do anything. All he had to do was let this moment happen. This *perfect* moment. This bloody, perennial show that had played out so many times before throughout humanity's history in the untamed, wild parts of the world. It was a very natural thing, Ben realized, as he felt the bear's growl thrum in the back of his throat.

This bear did not care about the individual *life*. It would shred and thrash Reid's flesh and bones until it deemed the man's physical resistance sufficiently diminished so that devouring him would be a more casual, less fussy experience. That violent process—this bear's morning feed—it was as natural as any other thing in the world.

It was as natural as both the five-day-old and five-thousand-year-old rockslides in this valley; the scars, gouges, and rubble from each were still clearly visible from where Ben stood. It was as natural as the morning hatch of mayflies whose birth was fusion-induced by the first beams of sun from the east. It was as natural as the frenzied dance over the surface of the burbling stream at Ben's feet those same mayflies would dedicate their entire, brief, twenty-four-hour life span to.

Ben no longer needed to plan an elaborate escape plan through this harsh landscape. He just needed to do nothing. He just needed to watch as this beast smashed into the man, ripped him around until pinning him into the wet dirt and grass beneath its razor claws. Just watch as it crunched and splintered the man's forearms and rib cage with its viselike jaws. Just watch as it found the soft parts of the man's body to begin peeling open and feasting into. Just watch as the man's struggling was reduced to desperate grasps at the bear's face with broken fingers and gargled groans from blood-filled lungs. Ben just needed to watch this perfect, natural moment unfold. Nothing more.

Unfortunately for Ben, as he looked over at Reid—who still held the bear's gaze and hadn't stopped working the sponge against the grime inside the pot—he was reminded that the whole corpus of things he had thus far enshrined as *natural* was either in need of serious revision or had just been terribly flawed all along.

Ben fell to his knees, his bladder released, and he felt his ears pop and his teeth begin to twist in his gums as he watched Reid smile at the bear.

Ben forced himself to look away from the man and back at the bear, whose posture began to change. Its muscle definition slackened, its rump lowered toward the ground as its rear legs appeared to lose strength and begin to wobble. It tucked its massive head back into its shoulders, turning his snout slightly and looking away from the man's smile, fixing its panicked, darting eyes on some vague area in the bushes along the stream. Ben could not hear the bear's growling anymore. It had been replaced by a steady, canine whine. He could see the bear's head seized into a fit of small, fast shaking, almost like a vibration. Blood began to drip and stream out of the animal's nose into the grass and bead down its fur from the ears. Its whining evolved into a frantic, desperate whimpering that came from its lips and nose in unison with jolts and blasts of blood-pinkened globs of froth and spittle.

Ben looked at the muddy patch of riverbank where he'd collapsed on his knees to see hundreds of worms and stonefly larvae writhing and twisting on the surface. A flash of movement in the stream itself caught Ben's eye, and he saw a group of cutthroat trout smashing their own noses against the jagged, flat face of a large, submerged stone. Again and again they'd let the current carry them back a foot or so before blasting their silver bodies forward to connect their noses against the rock again at full speed. A filmy murk of thin blood and tiny scales surrounded the fish; several already floated above the rest, bleeding and twitching on the surface of the water.

The bear suddenly exploded into movement. As though it had been released from a trap, it stumbled and fell over itself as it moved backward and tried to turn its body around, unable to move its joints fast enough to escape and move away from the man crouched by the river. It fell over several times before finally gaining its footing and sprinting away from the stream and down the slope into the large, open meadow faster than Ben had thought any mammal that size could move. Ben watched the bear maintain its sprint down the valley until it went around a rocky fold in the highland landscape and disappeared.

Ben then looked up at Reid, who looked amused as he stared out toward where the bear had disappeared and dipped the pot into the river several times, taking care to rinse all the suds from all its surfaces. He used a small camping towel to wipe it dry, then placed the bottle of soap and the sponge in the pot, put the lid on it, and stood slowly. Ben watched him gaze out over the landscape with a pleased, satisfied expression, then take in a deep breath before turning and strolling back toward camp. Strength returned to Ben's body as the man walked farther away. Ben could hear him start to whistle some familiar tune as he disappeared into the trees and made his way toward the fire ring to start breakfast.

Ben tried to collect himself, letting his lungs slowly empty through a thin opening between his lips, then crawled, scrambled, and stumbled his way back toward his tent, grateful that the other boys were not up yet. Once back inside his small tent, he took his boots off and removed his urine-soaked pants, long johns, and underwear. He stashed them deep in his bag, replaced them with dry ones, then fell back onto his sleeping pad. He wiped his mouth and nose and found a smear of blood, unsure which orifice it had come from.

The insanity, exhaustion, and impossibility of the morning and night before twisted into a surge of rage, confusion, and fear that coursed through him like an electrical fire. Ben turned over, buried his face deep into the folds of his down sleeping bag, and balled his shaking hands into fists.

CHAPTER 25

LIGHTNING CRASHED into the boulder field like an artillery barrage. The counselors saw the afternoon thunderstorm coming, and then the boys did. White sheets and squalls of rain frenzied at every possible angle from beneath a contiguous band of furious black-and-purple clouds, blanketing the distant peaks and valleys. All the boys were commanded to ditch their packs and anything else conductive to electricity, then file into a large overhang below a rock outcropping. Here they were instructed to squat down, keeping the rubber of their boots below their bodies as the only points of contact with the ground.

The increased volume of crashing thunder and its metallic thrumming aftershock was not the only way to tell the storm was bearing down on them. Neither was the change in the light, which seemed to be slowly draining away from the expansive alpine steppe that they'd been traversing when they sought cover, replaced by a threatening, flat grayness. In addition to the wind picking up into gales and the wall of fine, stinging rain, the boys could feel the electricity on the backs of their necks. They could see one another's hair starting to stand up on end. When the storm finally reached them, the actual electric *zap* of a close lightning strike could be heard just before the earsplitting roar of its wrath churned from the atmosphere above.

Some of the boys were white-faced and terrified, hands clamped down over their ears with eyes squeezed shut. Some were whooping and cheering on the deafening fusillade of white fire that punched down into the landscape all around them. Some of the strikes were so close that they'd temporarily blind the boys, who'd then look down and frantically try to blink away the flash scars floating in their vision. Counselors issued confident declarations of reassurance and calm, only somewhat audible through the scream of the storm.

This all lasted about seven minutes. Eventually the electrical heart of the tempest had passed over them and the weather began to relax. Vibrance started to creep back into the light, the steady wind ratcheted itself down into mild gusts, and the rain became lighter, its angle more vertical. The decreasing weight of collective tension could almost be felt in one's shoulders as it lifted away from the group. Several of the boys openly thanked God, then tried to wipe away evidence of crying.

During the real blitzing peak of the storm, Ben had to resist a strange but powerful urge to run from cover into the killing grounds. He could see himself standing out there among the lightning strikes, arms spread wide, staring up into the sky. He was jealous of this fantasized version of himself, envious of his freedom.

Earlier that day, at the top of what was probably the gnarliest, steepest bit of mountain topography the group had climbed up at any point so far this summer, there was a several-hundred-foot cliff down onto a section of the switchback trail they had just taken. It was a sheer, granite face that almost appeared to have been belt-sanded. Each boy took their turn standing at its precipice as they reached it, feeling the rush of vertigo and adrenaline that pumped through them as they took in the view down, until Mitchell—the counselor who'd been stationed there to keep the procession of exhausted boys from falling off—kept each boy moving along.

When Ben had reached that point on the trail and was staring down that cliff, he also felt a new kind of peace, similar to that felt in the lightning storm several hours later. He saw himself jumping, screaming in defiance as he did, and likewise felt jealous of the falling boy, envious of his strong will and his liberation. When the world came back to him, when he was ripped out of his fantasy, he realized Mitchell was gently squeezing his shoulder, saying *let's keep moving, buddy.* Ben turned his head to look over at the counselor with cold, emotionless eyes. Ben saw concern flush into the man's face. He cast his dead gaze onto where the man's hand rested on his shoulder. Mitchell, slowly and reluctantly, removed his hand from the boy's shoulder, and repeated his earlier directive to keep heading up the trail, but this time more quietly, with a hint of concern behind the words. Ben looked back down the cliff, then turned and trudged up the trail.

Since watching the scene unfold between the grizzly bear and Reid, Ben had felt like part of himself had died. He thought, standing on that cliff, that it was his will to live that had died. Later in the day after not jumping, and after not running into the lightning storm, he figured it was actually some other part of his soul that had taken its last breath. Perhaps it was the part of a person that toiled with concepts like *tomorrow* or *the future*. Perhaps it was that part of a person that ginned up *the point* in doing things. Whatever it was—since pulling his face from his sleeping bag that morning and wiping the blood from his nose, ears, and gums—Ben could feel that some formless, nameless muscle within himself had expelled its final, shuddering breath.

The group reached their last camping spot of this expedition an hour after the lightning storm had passed. It was a meadow several hundred yards below a mountain pass still above the tree line but only several hundred yards above the highest fingers of the pine forests that rolled outward as far as one could see. From here, one could see segments of the nine miles of trail the group would cover the next day as it ran its way down the ridges and draws on its way back toward the upper reaches of the valley where Bear Springs sat.

Ben finished collecting, sawing, and stacking some firewood next to the stone fire ring being assembled by several other boys, then sat on a stump below his tent to await a meal that he desperately craved, but wasn't exactly sure why he should bother eating.

He looked up the impassable wall of scree and boulders that rose above the camp to the south where a large, dirt- and silt-covered glacier sat. Ben had been surprised earlier in the summer by how many of these glaciers were in this high country year-round, nestled into their dark, cool, north-facing crags. He could hear the glacier's lifeblood running in trickles underneath the field of rocks below it, on its way to form some nameless creek until it flowed into some stream, then some river, then some larger river.

He wondered how much water from this specific glacier would actually be left to fuse with the Pacific as it flowed into the final brackish stretch in some foggy, oyster-reeking estuary to the west. How much of it would really survive seepage and evaporation or avoid getting slurped up by an elk or some growling, rusty irrigation pump to be blasted out over a hot cornfield. He figured maybe a tablespoon per gallon of what he now heard trickling through the rocks would actually, *finally* pass over that muddy tidal reach and into the gills of salmon and sharks. He wondered how long this glacier had been sitting there. How many summers had this ancient thing shouldered the antagonizing heat as it oozed braids of frigid water until the planet entered a more merciful stretch of its course—until its season of ice, wind, and frigid darkness finally returned.

Reid's voice cut over the hum and clamor of boys, birds, and bleeding glaciers.

"Bring it in, guys, bring it in, I've got some special news to share."

Ben pushed himself up and stared down the endless expanse of rocks and trees for a few breaths. What he saw was beautiful, but even after all this time, it still felt incredibly foreign. Never before had he missed the bayou and its sounds and smells as he did in that moment. He felt it in his bones as he turned and followed the rest of the group up to the center of camp where Reid stood.

The counselors Mitchell, Freddie, and Devin flanked him and were, for some reason, wearing their backpacks. Off to their side, grinning with sheepish embarrassment, were three of the boys. The first two Ben knew, Marcus and Charlie. The other was a quieter kid named Dean. Dean was from some small timber town in southern Oregon that Ben had heard him describe once as only having half the population it had twenty years earlier, as well as being *rainy and methy*. Both had one thing in common, in Ben's mind at least: they were the two biggest brown-nosers at the program.

Everyone looked to Reid when he began to speak.

"Alright, fellas, now, as you know, when a young man's time comes to face the crucible of self-control and maturity, we, the counselors of Bear Springs, can see it. A lot goes into making that determination, for each and every one of you. And every summer, *every summer*, we get a couple early bloomers. By early bloomer, I mean a young man who has come such a long way, has displayed so much integrity, and fully committed to the mastery over their mind, their body, and their will, that they . . . *are ready for their solo night.*"

All ten or so of the counselors who'd been on the expedition—as well as the now-jolly, dim-witted Joe—erupted into raucous cheering and celebration. The counselors clapped Marcus and Dean on their shoulders. Freddie grabbed Marcus's backpack and gently shook him from side to side. Blushes on both boys' faces could be seen even through sunburned cheeks as they smiled with genuine pride at all the praise and congratulations.

It was contagious too. Some of the watching boys had wonder and even jealousy in their eyes as they watched the jovial celebration of these two boys' setting off to reach the final milestone of temperance, self-control, and manhood. More and more of the boys began to join in with enthusiastic clapping and whistles. Joe skipped through the group of assembled boys, wordlessly beseeching their participation by clapping and smiling in their faces.

As this excitement and spirit spread through the group, Ben watched with a growing sense of dread when this began to serve as some kind of fuel for the counselors. It seemed to boost their collective mood beyond elation and into something more like a state of fervid delirium.

Mitchell began jumping up and down like some receiver who just scored a fourth-quarter touchdown in the playoffs, neck veins bulging as he blasted out a long, continuous scream. Pete stomped down the row of onlookers, violently pumping both fists toward the ground and repeatedly screaming *let's go boys, let's go boys.* Riley paced in a circle, heaving, as he used every muscle in his upper body to clap, eyes squinted shut in a smile that seemed to show every single tooth. Devin covered his mouth and nose with tented fingers as he laughed hysterically, rocking back and forth with tears streaming from his eyes.

Reid leaned into the faces of the three boys being celebrated and began ranting something impossible to hear over the ruckus, speaking almost forehead to forehead, pointing into their faces like some boxing coach. They had tight-lipped smiles and serious, listening, dutiful wide eyes as they nodded back at Reid's seething words.

Ben's dread and disgust grew as he watched this scene unfold. This zeal he saw in the counselors was something rabid and carnal. They had, once again, gone totally febrile. The group's excitement, hope, and enthusiasm for these three boys—or for this final ritual—it was serving as some kind of somatic slop the counselors had been ravenous for. It was like watching a group of hogs bite, squeal, and grunt over a bucket of moldy silage and compost.

Reid continued his little speech, but Ben didn't listen. He didn't need to. He didn't know the boy Dean that well, but he'd gotten pretty friendly with Marcus over the last two months. He stared at the boy's face, feeling only pity and then actual scorn as he watched an ignorant, delusional fucking smile grow across Marcus's face. Despite his previous conceptions of how he'd handle this situation when it finally came, now that it had, Ben was a bit surprised to find that he didn't feel much of anything for these boys. He didn't feel the urge to scream out a warning of what was *really* about to happen to them, nor shriek out enlightenment to the group as to what was *really* going on here. And Ben didn't actually know, specifically, what was about to happen. All he knew was that it meant they'd be gone forever, that there wasn't a thing in the world he could do about it, and that it would mean his own ruin to try.

He scanned the group for Billy, whom he found sitting on a rock at the edge of the gathering, leaning forward with his elbows on his knees, staring blankly at the doomed boys. He then found Trent and Rodrigo standing side by side, a few feet in front of where Billy sat, both staring back at him. Unlike Ben, he could see in their eyes, clenched jaws, and balled fists a fiery desire to do something, a reluctance to just stand by and watch this happen.

Ben looked at them, saw their angst, their drive to act, to do the right thing. For the first time since he met them, all he saw in their faces was raw, unbridled stupidity. He despised the idiocy and the objective *goodness* he saw.

He knew they grew up poor and in rough places, had tough lives in their own ways, but he had also gathered over the summer that both boys were inherently good, kind, empathetic people who had never had prolonged exposure to *true* evil. They hadn't been beaten bloody, locked outside naked overnight in the rain, fed cat food, stomped on, burned, tortured, or humiliated by someone they trusted. They hadn't had someone do those things to them and then still wept, begged, and prayed for that same person to eventually love them.

They had *faith* left. They still believed in the ability to *overcome* evil. They still couldn't see that evil is like weather, that it's just something you try to sidestep and evade until it kills you or you die in some other stupid, shitty way.

He was truly disappointed to see that faith in their faces now. He was *angry* at them for it. Angry at the accompanying realization that he didn't have any of that spark left in himself. He wanted to scream at them for their altruism, berate them for wanting to help these other boys, for still holding on to that which was *right* or *good*.

What on earth do you two dumbasses think you can possibly do about this? Ben pondered, screaming the questions in his own head. *What ridiculous, pointless, moronic action do you think we could we take right now that would make any fucking difference at all?*

Ben's emotions must've shown on his face. Lines of subtle confusion and surprise formed between both boys' eyebrows as they gazed back at him. Trent's head even cocked to the side a bit.

Ben shook his head slowly a few times in response to their looks, which appeared to only amplify their confusion at his resigned reaction to this scene—to this execution—unfolding before them. Ben saw Billy turn his head to look over at him from where he sat behind the other two, and he stared back into that boy's violent eyes with the same icy, contemptuous glare.

Reid had reached some benchmark in his banal monologue that prompted the group to begin cheering and applauding again, with even more participation from the boys this time.

Ben watched as a subtle, knowing grin spread across Billy's face. There was vindictive satisfaction in his smile. He smiled like a man who'd just coaxed a murderer into admitting that it wasn't just convenience motivating him to kill, but other, sinister things that giggled and shrieked in the darkness of your soul. Ben felt real hate for Billy surge into his guts as he watched the large boy rise and join the rest of the group, slowly clapping his two massive palms.

Billy did not look away from Ben. The group might have been applauding the pair of boys and this wicked ritual of their demise, but Ben knew Billy was applauding *him*. Billy was applauding the birth of a compatriot, another fatalist survivor. Billy was celebrating the death of Ben's idealism, and the disdain he'd just seen in Ben's eyes for the same in others. Ben hated him for it. He hated himself for it.

Ben held Billy's gaze as he uncrossed his arms, let a broad, empty smile spread across his face, and as he cast his eyes forward again, he began to clap as well.

Trent and Rodrigo looked between Billy, Ben, one another, and the group around them until something quietly and tragically began to dawn on them.

Trent and Rodrigo would not have described it in this way, but through Ben's eyes, Billy's eyes, and the maniacal display before them, they had just realized—perhaps for the first time—that there were actually certain moments in life when, for oneself, *doing the right thing* is just an absolutely horrible fucking idea, no matter the cost to others. They were confronted by this fact that, sometimes, maintenance of one's own personal continuity doesn't just require *not* doing that which one knows to be right or good, but also requires releasing your grasp of the concepts of *right* and *good* altogether. Letting them wither and die like a neglected houseplant.

For those who truly fail to understand that which is right and good in the face of evil, *doing nothing* isn't actually a choice. For those who do, it *is indeed* a choice. A costly one, at that.

It is a choice to condone the suffering of others. The alternative might be ridiculous, but an active choice it remains.

Trent and Rodrigo stood there and digested this very old and very terrible axiom, this long-standing precedent in the human's self-preservation calculator. This quandary has served with distinction as a primary accelerant for evil, misery, and wickedness throughout human history, and is a bedrock principle beneath both death and survival.

They glanced at one another again, silently confirming that the revelation was mutual. Slowly, they looked forward again as they forced benumbed smiles onto their faces and began to clap.

CHAPTER 26

THE BOYS were given an entire afternoon of downtime the day after the expedition. Ben was uniquely exhausted, in body and mind, with zero interest in socializing, so he went to his favorite place in this godforsaken hellscape: the library in the Great Hall.

To his immense relief, Nicholas was *not* at his usual table, and he had the large room to himself. There was really only one book left in the history section that he'd had on his reading list, and he'd been saving it. It was a semi-academic 1922 book with a half dozen authors titled *Chasing Legends*. Ben had thumbed through it before and was excited by the subject matter.

The book was broken into eight or nine sections, each of which covered a different treasured object or legendary place that men had sought for centuries, or in some cases even millennia. Many of these men, Ben already knew, died or lost their minds in pursuit of these treasures. Reading about this area of history was a comfort activity for Ben, perhaps in the same way knitting or cooking is for others.

He gently removed the old tome from the shelf, settled into his favorite reading chair, and cracked it open. He found the first to fourth sections covered the Holy Grail, the Ark of the Covenant, the Holy Lance, and El Dorado, respectively. He was skimming at top speed once he reached the El Dorado section. Disappointment plucked at Ben as he thumbed past names like Gonzalo Jiménez de Quesada and Francisco de Orellana and found he already knew virtually everything in this section. Then he moved on to the fifth section and was pleased to find it covered the Aztec Jaguar Lantern. Ben knew a bit about this legendary piece of treasure, but far less than he knew about the first four mentioned in the book.

The Aztec Jaguar Lantern, as Ben already grasped a bit, was a fifteenth-century Mesoamerican relic said to bestow magical powers upon any man who possessed it. Some of the nuance of the relic, which Ben did not yet know, was set forth in this old book. Allegedly, several warriors killed a massive jaguar and brought the beast to the Great Temple of Tenochtitlan as an offering to Tezcatlipoca, their central deity. It remained there until that year's Xipe Totec festival a short time later during the spring equinox. During the Xipe Totec festival, as was annual custom for centuries, war prisoners and boys were ritually sacrificed and then priests would carefully flay the bodies, taking great care to keep the skin as intact as possible. These skins were then worn by priests or other participants in subsequent rituals of the multiweek festival. Xipe Totec's name translates to "Our Lord the Flayed One." This symbolism was tied to the concept of renewal and regeneration. The shedding of skin by animals and plants and young men in the name of Xipe Totec served as a powerful metaphor for the renewal of the earth's fertility and the cycle of life and death.

Ben raised his eyebrows, amused, albeit in a very grim and resigned way, by the connection between this Mexican legend and Ben's most inane hypotheses about the very place he currently sat.

Toward the end of the festival, Ben read that, as legend had it, Xipe Totec was so uniquely pleased with the sacrificial offerings that he imbued the massive jaguar skull with magical powers, turning it into a lantern in which the flame of his pride burned.

The legend says that the man who possessed the Aztec Jaguar Lantern was given two powers: the ability to live without aging, and the ability to fully control the minds and actions of others whose trust he earned. This, however, was a Faustian bargain. In exchange for those two powers, the possessor of the lantern had to do two things, as well: keep the lantern lit as long as he possessed it and consume the souls of boys before the following spring equinox. For over a century, the lantern was possessed by the leaders of Tenochtitlan and the flame was said to be constantly tended to by a group of four specially trained priests who were fully controlled by the one who possessed the lantern and the powers it promised. Their job was to protect it from those who would seek to douse the flame, which, according to legend, could only be done with that which fed its master: the lifeblood of a boy.

While the powers bestowed by the lantern obviously remain uninvestigated, correspondence between Spain and Catholic clergy in the new world do paint an interesting history of the skull lantern once it fell into European hands. Several letters mention it being among the plunder from Tenochtitlan that was moved to a monastery in northern Mexico in the late 1500s. From there, in the early 1700s, it is again referenced in various correspondence as being among certain trophies that were moved to a private residence of a Spanish military officer somewhere in what is now New Mexico. This residence was destroyed and looted during a Comanche raid some years later, as recorded in the local governor's annual reporting. Thus New Mexico is where the trail of the relic becomes a true mystery that has tantalized the American public for centuries.

Ben leaned forward as he reached the next portion of the section so he could read it carefully, as it pertained more to his interests: those who sought these legendary artifacts and suffered for their ignorance.

In the late 1800s, S. E. Blackthorn set out toward the Rockies on a quest to find the legendary Aztec Jaguar Lantern. S. E. Blackthorn hailed from the immensely wealthy timber-baron Blackthorn family who made a fortune during the eighteenth and nineteenth centuries by milling and shipping from the hardwood forests of the northeast. S. E. served with distinction as an officer in the 2nd Maine Infantry Regiment where he saw action at the battles of Antietam, Fredericksburg, and Chancellorsville. He taught at Bowdoin College thereafter. While long held to be mere prophecy and schoolyard lore, in 1870, while passing through Virginia City, Montana, S. E. Blackthorn told a reporter from the *Montana Post* that he'd been given specific details as to the lantern's whereabouts from a mortally wounded Confederate officer, and Texan, whom he comforted as the man expired.

While the details from the dying Rebel were vague, they were tangible enough for Blackthorn, who was confident there were only a dozen places in the Western US where such topographical anomalies could be found, and that he intended to scour every last one of them. As is now quite famous, Blackthorn, sadly, has not been heard from since 1876, when he was last seen out Idaho way. He had passed through Driggs, Idaho, on a supply run and to send some correspondence to his family back in Maine, which would end up being the last they'd ever receive from the man. The tack store owner and elected sheriff in Driggs both reported the man seemed to be near the end of his sanity, with frayed nerves, and tragically underfed. Both men compared him to old prospectors they'd seen pass through that country frequently in decades past with a crazed ravenous fury in their eyes.

In 1877, the wealthy Blackthorn clan back in Maine posted a lofty reward notice in the largest papers in the respective territories, the *Idaho Statesman*, the *Montana Post*, and the *Cheyenne Daily Leader*, as well as in the *Rocky Mountain News* in the brand-new state of Colorado. The Blackthorns promised $5,000 in legal tender or gold in exchange for actionable information regarding S. E.'s whereabouts. The family suggested one way he could be identified was his habitual tendency to use his left pinky—which was missing its upper most digit—to scratch at the bottom of a scar on his left cheek received from a Rebel officer's saber during the war. This sum kicked off quite the furor. Countless individuals and even a number of well-provisioned search parties from between Boise and Miles City set off after the notice of reward was posted, but all returned unsuccessful, with nothing to show for their efforts other than—as Missoula saloon owner Ammon Willis reported—"sore feet and saddle blisters." A few months later, in early 1878, the *Idaho Register* reported that the once-legendary cavalry scout turned successful cattleman, Dan Bishop, had set off from Bear Lake County, Idaho, to claim the reward, stating to several locals that just days prior he'd heard tell from a reliable source that a man fitting S. E. Blackthorn's likeness was spotted to the north. With Bishop rode the equally famous gunslingers and bounty hunters,

Javier Lozada and Gordy Colton, as well the distinguished war hero turned beloved local teacher, Nicky Hart.

In what became one of the most delectable mysteries near the end of the real American West, these four legendary figures—who had struck fear into the hearts of hard, shooting men from Canada to Mexico, and San Diego to Shreveport—were also never heard from again. Additional search parties were mustered to track down the group, but all were unsuccessful. Thus, directly or indirectly, the legend of the Aztec Jaguar Lantern claimed the lives of Dan Bishop, Javier Lozada, Gordy Colton, Nicky Hart, and of course their quarry Mr. Silas Everett Blackthorn, thereby inserting itself into yet another chapter in the annals of—

Ben froze in place. He scanned the room for others, then frantically snatched the book up again and reread everything. He pulled the wooden note card with its warning message from his pocket and reread the first several lines in a whisper.

It's all so S. E. B. can keep the lantern lit
   Silas left a bit upstairs for the rustlers to keep them sane and tend to the flame
   Nothing left for them other men, they age, they're just S. E. B.'s working stock

This absolutely had to be it, Ben thought. *Absolutely.* This message, this warning from the former Bear Springs student, had to be referring to *Silas Everett Blackthorn*. Thus *Silas Everett Blackthorn*, presumably, *has to be Reid.*

Ben looked back at the book, then tore the pages he'd just read from their old binding.

He walked shakily out the doors of the lodge and into the ruthless, brilliant afternoon light. Almost all the boys and a few counselors had begun a large Ultimate Frisbee game right outside. Ben saw Reid as he ran toward him to catch the Frisbee. The man spent several seconds assessing his receiver options, then pivoted away from the boy trying to block him and threw it deep down the field into the running mass of bodies. Reid smiled at the game and raised a hand to shield his eyes from the sun.

Ben glanced down at the man's other hand and saw something that—somehow, even after all the diagnostic, analytical, borderline-manic assessment he'd done on this man—he was just now really seeing for the first time. The pinky abruptly ended right where the fingernail should've begun.

Ben followed the stunted digit as Silas Everett Blackthorn raised it to his face then used it to scratch at the battle scar someone had carved into his face during a war that ended 158 years ago.

CHAPTER 27

THE PAIN was no longer new, but it was still electric and hot, and lingered far longer than seemed natural. It didn't hurt like the first few times at the beginning of the summer, but it still made Ben grind his teeth and let out a long groan as he adjusted the leather brace on his left arm, pulling it back up into place.

When shooting a recurve bow or a long bow, the bowstring will whip past the bow staff when an arrow is released at invisible speed, and its first point of vicious impact is often against the sensitive skin on the inside of the forearm holding the bow. It's like ten hornet stings consolidated into one ruthless whip crack. Thus the advent of braces that archers wear on their bow arm to prevent such a thing.

Ben checked his shot placement as he rubbed at the pain and felt the shallow lumps of older scars and welts underneath from many such whip cracks he'd endured over the summer. His arrow had landed in the red circle that encompassed the yellow bull's-eye where he'd sunk his first four arrows. Four out of five bull's-eyes was fine with Ben, so long as the fifth was in the red.

"Lemme see that, bro. It's just gonna keep slippin unless you tighten it up, toss it over I can do it quick, just did it with mine."

Ben nodded, took the brace off his arm, and tossed it toward where Rodrigo was kneeling in the grass with his favored bow across his leg. The boys had all worked their way through the archery arsenal until they'd found bows with draw weights and lengths that favored them. Rodrigo caught the brace and began fiddling with the elastic cordage that held it to the arm.

Trent sank his fifth arrow into the yellow bull's-eye of his own target, then looked over at Ben's.

"*Daaamn, B*. That's what I'm talkin about. Gettin more deadly every day."

Ben did not say anything in response, just stared forward at the targets, waiting for Billy to finish his five-arrow group so that Jimmy would call a *cold range* and they could cross the firing line and go retrieve their arrows.

Trent and Rodrigo exchanged a quick glance. Since getting back from the last expedition, they had noticed a change in Ben. When the boys were all taking a break to eat lunch on their hike down the mountain toward Bear Springs from that last camp under the glacier—several hours after Charlie, Marcus, and Dean had returned from their *solo night*—Rodrigo and Trent had joined Ben where he sat alone at the base of a boulder away from the group. It was the first time the three had been together and out of earshot from everyone else since the boys had returned that morning, bringing with them dramatically new personalities and mannerisms, no traces of their old selves left other than basic facial structure. They intended to engage Ben in animated, conspiratorial debriefs.

They both rattled off a half dozen comments each about the condition of the boys. Trent pointed out how they had permanent smiles now, just like Joe and all the guys from the spring class, and how unnaturally chipper they were. Rodrigo commented on how abnormally helpful and jolly they had been in breaking down camp, even offering to carry other boys' gear. He mentioned how creepy it was hearing them give the other boys cryptic, motivational comments about *letting go*, and *surrendering to the program*, and the spiritual approach toward *their own solo night*. Trent added on to that topic, noting how they had calmly refused to divulge any specific detail in response to the inquisition from the other boys about how their nights went, how they would only talk about how magical and soul-shaping the experience was. Rodrigo mentioned how they seemed, somehow, to actually be a bit *taller* than they were a day before. Trent agreed, and pointed out how their skin glowed, how they just looked *healthier* somehow.

Ben had not said anything. Nor did he seem to even be paying attention to the other two. He just quietly ate his serving of freeze-dried noodles as they spoke, staring out into the trees. This third-wheel effect grew awkward, so Trent pressed him a bit, asking for his thoughts on it. Ben took another large bite, then tipped his tin camping mug up and drank the broth with bits of peas and chopped carrots that remained. After clipping his mug back onto his pack and putting his spork back into an outer pocket, he finally responded.

"Yep, well . . . would've been pretty surprising if all this *were not* the case. Doesn't seem to be any *new* information to glean from what Marcus and Dean have turned into, nothing we didn't already know."

The discussion of this program's malevolence ended then—with Ben wandering off a few yards to piss into the mountain grass that had started to toast into a golden yellow of late summer—and the subject hadn't come up again, with Ben at least.

In the week since, even now as they watched him stare down the archery range, Ben had been just as far away in his own head, just as reticent. When Ben had been in the shower that morning, Trent opined that he had just become depressed by the weight of this whole reality, maybe even suicidal; maybe he'd just given up. Rodrigo disagreed with this. Rodrigo said he thought Ben had just stopped trying to maintain an act, given up his front, and that who they were seeing now was the *real* Ben. They agreed that they'd confront him that evening to make sure he was still with them, still interested in trying to escape. If his head was no longer in the game, or if he was still giving them the creeps—or the *frissons*, as Ben would sometimes say in his strange dialect—they agreed they'd have to just forget about him and plan to strike out on their own.

Billy's last arrow sank home, matching Ben's score of four out of five in the yellow, with one in the red. Rodrigo and Trent did not offer any compliment on Billy's shooting. They looked at the backs of Ben and Billy as they silently stared forward, waiting for Jimmy to call a cold range. Then they looked over at one another, silently communicating their worry that Ben and Billy were so similar now.

All four boys in the *green fire circle* had gotten pretty good with the recurve bows provided by the camp at the archery range. The entire summer class had done archery together a half dozen times or so throughout the summer during their afternoon lesson time, but during downtime they were permitted to go shoot on the range so long as one of the counselors accompanied them to unlock the archery shed, equip the boys with their bows and arrows, and supervise by playing the role of range officer. The range was set up on the hill behind basecamp and removed from its ruckus and bustle. It was a pleasant place with a nice view of the camp itself and the landscape beyond to the east. Archery was also the only activity Billy agreed to participate in.

These four went up there as often as they could. The camp had nice wooden-limbed recurve bows, too, at least according to a kid in the class named Hector, from Iowa, who said he grew up bow-hunting whitetail deer with his dad and was the only one in the group who had any apparent familiarity with the weapons prior to arriving here. Hector had outshot everyone in the class early in the summer, but by the third full-class archery outings and all those that followed, the four boys of the *green fire circle* put on a proper goddamn clinic, eclipsing the skill of the other boys and even some counselors.

Jimmy's voice cut through the warm afternoon air.

"Alright, fellas, that's a *cold range*, go on down and collect your arrows, and this'll be the last five-arrow group, we've gotta head down and get ready for dinner. And remember it's an early night, we've gotta get packed up for tomorrow, our last big expedition of the summer!"

All four boys walked the stretch of grass between the thirty-five-yard shooting line and the row of large, foam targets. A wake of grasshoppers sprang up from every step they took to click and snap away on blurring black and yellow wings.

"Listen . . ."

Ben spoke the word with a tone and authority that even made Billy look over.

"When Jimmy goes down, Trent, you're gonna get Jimmy's key to the archery shed, where you're gonna go grab two things. First, there are three little green plastic boxes on the top of the shelves on the left side, maybe more than that, but I know there are at least three. The boxes aren't big, maybe four by six inches, grab them all. Second, grab a couple of the bow stringers hanging on the nail on the inside of the door to the right. Once you've got the boxes and the stringers, lock the shed back up, remember the key, and bring all that shit back to me."

Rodrigo, Trent, and even Billy had stopped at their targets and were just staring at Ben instead of beginning to work the arrows out of the thick, arrow- and weather-beaten foam.

"*Look alive*, assholes, Jimmy's watching."

They all snapped out of it and began to slowly pull their arrows, side-eyeing Ben suspiciously as they worked.

"Billy and Rod, you two are gonna grab all four of our bows, all the arrows we've got over there, should be around twenty-five or so, and our arm braces, and then boogie down the slope to the east, toward that grove of pine trees with all the bushes at the base. You're gonna stash all that gear there and cover em up best you can with leaves and branches and shit."

Rodrigo was about to say something but Ben cut him off.

"Trent, once you bring the key back to me and Jimmy, bring those boxes and the bow stringers down to Rod and Billy, and stash that stuff with the other stuff under the leaves, you understand?"

Ben turned his head to the left and then to the right to make eye contact with all three of them as he pulled his last arrow out.

"*I need to hear you all say you fucking understand.*"

All three were surprised by the snarl in Ben's tone. It was like some other guy they'd never met was speaking through him.

Trent said *I understand* and Billy said *copy* at the same time, speaking over one another. Rodrigo removed his last arrow and all four began walking back toward the shooting line. Ben glared at the silent Rodrigo waiting for a response, then looked up toward Jimmy, who was shielding the sun from his eyes with his hands and staring up into the trees at some bird or some other dumb shit he'd very likely point out to them in the next few seconds. Ben looked back at Rodrigo just as he hissed a question back at Ben.

"Tha fuck do you mean *when Jimmy goes down*, tha fuck are you about to do, man?"

Billy and Trent both looked over at Ben as well. Ben spoke as he looked back at Jimmy.

"I'm gon' glitch him out. Take it all the way this time. And if it goes how I think it'll go, Jimmy'll be none the wiser . . . I hope, at least. If it goes pear-shaped, if Jimmy don't get back up, just stash that shit back into the shed, lock it up, and I'll run and get help. We'll act all worried and concerned for him. However this shakes out, whether it works or not, there's no way we can lose. Just trust me."

The boys said nothing as they approached Jimmy and began to slow. They came almost to a complete stop, everyone except for Ben, whom they watched stride ahead toward the man gawking up into the trees. Jimmy looked over at them with his stupid smile, throwing a fist up with his pinky and thumb extended in the *hang loose* gesture he constantly used. He started to point up into the trees and form a word when Ben's voice cut him off.

"What's the last thing your parents said to you before you got sent to Bear Springs, Jimmy?"

The man froze, one hand pointing at the tree, the other displaying the *hang loose* gesture, completely motionless. Trent, Rodrigo, and Billy were almost as locked in place as Jimmy, watching as Ben went straight for Jimmy's front pockets, rummaging through both until he pulled out a leather key chain with the key to the archery shed dangling below. Ben turned with the key extended for Trent to take, and saw them frozen there, dumbfounded at the spectacle they had only seen once before but clearly hadn't become any less jarring to behold. Ben's eyes widened as he barked out harsh commands and stalked over toward them.

"Trent, key, shed, boxes top left, bow stringers inside door on right, *fucking now.* Rod, Billy, grab the—"

They all spun as they heard Jimmy's monotone voice.

"*We do not talk about our personal circumstances to Bear Springs students until after your graduation.*"

Ben waited to see the life flow back into Jimmy's body. When it did, when the man's eyes began to focus again on the four boys standing in front of him, Ben sent the question right back at him like it was a body blow.

"What's the last thing your parents said to you before you got sent to Bear Springs, Jimmy?"

Ben turned back to the three boys, not needing to see if it would

work this time. He snapped at them when he saw they were all fixated
on the man's new frozen position, forced the key into Trent's hand, then
pointed down the slope toward the grove of trees and bushes.

"*Yo*, this is time sensitive, *move, Trent*. Rod, Billy, bows, arrows, and
braces, stash em down there, *now.*"

Trent dropped his arrows and turned, sprinting toward the shed.
Rodrigo snatched those up and grabbed the clutches of arrows out of
Ben's and Billy's hands, then went over toward another cluster of backup
arrows they'd grabbed earlier and where the boys had left their bows
lying in the grass. Billy didn't move at all. He just stared at Jimmy, slowly
beginning to chuckle in amusement as he shook his head. After a few
seconds of this, he looked at Ben with his flat, gray eyes.

"Look here, swamp rat, don'chu be barkin no orders at me. I ain't a
part a'yer little Girl Scout troop here."

Ben rolled his eyes and turned away from Billy before the large boy
had even gotten halfway through his comment. Ben had not failed to
notice Billy's tone slow and his eyes widen in surprise as Ben made this
disrespectful move. Ben was already shouting over Billy's last couple of
words toward where Rodrigo was scooping up another one of the bows
into the bundle of archery equipment he now carried.

"Rod, you got all four bows and all them arrows and braces on your
own? Billy here's decided *he ain't part of our little team.*"

Ben added air quotes with his fingers at the end of his comment, then
turned back toward Billy. The large boy had narrowed his eyes, tilted
his head to the side, and his right fist was balled into a white-knuckled
mallet. He had taken one quick step toward Ben and was about to say
something when Jimmy's robotic chorus cut across the afternoon once
more, and both turned toward the man.

"*We do not talk about our personal circumstances to Bear Springs students until after your graduation.*"

Ben walked up to Jimmy now and placed a hand on his shoulder. He
looked straight into the man's eyes. This time Ben actually *felt* the life
come back into the counselor and saw the focus and dilation come back
to his eyes behind his fluttered blinking. Ben leaned into the man's face
and asked the question one more time.

"James, what is the last thing your parents said to you before you got sent to Bear Springs?"

Just as Carl had seen, the man fell into convulsive shaking almost immediately upon this question hitting his brain for a third time. Jimmy buckled down to his knees, and Ben used the hand he had on the man's shoulder to keep him upright. Jimmy's hypothermic muscle spasms worked up Ben's arm and into his shoulder and lungs. Ben heard Trent return and utter *what tha fuck is* but interrupted him before he could finish by extending his free hand out toward the boy, then looking over at him. Trent held four of the boxes he'd sent him to retrieve, as well as the bow stringers.

"Gimme the key, Trent, get that shit down to Rod and help him cover it all up, do it quick then get your asses back up here."

Trent complied, and Ben tucked the key back into the pocket of Jimmy's shorts where he'd found it. He looked back at Jimmy's eyes and found only glistening white marbles with streaks of bloodshot, his pupils completely rolled back into their sockets. A gargled humming noise had begun to seethe from his trembling lips along with a long strand of clear saliva that dangled from his chin as he continued to shake and convulse on his knees. Ben put both hands on his shoulders and began looking him over. A thin trickle of blood began leaking from each nostril. Ben looked at the side of his head, then the other, and saw a thin trickle of blood beginning to drop from each ear as well.

Ben reached a hand behind him toward Billy.

"Bandana."

Billy didn't put anything in his hand, so Ben turned around to face him.

"Billy, can I *please* borrow your damn bandana? You can kick my ass later. Just give it to me, for fuck's sake, man, finna deal with somethin here."

Billy, for the first time since Ben had known him, looked disturbed. He didn't look away from Jimmy as he removed the black bandana he always kept in his back pocket and then stepped forward to hand it to Ben. Ben used it to wipe at the man's nose and ears, rotating between each orifice as he worked to remove all traces of blood.

A minute passed until Trent and Rodrigo ran back up the slope and back to where the convulsing man twitched and spluttered. Both boys looked from the counselor to Ben and back again, with disbelief and shock on their faces. Just as fast as he had begun the seizure, Jimmy went limp. Completely limp, collapsing into the dirt and pine needles at their feet and sprawling out backward. Ben had been preparing himself to tackle the man if he appeared as though he were about to rise from his seizing position. He did not need Jimmy trying to smash his face apart on a tree, as one of the three counselors had done after Carl had shocked their systems with this same trifecta of questions.

Relieved, Ben bent down over Jimmy, working him over, moving his head from side to side and wiping away the last traces of blood from his ears and nose, the spit from his chin and neck, then bunching it up and plugging it deep into each nostril and ear cavity to soak up any standing blood that hadn't escaped. When he was satisfied he had gotten it all, and that Jimmy was done bleeding, he stood, keeping his eyes on the man's body. Trent spoke first.

"Looks like he's sleepin."

Ben nodded, watching the man's chest rise and fall.

"Supposed to only be out a few minutes."

Ben completely ignored the two or three questions sent his way asking *how in the hell* he knew that, not wanting to recite his conversation with Carl that felt so long ago. He looked around the area for a moment, then over at the three stunned boys, gesturing around them with his hands as he went through the plan.

"Alright, when he comes to, let's be standing over here, together, all staring at him. He's gonna wake up, and let's not help him up, let's just stand there. As he gets his bearings, and begins to stand up, we gotta just act like nothing happened, act like we just watched him stop for a moment, alright? We gotta play this cool. He's not gonna remember a thing, only thing we gotta do now is play this *nice and fucking cool*, y'all copy?"

They all did as Ben had asked. The stress began to mount, and the boys began to pace a bit as the seconds ticked on, but after about three minutes, the man finally began to stir. Jimmy looked as though he was waking up in a neighbor's yard after a night of drunken debauchery. The boys all exchanged nervous glances.

Jimmy finally rolled over onto all fours and looked up at the boys, then slowly began pushing himself up to stand, glancing around with wonder in his eyes as though he'd just been introduced to the power of teleportation. Ben spoke first.

"Let's go, Jimmy. We wanna shower before dinner."

Jimmy looked over at Ben as though he were speaking some impossible language. But as they locked eyes, he seemed to begin getting his bearings a bit. He whipped his head back toward the targets, then over at the archery shed. Ben spoke again, and pointed at the man's pocket as he did, snatching his attention back onto the group of boys.

"You didn't forget the key, did you? After you just locked away our gear, you didn't leave the key in the lock, did you?"

Jimmy seemed to come back to earth a bit at this question. He patted the outside of his pockets, then reached inside one and pulled the leather key chain out, inspecting it, and looking as though it brought some relief that flushed into his face and shoulders. Rodrigo spoke up this time.

"Jimmy, let's go, dude, we wanna shower before dinner."

Billy was actually the one to jump into the charade next.

"Bout to shit my pants over here, Jimmy. Let's roll."

Jimmy began to nod, slowly. Trent gave him a big, genuine smile. Rodrigo beckoned with one hand and pointed down the trail that led back to camp with another, looking annoyed, while Billy just began slowly backpedaling down it.

Jimmy glanced back at the archery shed again, then around the area of the shooting lines, then at the key in his hand, then up at the boys, and, to all their profound relief, he smiled.

"Yah, yah, let's roll, dudes, sorry . . . Sorry, I just felt kinda dizzy for a sec there."

Ben smiled at him now.

"It's all good, man, it's a hot one, let's head home and get some water."

Jimmy's smile widened.

"B-man, classic, yeah, let's all go get our hydration on, eh?"

They all turned and strolled down the trail back to camp together as they had many times before. They watched Jimmy closely at dinner that night, and back at their cabin afterward as they packed for the second and final six-day, five-night expedition of the summer, which they'd be setting off on early the next morning. It didn't seem there were any permanent effects from the strange, personal-question-induced paralytic seizure. That was good.

They'd been told there would be a couple more one-night camping trips thereafter, and maybe even one two-night trip at the very end to make sure everyone got their *solo night* completed, as the spring class had done, but this was the last big one. Their last deep ruck that would take them a significant distance from basecamp, and Ben had decided several days earlier that this expedition was also their last solid opportunity to make a good break for it.

When Jimmy hit the lights and went to bed, Ben waited until he could hear the man's noisy breathing slough into a rhythm that the boys had learned served as an assurance that real sleep had truly taken him. The others heard it at the same time, and they all slowly rose together. Trent and Ben began quietly putting their boots on, while Rodrigo tiptoed to the window, scanning the grounds at all possible angles.

Billy didn't move, he just watched the rest. He hadn't volunteered to go help retrieve the bows and arrows and other gear from where they'd hidden it, or to help Rodrigo keep watch. He also hadn't said anything as Ben showed them how he'd planned to stash the two limbs and grip of each recurve bow and as many arrows as possible into the large, concealed space between the aluminum frame of the pack and the synthetic material of the bag itself. Ben almost asked him straight up whether he intended to come with them or not but stopped himself. As they now prepared to sneak off and Billy just lay there, Ben was actually relieved to see that he was showing his intention to take his own course and let them take theirs.

Rodrigo nodded at Trent and Ben, then slowly slid open a window on the back of the cabin, through which Trent and Ben slipped out into the night. They moved carefully between structures, crawling on all fours a lot of the time and even low-crawling on their bellies, then finally reached the darkness of the forest and broke into a jog to reach the grove of trees up near the archery range where they had stashed the gear. They disassembled the four bows there in the woods, then used the lengths of paracord they'd brought to wind the bow limbs and arrows up into two bundles, then each took one as they slowly followed their tracks back to their cabin. The trip home was slower, but they made it back without raising any alarms.

Ben's idea had worked, and they'd been able to hide the three pieces of the broken-down bows as well as six arrows each in the large space between the frame and the liner of the huge bags themselves. Billy was angry at being woken up by the commotion of whispers and scuffs. Ben made one final attempt to bring him into the fold by holding a bow and clutch of arrows toward Billy's prone position on his bed. He looked back at Ben with a scowl then rolled over, mumbling out his previous assertion that he *wasn't part of y'all's little Girl Scout troop.*

Again, Ben felt true relief as he heard Billy's words. Earlier in the summer, he had considered the large, angry boy a potential resource, a violent one who could prove highly useful. Now he just saw him as a liability, and generally as a piece of shit. This was a team, and they were about to draw their cards, and there was no place for emotional insta-bility and social incompetence in a game as deadly serious as this one.

Ben stashed Billy's disassembled bow and the remaining arrows between his mattress and box spring, and then, finally, they all crawled into their beds.

Rodrigo's whisper cut through the darkness once they'd stopped rustling into comfortable positions.

"B, you've got a plan, right? A route for us to take when we split. I mean . . . are we really doing this, are we really gonna sneak off on this expedition and make a run for it?"

Ben nodded, unseen in the darkness. Given how they'd spent their evening, an affirmative answer to this simple question seemed obvious. But even so, before Ben spoke, a few long moments of loaded silence passed as all three boys felt the weight and significance of answering that simple question with a simple *yes.*

"We've got a few options once we're out there. Specifically *when* we split and from where depends on the camps they take us to, where we're at in the national forest, the route they choose, and a few other things. But I've got the map, and as far as whether we're really doing this . . ."

Ben propped himself up on his elbows and looked through the darkness toward Trent and then Rodrigo, who were already doing the same, staring back at him.

"I don't think we've got a choice, fellas. We packed the gear we need, extra food, every piece of kit we've stolen or come up on. I think there are a few reasons why we've got a better chance if we cut away *out there*, in the wild. There's other people around up there we might run into, individuals and big groups alike; there are hikers, campers, fishermen, forest rangers, hunters, guiding outfits, climbers, photographers and shit. I think that helps our chances. If we split from here, well . . . we're on *their* turf, and would be for a good long while. It's fifteen miles to the state highway just on the county road, which we certainly can't take. I also don't think we'd be the first to try that. Reckon they've got a nice little protocol worked up for huntin down runners who leave from here. *Up there*, our routes back to civilization will take longer, no doubt, but I just reckon our chances are better. If y'all got another idea, I'm all ears, let'er rip."

They all shared a long, solemn moment of quiet before lowering themselves back down and staring up at the ceiling, wrapping their heads around what was to come. Ben took their silence as agreement that it was the best play. Several minutes passed before Trent spoke.

"Wait, hold up, what's in those little boxes from the archery shed? All this crazy shit, this whole time I just never even thought to ask."

Ben smiled as he stared up at the ceiling and let his accent roll back onto his tongue as he responded.

"Those are broadheads, boys. Double-bladed and sharper n'shit. Ain't like those field tips we practice with and have on the arrows now. Field tip might kill a man with a *perfect* shot. But dem *broadheads* . . . they designed to punch through bone and organs, they designed to rip and tear and bleed things out. If you fixin to take down big game, dems whatchu wanna be usin."

CHAPTER 28

FROM WHERE Rodrigo stood, staring down the trail back at Ben, he looked like some blood raider in an apocalypse movie. The walking stick he held in one hand hung loosely, parallel to the ground, looking like a Comanche lance. A bandana and sunglasses covered his face. His massive backpack protruded from behind his body at every angle as its mess of straps snapped and danced in the smoke-filled wind. The afternoon sun baked into the smoke in a way that cast everything around them in a hue of orange and pink rust. Rodrigo looked like he was leading a group of survivors through irradiated fallout, away from a city that had just been nuked, the line of boys behind him disappearing into the ripping, dancing smog of incinerated trees.

It was the kind of mountain wind that was erratic and unpredictable; the kind that holds a steady sailing breeze for a full minute, then sputters into gusts before dying away into complete stillness, then chugging itself back up into a single hurricane blast that would fall away just as quickly. One can actually see the volatility and rage in mountain wind when the heavy, ash-ridden smoke from a forest fire hangs low enough.

The wind ripped almost laterally over the spine of the ridge they were hiking down, bringing thick plumes of darker smoke through the ambient sheet of it that already hung in a thick veil, obscuring the landscape all around them.

An hour earlier, the group crested into a saddle between mountains and saw the dramatic scene taking place several valleys over. It was enough to bring a low chorus of *wows* and *whoas* and *holy shits* from the group of boys. The counselors made the group stop and rest as a few began boiling water for an early lunch, and Reid and Mitchell hiked up to an open high point above them with their radios, presumably to get more information on what they were looking at.

A massive spire of smoke pulsed up into the sky from where a forest fire raged behind a mountain on the south end of the range, a long way away. The smoke built up into a monolithic cumulus storm cloud that surged all the way into the stratosphere. A veil of lighter smoke crept away from the fire itself, twisting and curling along drainages and draws in the direction of the group. Small black dots could be seen buzzing back and forth through the smoke—helicopters, a counselor had told the group, that were dropping buckets of water onto the flames, going back and forth between hot spots along the fire line and the river to refill for another run. At one point all the boys cheered as they watched C-130 aircraft fly into view. It appeared to be moving incredibly slowly as it hung right above the canopy of the forest, right above the flames themselves, then dumped a plume of bloodred fire retardant that careened out behind the aircraft before peeling away from the mountain at a wild angle.

Ben watched Reid and Mitchell talk and nod into their radios as they looked down at a large topographical map they held between themselves. Ben looked back at the fire and cursed it silently as he got a feeling that this might mean an abrupt end was coming to their six-day expedition, even though they had only set out that very morning and had only made it seven miles from basecamp to where they now stood. This route was different than the others they had taken. Usually they just went straight up to the tree line, taking a direct route up the valley from basecamp and then working their way through the lunar alpine country from there to link into the existing trail system that spidered throughout the national forest. This time they'd spend their first couple of days on a gradual trail as they made their way toward a different high mountain pass to the south. It was a nice change of pace, spending some time *below* tree line and actually hiking through the forests of tall, proud firs and lush meadows that thrive under that ruthless oxygen threshold. Beyond that line of death, those few trees that managed to survive ended up scrubby, gnarled, stunted things that looked like their existence was accidental, like they were being punished by the callous and unforgiving alpine ecosystem for daring to defy its selective design. Finding this habitat more charming and palatable made Ben *really* hope the expedition would not be called off.

Thankfully, Reid and Mitchell came tromping back down a few minutes later with smiles on their faces.

"Listen up, guys. We knew this fire was burning before we left and had been keeping an eye on it all last week. We just talked to basecamp, who contacted the incident commander directly. Despite how it looks, it's almost fully contained, and all the hand crews on the ground and the air assets you can see flying around are mostly just doing mop-up and control now. A rain cell just went through that area, followed by serious wind, so that's why it's so smoky and looks so gnarly, but we're all good, they are not concerned at all about our safety on the route we're taking. They did tell us that it would be getting pretty darn smoky for the rest of the day and into tomorrow morning until the wind direction is forecasted to shift. That means we're likely going to be dealing with low visibility, so let's stay close to one another, watch our footing, and keep being very safe, alright?"

Over the last hour or so of hiking since, the visibility had indeed begun to worsen, and then turned to shit entirely. The group had to keep stopping as the smoke got thicker so counselors could send head counts down the line. Now, staring up at Rodrigo, this version of the boy whom the environment had turned into some war chieftain of the apocalypse, Ben could hardly see more than fifty yards or so in any direction. As they continued down the trail, the counselors kept skittering back and forth keeping a head count of their *fire circles* and communicating with the next counselor down the line.

There is something unique about being in thick forest fire smoke for the first time, having it driven into your eyes and lungs by fierce wind. Ben reflected on this as he hiked down that ridgeline, trying to put it into words in his mind.

It heightened the senses and activated some kind of early warning system that rests on the outskirts of the fight-or-flight mechanism. It made a light start to blink somewhere deep inside, wherever that control room in the mind is where threats are evaluated. It flipped on some dull drive for the safety provided by clean air and good visibility, which hummed in the gut and behind the eyes. It was a quiet message that seeped from the brain into the nervous system—into the leg muscles and fingers—that *something* dangerous was nearby and slowly, relentlessly coming for you.

Ben thought about how uncannily similar it was to the feeling he got when Silas, the beast he once knew as Reid, sat down next to him at a table, or strode alongside him on a trail, or looked at him from across the Great Hall.

Over the next few hours, the wind died down considerably, and the visibility began to improve so that one could see more than one hundred yards. The smoke changed, too, taking on a characteristic much more similar to a springtime fog than the hellish color palette they plodded through higher up the mountain. The boys were able to take their bandanas off their faces and no longer had to wipe their sunglasses free of ash every few minutes.

That evening the group camped in an open area of forest at the feet of monstrous old-growth firs, adjacent to a decently sized stream loaded with rainbow trout. Dumb trout, it would seem, as they expressed an eagerness to attack every fly the boys threw at them in swarms. Even Ben caught a handful, who had not seemed to pick up the knack of casting the flimsy, long rods or timing the hook-set correctly. These trout seemed willing to eat anything. One could put a hook through a Nerf dart and they'd go in for a bite, Ben figured.

He had just finished using a pair of long, steel forceps to remove a fly's hook from where it had lodged on the inside of a trout's gill plate as delicately as he could, when he heard Silas's voice punch through the forest. Ben loosely held the fish down into the water, where it remained for a moment. He watched as it made one soft flick of its tail, and noticed how this movement seemed to wake it up to the fact that it had escaped from the dry, terrifying, poisonous hellscape above the surface of the river it had been torn into a minute earlier. A current shot through the small fish that felt like a jolt of surprise in Ben's palm—relief that it had been returned to its domain—and it blasted away in a silver flash, disappearing into the freestone bed of the stream.

When Ben stood and turned to find Silas, he saw the man standing near the fire ring at the center of the village of tents among the mammoth tree trunks, boys trotting in from all directions to form a crescent around where he, and the others, stood. Next to him were several of the boys wearing their large backpacks, smiling sheepishly out at the others. Hector, Sam, and Willy, whom Ben had developed conversational relationships with throughout the summer, but had looked down on because of their obvious desire to befriend the adult staff. They were always hanging off some counselor's arm, following them everywhere. *Fuckin losers*, Ben had concluded early on. The fourth kid was named Chris, whom he'd only ever exchanged a few words with. Chris was from Baltimore, and rumor had it that he got sent here after snapping one day at school and slamming a chair over the head of a substitute teacher who'd been scolding him. He was easily the quietest boy out of all twenty-eight, perhaps even more so than Billy. He did not seem to have developed any friendships, he never spoke unless asked a question first, and Ben was pretty sure he'd never seen the tall, lanky kid make eye contact with anyone. However, he had seen him, quite often, nodding along with a counselor's lesson, deep in focus.

Ben knew what was happening before Silas had to say anything. Ben saw the counselors Mitchell, Freddie, and Pete, with their lightly loaded packs also on their backs, flanking the four boys. He saw the embarrassed, excited smiles on the faces of Hector, Sam, Willy, and even Chris, their pride and elation at having been selected for their *big night*. Ben knew they were about to be ushered away by the three counselors and Silas up the mountain above or back down the valley below their camp. Ben knew the counselors would be lecturing the boys along the way, Silas likely leading that show with some absurd sermon about this *final step* in their path toward self-mastery, until they began splitting off to be led to preselected locations where they'd carry out their *solo night*. Whatever happened over the hours that followed, he did not know.

He only knew they would come striding back into camp the next morning, glowing with hysterical fervor, to regale the other boys about the life-changing profundity of their *solo night*. He did not know what happened, but he knew Silas was certainly not about to tell them. So he let the man's redundant monologue flow in one ear and out the other, leaving only the lowest-level filter and screen on in his brain so as to catch anything of interest that might be said, but very likely would not.

Ben did not need to look over at Billy, Trent, or Rodrigo to know that they stood there with the rest just as he did—adopting masks of interest and attentiveness, clapping when others clapped, laughing when others laughed. The three boys were finally ushered away by Silas and the other counselors, and Ben exchanged a quick, knowing glance with Trent and Rodrigo.

His demeanor this time was different though, something that he felt and the other two saw. He did not need to glare a warning into their souls; he did not need to attack them with his eyes, implore them not to do anything brash and ridicule them for even considering it. Ben looked at them with a tight-lipped expression, the best physical manifestation he could muster to convey the message that *it really is too bad*, without actually speaking. They looked back at him with acknowledgment, along with something that Ben thought was almost like relief, or subtle gratitude, in their faces. He looked away from them, not knowing how to respond to what he interpreted as his friends' silent conveyance of faith that maybe, *just maybe*, he had some humanity left in him.

Ben turned and walked back toward where he'd left his rod leaning on a tree on the bank of the stream. He took his rod back in hand and watched the water for a rising, top-feeding trout to make a cast at. He stood in that spot for several quiet minutes, the spot where he'd deceived the small trout earlier by playing on its most primal instinct, thinking about its experience, about his role in the little creature's life. Ben had stood right here as he ripped that fish from the only world it knew into a toxic, dreadful realm with an intangible essence that would torture the creature to death in a matter of minutes; a realm full of monsters that would tear it apart and eat it alive, and where the heinous forces of gravity and air also dwelled, roiling invisibly to paralyze its body and fill its lungs with fire.

He wondered if that experience would be painful for the trout. He concluded it most certainly would be.

Ben considered these things as he watched for the boiling water of a feeding trout. He saw one strike, upstream from him in a small eddy along the cutbank. He could still see the fish as it held a position in the calm current just a few inches behind where it had just eaten a bug and waited for the next. Ben's heart rate quickened as he made a short, neat cast, landing his fly inches away from where the trout had struck moments earlier to slurp in some gnat, caddis fly, or other unfortunate insect.

Ben watched his fly swirl around the surface of the stream, waiting for the trout to notice it, muscles coiled in anticipation of the bite. He considered the experience of the insect that trout had just devoured. Ben wondered how long that bug would remain alive as it was smashed and squeezed down into the trout's digestive tract. He wondered how long the bug would be conscious as the gastric secretion of acids in the trout's guts began roasting the sensitive nerve clusters in its antenna.

He wondered if that experience would be painful for the bug. He concluded it most certainly would be.

The trout turned, saw his fly, and flashed forward. The fly disappeared in a splash of water, and the rainbow trout actually came entirely out of the water as it struck the deceptive little fly on the end of his line. He set the hook properly and fought the fish for a minute or so before working it downstream into an inch of water along the bank, then scooped it up with his left hand, gripping its wriggling, slime-covered body tightly. He was able to easily remove the fly with his fingers, having hooked it right at the tip of its bottom lip. It was a larger one, Ben noted, bigger than any he'd caught in this stream so far.

Ben mused over the fish's present experience of this terrible world he'd brought it into, and that of the real insect this fish had just eaten before being deceived by Ben's treacherous fake one, confident the bug was still conscious at that very moment as it was being sucked and smushed through the fish's acidic innards.

Ben knelt down, laid the trout on the wet gravel at his feet, and smashed a rock down onto its skull. The trout bucked once with the impact, then slowly opened and closed its mouth before going still as its experience faded into black. *It's too bad for the bug though*, Ben thought, *the trout got off easy.*

The counselors had gotten a large fire going and made a big meal of trout fillets and some grilled veggies over rice. Ben had gutted and filleted his own trout under Riley's watch as he used the skinny man's knife. He'd done clean work, Riley had assured him. Ben used several small branches to roast the fillets over the fire, replacing them as soon as one began to burn through and blacken.

It was a fantastic meal. Maybe the best thing he'd eaten this entire summer.

The mood around the fire was light, the boys joked and laughed easily. The smoke hanging low in the trees and off the ground became more and more visible as the day faded and the fire became the primary source of light, pulsing and flickering through the smoke in a way that gave it new life and substance.

Ben looked down the row of boys as they sat, chatting and eating on their stumps and rocks. He saw Marcus, who'd already finished eating, taking a knee with his back to the fire, facing a group of five boys who watched him with full attention, nodding along as they hung on his words. Before his *solo night*, Marcus had been a goofy, gangly kid, a follower, never one to take it upon himself to engage or command the attention of anyone else, let alone a group of other guys. Now here he was, offering some impassioned lecture, using hand gestures he'd never used before, maintaining eye contact with them one by one. *The bastard really does look bigger*, Ben thought. His shoulders had filled out; the muscles of his back appeared rounded and full where his T-shirt hugged his shoulders and spine.

Before going to bed, Trent and Ben were able to get some information out of Jimmy with respect to their route, and where they'd be heading. They were a bit surprised to learn that they'd be spending the next two nights at the same camp, which they'd be hiking to the next day. This was because when they woke up after the second night, on the third day, instead of moving camps to a new spot, they would be doing a day hike to summit a nearby mountain peak. *Everyone who's ever graduated from Bear Springs has stood atop that glorious summit*, Jimmy had said.

Ben easily memorized all the names of landmarks, trails, streams, and lakes Jimmy mentioned, as well as any distances. Once back in his tent, he reviewed the map he'd stolen from the office at basecamp, then cut and pasted into his journal. He now had a good idea of where their camp the next two nights would be but could not be certain about where they'd be on nights four and five. He cut a small piece of string to match the mile distance on the map's key, then painstakingly estimated the distances of several different potential routes—centimeter by centimeter—between the camp and state highways and public trailheads surrounding the national forest.

It would be a mean fuckin slog either way, Ben concluded. If they split from camp night after next—their second night at this same location—they would have about forty miles to cover before they reached a public trailhead or a state highway. Forty miles was about two days of hiking at the pace this group maintained at this point in the summer, *on trails*. Ben, Trent, and Rodrigo would not be using trails, or enjoying the benefit of any bridges to cross the several streams and rivers in their way.

He lay back eventually and turned off his headlamp, letting the minutiae of a journey he hadn't even started yet wash out of his mind. It was going to suck, either way, and they would likely be making this journey while being pursued. He just needed to pick a route, make a call, time it right, and get moving. That's all they could do, Ben told himself repeatedly.

He could smell the thick musk of forest fire smoke in his hair and clothes. He had left his rain fly off and could see Hector's and Sam's empty tents a few yards from his own, their usual inhabitants off somewhere else *sleeping under the stars*, one of the few features of the *solo night* that were disclosed. He looked at those empty tents and thought of the four boys out there right now on their *solo night*. He thought of all the boys and all the *solo nights*. He wondered if Mitchell, Freddie, Jimmy, or any of the other counselors had any recollection of what Silas had done to *them* on *their solo nights*. What kind of things Silas was doing to rip the personalities away from the four out there right now, in order to turn them into the happy campers they all returned as.

Ben wondered if that experience would be painful for the boys. He concluded it most certainly would be.

CHAPTER 29

THE NEXT morning the boys ate powdered eggs and dried fruit as four new *men* strolled back into camp, with Silas and the other counselors. They were peppered with questions from the other boys, and congratulations from the other counselors.

Ben just watched Chris, who had left camp the evening before the same anxious, jumpy, quiet, introverted person he'd been all summer. The person he was looking at now was so dramatically different that Ben actually wondered how—after what he assumed were all his many, *many* years of practice—Silas could fail to take something like that into consideration when choosing the order of these boys to . . . *do whatever he did to them* up there in the forest. It just seemed like sloppy work.

Ben watched from where he sat, eating his breakfast, as Chris walked around the fire and greeted those he passed. He felt a pang of disgust and revulsion. Joe, Michael, the three from last week, Sam, Hector—had all returned as unspeakably different people. But this guy was *anatomically* fucking different. There was no more slouch in his shoulders, no more of his atrocious posture, no hesitation to look others in the eye. The way he walked had changed, the way he talked had changed, the way he swung his arms, held his shoulders, every single thing about him.

Rodrigo also looked at Chris.

"What . . . is it? Why them? What's the, like . . . criteria for being chosen?"

Ben stood and responded immediately as Rodrigo finished his sentence.

"Trust, Rod. It's trust. It can only work if they trust him."

Rodrigo looked from Ben to the newly minted *men* of Bear Springs, then back at his friend.

"So what happens to us? What happens to the ones who never trust him?"

Ben spoke as he leaned down to grab his pack.

"We clear the hell out."

The day's route had them continuing on the trail that ran along the face of the mountain range, maintaining a relatively uniform altitude as they kept to the sprawling forest of large firs. Sometime after lunch, the forest broke away as they turned west at the foot of a large, sprawling valley that cut into the mountain range and up into the alpine landscape above tree line. They took their lunch along a narrow, fast, and frigid stream that cut a white, churning line down the middle of the drainage that could be seen all the way up to where it bled out from another of the gray, silt-covered glaciers.

At the beginning of the day's long march, Ben had found the opportunity to confer with Trent and Rodrigo, individually, to tell them to be prepared to leave the next night, their second night at this next camp. Ben had just figured the second night would be a better play, after getting a more comprehensive lay of the land, but he also felt some emotional ease by setting it back a day, giving himself a bit more time, and by avoiding openly saying the word *tonight*. He was scared, and he knew the other two were as well.

Ben told them they'd be leaving their tents behind, as it would be near impossible to break them down and pack them up quietly in the middle of the night. They'd only bring their sleeping pads and their rain fly. This late in the dry summer, many of the boys had not even been using their rain fly to cover their tents and just left them packed in their bags overnight.

Both boys looked scared at Ben's message, but neither tried to make an excuse, neither suggested they wait another night. The trio spent the day in deep, anxious contemplation as they got closer and closer to the camp location up the valley that the counselors had begun pointing out. It was a vague, flat area right at the tree line, beyond which only smaller, stunted coniferous trees and clusters of aspens grew. It sat in the center of the valley near the top, only about a half mile or so from the mountain pass that loomed above the entire visible panorama directly to their west.

As they pushed up the last few hundred yards toward this meadow where they'd be setting up camp, Ben began to scan the landscape, comparing what he saw to his mental image of the topographical map he'd used to plan their route out of here the night before.

To the right and north of where they'd be camping, the land was broken, dramatic, and jagged. It was almost like a valley of its own *within* this massive valley. There were folds and breaks in the rolling grass, flower-filled meadows and glades that hung above the rest that appeared to have cliffs on all four sides, impossible to actually get to. Ben assumed the only way grass and flowers could grow in such places was due to a few seeds shat out by passing birds that happened to take root. There were massive rock outcroppings that punched out of nowhere while deep draws and gullies scoured through everything. *Someone could get lost in that mess for a week*, Ben thought. Getting through there in the dark would be a nightmare, and Ben was grateful for the detail in the topographical map that had allowed him to confidently write that area off as a bad option before even seeing it.

To the left and south of camp was a long, gentle slope of grass, boulders, and small rock outcroppings that reached well over a mile to the upper, nastier reaches of the larger valley where the incline grew dramatic until it reached rocks, spires, and cliffs that soared up like the wall of a castle larger than any ever actually built by human hands. There could potentially be a few spots up there where the boys might find a break in the valley wall with a grade casual enough for them to scramble through, but Ben could not see any, and knew it would take way too much time to find such a route in the dark.

As the group reached the meadow and began the now-habitual process of pitching tents and gathering firewood, Ben looked up at the large saddle that formed the pass in the ridge directly to the west. The sun had just crept behind it, igniting the grass, shrubs, and rocks at its crest into a burning orange-and-red outline that was almost too bright to look at.

This fiery line was about a thousand yards above camp, at the crest of a relatively gentle slope of grass and a few large boulders. That was the primary pass that led to all the best-looking routes Ben had considered. That was the path that led to freedom.

He nodded to himself and felt a sting of pride as what he saw with his own eyes substantiated the conclusion he'd reached some twenty miles away while only using his map, without ever having seen this place in his life. *I taught myself how to read a topographical map and used it to plan an escape from this goddamned desolate mountain range*, Ben thought, *but that don't mean much if I don't get away.*

Ben tried to imagine navigating through the terrain leading up to the pass in the dark, without lights. If they could get up there in the dark, without getting caught, they could get moving down the other side and give themselves a solid head start, five or six hours at least by breakfast, when their absence would, or *should*, first be noticed.

Ben pitched his tent next to a small cluster of aspen trees at the edge of the meadow closest to the pass. There was only a bit of flat ground in this area, and Ben made sure Trent and Rodrigo noticed that he'd picked this spot so the trio could have at least fifteen yards or so between them and the next-closest tent. Despite his instincts, he looked for Billy as well with the intent of trying to get him to join them, but found he'd already dropped his pack on the far side of camp.

When he finished pitching the small tent, Ben sat on his knees in the grass and pulled the journal out of his bag so he could compare what he saw before him in the daylight to what he'd have to work with on the map in the dark. He made sure to monitor the counselors' whereabouts as he did this, not wanting his stolen map to be discovered. Trent and Rodrigo eyed him from where they finished setting up their own tents. Trent's voice grabbed Ben's attention.

"What's the word, B?"

Ben looked up at the pass, down at his map, then over at the boys as he stuffed the journal back into his bag.

"Tomorrow night, we've gotta get up there in the dark, no headlamps, so get familiar with that slope this evening and tomorrow while we have light. Once we cross over that pass, we've got options, four or five routes down the other side of the mountain range toward Idaho. As the crow flies, it ain't all that far, but from what I can tell, on foot, we're lookin at about thirty-five or forty miles to cover before we reach any state highway or trailhead, and more like sixty or seventy miles before we reach any towns or businesses. All that aside, first step is gettin up and over that pass in the dark tomorrow night without gettin caught. Once we on tha other side and can use our headlamps, and if we ain't got caught yet, I reckon we in tha clear, at least till mornin when they notice we gone. So, from the minute we beat cheeks tomorrow tonight, we ain't gon' stop movin till our legs fall off. If we lucky we can put at least eight or ten, maybe's many as twelve mile between us n'dem fo dey notice we gone . . ."

Ben had felt his angst build as he spoke the plan out loud, somehow making it all feel very real, hearing his Cajun accent turn from a trickle into a flow. Trent and Rodrigo nodded softly in response but did not ask any questions. Ben watched their faces. Trent didn't take his eyes from the pass for a long while, as Rodrigo fiddled with something small in his fingers that he was not looking at.

Ben felt the same anxiety they felt; the same angst broiled in him as he confronted the reality of *actually, finally* making their move in just thirty or so hours. He knew they had to do this though, and he reckoned both those boys did too. Having seen the return of the four guys this morning, having been in close proximity to them all day long, it had a powerful impact on the trio's nerve. The four boys who went up into the darkness the night before were gone, and something else had come back in their place. The reality of that fact—the look, sound, and smell of whatever these four new guys were now—steeled their resolve. All three of them had also been dreading missing the boat, being one of the ones selected to set off on their *solo night*, before they had made their move.

They all knew that could happen to any of them and could happen any day now. They all knew it was time to quit fucking around. They all knew it was time to walk the walk and do or die. Trent broke the moment of reflection.

"I just thought some of the others would've picked up on what's happening by now, you know? I mean . . . how is it that Billy and us are the only ones who can see through what's going on here? How can they not see how different the other boys are after their solo night?"

Rodrigo nodded a few times at the question in a way that suggested this was a familiar quandary he had no answers for despite having already confronted it. Ben stared down at the map for a few moments before responding.

"Lotta these poor bastards, like me, ain't never had no one. No attention. No love. No role models. They're hungry for it, you know? They've gone anemic for it, they're starving for family or affection or, shit, I dunno, just simple guidance I guess. They don't even know what it's supposed to look like, they just know they need it. For most a'these dudes, this is the first time they've ever seen any kinda structure, so it's hard to blame em for buyin in. It's why they want dudes like us, at this age. I reckon they think little shitheads from poor families and fucked-up neighborhoods are the best candidates for, well . . . *trust*, best type a'dude to buy into their bullshit. Fucked-up thing about it is . . . I spose they probly right too. Dudes like us, at our age, we might just be the best candidates for brainwashin."

Fifteen silent minutes passed, and Trent, Ben, and Rodrigo were still milling around their tents when they heard Silas's voice cut across the expanse in which this band of misdirected youth and brainwashed Boy Scouts had just built their newest temporary village.

All three of them stopped what they were doing, but none looked over toward Silas, Ben looked up slowly from where he sat toward the pass to the west, Rodrigo stopped removing his sleeping bag and stood there motionless staring down at the compression sack he was pulling it out of, and Trent let his head fall from where he'd been staring out over the valley to rest his on his chest. After a long moment, they all looked at one another at the same time, casting around silent wishes for good luck, unspoken prayers that none of their names were called tonight. They stood and fell in with the rest of the group.

It would be four more boys, tonight.

Spenny, Nick, Chase, and Greyson.

Ben felt real sadness and loss this time, seeing Greyson up there. He had undeniably, in Ben's mind, gotten far too close to these adults than he ever should have, but this was still a guy who had real character, a real spark and fire in him. This was the kind of guy the world could do with more of. Ben looked over at the logs and rocks guys had hauled in around the *fire circle* to use as chairs. He sighed as he failed to find the throne of rock and stone. The glorious chair Greyson always put so much effort and care into building for himself to the great amusement of boys and counselors alike was absent from the lineup.

What a strange thing to grieve for, Ben thought—ridiculous and creative chairs, hewn and piled together with whatever was at hand in the middle of the mountains, by some shithead latchkey kid from New Jersey. What a strange but beautiful thing that was about to be taken from the world. Ben wondered what else this kid would've done with his life. He wondered what other talents and skills had been extinguished in the dark as the eight others in the class who'd already been taken were transformed by Silas. What others still remained in the twenty guys left, soon to be sixteen, that would be ripped away in the coming nights.

This iteration of Silas's sermon was mercifully a bit shorter than the one the night before, but the celebrations of the counselors and those boys who'd already gone on their *solo night* were even more fevered and disgusting to Ben. He, Trent, Billy, and Rodrigo clapped and smiled, as did two or three other guys from their class, but all the rest who'd yet to have their names called were jumping and cheering and whistling.

It appeared as though most of the counselors just openly cried now during these moments of repulsive revelry. Ben had noticed a few who hadn't been *actually* crying the night before, but tonight they all had tears in their eyes as they roared and clapped and jumped around in celebration of the doomed boys and this bizarre ritual.

Riley appeared to be openly weeping through an insane smile as he walked in a circle shaking his hands in front of him so hard it looked as though he'd break all his fingers. Pete was on his knees, fists in the air, repeatedly roaring out the word *yes yes yes*, convulsing each time. Jimmy was just shrieking through a toothy smile, running in place so aggressively his knees were smashing into his chest. Sam and Hector—two of the guys who'd come back from their big night out just this morning— bounced around on the balls of their feet, arms and hands limp at their sides, with a moaning belly laugh coming from mouths they held open as wide as they possibly could. Ben watched as eight or ten of the *normal* boys closest to Silas and the doomed quartet, those who hadn't even gone on their *solo night* yet, put arms around one another and began jumping up and down in unison, laughing hysterically.

Ben watched as Silas extended both arms up and out over the carnal, gyrating celebration, then slowly close his eyes as he looked up into the sky.

Trent and Rodrigo's clapping slowed, causing Ben to look over at them to find they were wide-eyed and apparently as repulsed by what they saw as he was. He amplified the intensity of his own clapping, catching their attention and making both look over at him. He widened his grin, and let out a loud oscillating whistle, nodding as he did this, trying to remind them to keep their act together, to not give themselves away. This was the homestretch. Both snapped out of their revulsion and played along, Trent jumping up and down a bit as Rodrigo cupped his hands over his mouth and began to cheer. Silas looked over at them eventually. Ben saw his eyes widen and his smile grow as he began to nod in approval at the trio of friends and their apparent conversion, their infection by the dark elation. Silas looked around the rest of the boys with that same face, appearing to approve of what he saw.

The furor calmed eventually, and Silas said a few more words of congratulations and well-wishes to the four who were then led away into the broken country to the north of camp to their big night out under the stars. Silas exchanged a few words with some of the counselors who'd be staying behind with the rest of the group, who began dinner preparations as Silas jogged up the slope to catch up with the others heading into the jagged rocks.

The campfire and dinner routine went like many others had before, with the exception of the fact that over a third of them were now indistinguishable from the counselors, personality-wise. At one point Marcus came over and sat down next to where Ben sat alone at the end of the row of boys, gently putting his hand on Ben's shoulder as he lowered himself down next to him.

Ben got that same feeling along his spine as he did when Silas singled him out. He felt the tingling urge to move away he'd felt before. He suppressed it and looked at Marcus when he began to speak.

"Ben, how are you doing this fine evening, my friend?"

Ben couldn't conceal his look of amused surprise at the greeting as it came out of the mouth of this goofy, often-cranky asshole who'd never have said anything remotely like that just two days ago. Silas wasn't here; neither were the other more watchful counselors who seemed to control the rest, Freddie and Mitchell. Ben glanced around to find no other counselors or post—*solo night* boys were within earshot. He felt the pressure to keep up his happy-camper facade fade a bit, and just let himself start to laugh in Marcus's face. The boy did not appear surprised by the laughing, but looked instead almost as though he were trying to mimic Ben's demeanor. Ben caught his breath and leaned into Marcus's face as he spoke.

"Sweet mother a'Christ, Marc. What'd he do to you?"

Marcus was about to speak, but Ben cut him off by holding a finger up and *shhh*'ing the boy.

"Don't bother, ol' buddy. I know you can't say. But still . . . I'll be damned, he sure does a thorough job. Framing, plumbing, electrical, whole new ground-up kinda build, innit?"

Ben leaned his face around the other boy's, looking him over as he would some sculpture at a wax museum. Marcus recoiled a bit but did not speak, just watched Ben's face with curiosity. Ben sat back a bit, did another scan down the line to make sure no one was within earshot, then looked back into Marcus's eyes.

"What's your momma's name, Marc?"

He saw the boy's eye twitch as some of the amusement melted from his face.

"My mother's name is Amy."

Ben nodded.

"Pretty name. You excited to see her in a few weeks? Sure has been a while. What's the first thing you gon' say to her?"

The twitch at the corner of the boy's eye began to flutter now. Marcus's breathing did not speed up, but it increased in volume and heft as the air went in and out of his nose.

"I will tell her that I love her."

Ben smiled, despite the chill he felt at hearing the robotic monotone in Marcus's voice.

"Tell me, you ever wanna work here? Become a staffer at Bear Springs?"

Marcus's voice remained flat and toneless, but he smiled as he stared past Ben's face and into the valley.

"I will always be ready and waiting for Silas's call to fill any role he needs me to fill here at Bear Springs."

Ben let his smile fade as he stared at the boy's face for a long moment, feeling the weight of what Marcus had said, letting its implications grow and warp into a twisted theory.

"Yah, I'd reckoned that's how it works . . . You do enjoy this *fine evenin*, Marcus."

Ben stood, watching focus come back into the boy's eyes as he smiled up at him.

"You as well, Ben."

Ben looked around the group and did not see Trent. He looked behind where everyone was sitting and found him standing alone at the crest of the meadow to the north, at the foot of the wild chunk of land where the four boys had been taken. Ben walked up to join him, once again begrudgingly smitten by how beautiful these mountains were as the very last night of day melted out of them. Trent looked over, holding out a pair of binoculars in his hand. Ben took them, turned them over, then raised his eyebrows as he looked back at his friend, knowing where the glass had come from. Trent grinned.

"Snatched em from Jimmy's bag this mornin, figured they'd come in handy."

Trent pointed up toward a clearing about eight hundred yards up into the rocks and crags.

"You see that opening? I just saw Mitchell and Greyson pass through there, Mitchell pointing ahead of them and down the slope toward something we can't see. I'm guessin that's where they're gonna have him do his little *solo night*. And look, over at the east side, that's a big cliff, ain't nowhere else they could go, it's like a bowl. And look here, at this little ridge runnin up to that crest above where we lost sight of em. I bet we can see right down into where he's at from up there, looks like a pretty easy walk up there too."

Ben confirmed what Trent had seen, then took the binoculars from his eyes and handed them back to his friend. He felt a jolt of apprehension.

"I don't know why we'd bother. Won't change the plan none. Besides, like I told you, that old game warden told me that if we know what *really* happens, then the counselors are gonna know. He said it's like a stink that wafts offa ya. I just—"

Trent interrupted him with an exasperated shrug and an eye roll.

"Come on, B, we're lightin out tomorrow night, alright? We're gonna be fugitives, cops will be lookin for us and shit and they're probly gonna catch us, too, we probly won't get sent back here so that's okay with me, but in twenty-four hours we'll be getting ready to make a big fuckin call, *a life-changin call*, and it's because we don't wanna face whatever that shit is goin on *right there*. I'm tellin you there's a spot *right there* where we can finally see what's really goin on here. You gonna try to say the *only reason we shouldn't* is because of what some cowboy cop motherfucker told you in a ten-minute conversation?"

Ben struggled to cook up a rebuttal in his head, and Trent could see he was trying.

"Nah, man, I don't wanna hear it. No part of our plan changes, alright? But I'm goin up there tonight. I at least wanna know *what* I'm runnin from, and what's gonna likely be chasing my ass through these mountains, okay? You can join me or not."

Trent gave Ben a patronizing pat on the shoulder and walked back to the fire.

Around three hours later, after the three boys had patiently waited for the last hiss of a tent zipper, and for the steady cadence of snoring to loft into the valley air, Ben was crawling up a grassy slope on all fours. He was following Trent and Rodrigo up the ridge to the little crest where they could look down on the spot where Trent was confident Greyson's *solo night* location had been chosen.

Ben had tried to talk them out of it. He'd tried to push the importance of what Mr. Rickert had told him. They wouldn't have it. They also did have a point he had difficulty denying the reasonableness of.

They were about to run from a program they got sent to by a judge in lieu of an alternative punitive course in state juvenile corrections—

a program that held lawful authority over them that their parents and guardians had knowingly approved and signed over. The consequences were real, no matter how this shook out. And while all three knew deep in their bones that juvenile corrections or legit prison would be far better than whatever was at the end of this Bear Springs path, it was fair to want to know what they were about to run away from.

So here these three were—wind whistling in their ears, hearts pounding in their chests, creeping up some ridge on a mountain in the middle of the night—about to find out.

CHAPTER 30

BEN CHECKED his watch when they'd reached a spot a few feet below the crest to catch their breath. Trent cocked his chin up at Ben, who knew this was a request to spin his wrist around, light up the analog watch, and show them that it was 12:13 a.m.

As the stars began to appear overhead, the group went silent. It felt to Ben like the nervous quiet before the first explosions fill the sky on the Fourth of July. Ben could hear his heartbeat in his ears as he scanned the clearing below them. They were a lot closer to the meadow than he thought they'd be, a *lot* closer. The shadows played tricks on his eyes as he waited for any movement. Then, he saw something. It was confusing at first, then it became clearer. Flames. Headlamps, bobbing up and down like lightning bugs between the trees. Ben looked over to make sure the other two saw what he did, and both stared down with wide eyes.

They emerged into full view. A group of counselors, walking two by two as they made their way slowly and steadily into the center of the clearing. Behind them followed Silas and Greyson. Silas's hand rested tenderly on the boy's shoulders as he led him forward.

"Holy shit."

Rodrigo's seething whisper caught the others' attention as a thudding impact resonated a few yards away. Then another. They looked around and then up. Something was falling from the sky. The percussive thumps continued to land around them when suddenly something hit the ground a few feet from Ben, scattering a small cluster of pebbles in each direction. He leaned over toward it, pushing aside a patch of dead grass.

It was a bird, a chickadee, Ben was pretty sure. Its wings bent and its neck broken from the impact. Birds were falling from the sky. The shock lasted only a moment as the sound of Silas's voice from below commanded their attention. The man stared up at the sky, arms extended up toward the heavens as he shouted.

"I taste his trust, the seed I need, to make him mine through fir and pine. Cast away his doubts and flaws, let me use him as my jaws. When boys lie and steal and cheat, they come before me as blank meat. In their flesh I leave my will, to live their lives under my thrill."

Greyson looked up at Silas, trembling. Silas's expression offered nothing back other than his ink-black eyes. Silas peeled off his shirt then, baring his chest to the night air. The counselors accompanying Silas dropped to their hands, their joints seeming to loosen as their frames took on a canine posture. Greyson began glancing around, looking as though he might make a run for it. The emotionless faces of the counselors on all fours around him seemed enough to keep him pinned in place.

"You will be troubled by your rebellious spirit no longer, boy. Take heed. See now as your soul passes to the great Flayed One. I offer you that he may be pleased. Your suffering, your bondage, my gift to him."

Greyson's mouth snapped open as he went to shout in protest, but no sound came out. His face twisted in shock as he struggled and failed to make even a sound. He began to tremble as though straining against some great weight. Ben's mouth began to hang open as he watched spiderwebs of blood begin to emerge from Grayson's eyes.

As his gaze met Silas's above him, every muscle in his body began to strain. Silas was looking down at him, his mouth agape. He continued to open it wider and wider, his lips splitting as the skin tightened around his jaw while it jutted forward and open wider still. The flesh of Silas's gums split open, blood running down his chin as a set of fangs emerged, the teeth surrounding them cracking and falling away. Silas looked down at Greyson, his maw wide open in a soundless wail. Silas suddenly threw his hands up over his head, locked straight at the elbow like a surrendering suspect. His nails began to extend from his nail bed into a grotesque, sharpened set of claws. He spread his fingers wide apart like a feline, the claws jutting out menacingly.

As he held this posture, Greyson's eyes darted around, scanning frantically as every other part of his body remained locked in place. When sound finally came bellowing from Silas's gaping maw, it wasn't anything one could have expected, certainly not from a man. Guttural and thunderous at first, it rose in pitch—reaching a distorted and off-key crescendo that sounded like a great cat snarling above its prey. The feline roar warbled into moments of high-pitched screeching that made all three boys clutch their ears in pain.

Silas locked eyes with Greyson, whose trembling resistance reached a fever pitch, his entire body rattling as he struggled against the unseen force that restrained him. On all sides, the counselors, still on all fours, began baying like hounds, snarling, and gnashing their teeth with such force that their gums began to bleed.

The sound coming from Silas's chest lowered, shifting to a bass-heavy roar that shook the ground. Pine needles in the trees surrounding the clearing began to fall to the ground as he continued. As the sound reached a deafening volume, Silas's back arched. His skin began to thin as his tailbone began to protrude from his lower back. It grew with a horrible crackling sound at first until the growth began to swing side to side—fleshy and vascular but frighteningly powerful as it whipped back and forth. A tail, greasy and dripping, spasmed and twitched until it appeared as though it synced with the other limbs.

Greyson's neck suddenly snapped back, his face now fixed upward toward Silas's, whose eyes shifted in shape—a jaundice curtain of yellow tint dropping over them and growing until they blazed a fiery gold as his transformation reached its peak. All at once like a great suffocating gale, Silas inhaled. Greyson's horrified eyes jittered in their sockets as though they might come to a boil. Slowly, the pupils and cornea began to distort, like a drop of ink evaporating from a tea saucer. They lifted off the surface of his eyes, leaving nothing but a white, pupil-less, and bloodshot eyeball. A vapor snaked out of Greyson's body—through his nostrils, mouth, and ears. Silas continued to inhale, absorbing the glistening, gaseous material that hung in the air like dust in a beam of afternoon light. All around them the counselors snarled and howled.

When the last wisp of vapor drained from Greyson, he slumped to the ground like a marionette cut from its strings.

Silas knelt down and ran a finger up Greyson's neck to his chin, then held his face in place, staring into the boy's eyes, and smiled. Greyson smiled back, shaking and beginning to weep, as he assumed a position on all fours and obediently began to bay and howl like the other counselors around him. The smile on Silas's face only grew as his cracked and bloodied lips expanded horribly across his face.

Ben was pulled out of the trance he'd fallen into watching this impossible scene when a hand gripped his shoulder. He turned to see Trent, Rodrigo already moving away from the ledge, crouched low. Trent didn't say anything. He just looked at Ben's terrified face, worried, unsure whether some vicarious evil had worked its way up and into his friend. Focus flooded back into Ben's eyes as he leaned into Trent's ear and pulled himself away from the ledge.

"Change of plans. *We're leaving right fuckin now.*"

CHAPTER 31

THE THREE boys crawled, rolled, fell, and ran down the ridge back to the edge of the meadow behind their camp. The only English words spoken throughout this flight were profane and seethed out through clenched teeth. They'd gone as fast as they possibly could in limited moonlight without kicking any rocks or slides of shale to go cascading down the mountain and likely waking up others sleeping in camp.

When they reached the edge of the meadow, they bear-crawled on all fours around the perimeter of the camp while maintaining a large buffer zone around the outermost tents. When they reached their own little aspen grove at the far side of camp, they stopped to listen and watch, making sure no one was on to them. The loudest noises they could hear, by far, were one another's heavy breathing. When they made their final approach, they had slowed down their pace considerably, making certain that they could get back to their gear in near silence without waking anyone. Everything depended on that, which Ben made sure to snarl into both of their ears before they crossed the final stretch.

When they reached their tents, all went about the process of unzipping them as slowly and as silently as was possible. Once this was done, they helped one another remove their large packs to lay them gently onto the grass outside. They each slowly folded up their foam sleeping pads and secured them onto their bags, anxiously scanning the darkness, keening their ears to pick up any noise that was out of the ordinary. Twice they had to stop and lie flat on the grass as one of the boys noisily left their tent, walked to the edge of camp, took a piss, then stumbled back.

When everything was packed up, they helped one another hoist the large packs onto their shoulders and silently secure the straps across waists and chests. Ben insisted that both other boys take their headlamps off and stash them in the small pockets on lumbar straps around their waists. Rodrigo asked why, but complied when Ben explained the consequences of accidentally turning one on and lighting up their location for anyone to see who happened to be looking at the thousand-yard stretch of open landscape they still had to cross in the darkness. Ben also hooked the can of bear spray he'd stolen onto the strap that ran across his chest. He almost tucked it into the fold in his bag he'd been hiding it in, then realized how silly that would be. Not only was there no longer any purpose in trying to hide stolen items, but he'd also need to be ready and willing to blast that can of hellfire straight into the eyes of those he stole it from, should they cross paths in the hours to come.

They all stood there, staring up at the pass to the west, then back at camp, no one ready to take the first step of their escape. Ben had known he'd need to step up and make calls if this was going to work, and now was as good a time as any. He checked his watch, saw that it was 1:21 a.m., showed this to the other two, then leaned in to whisper to them.

"If we're up and over that pass by 2:15, that gives us about five hours to put some miles between us and them before they realize we're gone. Let's move slow, move smart, stick close to one another, and get over that pass."

The other two had resolve in their faces, Ben was happy to see it, but unsurprised based on what they'd just witnessed. Even so, both held their gazes fixed on the far end of camp, and Ben knew exactly what they were looking at. He sighed, let his shoulders slump a bit, then whispered his thoughts.

"Look . . . I don't like leavin him behind neither, even bein the gloomy, cranky, *shit-kickin asshole* that he is, still don't feel right. But lord knows I damn well tried to get him on board with this a half dozen different times, y'all know that, *we all* tried to get him on board. I mean, shit . . . he told us flat out he ain't comin with, that he ain't tryin to be a part of *our little team*. He made that call, and he made it clear. So now, well, ol' Billy's just gon' have to live with it or *die with it*. That ain't on us. That ain't on you, Rod, and that ain't on you, Trent."

Both boys eventually, reluctantly nodded at Ben as he pointed into each of their faces. They all seemed to take deep breaths at the same time as they stared across the dark camp toward Billy's tent. Then all three turned, and filed past the aspen grove and into the meadow that ran up toward the mountain pass.

Ben was in front, then Trent, with Rodrigo at the rear. They made slow progress at first, Ben being overly cautious at every stretch of ground where the quiet grass gave way to gravel and rocks. After a few minutes, they had worked into a decent walking pace and the stars and purple-hued night sky above the mountain pass grew closer and closer.

One of the largest rock outcroppings loomed up ahead. Ben had made a mental note of it before the sun went down as a landmark that would keep them right on the path up toward the middle of the pass. As they reached the house-sized mass of jagged granite, they worked around its north side slowly. When they'd rounded its far side they could see open ground through a cluster of boulders that led straight up toward the center of the pass again, so Ben began to break away from the side of the large outcropping.

He'd made it a few steps when a soft light suddenly suffused everything around them. It made Ben jump in surprise and wheel around, already wondering which one of those two dumbasses had taken their headlamp out and flipped it on.

When Ben saw the two men to the right of Trent and Rodrigo, leaning up against the wall of the rock outcropping with a lantern resting on a small boulder a few feet off the ground in front of them, it made him jump again. Trent and Rodrigo as well, all three sucked in air at the unexpected start and flinched away from the two guys as though they were swinging bats toward their heads, but they hadn't moved at all. Trent almost fell over, and likely would have if Rodrigo hadn't grabbed his pack. The boys steadied themselves and backed up into the boulder behind them as they squinted into the light that cast the legs and bellies of two men wearing boots and hiking trousers into full daytime detail, but the angle of the lantern lid cut off all light from reaching anything above their sternums.

"*Bro-bros*, we've almost got the full green cabin *fire circle* roster, where you dudes off to on such a nice evening?"

A distorted version of Jimmy's voice sent ice into their veins as he stepped slowly forward into the light. The second man followed, and the features of counselor Riley became clearer—the dim witch light painting both of their faces from underneath.

Ben could feel Trent begin pushing him toward the opening in the boulders that led up toward the pass, but Ben's legs and feet were frozen in place. Ben reached up to the bear spray holster on his chest and started trying to unclip the lid to take it out, but had no idea how the hasp worked, let alone without looking at it.

"*Whoa whoa whoa* now, B-man, I'm not a bear, it's me, *Jimmy*, your friend, *your buddy*. Why don't you pass that over here, students *should not* have bear spray, you *naughty boy.*"

Jimmy took a step toward the boys as he extended an open hand toward Ben. They could see him more clearly now, and it wasn't a Jimmy they had ever seen before.

His pupils were pitch-black. His chin and lower jaw hung a full six inches lower than was natural, pulling his lips and cheeks down with it into tight sheets of skin where stressed veins stood out. His smile reached into parts of the face that were impossible, all the way up near his ears. He had a hundred small, round teeth on the top and bottom of his mouth. The fingers on his extended palm each had two extra digits and knuckles. Ben's eyes went wide as he heard Rodrigo utter *what tha fuck*.

The boys pushed their backs into the boulder as Riley took a step forward as well, with similar inhuman features that had taken over his face, and he spoke with a sloughed, breathy version of his old voice.

"Boys, boys, *boyyysss* . . . Reid is going to be *very disappointed* when we bring you back to camp and tell him where we *fooound youuu*. He just *hates* when anyone tries to *slip away*. It just makes him *so vewy vewy saaad, pwease come back wiff us, pweeease.*"

The baby voice Riley used at the end of his sentence was accompanied by a grotesque manipulation of his elongated facial features that, perhaps, this *thing* thought was supposed to imitate some operatic sad face. Both men had rivulets of clear drool and milky snot that poured from their unnaturally large mouths and nostrils and dripped down their extended chins. When Jimmy spoke next, he did so through one of his plate-sized smiles, ending it in a squealing giggle.

"Trust me, little dudes, you don't wanna leave before your *solo night* with Reid. They're *magical*, fellas, *they're absolutely friggin magical*, you've just gotta let him in, guys, you've *just gotta* let him in, and the more you trust him, *the better it feels!*"

Ben gave up on the bear spray and went for his pocket where he had the stolen knife and began trying to thumb the safety catch and open it with one hand. At the same time, Riley put one hand onto a hip as he began to pump his knees slowly and rock his hips back and forth, using his other hand to snap his long fingers. He sang his words in the melody of a song.

"Up on the mountain, *he-took-me*, where I joined the other boys for *eter-ni-ty.*"

Ben had to buy some time.

"Don't you mean Silas?"

Both Jimmy and Riley halted their antics and stared at Ben in the best version of surprise he figured these things were capable of, before looking at one another, then back at the boy. Riley spoke.

"What did you just say?"

Ben shrugged, trying, and failing, to look unafraid.

"Silas Everett Blackthorn, your *master*. Why don't you call him by his name, why do you call him Reid? Silas Everett Blackthorn. *Say it.*"

Jimmy quickly wagged his distended finger from side to side, then spoke with something that sounded like anxiety, which made Ben feel like he'd found a good, sensitive area to keep probing around.

"Uh-uh, stop, *stop it.* We don't use that name anymore, *Benny*, you understand? He's Reid now . . ."

Jimmy had just taken another step forward when a flash of movement and noise made the boys wince and flinch in fear yet again. The startling commotion that sucked the breath out of them was Riley's body crumpling sideways and hitting the ground so hard and so fast it was as if his head had been tied to a truck speeding away in the direction he fell.

Jimmy's eyes had just turned toward the noise of Riley's crash to the earth, but his head had not, just as a dark blur flew into the witch light behind him. The sudden snap of a wet crunch was what made the boys jump—now for the fourth time in the last minute—and flinch away from the source. As they looked back at Jimmy, they could see his head had parted down the middle from the top of his scalp to somewhere right above his top lip. Where his nose had just been, there was now a dark, glistening mass protruding an inch above his bottom jaw, which worked up once, and then down once, before the man's knees buckled and he dropped.

As he fell, another wet sucking tear punched through the still air of the rocky space and the boys saw Billy, standing behind Jimmy's crumpling body, wrench an axe from where he'd buried it in their former counselor's skull. He didn't even look at them before he turned, walked over to the prostrate form of Riley, hefted the axe into the air, and drove it downward into the man's skull right above his ear, bursting the top of the head open like an old tomato and somehow causing the one eye they could see to pop almost entirely out of its socket.

In the same second, speaking over one another, Trent said *Jesus, dude*, Rodrigo said *Dios mio*, and Ben said *fuuuck me*.

Billy looked at them with scorn, then down at Riley's destroyed skull, then back up at the boys as he pointed toward Riley's body with the head of the axe—the vitae- and brain-caked blade of which glistened in the light of the lantern.

"Oh, *forgive me*, would y'all've preferred for me to've left that thing alive? Y'all even seen a goddamned horror movie before? If ya haven't, lemme tell ya, not makin sure they're fuckin dead'll kick off some problems."

The boys stared back at Billy blankly, surprised by his assumption that the root of their explicative torrent was his decision to kill Riley, and not the vicious brutality of the act itself. Ben finally found his voice.

"No one's questioning that call, Billy. Just pretty sure that, until just now, none of us had ever seen a man's head explode . . ."

Billy appeared disarmed by this comment, and he met them halfway with a single nod of understanding. The boys now realized that Billy carried the large felling axe that one of the counselors always brought along on expeditions and were entranced by it as he began running both sides of its blade along the back of Riley's shirt, where it left dark, running skids of chunk-laden blood. He hoisted the large axe up onto his shoulder, then cocked his head toward the opening in the rocks that led up into the moon-silvered open ground below the mountain pass.

"Well, *let's get goin* then, boys."

CHAPTER 32

*S*HIT, YOU gotta hold still, man."

Rodrigo looked down at Ben with fire in his eyes, then gripped both hands on his knee and looked away. Ben brought the dressing back over the butterfly bandages pulling the deep, nasty gash in Rodrigo's thigh together. He did this slowly, then dropped it onto the wound, gently rubbing it onto the skin and bandages underneath so it sat flush. He did this again with another dressing, then used athletic tape they found in the first aid kit to wrap around the leg to hold it all in place.

Right before sunrise they had been working their way down the spine of a steep ridge when they ran into a massive, gnarled snag of a dozen big firs that had gotten blown down sometime in the last year and had landed in a tangled mess bigger than a house. They couldn't skirt around either side of it given the steepness on both sides of the ridge, so they had to remove their packs, passing them to one another as they went, and effectively boulder their way over, through, and down to the other side.

As Rodrigo pulled himself over the last large trunk, he slipped and went sliding down the thing. It led to a soft landing, so he should've been fine, but his leg caught on a hunting-knife-shaped stub of a broken limb, and it tore into the flesh of his thigh. It was a clean gash, but deep, and one that would *definitely* require quite a few stiches if it had been acquired somewhere near a hospital instead of deep in the backcountry.

The sun had risen a couple of hours ago, and it was now fully light out. An hour had already passed since the group addressed the grim reality that their absence could not possibly still be undiscovered by that point, if it hadn't been even earlier when one of the other demon counselors stumbled upon the butchered corpses of Jimmy and Riley.

Over the past few hours, Ben had done his best to explain how on earth he knew Reid's real name was Silas Everett Blackthorn, and why he hadn't told them earlier. Ben also told the guys about the 1917 message on the piece of wood he'd found in the library all those weeks back. He apologized for not showing them earlier, but that was behind them now, and they seemed to accept that as well. The guys had a ton of questions to start, but as soon as Ben got into the weeds and nuance of how he'd used the cryptic warning from the old student to cross-reference against geographical resources and history books about Aztec lanterns, their interest seemed to wane, and the questions sputtered away. Ben was grateful for that, and readily agreed when Trent asked if they could still just call him Reid, on grounds that the new name was *weird as hell and long as shit.*

Where they all sat now was on the bank of a small stream that trickled down at the far end of the open, alpine expanse they'd just finished crossing. The landscape was an alpine tabletop, no trees in sight, just clusters of shrubs and grass throughout a dozen small lakes that nestled in the smooth granite rock, small streams leading in and out of each. Rodrigo commented on how one could almost navigate across the mesa on a skateboard. There were sheer rock faces leading up to multi-spired peaks that stood sentry to their left and right. The drop-off ahead looked like a cliff but was a steep causeway of rock, scree, snags, and deadfall that led several thousand vertical feet down into the deep valley carved away by the stream they intended to cross before nightfall. Beyond that stream, on the other side of the valley, another massive line of mountains composed the ridge that dominated the entire western horizon. This monstrous dragon-back they would also need to cross, before dropping down the far western side into the rolling ocean of forest and sagebrush that ran for hundreds of miles, all the way from western Montana to the eastern foothills of the Cascades.

As they had walked into this otherworldly landscape earlier, something exploded up from Ben's feet and he gasped in fright, prompting deep, hearty laughter from the others. Ben had never seen a grouse until coming to Montana. He vaguely knew of the existence of these strange forest chickens from some hunting magazine he'd skimmed through a few years earlier. What he did *not know* was how terribly frightening they could be when you unknowingly approached a covey of them hiding in the understory and spooked them enough to trigger their loud, explosive flush into the air. It was almost like walking through a trip-line that blasted a cluster of the large birds out of a three- or four-barreled shotgun directly at your feet. On two separate occasions now this summer these treacherous mountain fowl had surprised Ben so badly he'd audibly yelped then tripped backward over his own feet.

This was the first time they'd stopped moving at all since they'd snuck out of camp eight hours earlier.

They hadn't heard or seen any sign that would suggest they were being pursued by the counselors, but they could all safely assume they were, indeed, being hunted. When they crossed over the first mountain pass shortly after their encounter with Riley and Jimmy, they took a moment to consult Ben's map as he showed them the four or five options they had to get from where they were now to Kaniksu Creek.

Ben knew they did not have much time, but a bit selfishly, he wanted them to be involved in picking the route as well so that it was not all on him. They agreed to take a general southwestern course for a number of reasons. First, it was neither the most direct route back to civilization, nor the most obvious or intelligible. In addition to that, it appeared to have a combination of the fewest places to get cliffed out, as well as the fewest number of mountains or steep ridgelines they'd need to climb as they made their gradual way toward the west side of this mountain range and eventually d'Oreilles Pass.

There was a state highway not that far from the Idaho border, which was one potential final objective; they could reach the highway and hitchhike or creep along it until they found a business or a ranch or some other kind of residence. There were also two trailheads on the east side of these mountains only a few miles apart that led up into different valleys. Both were marked with several little icons on the map that the key told them meant the trailheads had parking for horse trailers, bathrooms, running water, and emergency phones. In the boys' reasoning, this suggested the best likelihood for high traffic and popularity, even for spots this far away from cities, or even towns with more than a few thousand people.

Once they decided on their route, they began making their way as best they could in the dark. They could use their headlamps now that they were on the other side of the pass and thereby obscured from view, at least from their camp. This helped their speed and progress significantly, but it was still very slow going. They also had not grasped the size of the alpine landscape they were entering. A mountain range—at least this one—was not a neat and tidy row of individual mountains; it was a monstrous swathe of chaos where the earth's surface had smashed together then exploded upward into the sky, which was then carved away and hacked at by water and gravity for millions of years. This left a jumbled mess of peaks, valleys, draws, cliffs, and every other kind of feature that could complicate human passage.

Trent and Billy passed a bag of freeze-dried slop between them that they'd only let soften for a few minutes with cold water as they leaned over the map they'd laid out on a boulder. Ben showed them where Kaniksu Creek and d'Oreilles Pass were, then explained how those were actually Buckle Creek and Caravan Pass mentioned in the old student's 1917 warning. It was not a particularly intuitive map to use, as Ben had cut it into small pieces in order to hide it in the small pages of his journal and had to explain its organization to the boys several times. He'd arranged it from northwest to southeast, or upper left to bottom right, putting west-to-east cuts in order, then once that cross section of the full map was glued into the book, he'd mark a page and do it again with the next west-to-east cross section to the south. Thus, trying to evaluate full routes that ran north-south required flipping back and forth through dozens of pages.

"So just gimme a ballpark here, on this course, how many miles you reckon till we get to that last row a'peaks at the far east side a'tha range fore we start goin downhill the rest a tha ways into the woods and eventually to the highway or trailheads."

Ben had answered that question ten times in the last few hours, as well as shown the other boys how to estimate it themselves with the piece of string he'd cut to the length of a mile. However, he was trying to be patient with Billy; this *new* Billy whom he'd never actually met before, and for whom he had immense gratitude for saving their lives and rescuing their entire escape operation pretty much as soon as it had started.

This *new* Billy did not have the same rage boiling behind his eyes. He was still dangerous, *obviously*, and still had the energy of a coiled snake that shimmered beneath the skin of his massive hands and shoulders, but Ben had realized over the last few hours that he was not the only one putting on a bit of a front for the purpose of deceiving the counselors. Why Billy had wanted to amplify the character he'd chosen over the last several months to deceive them, or for what purpose that could possibly serve, Ben was not sure. Either way, this Billy was far easier to deal and communicate with.

"Well . . . reckon we just did about eight miles since comin over the pass above camp, not sure about the distance to the row of peaks, but so with that ground now behind us, that leaves somethin like thirty-one or thirty-two miles from here to the edge of the national forest boundary, where the trailheads and state highway are."

Billy nodded and looked back down at the map, flipping back and forth between two pages. Trent appeared to finish calculating something in his head before offering his hypothesis.

"So, that means we'd get there by what . . . tomorrow around lunch-time, maybe late afternoon?"

Ben did not look up from the arrows he was working on as he responded—removing the field tips and replacing them with the sharp broadheads they'd stolen from the archery shed. He reminded himself to be patient as he did.

"I doubt it . . . About ten a'them thirty-odd miles is through some nasty, rocky, steep shit, Trent. The kinda dangerous, ankle-breakin shit we never trekked through with the counselors. About ten more a'them miles is through some less nasty, rocky, steep shit, but still quite rugged all the same. The other ten shouldn't be too technical, but there ain't no trail to use, we could be scramblin over deadfall and shit the whole way, makin real slow time. On top a'that, we've got two sizable streams to cross along the way, and we've gotta do that in spots where it's pretty damn steep and water's likely to be movin pretty damn fast."

Rodrigo spoke up now.

"So, what's that timing look like then, what's your best guess?"

Ben pursed his lips before responding.

"Fifty-six and a half hours. Forty-nine hours *moving*. Taking rest into account though, which we'll surely need, no matter what we feel now, I estimate it'll take us fifty-six and a half hours."

Billy asked what the other two were thinking.

"How you figure that?"

Ben cranked another broadhead into place as he responded.

"Give the ten *ultra*steep miles two hours each, give the ten *very* steep miles an hour and a half each, then give the other ten to twelve regular miles, *let's say twelve*, an hour each. Add an hour on top a'that for each of the two river crossings, and you've gotch yourself forty-seven hours. I'm sure we'll cover some a'them miles faster'n that, but some'll be slower, so it's an average I'm comfortable with. Now let's say we rest one hour for every five we move, which I reckon we'll end up aggregatin pretty easy, that's nine hours and twenty-four minutes of rest to forty-seven hours on the move. Lump all that together and you've got fifty-six and a half hours once you add in that six-minute little catnap I'll just go ahead and throw in there for us as a courtesy, you understand. It's Tuesday, round 9:00 a.m., so if we stay on track we'll hit one a'them trailheads or that state highway right around suppertime on Thursday."

Ben finished cranking the broadheads into the threaded necks of six arrows and handed the group up to Rodrigo.

"And that's assumin we don't break any bones, bust any eyes, get sick, run into a bear, have to backtrack, get chased by wolves, get swept down a river, or end up havin to scrap with them demons on our tail. We steer clear a'those hazards and stick to that time frame, which is unlikely, escape and salvation on Thursday evenin's my best guess."

The boys all laughed at Ben, who laughed at himself along with them. Rodrigo slipped the arrows into a quiver he'd fashioned out of paracord and a few strips from one of their tents' rain flies they'd decided several minutes ago to relegate for use as scrap for whatever needs arose.

Rodrigo bounced the quiver up and down a few times, then pulled one of the arrows out, seeing if it caught on anything or slipped out smoothly, let it drop, and tried another arrow. He smiled, as Ben and Trent nodded, impressed.

"Attaboy, Rod. Can you whip another couple of those up for Ben and me?"

Rodrigo smiled, pride in his face.

"Already finished em, bro."

He hopped down from the rock he'd been sitting on and buckled under the weight of his wounded leg. He didn't fall, but he almost did, and he rubbed the fresh dressings on his thigh as he walked over toward his bag, then passed them each a new jerry-rigged quiver.

Trent and Ben assembled all their bows to carry along with them at hand. Once they'd filled up their water and donned their new arrow quivers, they all set off down the mountain.

The boys went about nine miles over the next eight hours, which they spent winding down the long, timbered slopes of the mountain cluster they'd just eaten breakfast on top of. This was dense fir and spruce forest with groves of aspens, some of which were crammed together so tightly they couldn't pass through them with their large packs and had to go around instead. On several occasions they had descended hundreds of yards down some steep drainage or draw to find out that it ended in a cliff, requiring them to hike back up and try the next one over.

The boys did not have a GPS or advanced land navigation training; they could not be certain precisely where they were at any given point on the map. All they had were their compasses, a couple of large mountain peaks to use as reference, and then the best assumptions they could intuit therefrom. As such, trial and error was something they were growing used to and frustrated by, in equal parts.

Trent shot two squirrels and a rabbit with his bow, then deftly gutted and skinned them almost entirely while walking. He hung the carcasses from loops of paracord, one on his pack and the others on Billy's and Ben's. When he shot the second squirrel, the arrow went through the animal and smashed into a lichen-covered rock beyond, where the shaft shattered with a loud ratcheting noise and the broadhead exploded into a shower of sparks none of them had expected. Trent commented on how it looked like a roman candle. This initiated a lengthy discussion about firework fights, which it seemed all four boys had been fond of, and anecdotes were shared until they compiled a lengthy highlight reel.

They'd already agreed they would not make a fire until twilight—that time of day when it's dark enough for a smoke column to be difficult to see, and light enough for the flames to not yet be piercingly visible in the darkness. This conversation only made the boys ravenous, so the loss of a single arrow, which brought the promise of a forthcoming meal of cooked meat, was something they were all entirely fine with.

At one point they stumbled into a herd of over one hundred elk. They had not realized what was actually going on as every one of the animals began blasting up from the shady beds they sought during the heat of the day and went crashing through the forest around them in every direction. The boys dropped at the first thrashing and commotion, all fearing that they'd hear the terrifying voice or laughter from the monster they had known as Reid. Billy planted himself behind a large tree trunk and held his axe like a batter preparing for a pitch. The other three boys scrambled to trees of their own and clumsily pulled arrows from their quivers, nocked them, grabbed their bowstrings, and began scanning the area for targets. Then they all began to see the flashes of the animals' brown and tan hides and their dark, long legs through the trees and undergrowth, and then eventually several full elk came into view as they made their frenzied exodus from the area.

When the stampede had subsided, the boys looked around at one another, quietly acknowledging the ungainly way they'd just all fallen into a defensive posture, silently acknowledging that if that had been the counselors, they'd have had their asses handed to them. This encounter reminded them where they were and what they were running from. The mood grew more tense for the next few miles, the joking and trading of stories mostly stopped, and the boys tried to stay as quiet as possible.

When the first tendrils of dusk began to creep into the light of the forest, they'd finally reached the bottom of the valley they'd been heading for all day. They followed the sound of running water and worked their way down a trickling but very steep tributary creek until they reached the first stream they had to cross. They all stood there, quietly looking at what was not a very wide stream, but roaring fast over a deep bed of jagged rocks and boulders, with no visible ford in either direction where they might be able to wade across on soft gravel or sand.

They all desperately wanted to rest, collapse at the bank, make a fire, and eat the cottontail and squirrels that had begun to look like they might even taste good raw as they watched them bounce off one another's packs over the last several miles. However, the knowledge, or at least the very reasonable assumption, that they were being hunted by terrifying things that defied their understanding of the natural world drove them onward. Crossing this particular stream was also a big milestone in their route, one that meant they had essentially made it to the halfway point between the camp they snuck away from the night before, and the bleak, winding state highway to their west that none of them had ever actually seen. Furthermore, getting this fast river at their backs was a good defensive barrier for them, at least psychologically if not geographically as well.

They had discussed the counselors at great length that day on their endless trundle down the mountains. They debated the difference in physical capabilities between the counselors and their master, Silas. This turned into a discussion of whether he was controlling their minds somehow, or if perhaps they were just extensions of himself, complete minions, satellite extensions of his own body and mind under his full control. This latter seemed improbable and was ultimately disregarded by the boys, due to Riley having said he would *tell Reid where they found them* and how disappointed *Reid* would be at learning they had tried to sneak off. They also wondered why Riley had refused to use his master's real name, Silas.

One thing that was undeniable was that Billy had butchered two of them before they even knew he was there. Billy was fast, *wicked* fast, and very strong, and he clearly knew how to swing an axe. But even so, if the counselors were capable of bizarre, supernatural physical feats, they likely wouldn't have been snuck up on so easily, or died so easily. This was a point even Billy made.

Despite the conclusions of this deliberation—the general assumption that, Silas aside, based on what they had seen thus far the counselors were still mortal and obviously able to be killed—they still wanted this river between them and the demon things hunting them. Besides, they would not even be able to properly relax or rest until this barrier was at their backs anyway, so they decided to set off downstream in hopes of finding a snag or log lying over the river to use as a bridge, or just somewhere with less of a scream and surge where they could attempt to wade across.

A few hundred yards down they found a pair of two small spruce trees that appeared to have fallen together across the stream in a recent storm, based on their still-green pine needles and the large, sandy root balls that had been torn up when the trees fell, visible in the rocks across the stream. The natural bridge was sturdy enough but was in a place where the water cascaded down a steep run in white, boiling rolls that licked and sputtered underneath the bottoms of the fallen trees. Below that there was a fifty-yard run of the stream where there was nothing on either side but ten feet of sheer, wet rock, until the river opened up again where some willows and shrubs could be seen lining the bank. They debated continuing down to try to find another spot, but Trent was adamant that they'd be able to get across here just fine, and that they were likely just going to come back up here anyway.

Ben went first, holding his bow out in front of him for balance and going very slowly. At the halfway point he wobbled a bit where the river screamed under the logs, spitting and flecking up onto his bare calves. He almost took a knee in order to proceed on all fours, but bending down to do so seemed even more dangerous under the heavy weight of his big pack. He just slowly put one foot in front of the other until he reached the root balls of the trees on the other side, which he scrambled over until safely away from the water and looked back across the bridge.

Rodrigo went next, whom they were all the most concerned about with his gashed thigh and steadily developing limp, but he went across much faster than Ben had and without any of the wobbling. Ben grabbed his hand as he reached the other side and hauled him over the root balls.

Trent insisted that Billy go next, and he went *very* slowly. He seemed to be taking a full deep breath after every step, but he did not wobble, he did not falter, and the other three boys just watched and waited as he took his sweet-ass time. When the large boy got a step from the end, he tossed his axe to Rodrigo, then lunged forward where Ben clasped his large forearm and helped haul him up and over the root balls.

Then Trent hopped up onto the pair of logs. He was surefooted, cat-like really. He moved fast, deftly putting one foot in front of the other as he moved quickly across the logs. He slowed a bit as he neared the other side. He looked down, checked his footing, then looked back at the guys as he tossed his bow to them. As he did this, his back foot slipped out from under his weight.

His front foot landed, and for a moment he teetered there on it, peg-legged as he probed for a new spot to plant his back foot, but they could see that his weight was not centered.

Time seemed to stop as the three boys onshore watched him slowly but relentlessly start to tip over to his left into the downstream side of the bridge. Trent looked over at them with shock and surprise in wide eyes. As he started to properly fall and his body passed the log bridge he made one last effort to reach out and grab for them.

His forearm smacked across the logs as he passed, but it did not slow his fall at all. He dumped into the water, which was churning so fast down the deep, rocky stretch that he just disappeared, swallowed entirely by the rapid. There wasn't even a splash.

CHAPTER 33

ALL THREE boys launched themselves downstream and began sprinting down the bank, screaming Trent's name and scanning the white water for any sign of him. Billy blasted ahead of the other two, not bothering to look into the water at all, but just making a direct line for the spot fifty yards down where the river opened on both sides and where he could try to position himself to grab what they assumed would be either a dead or unconscious boy as he floated by.

At one point Ben saw Trent, or at least his bottom half, when he appeared to be flipped over somehow as he went down the river—the boy's legs and butt broke the surface of the river, kicking wildly before he completed his rotation and went entirely back under the surface. About ten yards downstream he emerged again, along their side of the river, his head and arms visible now as he desperately raked his hands along the surface of a soaking-wet, near-vertical rock where the others could see he would never be able to find enough purchase.

He disappeared again, but there were only twenty or so more yards until the river opened up, to a spot Billy had already found near the bank to get into the river himself where he stood with water up to his waist, braced to grab Trent.

Ben and Rodrigo both jumped down into the bushy area Billy had used to get into the river, and each grabbed on to one side of his backpack. Just then Trent came dumping and rolling out of the last stretch of pure white water, end over end, backpack barely still secured on his shoulders. Billy lunged forward and grabbed him, landing one hand on Trent's ribs and another around one of his legs.

They all hauled him onto the bank, where he tore his head up, gasping for air and grabbing at all of their arms, appearing to think he was still about to get ripped away and sent down another stretch of river. It was a blur as they all clambered back up onto the tall bank and sprawled out in the pine needles and dirt, Trent gasping and coughing as he collapsed onto all fours. Ben and Billy were both yelling at Trent to calm down and tell them where he felt anything that hurt, while Rodrigo just started assessing the boy from head to foot.

Trent rolled onto his back, and they could see a deep cut on his forehead that bled badly, but all three boys knew—from considerable experience—that foreheads just bleed bad. Trent pulled his hands up to his chest where they could see him clutch his right hand in his left, wincing his eyes closed in pain as he did this.

"Lemme see it, bro, lemme see it, I needa see what happened, man."

Rodrigo gently took Trent's hands and slowly opened the left's grip upon the right. As he did, all three other boys could see the pinky and ring finger on Trent's right hand twisted unnaturally at the middle knuckle, protruding outward at a sickening angle. Obviously, both had been terribly broken.

Rodrigo looked over at the other two, then back at Trent.

"Alright, bro, where else does it hurt, your fingers are broken for sure, but I need to know about your legs, your head, your back, shoulders, try and think and feel where else it might hurt."

Trent sat up and cradled his mangled hand, then took a few deep breaths and began looking himself over as he rolled his shoulders and extended one leg, then another.

"I . . . I think I'm aight. Busted my head, but my hand hurts the worst, don't feel anything else, just sore, like I got hit by a car or some shit."

Ben, Rodrigo, and even Billy took this opportunity to laugh. Trent joined in with a few chuckles, then hung his head again.

The boys helped him up and took his backpack off, which Billy carried as Ben and Rodrigo helped Trent over to a boulder to sit on. They looked him over once more and had him do another self-check for pain or numbness. They all knew it was time that they rest and eat something, but they agreed that they needed to do that in a safer and more secure spot. Ben and Billy went up the ridge to scout for a place to make camp, as Rodrigo filled up all their water bladders in the stream. When Ben found a nice horseshoe of large boulders and big spruces, he yelled for Billy and then went down for the others.

They got Trent, his bag, themselves, and all their packs into the little protected alcove, and all collapsed onto knees and butts.

Rodrigo began to dig through Trent's bag to find him dry clothes as Ben began working on collecting twigs and other small feather fuels to get a fire going. Billy grabbed the packs, bows, and other gear to clear an area with enough room around the fire for them all to sit or possibly even lie down, leaning everything against the boulder on the far, uphill side from where they were all clustered. Trent even used his one good hand to begin pulling at the knots of his bootlaces, trying to remove his socks, which were soaked through with frigid water. Billy began removing the three small animal carcasses from their paracord stringers and wiping away the dirt and pine needles from the two that had not been thoroughly washed off as the one tied to Trent's bag had.

It was not clear which boy stopped moving first, as it seemed like they all did in the same moment, and as though someone had openly commanded that they do so, they all went completely still.

The noise they had been making up until the moment they went still—screaming Trent's name, the commotion of getting him out of the river, checking him over, the subsequent racket made while they got Trent and all the gear up into this spot—it all seemed to catch up to them in the same second. All the sound discipline they'd let fall away over the last twenty minutes, all the consequences of being too loud, boiled up into their minds now.

They all sat there motionless, keening their ears for anything and exchanging nervous glances with their eyes. Something about the realization of what they had just been through, how much noise they had made, almost losing Trent, caused a deep, hot, raw anxiety to hang over the group now. A solid two minutes passed as all four boys sat where they were in complete silence, not moving an inch, until Rodrigo finally spoke up.

"Should we move, should we keep going, find somewhere else farther away?"

Billy looked at Ben, then over at Trent. Ben looked at Trent as well, then shared his thoughts.

"We've got about forty-five more minutes in this twilight window to make a fire. After that we could be visible for a long ways off. Even if we are well hidden, all it takes is one little flicker of light sneakin through the rocks or trees. In this light, we can get one goin and get some shit cookin, a hot meal seems pretty suitable right now, and it will help Trent warm up. We go stumbling up that valley in the dark without resting at all we're liable to fuck ourselves up even worse."

All the boys nodded in response, either because it was reasonable, or because they were so exhausted and starving. Perhaps both.

Rodrigo and Ben now both focused on getting a small fire going, as Billy broke down the animals into haunches and smaller chunks of meat so that they would cook faster, skewering them with sticks he pushed into the rocky soil to lean over the growing fire. Trent went about removing his wet clothes using his one good hand and his teeth, then putting new ones on.

Ben went to remove his first aid kit. He cut four three-inch sections of a small branch from a sapling next to him and shaved the bark away as best he could with his knife, exposing the damp, bone-colored wood beneath. Billy looked at the collection of items in Ben's hands, nodded at him, then pushed himself up onto his knees and looked over at Trent.

"Time to deal with them fingers, T. It's gonna hurt, but if we don't lay em straight and splint em up soon, they gonna turn into white-hot fire that won't go away and'll take your mind right outta this."

Trent looked between the boys, frightened, but he nodded.

"They're already white-hot fire now, just get it over with."

Billy and Ben got onto their knees in front of where Trent sat, Ben laying out the splinting kit on the ground. Billy grabbed Trent's wet shirt down from where he'd hung it, bunched it up, and handed it to him.

"Scream into that, if ya gotta."

Trent's eyes went wide as he took the wet shirt. They could see his jaw starting to quiver. Ben took his shaking right hand and inspected the fracture and angle of the fingers. He'd done this before with one of his own fingers, and two of his little brother's. Two different incidents, but both caused by Aunt Nicki on nights when she, and her boyfriend, were in a state of belligerence that Ben knew meant they would suffer far worse if they asked to go to the hospital. Billy put one hand on Trent's shoulder and firmly locked his other around the wrist of Trent's busted hand, holding it in place in front of Ben. Billy looked over at Ben and spoke softly.

"You know ya gotta pull em outward first, then—"

Ben spoke over him without looking up into his face.

"I know it, Axe. I know it."

Earlier in the summer, Billy Axelson had promised Ben that he'd rip his eyes out if he ever called him Axe again. This had been the second time the boy had exhibited some emotion at being addressed by the nickname, and Ben had theorized, with a high degree of confidence, that Axe is what people had called his father. A father who, Ben had learned, Billy had killed under circumstances that were hazy to the authorities and staff at Bear Springs alike.

Despite the prior threats to his vision, Ben now used the nickname as an attempt to convey a silent message to the large boy, one he truly hoped sank home. He hoped the use of that nickname carried with it an assurance that *I've had terrible things done to my body and no one around to help, as well.*

He looked up and locked eyes with Billy as he prepared to work the first finger into place and was happy to find the faint traces of a smile, instead of rage, in the large boy's face.

Trent did use the wet T-shirt to scream into, quite a bit, as Ben pulled the fractured fingers outward from the joints and then twisted them back into relatively natural position, then gently probed them back inward a few times each until he could feel a more natural, flush connection between the fractured bones. Ben then wrapped the two fingers lightly in gauze, splinted the bound fingers between the four little twigs, then did another solid wrap job with more gauze and then athletic tape. He popped the aspirin from one of the blister packs in the first aid kit, made Trent take it, then removed Trent's sleeping bag from his pack and insisted he get inside as he warmed up.

Ben patted him on the shoulder.

"At least you'll still be able to shoot a bow."

Trent gave one snort in response, but did not speak.

Real darkness started to sneak into the forest around them, and the light from their fire began to jig farther and farther away from the flames. They removed the blackened hunks of squirrel and rabbit and doused their fire with dirt and gravel, smothering it aggressively until no more smoke seeped from the warm pile of earth. They devoured the mountain kebabs in silence, legitimately cooing over the great taste of it. They each then had one of the many fruit bars they'd packed away for this journey for dessert, and all polished off the last of their water.

Ben finally brought up the subject no one else wanted to.

"We should get movin up that mountain soon. We should keep movin no matter what until we're on the verge of death, because that's what we're runnin from anyway."

All three other exhausted boys staring back at Ben let their heads hang. Ben felt the same as they did. They had all woken up almost forty hours earlier and had hiked over thirty miles at high altitude over rugged terrain. They'd done sixteen miles from their first night's camp on the trout-filled stream to the second camp where they'd made their escape, and then another seventeen since making a run for it. They felt existential exhaustion in their souls and physical fatigue in every joint and muscle. But even still, no one had a rebuttal. They figured he was right.

"That being said . . ."

All three boys looked back up at him, not even trying to hide the excitement in their eyes, or the deep desire for him to just shut the hell up so they could take the stupider, deadlier alternative, but at least get some damn sleep.

"We never figured a good bearing after Trent went swimming, didn't get our heads around how to start moving up that mountain, which pass up there we wanna aim for. On top a'that, we'd have to use our headlamps, and as bone tired as we are, we'd be crashin our way up there makin all kinds of noise, lightin our position up the whole way, they'd be able to spot us from anywhere on any of them mountains on the other side of this valley . . . Let's stay put, rest up, but as soon as we can see enough to move without using our lights, which was around 5:45 a.m. this mornin, we gotta be already packed up and ready to start goin. I'll take first watch from now through midnight, who's takin second?"

Billy raised his big palm and agreed to switch with Rodrigo two hours later, who'd then get Trent two hours thereafter to take the last, shorter watch, who promised to have them all up by 5:30 a.m. None of the boys bothered to dig out their sleeping pads; they just curled up in the sleeping bags right on the hard, uneven ground and fell immediately to sleep with full stomachs.

Ben found a comfortable spot at the base of a tree a few yards away from the little alcove where the others slept. He had the bear spray on his belt—holster unclipped this time—and an arrow nocked on his bow that he rested across his lap. Ben strained his ears to listen for a snapped branch, kicked stone, or any other noise his imagination could conceive that a band of monstrous demons might make as they rooted these boys out like truffle pigs.

Although this was not very easy.

Ben had liked camping along rivers and streams throughout the summer. They had always been his favorite places; the sound of the moving water was a comforting white noise. However, the sound made by thousands of gallons of water gurgling and crashing through a stone channel was a loud thing, and as lovely as Ben found it, it did not help a night sentry's job of cautious listening. He wondered if or what Rickert knew about any of the information Ben had uncovered about Silas in the last few weeks.

As he strained his eyes into the darkness he thought back on old game warden Rickert's description of Silas as the *houndsman* and his counselors as his pack of bay hounds, his pack of lion dogs. The recollection made Ben shudder.

The roar of a mountain stream was a welcome song to those things that wake at moonrise; it's the sound that washes away all others made by things that hunt in the dark.

CHAPTER 34

B EN WOKE first. He rolled to his side, and something cold and sharp in his bag pushed him through that final, thin skein of sleep and into waking reality. He opened his eyes and blinked at the sunlight, looking around at his surroundings.

He was lying on dirt, gravel, and pine needles. He heard Billy's snoring, looked over at where the large boy slept on his back, then turned to see Rodrigo, curled up in his sleeping bag on his side with a thin line of drool running from his cracked lips to the dirt his face was planted in. Ben's eyes went wide as a flood of adrenaline surged through him. He was trying to stand up before he had even unzipped his sleeping bag, the commotion waking both Billy and Rodrigo, causing them to wince and turn away from the noise.

"Trent."

Ben hissed the boy's name as he scanned the area around them for some sign of his friend. The utterance of his name made Billy and Rodrigo cease their confused fussing, provided them some necessary context, and both of their eyes went wide as well as they began peeling themselves out of their sleeping bags and scanning around them as well. Ben snatched up his bow and knelt down on his sleeping bag to nock an arrow, Billy held his axe at the ready, and Rodrigo crouched and started making his way toward the opening to their little rocky alcove, outside of which was the tree that each of them had sat under during their respective watch shifts.

They bolted outside and felt soothing relief as they saw Trent sitting at the base of the same tree, bear spray loosely clutched in one hand,

Rodrigo's bow across his lap, twitching into wakefulness at the noise they caused. As the boys looked around themselves, then up into the sky, the relief was replaced by dread as they realized how late in the morning it was. Ben yanked his sleeve up to expose his watch and saw it was past 10:00 a.m., already over four hours over their planned departure. Trent looked up at Ben as he checked his watch, then at the others, then the area around him as reality sunk in.

"Shit . . . shit, I'm sorry, guys, I dozed off, felt like I only closed my eyes two seconds ago."

Billy scanned the trees below their position, then spoke as he looked up the slope above them, vaguely in the direction of the massive cluster of peaks and ridges that they had to climb up, over, and then down in order to escape this place.

"Don't matter now, we've gotta move, get your shit."

Within one minute they'd stuffed their sleeping bags into their packs, hoisted them onto their backs, buckled their waist and chest straps, and were stacked up in single file behind Ben, who was looking between his map journal and the nondescript mountains around them, trying to get his bearings.

They gave him a few moments to do this, and he finally handed Billy the journal to put into the top pocket of his pack already on his back, and spoke to the group.

"I don't know where we're at along the foot of this mountain, but that's where we are. I'll be able to tell better once we can see a bit more, higher up this ridge. All I can say from where we're at is that we've basically just gotta start goin straight up from here, keep heading west, and whenever we have to work laterally, we do so to the south."

They spent the next hour covering only around one thousand yards on a map but several thousand vertical feet up the steep slope. Every step seemed so loud to them all as they expected an ambush at any second, all clenching their jaws in anticipation of some grunt, jibber, or shriek from a nearby demon counselor to cut through the warm morning. On several occasions one of them dislodged a rock from underfoot that went smashing down the slope behind them and they'd all stop moving and cringe in dread for what felt like hours but was really only about eight or nine seconds until the rock came to rest. They reached a spot where the aspect of the mountain relaxed, and then turned into a fairly open, flat bench in the mountainside that appeared to run a long way to the north and the south. There were still some tall trees around and clusters of aspen, but they could actually see several hundred yards in every direction for the first time since before crossing the river the day evening before. Here they took a brief rest again as Ben worked with the map and compass and the others passed around dried fruit and a few energy bars.

They all awaited Ben's navigational call, no one saying a word. Finally, he closed the journal again, had Trent stash it in the top pocket of his bag above his head, and spoke.

"Let's move south on this shelf a ways. If we are where I think we are, it'll start going up and to the west a bit, and it should open up so we can see down into the valley and back up onto the saddles and peaks we went over yesterday. Then we'll know where we're at for sure."

They all kept a steady walking pace over the next several hours as they worked their way south along the open, meadowy expanse, with steep, dense forest dropping away on their left and climbing up the mountain on their right. They were able to move shoulder to shoulder, almost like a group of pheasant hunters, anxiously switching their gaze between their footing and the area around them. Once they'd started bearing west and up the slope, the landscape opened up considerably, and they walked out into an open bowl that seemed to encompass the entire face of this mountain and looked bigger than any stadium they'd ever seen. There were a few clusters of trees, boulders, and some taller rock outcroppings to break up the landscape, but for the most part the next mile—the entire east face of this mountain—looked like mostly just cheatgrass and sage. A tall, imposing line of basalt rocks with an apron of shale and scree below it rimmed the top of this expanse above the group to the west, which Ben pointed up to as he spoke to the others.

"We can't go up and over here, looks like that rim's blocking us all the way along the ridge, so we've gotta cross this open ground here in front of us. We could go back down to the stream and follow it south again, but I ain't gotta tell y'all that'll be a scramble, and we'll lose a lot of time. That's the bad news. The good news, I guess, is that I know where we are."

Ben extended his journal to the boys and pointed to a spot on the map that did not mean anything to them.

"Kaniksu Creek is that way, straight through that big, long open stretch. That's where we turn due west and head up toward d'Oreilles Pass. Get on the other side of that pass and it's downhill, whole way to the highway and trailheads."

The boys looked ahead, scanning the open, steep landscape they'd have to spend the next couple of hours traversing. Billy said what the others were thinking.

"We'll be awful exposed out there, for a good while too . . ."

Ben nodded.

"Yah, we will be, but any alternative is gonna add five or six hours, if we're lucky. I'm open to doubling back and looking for another route if y'all wanna do that, I really am, but I don't know where it would be."

Rodrigo spoke up, with conviction in his voice.

"Fuck it, man, let's do this. The pass to get outta the crotch of this mountain range we're stuck in is right up there. Spending hours out in the open is risky, but so is every damn thing we do up here, and we gave those fuckers almost twelve hours to catch up to us. We need to keep moving."

Rodrigo barely waited for any agreement to be expressed, and just punched out of the forest line, picking a path out into the open mountainside.

The group made good progress, despite spending the entire first three hours with their eyes glued to the opposite wall of the valley, letting their imaginations work up visions of the counselors standing where Ben had bandaged Rodrigo's leg the morning before, glaring down across the valley with their black eyes to where they now were. All four of them endlessly scanned the landscape for people, grizzlies, the demon counselors, or any movement at all.

It had grown hot, and windless. All the boys shed layers as they went, stuffing them into straps and folds of their large bags, until they all were in tank tops or shirtless as they side-hilled across the steep, dusty, baked expanse of summer-toasted grass and grasshoppers. Always, so many grasshoppers—a constant, living insect perimeter surrounded each boy as a halo of the things launched themselves up from beneath each stride, then boosted into their clumsy, uncontrolled flight lines on their snapping wings. Rodrigo had commented on how similar they sounded to the Taser the cop had used to drop him when he got arrested, bringing a much-needed laugh to the group, but then all they could hear again was the buzzing snap of electricity as they rucked along the hot mountain slope.

Once they'd finally reached the point where the mountainside started to round, curling in toward the west, they could now begin to see up the new monstrous valley that led toward the saddled d'Oreilles Pass, which was their final alpine crucible toward freedom. The evening vibrance of light made it stunning to behold. They came upon what was actually a very defensible little fortress of boulders a few hundred yards up the slope from what sounded like a small waterfall below, which Ben assumed would be the confluence of the stream they'd almost lost Trent in and followed all day and Kaniksu Creek. They collapsed into the small area and untangled themselves from their large packs.

Rodrigo was put on cooking duty—boiling water so they could have some hot freeze-dried food—while Trent worked on redoing the now thrashed and tattered splint on his own fingers, and Ben and Billy went down to the stream to fill up all their water bladders.

Ben and Billy both took their boots off and cooled their feet in the stream as they washed all the blood, sweat, and grime from their bodies. Neither spoke as they did this, or as they plodded back up the slope loaded with water. Their spirits rose a bit as they reclined around this little recovery dojo they'd found and shoveled the hot packets of slop into their mouths. Eventually they boiled one more pot of water to make a large batch of tea with juniper berries and rose hips Trent had been collecting throughout the day.

That tea was, so far as any of them could recall, the most soothing, soul-warming thing any of them had ever consumed in their lives. Right before dark, they smothered their little cooking fire thoroughly, and all sat on their sleeping pads, sipping their trapper tea, staring out across the landscape. They all watched silently until the landscape was covered by the night. The near-full moon cast the landscape in a silver hue and made long, dark shadows of everything. Ben offered to take the first watch, which the others gratefully accepted, and he took his bow and the bear spray and went a few yards above their rock fortress to sit against a large stone where he had a commanding view of everything around them.

Five minutes later, Billy strode up toward Ben. He passed his tin cup of still semi-warm tea to Ben as he sat down next to him. Ben accepted it, took a few sips, and passed it back. Several silent minutes passed before Ben spoke.

"Folks used to call your ol' man Axe?"

Billy was looking across the valley, up toward the mountains they'd had breakfast on the morning before, but Ben could see the large boy smile.

"*Yup*, you had that one figured early, eh?"

Ben did not reply right away. He came very, *very* close to asking Billy about his dad's death, his uncle's death, about the true story behind why he'd killed them, whether it really was an accident, but he did not. He went with something else instead.

"You told Silas, all those weeks back, that your dad can't say nothin, because that son of a bitch is dead. And you're right about that, he can't, he's dead, and you're his boy, so you get whatever he left behind. That's how it works. That might not a been much, but you can sure as hellfire *take that fuckin name*. Ain't his no more, it's *yours*."

Ben fused some exhausted passion into those final words, enough to make Billy look over into Ben's face, his expression unreadable. Ben went on.

"After last night, saving our asses like that, you damn well earned that name, Billy. If anyone's ever earned the name Axe, a real Axelson or otherwise, it's you."

Ben heard the large boy let out a single chuckle. He could see him nod a few times, then look back down the valley toward the dead counselors.

They sat there in silence for a while until a bone-chilling sound pierced the air. When it started, it was something low, something that could've been mistaken or disregarded, but as the wolf's howl worked itself up in pitch and volume it blasted across the valley.

It came from the massive expanse they had spent the day crossing. Over the next few minutes, the wolves howled more, until they were blasting one off every few seconds. Ben and Billy heard Trent and Rodrigo hissing at one another, then up at Ben and Billy, so they went back down into their stone fortress.

They all huddled together listening to the symphony.

"They're about to start eatin somethin, and *you'll know* when they finally do."

Billy's uninvited hypothesis was chilling, and no one responded. Eventually, presumably when one of the wolves worked up the nerve to take that first bite into the haunch or neck of the elk or moose that was about to die, a feeding frenzy began as the wolves barked, snarled, snapped, keened, and roared at one another, fighting over the fresh meat. It lasted for over an hour until it finally began to die down.

The boys were grateful for the silence that followed. It felt like it did when the furious heart of that lightning storm had finally passed them by a few weeks earlier. They'd all begun to breathe easier just when a single, lone wolf's howl punched through what had finally become a quiet night. The beast was not more than a hundred yards above their little camp. Then a second came, from the same distance *down* the slope, below them. Then to their east, then their west. Before long, all they heard, from every direction, was the unique sound made by a pack of wolves that had just finished devouring something alive but had then decided that they were not, in fact, finished eating.

When the first gray light of dawn finally rimmed the eastern wall of mountains, all four boys were sitting in a tight bunch, back-to-back, facing outward, each covering a ninety-degree sector. They'd heard the last, single howl from above camp just about thirty minutes earlier. The wolves had stayed with them all night, falling into a lull at times, then working themselves back up into a snarling frenzy just beyond the rocks that formed the boundary of their camp, making it sound like boys were in the middle of some beastly, hellish carousel. They'd each spent so long with one of the sharp arrows gripped in one hand, a knife in the other, all their hands were numb. They could feel the tension and dread build through one another's backs and shoulders as the wolves worked closer and closer.

They all sat there, bloodshot, desperate eyes staring outward, as they had for every single minute that had passed since they'd woken up the morning before. Eventually, once there was enough light, they all quietly began packing their bags.

None of them spoke.

Something quiet but catastrophic had happened inside them all through that terrible night. Something had changed, irrevocably. They all had realized, in their own way, that they were either going to die in these mountains or escape them, but there would be no easy or painless moment to come until one or the other finally happened.

CHAPTER 35

THEY WERE packed quickly, but when Trent proposed they all have some more of that trapper tea from the night before to give them a little boost after a sleepless night, the other three sat back down.

Ben surveyed the map, Billy propped his elbows on the rocks and peered into the new valley they'd be entering with Trent's stolen binoculars, Rodrigo gently rubbed the skin of his thigh around the deep gash, and Trent cradled his throbbing, fractured fingers. They shared a small meal of nuts and jerky in silence for several minutes as their east-facing mountainside erupted in light when the sun finally crested over the mountains.

Billy's urgent whisper cleared every other thought from their heads immediately.

"There, somethin's over there, somethin's movin, it's white, right under that big stand of trees that's diamond shaped, across this creek up ahead in the middle of the meadow on the other side."

The other three boys spun and hunkered themselves up into the rocks on the south side of their natural bunker, scattering a group of small sage lizards who'd just emerged for their morning sunbath. They peeked their heads and eyes over the warming, rough stone to scan the massive space ahead. Billy was pointing toward an area ahead of and a bit below them, on the other side of the new valley.

"Oh, *whew* . . . it's deer. It's a group of deer. Eight or nine of em."

Trent snatched the glass from Billy to confirm for himself, then let out a long, relieved exhale.

The mood lightened again as Rodrigo took a turn with the binoculars and made a joke about how they were all just as jumpy as deer, giving everyone an opportunity to laugh out some tension from the long night. He passed them to Ben, who had to take a moment to locate the animals through the shimmering heat distortion that pumped up from everything in the baking landscape. But there they were, a group of mule deer grazing lazily in the shade.

Ben had just counted the eleventh doe in the group when all the deer he could see, in the exact same split second, whipped their heads up and over to stare directly at the group of boys, and went completely still. Something about it made Ben's heart skip a beat.

"They just spotted us, all at the same time."

Ben lowered the binoculars from his eyes, joining the rest of the boys in staring down at the small herd with naked eyes. After a long moment, and just as quickly as they had looked over and frozen, the deer spooked and exploded into motion down the slope toward the dark timber of the valley floor. They moved at incredible speed, taking long, deep bounds they appeared to use all four legs at the same time to launch themselves into.

"Things must have some *damn* good eyesight."

Billy shook his head, disagreeing with Trent's comment as he watched the last deer disappear into the trees.

"Nah, way they all spooked at once, they must've winded us."

All four boys heard something that made them turn. It was like the bleating of a goat, but deeper, more rounded. They scanned the grassy expanse to the north they'd just crossed and saw the movement at the same time. It was on top of a crumbling boulder about four hundred yards behind them, something with four legs. It sat too low to be a deer, elk, or mountain goat. Rodrigo asked the question for everyone.

"Tha fuck is that thing?"

They watched as it brought its head up, pushing it forward and away from the profile of its ambiguous body, and trumpeted out another of the strange, bleating cries. As it did this, they could see it was not an animal's head. It was a human, it was a person on all fours. It looked in the direction the boys were looking, into the mountainside they had just hiked through. A responsive call of the same kind came echoing up from farther away to the north, beyond a fold in the slope that obscured their morning's route from view.

They instinctively took a step backward as the thing, *the person*, on the rock whipped its head around to seemingly glare directly at the group. It screamed out a new and different kind of sound then. It was still animalistic, but a distinct human voice was deep in it somewhere beneath the wet, gargled oscillations. It was part screech and part roar, just a single syllable, but it had distinct excitement in it, as well as what was unmistakably, chillingly, a single word.

"*Boys.*"

It scrambled down off the rock and then began bounding toward them, running with the gait of a dog. The grass obscured its body, so they could only see its head bobbing up and down as it increased speed into a full charge. As it came on, the boys heard the same word—the same bone-numbing, squealing roar from several different mouths somewhere behind it. *Boys, boyssss.*

Rodrigo and Trent had already turned to get their bows before Ben had looked away from the *thing* galloping toward them. Billy yanked Ben's shoulder backward, snapping him out of his trance and smacking the third bow into Ben's hands. Trent hauled both his and Rodrigo's arrows out of their quivers and dropped the clutch of nine arrows on the ground between them, Ben did the same and dropped his arrows onto the ground to his right. Each boy took one, nocked it, then turned to stand shoulder to shoulder to face the galloping *thing* that was now bearing down on them.

Billy stood to their left, rolling his shoulders and adjusting his grip on the large axe, appearing perfectly calm, and sounding that way as well when he spoke.

"Wait till I call the shot, you hear me? You shoot on *my command*. I'm a let him get close, real damn close so you can't miss, these first shots count the most. Once you shoot, I'll make sure it's down, you just get another arrow nocked, we got more comin behind this one."

The boys could see the bobbing heads of more of these canine humanoids come into view following the first one they'd seen on the rock, which was only around one hundred yards off now. It moved with the speed of a running man, but no human should be able to gallop that fast on all fours. The things continued to bleat, roar, and squeal as they mobbed over the grass toward them.

They could see the closest one now. It was a man alright, and a man they began to recognize. The sun lit up his face, which suffered from the same distortion that Riley's and Jimmy's had. The thing smiled with its massive mouth and began barking like an actual dog. Drool and froth formed racing stripes that caked back along both sides of its face. It kicked up clumps of dirt and dead grass as it charged forward, a cloud of fine dust hanging in the air behind it.

When Billy spoke the word *draw*, a certain amount of calm fell over the three archers. There was no relief from the panic that gripped them as they watched this beast charge forward, but it was the type of calm that accompanied the performance of something from muscle memory. They'd all used these same bows they now held in their shaking hands to shoot thousands of arrows over the last months. Their hearts still thundered, their throats still closed, their minds were nothing but shrieking dread, but as they brought the fletching of the arrows to the corners of their mouths and aimed down the shafts at their target, their hands did not shake.

"*Shoot.*"

It was not clear whose arrow was whose, but they all could just *feel* that they'd landed their shots without having to actually see it. They'd felt the same thing on the range before; sometimes, somehow, the brain doesn't need the eyes to know it's a bull's-eye.

Counselor Pete was midgallop—long-fingered hands still in the air in front of him—as all three arrows tore into him within the same half second.

The first arrow struck the man right above the right clavicle, the broadhead tearing all the way through the muscle, lung, and punching into his liver—a couple of inches of the feather fletching was all that protruded from the wound. The second arrow snuck right under his elongated chin, where the broadhead shredded into the Adam's apple and trachea, and shattered against the spine. The third arrow hit Pete in the face, the tip of the broadhead entering directly into his tear duct then punching out the back of the man's skull.

This final arrow had whipped Pete's head back so hard it sounded like a vertebra in his neck cracked. It was as if they had shot him with a shotgun loaded with three steel slugs. Every muscle in his body went limp before his face had even crashed into the dirt, doing a full cartwheel before coming to rest ten feet in front of the boys.

Billy barked at them to nock their arrows, which they did with numb hands as fast as they could.

The next two were about one hundred yards off now, side by side, with the other pair about another hundred yards behind.

"Same thing this time, but aim for the one on the right. I'll take the one on the left."

It was Freddie on the right, and one of the other cabin counselors, Jake, on the left, surging ahead like dogs just as Pete had. Their impossible smiles faltered and their black eyes widened as they saw the corpse of Pete piled up in front of the boys, and their sickening glee morphed into fury as both let out a jittery squeal and appeared to speed up. Freddie was a massive man even before he'd turned into this repulsive demon version of himself.

The boys barely heard Billy's *draw* command over the beastly noise, but they heard *shoot* clearly.

Again, it was impossible to tell whose arrow was whose, and all arrows flew within the same half second, but one arrow clearly missed, soaring just an inch over Freddie's shoulder and gouging a blast of dust into the air twenty yards behind him. The second arrow went straight into his roaring mouth and punched out the back of his neck behind his right ear. The third arrow hit him in the top of the massive left shoulder, the broadhead buried into the joint with a sickening thud, and the man crashed down when he landed his stride. The weight hit his useless shoulder, rolling him toward them in an explosion of dust.

The boys glanced to the left just as Jake began lowering his shoulder to slam into Billy, and Billy's timing was perfect. Right as Jake tucked his head down, Billy's axe fell, its entire head disappearing into the muscle and meat between the man's left shoulder blade and spine. The blow shattered ribs, shredded through the lung, and burst out from Jake's chest. Even so, Jake had been charging so fast that his weight bowled

Billy over, tore the axe from his hands, and both disappeared into a rolling ball of legs, arms, dust, and yellow summer grass.

Their attention returned to Freddie, who was abandoning his qua-
drupedal approach and pushing himself up onto two feet with one
hand as his left arm hung completely limp and useless below the arrow
buried in his shoulder and jutting upward toward the sky. He was huge,
weighing as much as two of the three boys who now faced him, and as he
attempted to gain his feet, they could see he was even larger now. Blood
poured from where the arrow stuck out the back of the man's neck just
below his ear. He tried to remove or break the arrow by gripping the
fletched end protruding from his mouth but abandoned the effort as he
saw the threat approaching him.

Ben was sprinting at Freddie before Trent and Rodrigo had fully
focused back on the massive, wounded man. It even seemed to surprise
Freddie. Ben did not realize he was screaming, *roaring* until he'd already
slammed into the wounded counselor, driving his shoulder into the
man's sternum just as he rose onto two feet, slamming him backward
into the dust. He barely remembered pulling out the pocketknife and
flipping it open, but found himself now on top of Freddie, straddling his
upper body and slamming the blade into his throat and eyes repeatedly.

Ben only noticed the fourth and fifth counselors bearing down on
him when they let out piercing, agonized squeals. He looked up just
as the one closest to him stumbled, kept his footing, then crumpled
forward.

It was Gordon, one of the elder men who'd come all the way to
Louisiana to yank Ben out of his home. Something about his demeanor both grounded Ben and perplexed him. The man looked
almost confused as he began crawling, then sat up onto his butt
and stared down at the shaft of an arrow that he clutched where it
protruded from his belly. Ben saw he had a wide leather belt on the
outside of his button-down shirt, and his eyes went wide when he saw
a pistol holster on his right hip where a worn, wooden pistol grip was
nestled. Ben was not sure when he'd climbed off Freddie's butchered
corpse onto his feet, but here he was, sprinting toward Gordon, then
diving headfirst toward his gun. To Ben's surprise, the man did not

make any effort to resist the boy as he wrenched the old six-shooter from the holster, then scrambled away.

As Ben made his move on Gordon, counselor Devin—another real dipshit they'd all hated *before* he'd turned into whatever this thing was—came surging forward. Trent had put an arrow through his waistline somewhere in his lower belly and it was pouring blood down his pants, but he still stumbled forward toward Trent. Rodrigo dropped his bow and rushed him, falling into his boxing stance as he moved, easily weaving away from the monster's wild haymakers and attempts to grab him. He'd sneak inside the man's reach and send hammering flurries of jabs and crosses into the man's face, then bound away. He sent whip-cracked uppercuts from his hips and shoulders, one of which audibly crunched Devin's jawbone.

Devin made a flailing dive toward Rodrigo and, despite paying for it with three hits to the nose, he did get his hands around the boy's ankle. He began barrel-rolling like an alligator and thrashing the boy's leg around as Rodrigo went down, kicking to break free. Trent ran toward the grappling pair to help, but Billy came out of nowhere in a blur.

Every inch of him appeared covered in dust-caked blood from his tangle with Jake. His first axe blow sank deep into Devin's lower back, right above his beltline, and seemed to paralyze the man in some way. His mouth and eyes went wide in anguish and shock but no noise came out. His grip released on Rodrigo's ankle, and immediately after Billy wrenched the axe from his body he began to convulse and whimper. Billy took a massive golf swing with the axe that tore the blade into the back of Devin's neck, abruptly ending his panicked noises and spasming.

Trent, Rodrigo, and Billy all noticed Ben sitting several yards away from Gordon—the last counselor alive—as the man began rising from his seated position onto shaky legs. He faced away from them, strangely, and as soon as he stood, the blur of Trent's arrow shaft screamed through the air. Ripples of impact roiled through man's entire body as the broadhead smashed into his shoulder blade, shattering the scapula and sending a loud crack out over the valley. It knocked Gordon forward onto his knees.

"Wait!"

Ben was surprised by his own voice and the fact that he was holding a palm out toward Trent and Rodrigo, who each had arrows nocked and had just begun to draw their bows back to send two more arrows into this final counselor. Billy had also been stalking toward Gordon with his axe held at the ready. All three boys looked at Ben, surprised by his command, and then by the gun in his hand, but went forward behind him as he rose and worked around the groaning, miserable form of Gordon to approach him from the front. Ben had the sense to toss the gun into a sage bush before entering the kneeling man's striking distance.

"Gordon, look at me."

Gordon did not move for a long moment, but eventually pushed himself up and rocked back onto his knees, lifting his face toward the sun. Ben was briefly fascinated to find that this man's features were not actually very distorted like the others'. Gordon remained there, breathing heavily, kneading the shafts of the arrows protruding from his guts, and the boys felt some of the murderous frenzy slip away as they watched real, deep, human pain contorting hisfeatures.

"You Gordy Colton?"

Trent, Rodrigo, Billy, and even the miserable Gordon looked at Ben's face when he said that name out loud.

The man held Ben's gaze for a long moment, then stared back down at the arrow sticking from his belly.

"*Yup.*"

Ben heard one of his buddies begin to ask him a question just as he sent one of his own toward Gordon.

"You remember anything from 1878, or before then?"

As though he'd let some veil fall away, Gordon spoke with an older accent now, one that almost sounded like game warden Rickert's.

"Bits n'pieces, I spose."

Ben glanced to his friends as he thought of his next question, finding them wide-eyed in disbelief, then back to Gordon.

"Reckon you and your buddies ended up findin ol' Blackthorn, then . . ."

Gordon looked back up at Ben with genuine humor in his eyes, letting out an amused chuckle as Ben went on.

"So I gotta assume he'd already gotten that ol' lantern burnin by the time y'found him."

A lance of pain appeared to boil up from where the broadhead tore and perforated Gordon's intestines and stomach. He looked down at the arrow again, and eventually he spoke through clenched teeth, dark blood dripping from his lips into the dirt.

"That he did, son. *That . . . he did.*"

Ben knelt before the man, nodding to the horizon as he spoke.

"Silas out there, then? He out there with a whole new platoon a'dogs, huntin us down?"

Gordon shook his head as he spoke but did not look up.

"He's huntin y'all alright, but *nah,* you four broke the order. *Harvest can only happen once the seed of trust begins to ripen,* as he put it. Once y'all lit out, well . . . it spoiled the rest a'tha root stock. Trust was fractured and doubt was sown in the minds a'the rest. Too late in tha season to start over, so . . ."

Ben leaned into his face when the silence began to stretch.

"So . . . *what?* Tha hell's that sposed t'mean?"

Gordon looked blankly past Ben, speaking out into the valley.

"Well, when a crop takes to rot, you *wipe it out,* root and stem, then burn it . . . Only ones he managed to harvest was those he'd already turnt fore tonight. Y'all's the only bad crop left. Haven't had a yield this small since back in '31 . . . Ol' boy's awful worked up, *tell you what.*"

Ben looked over at the others, who all stared back at him with awe and exhausted confusion.

"Javier, Bishop, Hart, your buddies, where they at?"

Gordon gestured toward the mountains to the north with his head as he spoke.

"Jav-Zada's out with tha boss, huntin y'all down. Bish and Hart's back at camp on flame watch."

Ben went on with a question somehow even more cryptic and meaningless to his friends than those he'd asked thus far.

"How do we destroy it?"

Gordon shook his head slowly.

"Can't tell you that, young'n, even if I wanted to."

Ben thought for a moment before changing course.

"Then how do we *put it out*?"

Gordon nodded.

"Lifeblood a'youth to start it up, *same to douse it out*."

Trent's voice surprised Ben.

"Alright, B . . . you have *got* to tell us what *in the hell* you two are talkin about."

Ben nodded at his friend and extended a finger, hoping that would serve as a humble request for a bit more patience.

"Where's it at, upstairs at the lodge someplace, behind them big, locked doors at the end of the hall?"

Gordon looked at Ben and smiled with a closed mouth.

"Nicky said you was sharp."

Ben nodded in understanding and stood, asking his next question out into the valley.

"How you able to tell me all this? How'd I get your gun fore you even took a shot? What about all that business about Silas having *full dominion and command over men* once he has the lantern?"

Gordon appeared to sincerely consider this for a moment before responding with a hint of wonder in his voice.

"Ain't all that clear to us, the counselors, the dogs, those he plants that trust seed into, anyone he gets close enough to take over. He gave us *lots* of orders we can't break no matter how hard we try. All I know is Jav-Zada, Bish, Hart, and myself are differ'nt. We, well . . . we're just not like all the rest, we ain't full puppets I guess, don't age. First thing he ever told me to do was to protect the flame, and I have. He told me to find y'all once you lit out, and I did. But he never said to draw on nobody, and he never told me not to answer this kinda query if asked. I spose . . . well, I spose Silas Everett Blackthorn juss got shortsighted. The ol' boy juss never spected anyone to ask this kinda stuff."

Ben stared down at Gordon for a good, long while before speaking.

"You wanna hand, or you wanna see this out on y'own?"

Gordon closed his eyes.

"*Boy*, I been ready for this for a long, *long* time. If'n it's all the same to you, I wouldn't wanna stall another minute."

Ben startled the other three boys as he abruptly closed on the man.

He slowly gripped Gordon's hair in his blood-soaked left hand and pulled it back, forcing the man's face to stare up into his own. As soon as he saw the man was smiling with tears in his eyes, Ben plunged the blade he'd used to kill Freddie deep into the side of Gordon's Adam's apple. He wrenched the knife back and forth several times, then yanked it free. Gordon looked, of all things, genuinely *relaxed* as Ben planted his boot into his chest, slamming him backward. The last thing Gordon saw in this world after a long, *long* lifetime was a glistening arc of arterial blood trailing out of him into the air right before the back of his skull connected with the rocks.

Ben looked over at his friends, who were beyond confusion at this point and had fallen comfortably into the realm of raw disbelief.

"Boys, I'm sorry, but I can't keep heading west. I've gotta adjust course, and I ain't askin for y'all to join me. In fact, you'd be stupid to follow me, *real* stupid. Right up there is Caravan Pass; on the other side it's all downhill to the highway and back to civilization. I know you're exhausted, but if y'all left right now and hydrated like crazy all day, I reckon you'd be up and over by lunchtime."

The expression on their faces subtly changed from disbelief to resignation. Billy was the one who spoke.

"You're thinkin about goin back to Bear Springs, aren't you?"

Ben met his large friend's gaze and chewed the inside of his cheek for a moment, then stooped over the old, dead cowboy and began removing his gun belt as he responded.

"Well past thinkin bout it, Axe. *I'm goin*. I don't like endin things like this, but I ain't got no choice. I know you'll scoff at it, but this time, I . . . I gotta just do what's right. Can't leave this place operational, just can't. Wouldn't be able to live with myself."

The other boys did not speak as Ben finally slid the gun belt out from under the dead man, then walked over to where he'd tossed the pistol into the sage bush. He found it then brushed some dust off, exposing S&W MODEL 3 .45 SCHOFIELD engraved into the old metal. He inspected it for a moment, then pointed it away from himself and fiddled with the latch on the frame until the gun broke open, exposing the rear of the fully loaded cylinder. He checked the six rounds therein, slammed the weapon closed, then counted at least eighteen additional bullets in loops around the belt. He looked over at his friends and was surprised to find a grinning Billy had taken several steps closer to him.

"You really think we can beat Reid, or *Silas,* back to basecamp?"

Ben looked to the east and took a deep breath.

"Yes. We took a goddamned circuitous route to get here, zaggin and ziggin with the counselors for three days around the mountains before we lit out. If we leave now, I wager we can get back there before they stop lookin for us. Silas is still out here huntin us. I don't see why he'd expect us to go backward. Reckon he eventually sniffs out these dead bastards sometime this evenin, then figures us for long gone with the pass right up there. Either way, as the crow flies, camp's a straight shot thataway, and I think we beat him back there."

Billy nodded and looked over as Trent and Rodrigo approached to stand next to him. Both boys looked at Ben, almost appearing relieved. At what, Ben was not sure, but he figured it was his admission that he'd not entirely lost his grasp on that which was right and good in the face of evil. Rodrigo spoke.

"Let's roll."

Trent smiled and nodded his agreement.

Ben looked down at the old gun as he wrapped the ends of the belt around the holster, then held it up as he addressed the others.

"Any of you three know how to use this thing well, and by *well* I mean with *some* level of proficiency?"

Trent, Rodrigo, and Billy, appearing a bit less fatigued, all eagerly raised their hands in the same second.

Ben was unsurprised, and pleased. He smiled at them through bloody teeth.

"Well, *good,* cause we're goin back to Bear Springs to throw down against some gunslingers. *Real ones.*"

CHAPTER 36

THE CUTS all over Charlie's face were deeply packed with dirt. His nose, lips, and eyebrows were gone, as well as most of the outer skin on his forehead, cheekbones, and chin.

His hands had been mostly frayed away into bleeding stumps where only the thumbs and a few other small bones remained. All the skin, cartilage, and muscle was either compacted into a dirt-caked meat around the few remaining bones of his hands or had been flayed away entirely. There was *some* skin remaining in shredded, dark, strips that hung from increasingly tenuous connections to the skin of his wrists.

Silas had cut young Charlie loose on their scent the morning they found Jimmy's and Riley's corpses. He knew such a strenuous hunt would destroy this fresh new boy's body.

That was alright. Hunts like this had truly become a *rare thing*.

He whispered his wishes and commands into the ear of Charlie, and off he went, galloping away on all fours to find the location of the four deviant escapees' first camp.

Silas was very clear with this fresh new boy that he was *not to leave* the location once he found it, and that he was to stay there until Silas came to him to retrieve him. He could not trust a fresh new boy to find a scent and then make it all the way back to him and still remember where he'd found it. They were just too raw in their first few days, their new form, their new mind, it was all just so new for them. It took time to mold a fresh boy into a *good, smart boy*.

Charlie had found it within about six hours, and as father had commanded, he spent the next thirty hours finding *every last trace* of their scent on every rock, every boulder, and every stump. By the time Father had arrived, Charlie had been a very good boy indeed. He smashed his nose and furiously clawed and dug at *every last trace* of their scent.

He'd also sent his fresh new boy Dean to find the first spot the escapees had eaten a meal, several hours before he'd cut Charlie loose. He told Dean, as well, to wait there and find *every last trace* until Father arrived to collect him.

But Silas had already gathered, through other means, where that was—up on the crest of the other side of valley across from where he now stood rubbing the back of his hand along his proud Charlie's skinless face.

Silas looked up and smiled as he whispered *that's a very good boy, I love you* in the direction of the gully where Ben had bandaged Rodrigo's gashed knee—where he knew Dean had been digging and thrashing and gouging his hands and face against rocks and stumps for the last thirty-five hours. *What a shame, what a loss.* Alas, it had to be done, and *Dean will go to sleep soon*, knowing he'd been a very good boy.

Unbeknownst to Silas, Dean had actually died of blood loss seven hours earlier as he'd eventually severed too many arteries while he dug down, down, and down, below the spot where several drips of Rodrigo's blood had fallen.

Silas *always* lost a few of his fresh new boys after every feasting season. Some hunts, Silas knew all too well, would just destroy the body of a new hound. A hound needed time to learn how to exist in their new form, and he'd make sure some of them got that time, but just like packs of bear or wild boar hunting dogs, every ruthless hunter knew that a certain number would be lost, especially if there was a good hunt underway.

Silas went up the slope, toward the long open bench the escapees had taken toward the open mountainside, with Mitchell, poor, mutilated Charlie, the rest of his fresh new boys, crawling along behind him on all fours, and of course his loyal Javier. He glanced over at Javier, his dear, sweet, ruthless hunter. His personal favorite *keeper of the flame* of the four. They'd been through so very much over the last century and a half.

He did not make his *keepers of the flame* crawl like the rest of his dogs. He let them, if they so chose, which sometimes they did, but on hunts like this, he would let his *keepers of the flame* have their old guns back; their *beloved guns* that they used so masterfully in his name over the years. Danny, Gordon, Javier, even old Nick, they were like dancers with their guns when Silas commanded them to kill. It was *glorious* to behold, and such a rare thing these days. He'd forgotten to command Gordy to use his gun to kill the boys if he found them, but no matter, he hunted in a pack with some of his most ruthless dogs.

Javier stood next to him, stroking his thumb along the ivory hilt of his pistol as Silas stroked *his* thumb along the chin and lips of his dear, sweet Javier.

Even after all this time since he'd used the power of the lantern to bring the four cowboys into his stable, he could see Javier would *still* quiver and shake with rage as Silas would touch him, as Silas would *take him*. It's why he cherished Javier so much. That zeal, that rage. It was irreplicable. *How had he been so lucky to find these four talented men so early along the jaguar path*, Silas often wondered.

It took Silas and his pack a few hours to reach the site where five of his best boys had been butchered. He could smell their death and rot from a long way off.

Silas shook with rage as he bent down over the destroyed face of his good, sweet boy Freddie. Silas could still see some of the knife wounds in his eye sockets and throat that remained even after the vultures had spent their day going to work on him. Then he saw Gordy. His precious Gordy, who'd been with him since the beginning, one of his *keepers of the flame*, he had never lost one before. He jabbered and shrieked as he made his way over to sweet Gordy's corpse. He saw the deep, lipless wound in his neck with great dismay. Silas slipped his tongue into this wound and tasted Benjamin Thibodaux. Then he saw it, something peeking out from inside Gordy's mouth, which he removed with two shaking, clawed fingers.

It was an old photograph, one from a very, very long time ago, showing him and some of his *first* good boys.

Silas's rage boiled over at the insolence of this Benjamin Thibodaux. When he got control of himself again, when he ceased his wailing and shrieking, and realized what he was doing, he released the clump of meat and shattered bones he clutched in both massive fists. He looked down, startled, to find his poor, *poor* fresh new boy Hector's destroyed corpse below him. He looked at it with astonishment, gently laying it back onto the rocks where he'd been smashing it for the last several minutes.

He had not lost himself like that in many decades, Silas pondered. This was a terrible, terrible day. He took deep breaths as he thought back to the din, roar, and wailing of Antietam; back to writhing and wiggling his body deeper and deeper into sea of corpses on that hill of butchery at Fredericksburg to escape the wall of steel and fire above. He recalled the stench and blood and screams and felt some measure of calm return to his bones.

He turned back to his pack, who still sat on all fours and panted, staring blankly at the bloody rocks at Silas's feet.

Mitchell, Silas's *best* boy, grunted. Silas looked over, followed his best boy's gaze, and took a deep whiff. He smelled it then too. *Ahhh,* those poor, stupid, *bad* boys went up toward Caravan Pass. Silas stepped over toward his dear Javier, then put his clawed hands on *his* fabled gunfighter's shoulders. Before he spoke, Silas leaned down and ran his tongue along Javier's neck, relishing the shaking rage he felt in this fiery man's spirit.

"Do you concur with Mitchell, *flame keeper*? Did these stupid boys make for the *passssss*?"

Javier nodded. He eyebrow twitched as he responded.

"Can't say for sure till we get up there, boss, but it seems likely."

Silas smiled maniacally down at Michell with his hundreds of needled teeth, and nodded, releasing the dog and his remaining pack of fresh new boys and sending them up after the escapees, who he hoped would be exhausted and scrambling toward the pass now.

Silas strode forward on his feline legs, slowly beckoning Javier to follow with one long, clawed finger.

"Come now, *flame keeper*, I'd like to see you use your gun today. It has been so *very long* since you've put on a good show for me with it, and *these boys are close.*"

CHAPTER 37

RODRIGO SUPPRESSED a gag as he took the binoculars from his eyes. He looked back at where the other three were repacking their bags after ditching some gear and going over the plan for the fifth or sixth time since they'd finally settled on one. This final plan was expeditiously deliberated over the hours since leaving the corpses of the counselors behind and heading back east, back up the other side of the valley to the saddled mountain pass where they now sat. The others looked back at him, Trent asking the question.

"Did they buy it?"

Rodrigo shrugged.

"Looks that way. They're a few miles away so I can't tell much, but I can see that it's Silas, Javier, and at least six or seven of their dogs. They just left the bodies and are headed up toward the pass."

Billy nodded.

"They bought it alright. We'll have enough time. It'll be close, but we'll beat em back to camp if nothin goes wrong."

Before they'd left the bodies in the valley behind, Ben and Trent each soaked shirts in the blood of their collective wounds sustained during the melee with the counselors. One went about a mile up the north side of Kaniksu Creek; one went a mile up the south. It added an hour onto their departure time but would now hopefully stall and confuse their pursuers for even more than that. It was a bargain, one hour in exchange for hopefully three or four. They'd find out later if it was worth taking, but it was working at the moment, so they had to move.

What their plan depended on now was speed, and quite a bit of luck.

They had fourteen miles to cover, but on easier ground than any they'd traversed in the previous days, and mostly downhill. It would be a tall order, but entirely possible, so long as no one got hurt moving in the dark. They had the water, they had the food, they had the will, but they were all exhausted.

Billy, who apparently had done a fair bit of deer and antelope hunting in West Texas growing up, read the wind now constantly, leading the group on slight deviations from their course to play the environment. By playing the wind, by keeping a good pace, by staying hydrated and focused, they could do this.

The boys each took a sip of water and looked at one another, then toward the west, toward freedom. They'd followed him this far, on faith, and now he was asking them to push on toward their likely death. No one wanted to take the first step back toward the prison they'd worked so hard to escape, but these guys were committed, Ben could see that. They were here of their own volition, here to do the right thing in the face of evil, no matter the cost. This was a group of young men right on the edge; the edge of what, Ben did not know, but he knew it was something already programmed deep within each of them. They didn't need *encouragement*, but they did need a belly full of fire and rage, and Ben was prepared to give them that. He was *born* to give them that. When he was done, they'd be ready to eat glass and destroy cities.

"We think smart, we move smart, and I'll bet beaucoup scratch we can be in position before sunrise, before they open up the lodge. Once they do that, we've got one straight shot. If they don't, then we'll just use that hand cannon to blast through that door as we discussed. *Look . . .*"

Ben leaned in, closer to the other three. They all stared back at him with red-rimmed, wired, violent eyes.

"We *could* run, but we ain't. We're goin back there and endin this wicked Aztec mountain *gris-gris* for good. We're not goin to *fight*, this ain't some stand-up squabble, this ain't some honorable cowboy bullshit. This here . . . this here's a *kill mission*. We're on our way to *rip the life* outta somethin. Somethin truly evil, somethin that needs killin, somethin that can't cause no more hurt once it's dead. That's up to *us now*, whether Silas Everett Blackthorn keeps causin misery and terror, that's *our fuckin call*."

As Ben went on, the boys began to rise, pushing themselves up onto their knees, and then their feet. Ben wiped his eyes, took in a few deep breaths, and felt life and fire flow into his body with each.

"And that's what I'm doin, I'm just here makin a call, *goddamnit*. That ain't somethin I've had a lot a'chances to do in my life. I'm here claimin this mission for myself, and I'm standin my ground, no matter what happens back at camp. That is *my goddamned* camp, and I'll fight and die here, but that's *my call*, not his, not *no one else's*, it's *mine*, and I'm *fuckin ready*. He can snatch the life right outta me, but I ain't dyin as one a'his dogs, I ain't dyin with his dogs on my heels, and I *sure as hellfire* ain't dyin a long way off *knowin* he's still out there."

The expressions of resolve and defiance that came from the combined faces of Trent, Billy, and Rodrigo made Ben's stomach flip with butterflies. All three other boys seethed breath through clenched teeth and gripped their weapons with white knuckles.

"We're headed to remove somethin truly evil from this world. That's a rare opportunity. Even more rare is when that opportunity presents itself in a way that can only be taken by the use of violence, rage, blades, fire, *tooth and fucking* nail to do it. No diplomacy, no negotiation, just violence of action, boots and fists and killing. The leash has been cut. fellas, everything back at that camp is pure corruption and hate, *pure evil*. Let's go stand against it then *drown it in its own blood*."

The boys knew they had to stay quiet, and did so for the most part, but for a solid minute or so they *screamed* war cries in whispers through locked jaws and shook one another by the arms and collars. No one had to take the first step back toward Bear Springs; they were just moving. Fast, and silent. They weren't even human anymore, just hands, eyes, teeth, and violence. Not only had they *become* the wolves from the night before, but nothing would bring these boys more bliss and elation than a confrontation with those same canine beasts; an opportunity to scream and hack and carve into something that wanted to try to stop them.

They were different now and would be forever. Perhaps it happened at some point during the excruciating terror of the night before with the wolves, the longest night any of them had ever lived through. Or perhaps later that morning, during the insane butchery and exertion of the fight.

Perhaps it was just the psychological by-product of everything these boys had been through over the weeks leading up to this: having their grasp on reality and the natural world turned upside down, watching men turn into monsters, watching the souls of their peers ripped away, the act of killing other people up close with their hands. None of them knew specifically when it happened or what made it so, but at some point within the last few hours, they'd all fallen into the fatalistic mindset of a kamikaze pilot, a gladiator, a soldier leading the Forlorn Hope.

There was something deeply empowering about a collective mindset of crazed violence among a group of young men. Something ancient and primal and tragic and pure. Perhaps, Ben thought, there was nothing more dangerous and destructive in the history of mankind than a group of young men in this state. It took a lot of *letting go* to get into this headspace, a lot of shedding away certain conditioning. Some of that conditioning is even healthy and nice and, at one point, before this moment, provided stability and peace. But once there, once exposed and raw enough, an honest communion can be held with the chaos of bloodlust, and something kind of magical happens, something that just feels so deeply, beautifully *right*. The violent electricity that buzzed among a group of young men unified in their commitment to unleashing violence was, in a dark way, almost therapeutic. This energy easily could be—and often enough throughout history *had been*—unleashed in a way that brought horrifying, society-shaking consequences.

But the appalling, heinous, rapturous power of that energy was undeniable, to those facing it and those enjoying it. Hopefully, here, in these mountains, it was about to be put to good use.

CHAPTER 38

D AN DIDN'T really sleep, at least not like he did before that day in 1878, before Silas, before the lantern. Even so, sometime around moonrise on those nights when he wasn't on flame watch, he'd strip down to his long johns, get into bed, and become *less* conscious. On unique occasions, he'd even dream. He awoke in his little bedroom upstairs in the lodge after one of those rare nights. He'd dreamed of his daughter, that last time he'd seen her, run his hand through her hair, the morning he set off to find Silas. *He couldn't remember her name.* He felt longing and pain, knowing that even if she'd lived a long life, she'd still be long dead by now. Even so, it was a dull, fleeting kind of heartache. Almost like the *memory* of heartache, long, long ago.

He got up and dressed himself, then strapped on his gun belt. The boss man had given them back their guns for the first time in decades. Something big must be going down, he and Nick had mused the evening before. He felt brief satisfaction when the familiar weight of his gun tugged on his hip and tied down the holster around his thigh with practiced hands, but that faded. He felt some enjoyment as he inspected his pistol and checked its loads, but that quickly faded as well. He thought again on what might be happening to warrant gunplay, then didn't care anymore.

They did not have a desire to find out *what* was going down, or even the cognitive toolbox to attempt that if the desire were there. Since finding Silas, since sitting with him at his fire in that beautiful meadow and listening to his story all those years ago, that's just how things went. Everything he thought or did, it just . . . *was.*

Like now, he knew, somehow, that the sun rose in fifty-eight minutes, and that he'd like to be on the porch well before then to keep an eye on things as soon as the wolf-light of dawn allowed his eyes to do so. He walked out into the temple where Nick sat, staring into the lantern. He remembered helping Nick bury his wife in that cold, hard winter dirt, and that night they realized they'd actually been fighting on opposing sides during the battle for Kennesaw Mountain. Then those memories faded, or perhaps they just didn't matter. Nick looked up at him. In that brief moment when their eyes locked, Dan knew they both wanted to say so many things. He knew these were urgent, desperately important things, and could even begin to recognize what those things were, but then they faded away, and both men's eyes dulled, and they just nodded at one another.

Dan was not sure *why* he wanted a cup of coffee and a muffin, but he knew he did. He unbolted then opened the doors above the large stairs that ran down to the lodge's front entrance, thought about closing them, but remembered the boys were gone and Nick was in there, and no specific reason or order from the boss to close them filled his mind, so he didn't. He stomped down each step of the large staircase then lit the oil lantern on a side table at the end of the carved banister. Dan shook the flame from the match he'd used as he walked to the kitchen, where he grabbed a muffin and poured himself a cup of coffee. He vaguely enjoyed the warmth of the first sip moving through his body into his gut, then the warmth faded.

He walked outside and saw that thin line of gray over the land to the east, then leaned his back against the pillar, adjusted his gun, and took another sip of coffee. He felt a very subtle bite of cold on his nose and fingers, heard the way the breeze rustled the aspens nearby, and smelled something in the air. He knew these things meant autumn was coming a bit early, and he was briefly pleased by that. *So many* autumns in these mountains, he thought. He gazed back to the east, awaiting the sun.

He remembered it was the early autumn when he'd been chasing the Nez Percé and Chief Joseph around the Montana territory, how smart and tricky they'd been. He remembered being so proud to serve under

General Sherman in the Civil War, and how disgusted he felt serving under him out west against the Natives. He did not feel pride, or disgust, just remembered those feelings existed. He remembered what Nick had said a couple of weeks back about one of the kids in the new batch, Ben was his name. How smart that kid was. He'd said something about General Sherman to Nick that really tickled the man.

Dan stopped caring about that smart boy, Ben, or what he'd said to Nick. He watched the light creep across the land for a while, then pulled out his tobacco and papers. He rolled a cigarette with expert precision and acknowledged the smoke warming his lungs. Dan did not remember when he'd started rolling cigarettes, but he knew a Comanchero had taught him while he'd been on a drive down in Texas.

Ben had been a fighting man since he was the age of the boys who came through this here camp. By the time of the Nez Percé war in 1877, there were few left in the West who could read sign or shoot a rifle better than him. Be that as it may, his fighting days had slowed, considerably, over the last 140-odd years. Truth be told, over the last sixty or so, he'd barely done much fighting at all, minus the odd dustup ol' Silas got them into, but those were increasingly rare. His blade was a bit dull, as it was said, and he didn't pick up on the subtle movement in his periphery that he'd have pegged from a mile away in his prime.

Dan was pondering how long ago it had been since Silas let them take their guns out, just as a blur of movement activated his fighting mind, as rusty as it was.

An arrow—a goddamned *arrow*, Dan briefly mused—slammed into his sternum, knocking the coffee mug from one hand and the cigarette from the other. Before the cigarette had even made contact with the ground, a second arrow took him high in the chest. So high, in fact, he wondered briefly if it had missed the lung, which he'd seen several times before. Before he could finish his thought, a third arrow hammered into his waist just below the gun belt and splintered part of his pelvis.

Dan was still a fighting man. Some instinct can't moss over and die. He knew he needed cover, and backup. He began to spin toward the lodge just as he heard the footsteps coming down the porch, and only had enough time to glance up at what was rushing him. *It was the big, ornery-lookin bastard from this summer's batch*, Dan realized.

That was the last thing Dan ever realized. Any further thought was cut short by the axe blade that connected with his face right above the bridge of his nose. Dan's lights went out just as the axe proceeded onward through the nasal cavity to rend the old, *old* man's brain into slurry.

CHAPTER 39

NICK SAT in the temple and stared at the flame as it flickered in the lantern, just as he had on so many mornings throughout the previous months and years. *Lifetimes.* Just as he had on all those mornings staring into this Jaguar skull, he felt the urge to scream, run, or smash the lantern. That urge would pass, then come again, then pass again.

He was a *keeper of the flame*, and no matter what Nick felt, keeping this lantern safe and aflame was his duty, one he could not betray even if he wanted to. Which he did want to do, so very often, but that feeling would pass, just like all the others.

Dan came from his room into the temple. When he saw him, he remembered watching Dan kill a man trying to rob the tack store up in Victor, remembered seeing Dan weep tears of joy after his daughter was born, remembered teaching that same girl her letters in his classroom several years later. He looked up and locked eyes with him.

He wanted to scream at him, curse him to hell and back for taking him along to find this Silas Everett Blackthorn, beg him never to leave him here, alone, tethered to this beast. No real emotion motivated these desires, just flickers of them, which blew out in the wind as soon as he'd noticed them. He nodded at his old friend, who nodded back as he left the room. Nick watched him unlock then open the large doors across the temple, then disappear as he descended the staircase on the other side of the doors, down into the belly of the quiet lodge.

Nick stared at the lantern, at the altar upon which it sat, burning. He'd set his pistol belt there, grip facing him, of course. Somehow he knew it was easier to draw that gun from the altar than it was to draw it from his belt if he were sitting next to it.

After several minutes, Nick stood and walked to the tall windows behind him. These sat below a series of stained-glass panels that cast the room in a foul, unpleasant light when the morning sun hit them. Nick stared out into the gray, dawn landscape below. He knew autumn was near. He assumed he would soon start to hear the piercing bugles of bull elk as their rut began. He remembered enjoying that sound, and the season it ushered in.

He remembered hunting those massive beasts when he moved out to the Montana territory after the war. He remembered seeing an elk bugle once; he had stalked in so close to it that the cloud of steam from its lungs licked his cheeks and nose. He remembered not being able to pull the trigger to shoot that animal, and the reason why. The *many* reasons why. He remembered the heaps of screaming Yankee boys, writhing on the forest floor in the mountains of northern Georgia. Their faces contorted by terminal pain. He remembered them begging him to just kill them.

Those thoughts passed through his mind, as they always did. For a while, he thought about nothing much at all. Until he heard a strange noise downstairs. A thump, then a wet, sucking tear. He'd heard that noise before, but could not place it. He did not think it was a good noise. It activated some old memory, one of the many he knew was in there but could no longer grasp. Nick stood and crossed the temple toward the doors into the cathedral that was the central room at the lodge.

He stopped at the top of the stairs. As he expected, he found the large double doors at the bottom of the stairs both stood ajar, letting in the cool air of the morning and the silver light of dawn. However, he *did not* see Dan leaning against his pillar having his morning cigarette.

"*Dan.*"

He waited several seconds for a response, then descended the stairs to the large landing halfway down.

"*Hey, Dan.*"

No sound came in response. Something else did, though. An arrow, shot at an angle from some shadowed nook of the large room below him, punched into the ribs on his right side. The force of the impact sent him staggering backward several steps. He looked down at it in momentary disbelief and confusion, just as another arrow—shot from directly ahead, outside the front doors—slammed into his body above his belly button, which then seemed to flip some terribly important switch in his body. He collapsed to the ground, just as a third arrow whistled inches from his ear to clang and ricochet off something behind him.

Nick did not know that the L2 vertebra in his lumbar spine had been splintered. All he knew was that his lower legs no longer worked.

You are the keeper of the flame.

This realization triggered action, and he began using all his upper-body strength to pull himself up the stairs, back toward the lantern and its precious flame. *Nothing* mattered more in the world.

Before he'd cleared the top of the stairs, another arrow punched into the back of his thigh. That was the first time he'd felt real pain in a long, long while. It brought a wave of such powerful nostalgia for so many other sensations, he shuddered and smiled. Nick toyed with the idea of going for his pistol, but only for a moment. He decided to go for the bell. That was his duty. He could not walk, he could not see or count the attackers, he needed backup, and when that situation arose, he was to ring the bell. *Nothing* mattered more in the world.

He got himself back into the temple and then crawled to his left where the tall armoire sat. He ripped the door open, which exposed the thick, black rope hanging down within. He reached for it, took it in both hands, and began to pull.

The ear-shattering *clang* of the old, massive bell tore across the landscape around Bear Springs Basecamp. The silence of the early morning seemed to only amplify the volume of the bell into something so loud it did not seem possible. Nick could hear that the tolling of the bell seemed to awaken some urgency in the attackers below, as their voices grew frantic with haste, and many pairs of feet began pounding up the stairs toward the temple.

Nick had done his duty, so he let the rope fall from his hands and flipped himself over. As he did this, he drew the bowie knife from where he kept it on his lower back, sheathed lengthwise along his belt.

A Frenchman who'd fought for Napoleon against the Brits at Waterloo, then for himself against the Blackfeet on the upper Missouri River, had taught Nick how to properly fight with a bowie knife. He'd first used a bowie knife to kill a man on a Mississippi riverboat after a card game. Having it in his hand made him calm.

He saw his attackers then.

You are the keeper of the flame.

They were young, he knew them. The one coming ahead of the rest was the large, angry lad, Billy, he'd noticed early on. Behind him came Ben, the sly one from the library who didn't think Nick knew he was stealing books. With practiced skill, Nick feinted a move as Billy came upon him and—as it had so many times before—it worked wonderfully once again. He ripped the blade in and across the large boy's abdomen and knew, from considerable experience, that it had tasted large intestine and even a bit of liver. Billy writhed to the side, away from Nick, and the others came on.

Nick could see very clearly that fighting with blades was something very new to them. He could also see, however, something else. Something he hadn't seen in a long, *long* time.

Real, true, unbridled *rage*. That, Nick knew all too well, could *sometimes* make up for a deficit in skill.

Nick felt Billy clasp both hands around his wrist above his bowie knife just as the others set upon him. They were like furious hornets. He felt blades pierce his stomach, neck, and gut. He felt one blade bite into his kidney, then start getting jackknifed side to side. He *screamed* like he hadn't in over a century and arched his back as white-hot electric pain surged through his entire body. One of them got a knife into his left eye and his view of the world was cut in half.

The last thing Nick saw in this world was the face of that sly boy from the library, Ben, contorted with murderous rage as he drove a knife down toward his face. The last thing Nick thought in this world was *finally.* The last thing he felt in this world was peace.

CHAPTER 40

SILAS AND Javier walked side by side through the large trees just beginning to take color in the early light of morning. There was a new chill in the air, enough to produce a faint cloud of fog every time they exhaled. The *dogs* moved along with them, farther off in the trees, grunting and snuffling as they trundled along on hands and feet.

The rage Silas felt at having lost the four boys had not begun to ebb, but he had been able to channel it into something more focused. He was quite certain the treacherous boys had deceived the noses of his dogs with trickery back there at Kaniksu Creek, and he knew this had bought them considerable time to put distance between themselves and his pack. It had not been an easy call to turn back to camp. Doing so, letting those four escape, made his skin crawl and his eyeballs throb. He could feel the disappointment of Xipe Totec, he could feel the flame in the lantern dim. But he'd had boys get away before. Some of them he'd found, later, thinking they were safe. Those moments were glorious, the look in their eye. He would dedicate quite a bit of off-season energy to finding these four. Or perhaps he'd just focus on that snake Benjamin Thibodaux, and that brutish ox of a boy, Billy Axelson.

This had been a truly *disastrous* season. He'd had smaller soul harvests, to be sure, but never in conjunction with such loss and waste. That repulsive little orphan twit from the swamplands of Louisiana, how terribly Silas had misjudged him. He'd taken six of his best dogs and *Gordon Colton*. One of his *first boys*, one of his four *keepers of the flame*, the only four he'd ever had, ever *needed*. It did not seem possible.

Silas would have to call upon more of his dogs to come home from wherever they were around in the world following his ambient directives to be helpful, courteous, and selfless. This was always a headache to do, a time-consuming process, making up their excuses for their families and communities back home as to *why* they were coming back to *work* at Bear Springs, tying up all those loose ends. Alas, he had no choice. He needed to replenish his pack, and he had *so many* dogs out there in the world, still *thousands* of them, he assumed, just awaiting his beckoning.

He could not yet see Bear Springs through the forest, but he could smell it. He could feel the warmth of the lantern. It brought a sense of calm to his bones.

This calm was shattered like glass when he heard the bell. *The* bell. That tolling that meant danger was nigh, that the lantern was in trouble. Neither he nor Javier needed to say a word or even exchange a glance.

Both began sprinting through the forest back toward camp with their pack of blood dogs, baying at their heels.

CHAPTER 41

*S*HIT!"

Trent cradled his burned hand after another unsuccessful attempt at extinguishing the flame in the Jaguar skull.

Ben cut strips of clothing off the dead man Nicholas and bunched them into wads that he pounded onto Billy's stomach wound, one on top of the other.

Rodrigo paced at the windows around the temple, frantically scanning between the landscape, Billy's stomach wound, and the flame in the lantern that they could not find a way to put out.

Billy sat propped up, staring calmly down out the doors to the temple and down the stairs into the lodge as Ben worked on his wound. He could only see the top few inches of the doors below from where he sat, which they had decided to close, lock, and quickly barricade with a bit of furniture before surging up the staircase to attack Nicholas when they heard him begin to ring that terrible bell. Billy leaned against the altar where the lantern had been nestled among candles and other grotesque figurines made of wood, stone, and ivory when the boys fought their way into the room.

Trent was now slamming the lantern onto the stone floors of the strange temple room they were in. He had the Jaguar skull in both hands gripped onto its lower jaw. He brought the relic above his head, then slammed it down on the floor with all his strength. Again, and again. Over and over. Nothing happened; not even a granulate was altered or flake of dust expelled from the bone structure of the lantern. The flame burned on.

Rodrigo started shouting.

"*Fuck*, guys, it's Silas, and Javier, they're here, they're sprinting from the forest toward the lodge right fuckin now. There's others, too, running on all fours, some of the counselors and, oh shit, man, some of our classmates."

Trent's and Ben's eyes went wide at the news.

Rodrigo gave up his sentry post, having seen all he needed to, and took a knee on the left side of the temple behind the large, oaken door frame. He took the pistol from the old gunbelt he'd taken from Dan's corpse outside, which he now wore strapped above his waistline and over his filthy cotton hoodie. He stared at the heavy six-shooter as he brought the hammer back, then took it in both hands as he aimed it down the stairs. Trent, wearing Gordon's gunbelt in the same manner Rodrigo wore Dan's, snatched the other large pistol they'd found lying on the altar and tossed it to Ben as he jogged across the room. Trent went to the right side of the door frame and took up a defensive position opposite Rodrigo.

Ben slid the gun to the side, then grabbed Billy under his arms and began pulling the large boy out of the open, toward the wall behind Trent. Billy wailed. All three other boys looked at him, never having heard him in pain before.

As Ben took stock of his new gun, relieved to find it was the same kind as the one they'd taken off Gordon, he realized Billy was trying to say something and went to his side.

"*The Lantern* . . . you stupid . . . sons a'*bitches*. You gotta . . ."

Billy winced in pain and began to tip over to the side, both red hands clamped on the deep knife wound to his belly that oozed dark blood all over his lap. Ben held him upright as he took several deep breaths and spoke through clenched, bloody teeth.

"You gotta use . . . blood . . . *blood of a boy, to light it and douse it* . . . Gordon already . . . He already fuckin told us how to put it out, you *useless shit for brains.*"

Ben, Trent, and Rodrigo all froze in embarrassment and realization. Billy was right, how had they forgotten that completely over the last three minutes. Rodrigo dove for the lantern and began squeezing blood from a fresh gash on his arm into the flame. It wasn't bleeding enough, though.

Trent and Ben both flinched as Rodrigo took a knife from his pocket and ripped a deep gash down the center of his palm that began bleeding immediately. Just as he reached for the lantern, an explosion rocked the lodge at the bottom of the stairs, causing all four boys to flinch.

The couch, desk, and several armchairs the boys had barricaded the door with shattered to pieces and blasted around the room. For one, long moment, the only thing they could see was dust, illuminated by the silver morning light outside. Then they saw their classmates.

They came pouring in on all fours, braying and shrieking like a pack of hyenas. All three began shooting the heavy, double-actioned revolvers at the same time. The guns *thundered* in the confined space.

Two of the boys, Hector and what appeared, *maybe*, to be a terribly deformed Charlie, were ripped backward by the heavy bullets where they crashed into the detritus of the former barricade, shrieking and flailing on the ground. The others rushed over them, stomping their faces into the floor, and came up the steps in a mass. This, the boys realized, was rather convenient, as it pinched them together and slowed their movement a bit. They poured fire into the wall of deformed bodies, into the faces and necks and guts of their former classmates. One of these bullets passed through meat and bone then shattered the lantern at the base of the staircase, creating what appeared to be a small explosion as fire leapt after the oil and glass showering the old wooden floors and staircase.

One shot appeared to tear Marcus's arm off all the way up at the shoulder, while one took Sam's head off above his upper lip. Another punched into the sternum of the once-quiet Chris, who appeared to lose all control over his limbs as he dumped forward into the landing halfway up the stairs and began seizing and groaning horribly. Their fire slackened as Trent went about reloading his gun, and then even more as Ben's gun ran dry and he did the same. Rodrigo took his last shot, then went back to trying to douse the flame of the lantern with the blood that now poured freely from the deep wound in his palm.

The smell and sizzle of blood drizzling into the flame was nauseating in the small space of the temple. Rodrigo looked at the others with wide eyes.

"It's not fuckin working."

Trent stared back at Rodrigo, unsure what to do, then began firing into more of the *hounds* plodding over their fallen brethren and up the stairs. Billy's voice cut through the chaos.

"Give it to me."

Rodrigo hesitated for a moment but then slid the lantern toward Billy, but it did not make it across the room due to the bloody mess covering the floor and came to a stop several feet out of his reach. Ben saw this problem as he kept reloading his weapon with shaking, numb fingers.

Mitchell, one of the lead counselors, broke through the twitching and shrieking mass of bodies to come bounding up the stairs more like a cat than a dog. Trent took his gun up in both hands and took careful aim. He closed an eye, stuck his tongue out the corner of his mouth, and just as Mitchell reached the top of the stairs, Trent shot him in the face. While the bullet left only a neat little hole in the man's forehead, the force of the impact did something else entirely on the inside. The overpressure blew one eye out of its socket, and somehow triggered a *torrent* of blood to come dumping from the man's nose and ears. The deadly shot put an abrupt end to Mitchell's screeching and sent his limp body tumbling down the stairs.

Rodrigo pushed back up toward the door, joining Trent as they poured a thundering fusillade of hot lead down into anything that still had life.

Something downstairs had caught fire, and light smoke began to feather into the room. Ben looked at Billy, who appeared very pale but quite calm as he spoke, as though most of the pain had passed. Ben did not think that was a good thing.

"Lifeblood, dumbass, and *you're* supposed to be the smart one."

Billy could see the weight of his words hitting home on Ben's face.

"I'm done for, ol' buddy. Bastard stuck me good. Ain't no comin back from this. It's *lifeblood* of a boy that douses the flame, not just *any* blood, you said so yourself, read it in that little book a'yours. Gordon said the same."

Ben nodded once, then slid his gun toward Trent, who scooped it up wordlessly and began blasting it down the stairs.

Just as Ben made a move for the lantern, an eye-shaking, earsplitting scream punched into the lodge in that moment. All the boys dropped anything in their hands to clap their palms to their ears. They stared down into the carnage of the lodge through squinted eyes. The noise came from outside. It had so much force it began to shake and rattle the pile of twitching bodies, bleeding limbs, and gore blocking the stairs, growing with intensity until they began sloughing away to both sides, leaving a clear lane up the center toward them.

Mercifully the noise finally stopped, but in that same moment, Silas Everett Blackthorn stalked through the front doors into the lodge. Into his home. Javier came in behind the monstrous thing on its flank.

Silas pointed a clawed hand up toward the four boys.

"IN MY DOMAIN?"

Every word Silas spoke had a despotic effect, each syllable a complete assault on the boys' senses. It made them dry-heave and gag, made their eyeballs burn and vibrate. Their bladders released. Trickles of blood began to drip from their noses.

"You stand here, in my domain, wielding simple hope against a power as limitless as mine? Men stronger than you have tried, their screams and pleading still echo in the abyss of my memory. I can still taste them . . ."

Silas spread his arms wide as though embracing the sky, closed his eyes for a moment, and waggled his hideous tongue in the air as he began ascending the stairs toward the paralyzed boys. The fire down-stairs was growing, and the smoke and flames themselves jumped and quivered to the beat of his words. His voice had both a snakish hiss and a guttural timbre. It didn't come in through their ears but outward from their brain stems.

"There is a choir in my shadow, boys. The wailing and shrieks of count-less souls form this choir's hymns, chants, and chorus. The arrogance of youth is my most cherished fare. Without the sweet nectar of trust, your souls cannot sustain me or please my lord. However, the sweet taste is unspoiled. I shall still shudder and squeal with delight to consume you."

Ben looked at Billy, eyes wide, then ripped his hands from his ears to grab the lantern from Rodrigo. The unrestricted flow of noise pushed Ben to the dark edge of consciousness. He launched himself back toward

Billy with all his remaining strength, planting the glowing Jaguar skull into his lap.

Billy tilted the skull to the side with one hand and took the other from his belly, where Ben could see coiled intestines *barely* holding their coiled form behind the wound. Billy reached into the Jaguar's mouth with his blood-dripping hand and clamped down on the blackened wick beneath the flame.

Something profound happened then.

It was as though the entire lodge itself expelled a deep, hot, elemental exhale that blasted outward from its foundation. The boys felt like they were in complete free fall at the same time, blinded by extreme velocity and pressure with stomachs in their throats. Every window in the building exploded. All the debris, bodies, and gore in the large room below smashed against the walls. As the torrent of invisible force burst and pealed out and away from the lodge, it shattered cabin windows and lanterns and shook even the behemoth old-growth trees throughout basecamp.

Then, everything fell into a stunned, oppressive silence.

CHAPTER 42

THE ONLY thing that moved was dust. The silence almost took on a noise of its own. The boys slowly opened their eyes and stared down the staircase where they'd last seen Silas.

Silas was still there, but not in the same way. He was just a man again. A tall, formidable man, to be sure, but a man, with no trace of his monstrous affect left behind. He was at the landing, halfway up the staircase, holding himself up on all fours as he breathed heavily toward the ground. He slowly lifted his head to look up at the four boys.

He had despair and raw anguish on his face. Tears flowed freely from his eyes and down his cheeks. It all slowly turned to fury—that perilous and unstable kind, the kind one would find in the face of a father who'd just watched his child get murdered. He rose onto two feet and began slowly advancing as he snarled at the boys, venom dripping off each word.

"If I can't take your souls, then I'm coming up there to take *every other fucking piece of you*, and I'm gonna do it *slow*."

Another voice roared across the massive room and into the temple, carrying with it a single word.

"Blackthorn."

The voice that spoke the word was like nothing the boys had ever heard. The word was spoken like a statement but was somehow just as loud and abrasive as a scream. The tone was brutal, severe, and tyrannical. The tone also had the grim resolution of a final decree, a solemn vow.

Silas slowly turned to face the entrance to the lodge and source of the voice, and the boys rose onto their knees to follow his gaze. As he turned, he exposed the form of a man standing directly behind him at the bottom of the stairs. He was standing perpendicular to Silas, right foot on the floor of the room, left foot on the first step of the large staircase. The man's left shoulder was the only thing pointed up the stairs, until he slowly turned his head and looked up at Silas.

Very few people who have ever walked this earth have seen the kind of hatred that broiled behind the eyes of Javier Lozada as he stared up at Silas Everett Blackthorn. It's just too difficult for that level of hatred to spawn within someone in a single lifetime. Even a lesser form of hatred would drive most men into a state of mumbling, pants-shitting insanity, or just suicide. But there it was, they all saw it, like fusion harnessed from a star, churning in eyes shadowed under the brim of his gambler-style cowboy hat.

"I'm callin you out, Blackthorn."

The man spoke with the same relaxed, menacing violence as before, and each word carried the steely permanence of a railway spike.

"Your yelluh ass has been livin' on borrowed time awhile, Blackthorn. Today, *that debt comes due.* I've been waitin a *long* time to make you hurt, watch you beg. This land remembers every sin, Blackthorn, every soul taken, and for years now *I've been hearin it screamin for yours.* Today, I answer that call."

Silas's eyes went wide as he held both palms out toward Javier, then stuttered for a moment before he could form a sentence.

"W . . . wait, Javier, *just wait.* Think about what we've gone through together, all our adventures. Please, *please.* I'll walk away *right now*, you'll *never* see me again, I swear to God. *Please*, just let m—"

The bullet shattered the joint and bones of his knee, which bent inward unnaturally as Silas's weight fell upon it and he collapsed onto all fours. Javier had drawn his gun, turned his body, and taken the shot at lightning speed. If he'd have dropped a nickel from his shooting hand before drawing the gun, the bullet would've smashed into Silas's leg before the coin hit the floor.

Silas let out a terrible scream of anguish and disbelief. He looked up at Javier, drool pouring down his chin, and looked furiously indignant and offended, as though Javier had just broken a sacred promise.

Javier held his gun at waist height, pointed directly at Silas, and while he began to slowly advance up the stairs, neither his head nor his gun moved at all.

"*That* one's for Gordy, and *this* one's for Nick."

Silas had raised his left hand toward Javier as though it could protect him, and that's where the next bullet landed. Several fingers spun away from the sudden burst of blood and bone. Silas yanked his ruined hand into his chest to cradle with his remaining one, then rolled onto his back. He stomped at the floor over and over with his good leg like a child having a tantrum as he screamed. Unlike the last, this scream spoke of simple pain. The stomping ceased abruptly when another bullet burst through Silas's remaining, intact knee.

"*That* one's for Dan Bishop."

Silas grunted when his other knee exploded, but then his screaming became jittery and higher in pitch. There was panic in this scream now, *as well as* pain. It was the screaming of someone being eaten alive. He flipped over onto his belly and started crawling across the landing toward the next set of stairs that led toward the boys, whom he looked up at with eyes wide in raw terror.

Even though they felt *zero* empathy—and wanted nothing more than to enjoy every detail and moment of this beautiful spectacle of suffering and retribution—the boys, even Billy, winced and flinched away as the next bullet struck home.

They could not see the impact, but they could hear and almost *feel* the deep, muffled *thwap* of the bullet as it tore into the man's undercarriage, somewhere deep between his legs.

"*That* one's for all the boys."

Silas's screaming stopped momentarily as that bullet struck him. His mouth went wide, his pupils almost disappeared back in the sockets, and his head craned upward as though he were trying to inspect the ceiling directly above where he'd been crawling. The veins in his neck bulged and throbbed, and a rough whine was the only noise coming from his throat. His head eventually dropped back down as he began to vomit.

Javier still came, and it seemed to the boys that nothing in the world could've stopped that. He was an inevitable force. He was like the glaciers that sat in the dark crags far above camp, or a forest fire that burned and churned its way across a dry, summer-scorched mountain.

Silas rolled onto his side and then his back as he began openly weeping now in slow, pathetic sobs. As Javier reached the landing, Silas extended his hands up toward his former slave, one of which was just a flower of blood, skin, and splintered bone. Javier only stopped once he loomed above the weeping, destroyed body of his former master. When Javier stared down at him, Silas began to shake, and the tremors grew into hypothermic convulsions. He began hyperventilating as well, chest and belly heaving up and down at unhealthy speed. The boys could see he was trying to form words that only came out as whimpers and bursts of spittle.

"And this one . . ."

Javier drew the hammer back on his pistol and pointed it down into the other man's face in one fluid motion.

"This one's *for me*."

This final gunshot seemed much louder than the others had, but perhaps that was due to the weight of the heavy silence that followed. The bullet struck Silas directly between the eyes, slamming his head down into the floor, where it connected so forcefully that a halo of blood, skull, brain, and dust kicked out in every direction.

Several long moments passed as the boys and Javier all stared down at the corpse of Silas Everett Blackthorn, the only noise the growing cackle of some fire in the room below as it found some fuel that excited it. Eventually, Billy's rough voice cut into the stillness.

"*My whole life* . . . I ain't *never* seent nothin *that* cool."

The voice, and then the image of Billy, snapped everyone back into reality. Ben ripped his shirt off and pressed it into the gaping wound in Billy's gut just as Rodrigo used both hands to apply pressure to it. Trent whipped out his knife and began ripping strips of clothing away from the corpse of Nick to use as more gauze.

They all glanced up at Javier as he approached, comfortable enough to accept him as their ally after what he'd just done to their mutual tormentor, but still unsure what to say to such a person. Billy smiled up at him, though, and nodded approvingly.

Javier cocked his head down the stairs as he spoke.

"That fire's movin on its own now, this place is gonna come down, let's get this guy outside."

Before they could protest, Javier had taken a knee at Billy's side, put one arm under his knees, one arm under Billy's own, and lifted the large boy into his arms. Javier grunted with effort as he rose to his feet, then strode confidently out the doors of the temple and down the large staircase, the far side of which was now on fire due to some spark from the hail of gunfire into the old, dry cedar.

Ben, Trent, and Rodrigo hastily grabbed up their three pistols, gun belts, and a few loose bullets and went for the stairs. As they reached the landing, they all stopped and stared down at the milky, dead eyes and thrashed corpse of Silas Everett Blackthorn. It was underwhelming, seeing him dead. Perhaps their rage toward Silas had faded with his death, or maybe it had just been burned out by Javier's cataclysmic hatred for this same man.

They left the brutalized corpse without a word and followed the old gunslinger as he carried their friend away from the fire and into the morning light.

Javier carried Billy out to the Lodge Pole, where he set him down, the boys back leaning on the physical totem of this now-burning camp. The two of them locked eyes for a brief moment, completely unaware of the fact that they'd both been born only fifteen miles from one another in the wild, mesquite-covered country of West Texas. Javier patted Billy on the knee, as he'd done to many dying men before. Billy nodded.

The other boys trotted up and surrounded Billy.

The west side of the lodge was fully engulfed in flames now, crackling loudly and emitting occasional deep booms when a truss or beam fell. A few small spot fires had also caught in the meadows and woods around camp. These had begun to creep their way up the mountain as they feasted on grasses, pine needles, and other fuels along the forest floor.

Billy's face was ashen gray. His three best, his three *only* friends in the world, knelt around him with hands on his shoulders and forearms.

Ben had abandoned his effort to hold back tears, as Trent and Rodrigo already had. Billy was close now, they all knew. Perhaps even seconds from death. This realization sent a bolt of panic through Ben. He clamped a hand over Billy's deep wound.

"*Come on*, Axe. You can't go, man, not after this, not after we took him down. *Please*, man, stay with us. You're finally *Axe*."

This raw, unchecked emotion from Ben made Trent and Rodrigo break down into open crying. Billy gently removed Ben's hand from the wound on his stomach and took it into both of his own. His voice was barely more than a raspy whisper. He did his best to smile as he spoke.

"If *I'm* the Axe, then *you're* nothin less than *Paul Bunyan*, buddy."

The other three laughed through their tears for a moment.

"*Ben*, listen, *I'm ready to go*, and we'll be catchin up later, don't chu worry bout that. You just worry about your *brother* now, you get him somewhere *safe*, and look after him. *That's* your job now."

Ben hung his head and shook with sobs but did not let go of Billy's hand. None of them took their hands off Billy, who gazed off to the east, toward the new sun of the day.

"*Stand up . . .*"

All three boys looked at Billy when he spoke the words, prompting him to keep talking. He did not lift his head, or open his eyes, which had closed several minutes ago, but he did squeeze their hands with his last burst of strength.

"*Stand up to evil, always, no matter the cost. Nothin good comes from accepting evil as just another part a'life, because it ain't, Ben. Evil ain't supposed to be here, not in the heart or mind of a man. It ain't supposed to be considered a natural thing in this world. Wherever and whenever it rears its head up, you just gotta fight it . . .*"

No one said anything. No one had to. Billy "Axe" Axelson slipped into death as soon as he'd finished his final words.

His final *command*.

EPILOGUE

A T THE exact moment Billy Axelson extinguished the flame in the lantern and Silas Everett Blackthorn lost his powers, there were around two thousand men around the world, between the ages of fourteen and 104, who had graduated from Bear Springs Academy.

The effects they experienced when the lantern was extinguished varied somewhat, but there was one collective sensation all would admit to—the jarring feeling of being suddenly naked in public after spending years chained up in a dark room.

Some of them simply collapsed to their knees and wept. Some began to vomit and convulse. Some fell into states of silent shock. *Many* promptly found a way to kill themselves.

Graham Thompson, a fifty-four-year-old in Traverse City, Michigan, slammed on his brakes, pulled his car over, fell into the grass along the road, and began to weep tears of dread. Paul DeAngelis, a thirty-three-year-old in Phoenix, Arizona, embraced his two-year-old son and wife and wept tears of joy. Kevin Clark, a seventy-six-year-old in Riverside, California, had a heart attack at his desk in the call center where he worked. Frank Davis, a fifteen-year-old in Lafitte, Louisiana, seemed to freeze in place where he'd been walking along Highway 45, until he stepped out in front of an oncoming truck just about a mile from Aunt Nikki's trailer, where Wade Thibodaux was staring out a dirty window and thinking about his big brother.

Javier Lozada, a 191-year-old in the mountains in northwest Montana, just stared at his hands for a while.

He flipped them over, slowly, as though looking for a tick, and then let them fall to his sides as he looked up into the bright morning sky.

"What're you gonna do?"

The question surprised Javier. He looked over to find the one with the watchful eyes standing at his side, also staring up into the morning sky. *Ben*, that was his name. Javier was not sure how to answer that question. He felt overwhelmed, almost panicked by it. Javier had not made a decision for himself in almost 150 years. It seemed the boy could sense this.

"There's a fella camped west of here, name a'Rickert. He's a game warden, manages the elk and deer populations and whatnot, hunts down poachers. He'll be up there through the end of archery season, another month or so. Reckon he could point you in the right direction."

Javier looked at the boy, unsure of what to say. The kid cocked his head toward his friends, who were walking back from a barn with some shovels.

"We're gonna give our pal a proper burial, then split on outta here."

All Javier could think to do was nod in understanding. He was surprised to find that he did, actually, understand that. That's not something he'd felt in a long time. The boy spoke again as he considered this.

"Give us a hand?"

Javier nodded again.

They buried that boy under the Lodge Pole. They said their goodbyes, and Javier watched them hike off into the forest to the east. Javier stood there, alone, watching the wildfire blossom into something massive and unstoppable as it ripped up the mountains to the north. He felt the old, familiar weight of his gun belt, and the excitement that had always hung over an empty trail to the west. He felt good. He felt pleasure. Those things he had not felt in a long, *long* time.

The last *real* gunslinger alive removed his hat, ran a forearm across his dirty face, then scanned the grounds of Bear Springs Academy one last time. He spit into the dirt, put his hat back on his head, then turned and started west.

ACKNOWLEDGMENTS

Our most sincere gratitude and acknowledgment to our family whose support and love have been invaluable: Amy, Robb, Dana and Dave, and our endlessly supportive and inspiring partners, Sonya and Chelsea.

We are endlessly grateful for the guidance of our representatives Scott and Liz and the rest of the Ground Control and Verve teams.

And lastly, we are so fortunate to have the collaboration and wisdom of our publishing and editorial partners at Atria Books—Lara, Hydia, and of course the amazing Emily Bestler, without whom we would be a pair of wayward boys lost in the literary forest.